REQUIEM

Also by Frances Itani

REQUIEM

FRANCES ITANI

Grove Press
New York

Copyright © 2011 by Itani Writes Inc.

All rights reserved. No part of this book may be reproduced in any form or by any electronic or mechanical means, including information storage and retrieval systems, without permission in writing from the publisher, except by a reviewer, who may quote brief passages in a review. Scanning, uploading, and electronic distribution of this book or the facilitation of such without the permission of the publisher is prohibited. Please purchase only authorized electronic editions, and do not participate in or encourage electronic piracy of copyrighted materials. Your support of the author's rights is appreciated. Any member of educational institutions wishing to photocopy part or all of the work for classroom use, or anthology, should send inquiries to Grove/Atlantic, Inc., 154 West 14th Street, New York, NY 10011 or permissions@groveatlantic.com.

First published in 2011 in Canada by HarperCollins Ltd.

Printed in the United States of America

ISBN-13: 978-0-8021-2123-3
e-Book ISBN:978-0-8021-9460-2

Grove Press
an imprint of Grove/Atlantic, Inc.
154 West 14th Street
New York, NY 10011

Distributed by Publishers Group West
www.groveatlantic.com

13 14 15 16   10 9 8 7 6 5 4 3 2 1

For Tate
For Campbell
For Frances Michiko

With much love

And for all of those whose memories
have been weighted with silence

THE FATES

Speak of a man and his shadow will turn up.

B lack outside. A solid blur of black. A wall of mountain behind. A man moving about out there would instinctively raise his hands to push his way through the dark.

Inside, lumps and shadows cast by the kerosene lamp. Twigs of frost to be snapped off in the morning, suspended from the seams where wall and ceiling meet. The drone of First Father's voice from his chair in a corner of the shack.

I had heard the fates many times before, but he insisted that I pay attention when he picked up the palm-sized book with the red cover. He read back to front, top to bottom, starting with my older brother.

"Hiroshi. You are number-one son, born in the year of the monkey. You are a strong boy and you will grow up to be a strong man. Because of your fate, you will be skilled at whatever you choose to do."

He paused, and I waited for Hiroshi's intake of breath.

"But sometimes you will not finish what you set out to do, and this will make you angry with yourself. Remember that you should never marry a woman born in the year of the tiger."

Hiroshi frowned, looked down at his already muscular arms and was momentarily quiet.

"Bin," said Father, because I was always second. "You are youngest, number-two son, born in the year of the tiger. A tiger may be stubborn, but can chase away ghosts and protect. If careful, a tiger is capable of amassing a fortune."

My brother and sister perked up, knowing what was coming next.

"But because your time of birth was at the cusp of the year of the rabbit"—he added this as if he'd sired a child who could not be helped—"you are destined to be melancholy, and you will weep over nonsensical things."

Hiroshi and Keiko leaned back on the bench and hooted with laughter, as they always did. Father cleared his throat and ignored the interruption.

I remained silent and glanced over at Mother, who was making sushi from egg and rice. The outer wrappings, rinsed cabbage leaves, had been stored since fall, salted, folded and packed in a jar. If a leaf tore, it was expertly repaired with a patch from another leaf. When the rice was tucked in—not a grain wasted—she rolled the bamboo mat, the sudare, and sliced the sushi in bite-sized circles. She caught my glance and gave a quick nod that also meant, Pay attention to your father.

Keiko's fate was last to be told, though she was middle child. But she was a girl.

"Keiko, you were born in the year of the rooster. You will be ambitious and work hard, but you must learn to trust. Even though you will want to tell people exactly what you think, you cannot be right all the time. Still, you will do well and you will earn respect."

Keiko preened, with a frown. Her cheekbones flushed like matching purple bruises.

Did this moment take place during the first winter of our internment, 1942? No, it had to be later, when I was older—the third year, perhaps. We were in the camp five winters in all. We were sitting as close to the wood stove as we could position ourselves, bundled in layers of sweaters that had tumbled from Mother's needles. Because new wool was scarce, she had unravelled sturdy fishermen's sweaters so that she could reknit the coarse wool into smaller items. Pattern was of no concern, nor was colour. It was warmth that mattered. We were living in the mountains, after all, partway up the Fraser, the great river that defined our lives in the camp. We were inland, more than 150 miles from the river's mouth and from the southern channels of the delta, where it spilled out into the Pacific, just north of the boundary with the United States.

Even farther from us was the west coast of Vancouver Island and the house Father had built with the help of his brother, our uncle Kenji. It was a fisherman's house, propped on massively thick stilts. Stilts that Father had sealed, by himself, to prevent rotting, and that defended our family when tidal waters swept up the bay and drifted in soundlessly over a thin strip of barnacled beach between house and shore. But all the while, hidden undercurrents had been making their own incursions with the tides, in and around and under the house. The house from which we had been forcibly removed, and that none of us, as it turned out, would ever see again.

CHAPTER 1

1997

The call from my sister, Kay, comes in the evening. Second call in a week.

"He isn't dying, Bin. I want to make that clear. He sits in his chair, facing the door, as if he expects someone to walk through. He asks for you every time I visit. I've driven to B.C. twice in the past six weeks—it's a long drive from here. But he won't budge from his place."

"First Father?" I can't resist, though I'm not proud of saying it like that.

"I wish you wouldn't call him that."

"That's what he is."

"You still have anger." She says this softly, but impatience is there, underneath.

"Don't you?"

"Not about the same things. Anyway, I try not to hold on to it."

I want to snap at her when she talks like this. I want to say, *Get angry yourself, why don't you. You deserve to.*

"He's old, Bin. Well, getting old. In his eighties, after all. I'd bring him here to Alberta if he'd agree to leave that tiny house of his."

"But he won't," I say. "And since Mother died, he insists on living alone—or so you keep telling me."

"You've never seen his house, because you refuse to visit Kamloops. In summer it's stifling, take my word for it. Another month or so, and it'll be scorching there."

"Why doesn't he go to the coast before the weather changes?"

"He won't. Not even with his own brother, though Uncle Kenji has offered to drive him, countless times. Father just sits there staring at the door, or out the window at dry mountains." She pauses and adds, "He needs to see you."

I choose to ignore this and remain silent for a moment. *He made his choices,* I'm thinking. *More than half a century ago. His needs are not my concern.*

I feel Kay bracing herself, ready to argue or persuade.

"As a matter of fact," I tell her suddenly, "I've decided to travel—west—to British Columbia. As far as the Fraser, to the camp. Well, there is no camp, but whatever is there now."

This announcement surprises me as much as it does her. There's a longer pause and I wonder, foolishly, if she has hung up.

"I won't be in your part of the country for several days, of course." I'm making this up, now, as I speak. "I'll be leaving in the morning, but I probably won't reach Edmonton for a week—more or less. I have things to do along the way."

Basil has been listening and pads by in the hall, his nails clattering against hardwood. He tilts his shaggy head at an angle, enough to ensure that his expression of reproach has been noticed. Nose to floor, long ears dragging the dust, he disappears into the kitchen. I'm certain he does this—the ear-dragging part—on purpose.

"What things?" Kay, as usual, has recovered quickly.

"Work things." I've never liked explaining myself, not even to my wife, Lena. "I'll phone when I get close."

"You're driving. All this way. By yourself."

I hear a long sigh and have a sudden image of Kay standing at a picture window in her Alberta home, looking out at a disc of sun hovering over flat, golden plain. No, there will be nothing golden this time of year in Edmonton. Last summer, when she moved from one neighbourhood to another, she wrote to say that her new house is close to the ravine and the University of Alberta—where she has worked as a counsellor for many years. For all I know, she might be staring into the depths of a crevasse, or at rows of houses, or at spring snow melting in a parking lot. After the enforced years in the camp, Kay has always hated the mountains. She feels squeezed between them every time she drives to B.C., says the mountains press in on her lungs until she's short of breath. Maybe now that her children are grown and on their own, she's finally found a place where she can breathe deeply, no dips or peaks to interrupt her view. A place where she can retire in a year or two, in peace. Her husband, Hugh, has already retired, and Kay has told me that he loves having his time to himself now. He has all sorts of projects going, though she's never said what kind of projects these are.

Basil reappears, having circled kitchen, laundry, dining room. His face looks up in innocence, but something is drooping from his jaw. He drags it across the floor and, without stopping, plops it at my feet and carries on. I watch his low-slung body disappear, sixty pounds of Basset Griffon, the Grand version. He's predominantly white, with a mix of grey, black and apricot markings, the apricot showing through from a thick undercoat. He circles again, this time reversing direction. He's been sticking his nose in the dirty laundry again, probably feeling ignored. Loping his way through an existential dog nightmare, perhaps.

"I'll be alone," I say into the phone. And now it's Kay's turn to be silent.

Who else would be with me? Lena has been dead more than five months. Greg returned to his studies on the East Coast and is back to living his own life. He left a week after the funeral, in mid-November. He was home again at Christmas, and we managed to get through muted festivities at Lena's sister's place in Montreal. Greg flew to Ottawa first, and we travelled together by train to Montreal. Neither of us wanted to drive because the roads were hazardous, covered in snow and ice.

Once in Montreal, we did our best to keep well-meaning relatives at bay—or were surrounded. One and the same, perhaps. There were always people around, people in every room. Was that by accident, or was Lena's family orchestrating our grief as well as their own? When I think of those few days, I remember chairs crowded around the kitchen table, lineups for bathrooms in the morning, music turned up a little louder than necessary. I particularly remember the Sanctus of Berlioz's *Requiem*, only the Sanctus, a solo tenor voice. It was a blend of pain and beauty, and I felt that the tenor, after singing, could only go offstage and weep. As for the answering women's choir, they were intent on bringing solace from afar. The women sang as if something clear and important had to be said. Perhaps that is when something I was holding back fell away. Perhaps that is when I began to allow myself to grieve.

As soon as Kay and I hang up, I phone Greg to tell him about the trip—before I change my mind. It's an hour later on the East Coast but he's up, studying. He, too, is surprised at my sudden announcement.

"Hey," he says, "you're really going back? Through the mountains? All the way?"

"Through the Rockies," I tell him. "As far inland as the camp, but not all the way to the Pacific. Do you want to come? It's been a while since we crossed the country by car."

"I'd love to, Dad, but I have term papers to finish. After exams, I have to prepare my research project."

Greg has a spot in a summer fellowship program in Massachusetts—exactly where he wants to be. He deserves to be excited about this.

"I don't have all the dates figured out yet," he says. "But maybe we can get together in Cape Cod while I'm there. Or even earlier. I'll let you know as soon as everything is confirmed."

During the conversation, while he tells me what he'll be doing at Woods Hole, the Oceanographic Institution, I find myself calling up a memory of a time when he discovered a dolphin skull on the shores of Passamaquoddy Bay. Almost eleven years ago. The Fundy tide was low; we'd been beachcombing. The skull had washed up on brown and slippery rocks, the elongated bones of its distinctive rostrum bleached by the sun. Greg easily recognized it for what it was, a perfect discovery for a ten-year-old. The skull stank for months, but we dried it in the sun in the backyard an entire summer, until it was odourless enough to be in his room. It's still there, on a shelf with his other marine treasures.

We say goodbye, I hang up the phone and lean forward to see what Basil has dropped at my feet. It's a message, a dismembered sleeve, a rag, a duster tugged up and out of the hamper. Part of a sweatshirt Lena used to wear around the house.

I recognize this as a measure of Basil's distress. He's a pack animal. And a member of his pack—our pack—is missing.

CHAPTER 2

Five-thirty in the morning and I've been dreaming of Lena. She was sitting on the edge of the bed, wrapped in a cream-coloured robe that I don't recall, her bare legs crossed at the knee. It was the way she always sat: on kitchen chairs, on the chesterfield, in the seats of airplanes. But there she was, in the dream, her dark hair pushed back behind her ears. My first thought was: *Lena is okay. She can move, she can speak.* She was teasing, telling me I'd slept the sleep of the high-strung and uneasy. Before that, she curled into my body deliberately, her skin as soft as it was when she was in her twenties, when I first met her.

Then I woke, or thought I woke, to see her sitting beside me. She raised an eyebrow, as if waiting for me to say something. But when I reached for her, she was gone. Did I call out? Perhaps that was part of the dream—believing I had.

I glance at the clock, 5:18, shove back the covers and force myself, will myself, to get up, even though it's still dark. I go to the window, naked, and pull back one of the curtains. Search for the line of river on the northern edge of the city and feel the disappointment as I realize, in the fog between sleep and awareness, that this is not the river of my childhood after all. So real is my childhood river, I can call up at any moment its steep banks, the steady rush of fast and muddy water, the ribbon of blue-green coming in from the side.

I push down the fluttering, the extra beats inside my chest, try to smother the sense of panic. And as I stare out, I recall an earlier dream. Or perhaps fragments of the same dream, a prequel of sorts.

I had been moving from one place to another, as one's dream-self does, changing scenes in a way that makes no sense to the conscious mind. I was walking in drizzling rain, searching for the Fraser River below the camp. As I descended the steep path, I caught glimpses of a horizontal rope of cloud stretched low above the tur-bulent water. I was wet and miserable and fatigued, and lay on the ground in that damp, leaden air, hoping to rest. When I woke, it was to find myself at the river's edge. Again, Lena was there, her body curled into mine.

Let it go, I tell myself. *Let her go.* I release the curtain and make my way downstairs in bare feet. Open the door for Basil, who streaks past in a grizzled mass of coiled energy and, just as coiled, returns. For a dog who is ten years old, he has surprising vigour. I pour pellets into his dish and turn away while he gallops through his food. The pellets resemble swollen cigarette butts stripped of their papers, an image I can do without so early in the morning.

A thin light has begun to filter down over the street. Next door, in the backyard of my elderly neighbour, Miss Carrie, a chaotic tan-gle of gooseberry bushes has emerged from under cover of melt-ing snow. The snowbanks have shrunk to grass level now, but it's a stretch to believe that bulbs are pushing up under that layer of slush. Years ago, Lena planted crocuses in our own backyard and, every spring, delicate purples and yellows defy the weight of winter and reappear like tendrils of hope.

Basil nudges my leg, my cue to pour water into his bowl. I wonder when to tell him we're going on a trip. If I say the word, or even spell it aloud, as Lena and Greg and I used to do—though he quickly caught on—he'll begin to run in tight, frantic circles until it's time for me to say: *Get in the car, Basil.* From the way I'm being watched, I suspect he already knows. He's tensed and ready, waiting for the words.

Despite his canine intuition, I make an effort to behave as if this is a morning like any other. I leave him in the kitchen and go back upstairs to dress, shave, pack a duffle bag. Shirts, socks, underwear, rough clothes for hiking that I can throw into a machine at a laundromat along the way—but only when necessary.

I add a couple of extra razors to my shaving kit and go to my studio, same side of the house as the bedroom. The blinds are never closed here. Clouds are tilted on their edges out there, a fleet of sails tucked to one another, news gusting from afar. With daylight lowering into the cold glint of city, I can see the Ottawa River more clearly now, a winding strip of darkness that defines the borders of two provinces. The Peace Tower erupts to the left. Old and dun, it lauds the sky without assumption, while the seats of power, the offices of Parliament, reside on either side. Not a scene I relish when I think of how the power was used in 1942. I focus, instead, on the smudges of pewter that are trees and bushes along the edge of the river as it disappears into an outline of hills behind.

I look down at my work table, knowing I've left the most important part of packing to the end. Every journey begins the same way. With reluctance, holding part of the self in abeyance, a distancing until I'm ready. I'm caught by this feeling, no matter what the destination. It's a suspension of the *want*, the real work, the getting serious, the facing up. But facing up also means admitting the dark places that are only too ready to seep from the shadows. It occurs to me that I'm not unlike Basil, turning circles inside the front door as soon as he imagines a hand reaching for a jacket.

I stand, hands extended over the surface, ready to choose. Floor lamp to one side, small easel before me, supplies laid out as if I'd been painting only yesterday. Two plastic containers, water in one. Striped socks, a contrast of cobalt and dusky blue, slit lengthwise and made into rags that hang from hooks at the side of the table. A bar of Sunlight soap, worn flat in an old sardine tin. Brushes of every size laid out side by side; a dozen stubby bottles of acrylics in colours I've blended myself.

The truth is, I haven't been in this room for weeks. The truth is, I haven't cared about this room or the paintings in it. My heart lurches as if my thoughts have just created a zone called *danger*.

Across the room, an abandoned abstract leans into the larger of my two easels. From here, the edges are dark and menacing. Tentacles grope along the lower half, trying to slither into position. At the top left, oranges and yellows spill from what could be a split gourd, a generous, big-hearted offering. I feel a jolt of something stirring, some earlier sense-image. I'm struck by the balance of the whole. But just as quickly, the glimmer of satisfaction is gone. A broad, pumpkin-coloured sweep wants a push to the centre; it wants . . . or maybe it's all right as it is and should be left alone.

When did I have the desire of those oranges and yellows inside me? I try to recover the feeling I had when I began to work on the canvas. Because here's the proof that I was making an effort, even if it turned out to be an aborted thrust. Stab and pull back, stab and pull back.

Anger is not so easy to disguise to the self.

My sister, Kay, would have something to say about that—if given the opening. She fills the silent spaces, has a name, a theory, for everything. As a child, she was always a leader. But she's more authoritative now, her ambition to the fore. It's partly her job, what she deals with every day in her work as a counsellor. She has to define problems, probe for solutions, solve problems. Sometimes I picture a sleep-deprived student facing her across a wide desk, fumbling, looking down at his lap, inventing answers he thinks she would like to hear.

And what about Greg? Has he been seeing a counsellor at his own university? He wouldn't tell me one way or another. Not that I would ask. I don't push my way into his territory unless invited.

At the beginning, after Lena's death, after the funeral in November, he phoned home every few days. His grief was raw and undisguised, the calls painfully brief. They are less frequent now—more like every few weeks.

"Dad? Are you working yet? Are you okay?"

I wasn't able to help him and didn't know how anyway. Greg has been a worrier, a *Gramps,* from the day he was born. Remembering the waver in his voice during one of those calls makes me think of another episode from his childhood. He hadn't yet started school and I was away on assignment, doing illustrations for a natural history magazine that paid extremely well. I was staying at a motel in Alberta's Badlands and had been gone almost two weeks when I received a letter from Lena. In those days, we wrote when either of us was away. Or sent cards.

You've been missed from the moment you boarded the plane. All the way back from the airport Greg stared glumly out the side window of the car. He said, *"It isn't funny, you know. It isn't one bit funny when the family is split up like this."* When we returned to the house, he spread his palms—*truly indignant*—and said, accusing ME, as if I were the one responsible, *"Now there are only two."*

And how, Lena continued, *am I supposed to handle that?*

A picture from Greg was enclosed, three large crayoned stick figures holding hands. It was labelled FAMBLY. A multicoloured rainbow arced across the upper right corner. At the bottom left were a stick-figure dinosaur and a hoodoo, both tiny, as if to let me know that the work I was doing was small, in comparison to FAMBLY.

Well, we are two again, but a different two, and Greg and I are stumbling along, but in separate parts of the country.

I look around my workroom and wish for what I cannot have. A time warp, a few moments when the three of us are living under one roof again. A light left on in the hall for the last person to come in from the dark. A meal of heated leftovers, nothing fancy. A note from Lena on the fridge door telling me she has taken Greg to his swimming lesson. The music of Benny Goodman floating out from the living room, announcing that Lena is home from work. Our bodies touching, by intent, as we brush past each other in the doorway.

A sharp bark from Basil at the foot of the stairs gets me moving again, and I begin to slide items into a shoulder pack from shelves above the table. A bound sketch pad, India ink, bamboo stylus that I probably won't use but will bring anyway. A wooden box with a hinged lid that Greg unearthed at a flea market in Halifax two years ago and gave me for Christmas. A faded list, pasted inside the lid, shows that the box was once used to store medical slides. In thin lines of penmanship, the list reads: *Blood, Cardiac muscle,*

Trachea, Tonsil, Tooth. I've left the list in place because I like the idea of objects in their original state. And I use the box now to hold charcoal, graphite pencils, jackknife for sharpening, soft eraser, quills. I take these on the road with me every time I travel. When Greg came home during Christmas break that year, he packed the box inside a carry-on suitcase he'd built from cardboard. There had been snowstorms on the East Coast and these had caused airport confusions, cancellations, rebookings, a bleary-eyed son arriving hours late. A son who was proud of his homemade suitcase and had Lena and me laughing the moment we picked him up and took a look at his luggage.

I stuff more bits and pieces into the side pockets of my pack. I'm not exactly sure what I'll need, but I'll figure this out along the way. More slit socks for rags, a capped container for water. Some of my river drawings are abstracts in graphite; some have been done in pen and ink. The larger acrylics were done at home in my studio. My upcoming show will be a mixture of the three.

I add a second sketch pad, though it's a joke to think I'll fill two. This isn't a trip to the other side of the planet. The overseas work was done—sporadically—during the decade before the idea became a proposal. *River themes* was the way Lena referred to my project, long before the work revealed its true shape to me.

I cast my memory back over countries visited, histories read, tales of rivers listened to and told. Not to mention the stack of drawings and paintings that has accumulated. My friend Nathan, who owns the gallery where I exhibit, suggested the show while I was still seeing the work in its separate parts.

"Join them up," he said. "Why not?" And then he began to talk quickly, as if he had a plan, as if the words might stop if he slowed down. "Put the ink drawings and some of the acrylics together," he said. "Just the river series. You select, you decide. The theme is fabulous, Bin, it's a great sequence. Every painting, every drawing is different, but with a mood or form that sets it apart. Totally recognizable as an Okuma abstract. I especially love the sensation of movement. The work is poetic, lyrical. And we can link the exhibit with publication. Otto will do the catalogue, I'm sure of it—he has the money. You can add short personal accounts if you want text. Leave that part to me; I'll discuss it with Otto. He'll probably want to write the introduction himself, he knows your work so well. We'll have the show and launch the book at the same time. We can celebrate, have a grand opening."

Nathan's gallery is close to the market, a modern building with three rooms and great lighting, great space. He and Otto have collaborated this way before. The exhibition I've agreed to is scheduled for the last week of November, seven months from now, and it's true that most of the work is complete, drawings and paintings delivered. But Otto has begun to ask for extra information, details, discussions on individual pieces. I haven't settled on a title yet, for the catalogue or the show—though it will be the same for both. We've tossed ideas back and forth since fall, and both Nathan and Otto are waiting for me to make up my mind.

All of this has become a disturbing weight in my head. But I'm thinking clearly enough to know that the trip, sudden though it might be, has to be a good idea. I need to get away from here, if only for a few weeks. I'm not in the mood for the company of friends—Basil excepted—and I don't want to fly. It will be better to get behind the wheel and point the car west. I'd drive non-stop if I thought I could stay awake.

I recognize the buildup of energy that has to be released, energy I should be putting into my work. *So,* I argue with myself. *Run away. You aren't going to hurt anyone.* Again, I have a flash of the old surge through the limbs, a feeling that I should be working on three canvases at once, an urge so strong, I could run in any direction and create while on the move. Until I'd be forced to stop and think, and then I'd start to feel like an imposter. There's a fragile line between the desire to create and the act of creation. An idea can so quickly lose its lustre—and so easily disappear.

I look down at Otto's most recent note, lying on my work table.

Would you add half a dozen lines to this, Bin—so we can write up a brief description for the jacket? Send it back as soon as you can. Your own words. We'll tidy it up and do the rest.

He has already begun:

RIVERS (working title only, I know, I know)
EXCITING NEW OFFERING FROM CELEBRATED ARTIST
BIN OKUMA

After that, blank space.

Trying to reassure, no doubt. I'm betting that Nathan was in the background when the note was sent out. If I were to imagine conversations between the two men, I'd be weary. Uncertain. About the entire project—dual project, as it's now become. But they are both loyal; I know this. And now that the momentum is underway, they'll see the project through to the end. Even with Otto distracted by his new girlfriend.

Twice divorced, Otto readily admits his weakness for phases. The present phase began with dreams of geisha, he told me. And involves all things Japanese, including Miki, who emigrated from Japan a year ago and has now moved in with him. She is teaching him to make *sushi* on weekends, he says, and he's become an expert. They eat out in Japanese restaurants twice a week, and I've joined them a couple of times. A month ago, Miki brought along a friend, a woman who works at the Japanese embassy. I didn't comment when Otto called me, next day. He has also begun to track down woodblock prints, and attends auctions seeking more. He'll be travelling to a Buddhist retreat for two weeks this summer while Miki visits her family in Japan. I swear he would turn Japanese if he could. I think of the years I looked into the mirror, never liking the person I saw, wishing to be anything—anyone—but. And marvel at the leap through time. So many Japanese Canadian men of my generation turned away from Japanese women. They made friends with and married *hakujin*— "white" girls. And I found Lena. In Montreal. We found each other.

I should be happy to have the support of Otto and Nathan, happy that the show will take place at all. And it is time for a show. My work has been changing over the last four or five years. *A natural evolution,* Lena told me a couple of years ago. *Look at you. An idea, a shape, a brushstroke, a mood: one begets another, begets another. It's so organic, so much about form. It's all about challenge and risk with you, isn't it?*

Challenge and risk. That sums it up. Or did. Because, lately, my biggest worry about the project, the one that has gnawed up the side of me with depressing persistence, is that the spirit of the whole has not been realized. Not on paper, not on canvas, not at all.

There was a time—it now seems long ago—when I cared about all of this.

I did not complete the catalogue description for Otto, nor did I send it back.

I think of Otto at the funeral, a quick pat on the arm, his hand resting on my sleeve. "It will be good for you to finish the river project, Bin. Get it done once and for all. You've dragged it behind you long enough. You need to sink into it again. It will give you something to do."

His use of the word *sink* unnoticed by him, even as it was uttered. He didn't mean to discourage or offend, I know. But while he was speaking, I could see over his shoulder the rectangular box that held Lena's ashes, three feet behind him on a polished wooden stand. That was immediately after the service, before everyone assembled to walk through the cemetery's convoluted paths that led to the "garden" where the ashes were to be interred. There was initial confusion before people fell into some sort of procession. Feet moving in different directions until a leader emerged and order prevailed. Who was that leader? Someone to the left of me, someone from the funeral parlour, perhaps. Voices were subdued, people half-nodded to one another. My brother and sister had arrived, and Lena's family, of course. They had to be there. They *were* there. It must have been Greg on my left. We were trying to look out for each other. Keep moving. Silently. No obligation to say anything to anyone. Made insensible, insensate, made useless by grief.

I go to the rolltop desk in the corner of my studio and open the long drawer beneath its extendable surface. There's a small Japanese scroll in there and, beside it, a manila folder with printing along the top edge: FRASER RIVER CAMP / REMOVAL FROM PACIFIC COAST. Lena gathered and compiled the contents. Her signature—familiar, flowing, at a forward slant—is written across the bottom. All the differences between us are blatant in that signature. My own, in comparison, resembles hidden tracks. I take the folder out of the drawer and shove it into my pack. A folder I have not, until this moment, intended to bring. Now it will be with me, whether I decide to look at it or not.

Keep river as your focus, Lena said, often enough. She repeated it like a mantra. Through the weeks and months and many summers that she, and sometimes she and Greg, accompanied me on my travels. *This is an important project for you, Bin. Keep river as your focus and the work will get done.*

I do a final check of the room from the doorway, glance back and see what I have not been looking for. Along the windowsill, my array of *smalls,* collected over the years. From Long River in Prince Edward Island, a sandstone quill holder, brownish red, plucked in its natural state. A tiny glass whale with jagged flukes from the Saguenay. A palm-sized burl picked up on a trail near the Saco River in Maine. A delicate Bourgault carving of a man in a green toque, from Saint-Jean-Port-Joli on the St. Lawrence. I had settled on a large rock behind the *auberge* in that place and was watching the tide push back the great river. It was a summer night, and a yellow band of light floated above the waterline. The evening was so layered, so exquisite, I sank into it and couldn't leave. By the time complete darkness rolled up the river valley, all that remained visible was a band of woolly cloud joining west to east. A grove of trees to my right had blackened in silhouette, and Lena stepped out of that blur of darkness and made her way down the slope. She was shaking her head. *Did you forget you were to meet me in the dining room? I might have known.* But she came to sit with me, in the dark.

Here, too, is my tiny clay seaman, his left leg snapped below the knee. Created to sit on the edge of a shelf or sill, he is ruddy and elegant, even with a peg leg. Lena and Greg chose him in a pottery shop in Cornwall while I was sketching outcrops on the lower banks of the Helford Estuary. It was a working holiday for me. We had sailed, embarking in New York and docking in Southampton, where we rented a car. We were almost five days at sea before reaching England, and Greg—who was eight at the time—spent much of the voyage asking about ocean tremors, canyons, earthquakes. He was fascinated, but full of worry, too. *Are we crossing an ocean ridge right now, an ocean trench? Will our ship be lost at sea?* I gave him a compact sketchbook of his own, a blue Hilroy, and he drew pictures of wrecks all the way across the Atlantic. In pencil and ink he created ships with flags, primitive lifeboats, our cabin porthole, spray and blue froth, sailors and pirates, undersea creatures, shark and octopus, giant fish eating smaller fish, a narrow trill of waves inked and glued separately beneath a ship as if in afterthought—or maybe a carefully planned collage. All part of his vision. He also drew a spewing ocean volcano in menacing black and red crayon. Two ships bobbed on rocky waves to the right of the picture. An explanation accompanied: *The big ship is helping the little ship to get by safely.* Someone was often lending a helping hand in Greg's drawings.

Later, the same afternoon I'd been sketching in Cornwall, we drove the car to Helston and sat on a stone wall at the top of the hill and ate Cornish pasties purchased from a street vendor. That was when Lena and Greg presented me with the clay seaman. But shortly after we returned to Canada, my sleeve brushed the cap of the tiny man as I reached towards the window, and I knocked him to the floor.

Bin, protector of fractured and broken goods. Lena laughed at my collection of smalls, even when she herself was fractured and broken. Though neither of us knew how broken she was. Nor did we know that the stroke that took her life had already announced its arrival, in the weeks preceding her death.

CHAPTER 3

I haul things out to the station wagon: Thermos, cooler with the green lid, road map on the passenger seat, camera, a bottle of Scotch in its sturdy cylinder, Beethoven tapes and some of Lena's Benny Goodmans. Books to read in motels along the way, placed on the floor, passenger side: Ishiguro's *An Artist of the Floating World*, which Greg has been urging me to read for a few years; essays by Heinrich Böll; Beethoven's letters. I'll be lucky to finish any one book completely, but at least I'll have choice. I give silent thanks to Okuma-san and wonder, as I often have, if without him in my life I'd have come to music, literature, even my own painting, in the same way.

Basil, now certain of an upset in routine, is executing tight circles in the front hall. There's a blur of shades on his haunches as he hurls himself at the door every time I go outside with a load.

"Hang on, Basil, hang on," I call out, but he continues to half-whine, half-bark until he hears the words *Get in the car, Basil*, at which he bolts off the steps, stands panting beside the car until the trunk is open and launches himself from a standing start, up and into the back.

Because of his odd body shape, it always seems that he won't get off the ground, but he ends up inside first try. Low and heavy, three feet long, nose to tail, is my hound with the grand name and the heavy paws. He'll continue to turn circles in the confined space of the car and won't stop until we're past the turnoff to the kennels, a road the two of us know well.

The back has been flattened to give him plenty of room. I've thrown in a worn piece of mat, a couple of ragged towels, a bag of dog food, pouches of meat, leash, hide chews, his Kong, a sealed container of water. Most of this is stacked on the floor behind the front seats. There's more baggage for Basil than there is for me.

I slide into the car and take a last look at the house. And there is Lena at the front door, her face expressionless. One hand rests against the edge of the door as if she can't wait to push it shut, the other is at her waist. I know the stance; we were married twenty-six years. Didn't she say, somewhat mysteriously, that the trip had been put off long enough? When? When did she say that? The trip was postponed so many times. But postponements didn't stop the subject from coming up. It was clear all along that Lena wanted me to go back. Back meaning farther than Alberta, farther than the homes of my sister and brother in Edmonton, where we have always come to a full stop. Back meaning all the way back, through the Rockies and as far as the inland camp on the Fraser River. Or maybe farther still, to the West Coast and the Pacific, where my own journey began.

None of this was surprising, given Lena's penchant for gathering history. She taught the subject at the University of Ottawa and, in her spare time, filled an entire upstairs closet with the genealogical history of her own family—photos and documents of generations that preceded her. Maybe, if asked, Greg will deal with those covered containers someday. But not now. What twenty-year-old is interested in his parents' family history? *All in good time,* Lena used to say. Greg might even decide to turn the task over to Lena's sister and brother. Let them sort it out.

Of course, it is not Lena at the front door. How could she have had a stroke at the age of forty-nine? It's difficult not to keep asking the question. How could anyone who is not yet fifty have a stroke? What didn't we know? Why didn't she tell me what was going on?

The front door is firmly closed and locked, the spare key given to Miss Carrie, who, with her diminutive frame, now emerges from her own house next door and stands at the top of her veranda step. She offers a regal wave in farewell. She has thrown some sort of greatcoat over her back, and its weight tips her forward more than usual. She has one hand on her walker and tilts her eyes upwards as if to acknowledge a neck too fragile to support her head and its thickness of white hair. She has declared, in the past, that she is the same age as the stone house she lives in, though she's never divulged how many years that is. Ninety-something, no further details. The house was inherited from her late father, a General of the Great War, whom she looked after in his old age. Although he's been dead for decades, his presence fills the house and she still refers to him as "Daddy." "Mommy" died ten years before "Daddy." All of this happened before we moved into the neighbourhood. Miss Carrie doesn't seem to have much ready income apart from her pension, but she is surrounded by ancient furniture and memorabilia. During the seventies, when we bought our house, she adopted us as family and later became an honorary, close-at-hand grandma to Greg when he was born. Now she's the only "grandmother" he has. When I phoned last night to tell her I was heading west on a sudden trip, she offered to bring in the mail and keep an eye on things, as she usually does.

"I'm nearly blind," she's been saying for two decades. "Blind as an underground mole." But there isn't much Miss Carrie doesn't see. And she insists that she's capable of checking my house, casting out junk mail, watering indoor plants. She'll do that with love and care, in the same way she goes outside with a small wooden bucket on summer evenings to water a scraggly maple, which, against odds, has pushed up through cement on city property in front of her house. "Poor tree," she mutters while she pours water to its roots. "Someone has to help you stay alive."

I wave to her now and start to back out of the driveway, feeling that I'm the one who has the eyesight of an underground mole. And it's impossible not to hear Lena beside me, steering me along.

"What do you want?" I ask the air inside the car. I even turn my head to the right. Somehow, Basil knows I'm not addressing him. It wouldn't be the first time the hound reads the human mind.

What do you? the silence replies.

Once on the street, my foot drops heavily to the pedal, though it's not my intention to depart in a roar. Too late. Miss Carrie has seen my lips move before I pull away. She's caught me talking to myself. Not that she doesn't do the same. She speaks her thoughts aloud, laughs as she does, makes no apologies.

She'll think I'm talking to Basil. Still, I'm distracted. By the belief, momentary as it was, that Lena really was there. First at the door, and then beside me. As vivid and real as she was in my early-morning dream.

Music blasts from the car radio and I'm on my way. What I hear is a burst of chaos. The middle of something I can't immediately identify.

A violent clash of sounds. Notes brought together against their will. Dissonance. And then, I recognize *Eroica,* first movement. The chaotic climax is reached, followed by pulsing, shrugging, withering steps. I know the symphony in its entirety thanks to Okuma-san, who, for so many years, tried to teach me about grand themes.

I turn the corner at the end of the street, relieved that Miss Carrie's house and my own can no longer be seen in the rear-view. *Leave it behind. Leave it all behind.* Lena's voice in my head. I've read that soon after a loved one dies, the person's voice will no longer be remembered. But this hasn't happened to me, not at all. Not even after five months have passed.

As *Eroica* continues, I think of Beethoven, who must have known a great deal about chaos and suffering and grand themes. He died in his fifty-seventh year, younger than I am now. What did he know of the human condition to be able to write the last movement of the Ninth Symphony? What did he believe—believe in—when he chose the poetry of Schiller, whose work he so much admired? He declared Schiller to be an "immortal" and worth the trouble of setting his words to music. *Oh, you millions! . . . above the canopy of stars . . . a loving Father surely must dwell.*

It's all so bloody complicated. The persistent attempts to put something meaningful on canvas—or into music, or on the page.

"Sex and death," Otto said during one of our early meetings to discuss the river project. "*Eros, Thanatos.* Think of it, Bin. Every book I publish is ultimately about sex and death."

But he hasn't said that since Lena's funeral. And he's never mentioned the word *love.*

I stop at a light, do my best to shove everything sideways out of mind: my sister's phone call, First Father asking to see me, the last of the river drawings—due and overdue.

At my most recent meeting with Otto and Nathan, Otto said, "Could we settle on the middle of June at the latest, Bin? For a final deadline? For the sake of the catalogue? It'll be stretching things with the show in November, but we can do it—if we all agree. Of course, the last bits and pieces have to be tidied up."

Otto, Nathan, myself nodding silently. The solid handshakes that followed. The perpetual need to tidy up.

Again, I try to clear my head, to focus on the drive ahead, to imagine a destination. But the thought of destination, the word, the sound of it, makes me wonder what my real destination is: The camp? First Father? Final drawings for the show?

Why am I leaving?

You're trying to force things to matter.

I want to work.

Which means? A hope that your life will change?

I have the distinct sensation that despite the wheels of the car rotating as they should, I'm suspended in a kind of punishing no man's land. I narrow a slit in my mind, try to block everything but the continuing music of *Eroica*. Grand themes. I've lived enough for a lifetime and I'm not an old man yet. But because I'm making an effort not to, I think of Lena again. It's the Beethoven. One of my favourite pieces is his *Leonore Overture III,* which reminds me of Lena and not only because of the name. It's the opening. The extended note. The descending scale that levels in a thickening of darkness. And then, a flute entering from far away, leading up into the light as if announcing its arrival through a long tunnel. Joy rising from an underground spring, that's the way I hear it. Far and near, far and near. Whatever it was that Beethoven intended, he understood about life setting up patterns. Even so, Leonore transcends pattern, so woven is it with rivers and peaks. Always something hidden and receding. Always the flute, beckoning and bringing a glimmer of light. After that, turmoil, frenzied and exuberant. The breaking of pattern. And then, the notes ascend again. That would be Lena, all of those things. I am the receding part.

I think of Okuma-san, who shared his knowledge of Beethoven with me. It was his singular passion. Okuma-san, whom I once believed to be old. But anyone over thirty would have appeared old to a child. How could I have known, when I first met him, that he was only in his mid-forties? Numbers meant nothing. Hiroshi and Keiko and I referred to him as the old man who arrived in camp without a family. The man who'd been hiding out in Vancouver, looking after a sick wife. When she died, he came out of hiding and was promptly arrested a block from Powell Street in Japtown, as it was then called. Now, more kindly, more politely known—historically, for the tourists at least—as Japantown. Childless, Okuma-san arrived at our place of internment above the banks of the Fraser two years after everyone else. I could not have understood this at the time, but he must have appeared older than he was because of sadness and grief.

I shift gears, nose the car up an incline and down again. Realize, with no surprise, that I've pointed the car towards the Ottawa River. A detour across the bridge and into nearby Quebec, to an oasis both quiet and turbulent, a place I discovered years ago and to which I often return alone. Not always alone; Lena came with me on several occasions.

"You always bring me to water," she once said. "No matter what else you invite me to do or where we do it, we end up walking trails beside a river. Or crossing a bridge and staring down at one."

"Maybe," I replied. I was weighing this as a new idea, wondering if it was true.

"Remember the Enz?" she said. "When we took Greg to the Black Forest?"

"I do," I said. "The tiny river with the large roar." I was remembering ice formations, horseshoe shapes that clung upside down to branches along the banks. In my mind I saw frosted white against the steel-hard blue of rushing water.

"And what about wading the length of a river? Being knee-deep in the Nerepis, surrounded by eels?" She shuddered as she brought the memory forward.

I hadn't thought about the eels for a long time, thick brown bodies of spawning eels that had come in from the sea and camouflaged the bottom of the shallow Nerepis. When we disturbed them, not knowing they were there—but they were, by the thousands—they reared their heads in rapid, wide-fanned splashes. There was something monstrous, something truly horrifying about the scene. But we had already waded some distance and couldn't get out of the water for another quarter mile because of the tangle of scrub that had grown to the edges of the riverbank. There was no trail to climb to and no turning back. How could either of us ever forget?

"There were better places," said Lena. "The Adirondacks."

"The upside-down mountains in the Au Sable. Morning air like polished silver."

"Or brooding across a dark surface in the evening," she said.

And I thought of shadow. Of shadow and light.

Now, the sight of the Ottawa River up close brings a surge of old energy. It will be easy to recross and join the main road again before I head for the Trans-Canada Highway. I might do a quick sketch before I officially depart for the West. Make an attempt to capture the spring rage of gathering waters.

First day out and, already, I want to draw. But this is not about sex and death. Or do I deceive myself? If Otto were present, he would look away, sagely, cautiously. Otto, who has found Miki and who is searching for answers in things Japanese.

Basil has settled down, knowing we're safely past the road that leads to the kennels. I glance in the mirror and an exchange takes place—his cheerful, shaggy face greeting my own. The hound's permanent expression is one of enthusiasm, of being pleased with himself, though he can alter this at will. I'm convinced that he hears sadness, smells detachment, knows grief. Reading my mind again, he sniffs and lowers himself out of sight behind my seat.

Basil has always preferred Lena's company to mine—*I was born in the year of the dog,* she used to say. *That has to count for something. Right, Basil?* But Basil loves a trip, and he won't complain about my company. I've arranged to drop him off at Kay's, in any case, once we reach Edmonton, five or six days from now. From there, I'll travel alone and pick him up on the way back. Kay has a snappy little dog, Diva, who will keep him in line. Diva is half his size, but wicked.

I turn off the radio. *Eroica* is over but I don't know when I stopped paying attention, or whether a subconscious part of me completed the piece. Did I switch to Leonore in my head? I park the car on a dirt road beside a thin stand of poplars. No one is around. Patches of snow have begun to melt into last year's wild grasses beside the road. Along shore, jagged pieces of ice have been shoved up onto layered shale. I lock the car, zip my jacket and look out over an expanse of river that is both solid and free-flowing at the same time. It's been a long winter and part of the river is still frozen, even this late in spring. Stray bits and pieces of ice are floating past on the current. Farther upstream, where the river is wider, the surface looks static, the dullest of greys. Close at hand, the smaller floes hold a tint of the palest blue. There must be cracks in the large sheet upstream. I know how fast the current can be. It's a dark, continuous force, an unending murmur under ice, rushing towards open water.

I begin to walk in the direction of the current, downriver, towards an elevation of land. There's an open stretch and I hear the roar of rapids in the distance. The river never freezes over white water there, no matter how cold the winter. Gulls wheel overhead. Basil, immensely pleased at being out of the car so soon, has found enough melting snow to roll in. His long back, his short legs and huge feet make me think of a hairy weight sinking through earth. He'll follow when he's ready, good hound that he is. We'll take our chances on ice balls building up between his pads.

I walk for ten minutes under low cloud. Follow the path worn down centuries ago by Native Algonquins as they brought their furs to scattered trading posts. The portage was established long before the arrival of the *voyageurs,* who sought furs and adventure as they headed west, in the opposite direction. I climb the slope that looks out over fast water and ragged shore. At the highest point along the bank, I turn and look back.

In the short time since I parked the car, the huge grey mass upriver has begun to rotate. After being so tightly lodged all winter, it has made a distinct but sluggish shift, as if the river itself is threatening to turn sideways. Freed at the edges, caught by the current and with nothing to impede it, this vast floe is already picking up speed. I consider running back to the car to get the camera or my sketch pad, one or the other. But if I do, I'll miss the spectacle that's about to unfold.

I scramble to lower ground and wait. The river is impossibly narrow here, too narrow. The approaching ice will not have enough space to manoeuvre and will have to grind itself against shore. As it approaches, the sound is one of a persistent, slurring mush. Basil has caught up and pauses beside me, alert. He hears it, too.

First, there is sound. This is the order of things.

The sheet is wide, its farthest edges a blur. The ground shudders and ice crashes simultaneously through current and against shore, piling up layer after layer of harsh, metallic silt. What first appeared to be slush has become a chain of high, grating hills. Never again will I witness the purity of this shade of blue.

The immense portion of ice that remains in the water now flows swiftly by, but everything has happened so quickly I have difficulty separating detail. When I step back, I realize how cold I am, and pull up the hood of my jacket. I dig at a heap of newly stacked ice with the heel of my hiking boot and watch the mass explode into hundreds of candled segments, the result of days of sun preparing the melt over the river. Crystals scatter like spears from dismembered chandeliers. One form becomes another and another.

I know how impossible it would be to try to capture what has just taken place. A light rain is beginning—I can hear and feel the patter of drops on my hood. Gulls fly drunkenly into the wind. Some have begun to lift off the shore in groups of twos and threes, and are about to settle on chunks of ice that have broken away from the main floe and now trail in its wake. Each chunk is no more than a foot or two in breadth; each appears to be specially carved for riding out the waves with a bird on top. And this, before my eyes, is what the gulls now begin to do. They are hitching rides. They even seem to be selecting the best shapes. All for the purpose of partaking in some adolescent feathered rite.

Lena's voice in my head again. Speaking French, as she was sometimes wont to do—having grown up in Montreal. *C'est comique. C'est vraiment comique.*

The chunks pick up speed, swirl and bob in the direction of the rapids. With split-second timing, the gulls lift to safety precisely as each piece of ice beneath their feet reaches white water and flips upside down. From there, they fly upstream and ride down again.

It's the bird midway at the fair. They don't seem to tire of these daredevil rides that tease danger. Faster and faster they travel under layers of descending cloud. And then, a last flat sheet of ice shifts and turns with a mild roar, dips to the whitecaps like a salute and is gone. Out of sight, beyond hearing. The river, still swollen, is dark but free.

I don't know how long I've been standing here. I do know that this is breakup, what I have just seen.

At the car, I remove my wet jacket and open the trunk for Basil, who takes his time about climbing in. He'd run miles if I let him, even in the rain. Especially in the rain. I start the engine and turn up the heat, full blast. Glance out the side window. The gulls are circling aimlessly above the river, as if suddenly bereft.

Basil pokes his head over the back of the seat and rests the weight of his damp and hairy chin on my shoulder. A thick fug of warmth permeates the inside of the car and mixes with the odour of wet dog. I look out the window again at the gulls and imagine beginnings: the way I'll shape angular chunks of ice, the overwhelming greyness, a flash of wing to hover over speeding darkness while the river discharges its winter debris. I think of the Fraser again, my childhood river, and a rush of images floods up so suddenly, I'm caught off balance. *It happens,* Kay's maddening professional voice once said over the phone. *It's always there, the camp, close beneath the surface. For all of us.*

It is when I feel the cold touch of Basil's nose against my neck that I curse the fates, lower my head and weep.

CHAPTER 4

I'm on the road, seriously on the road, enjoying my hands on the wheel, the liberating sense of moving forward. "Travel does that," Lena used to say. "It clips the fetters of routine."

Every time we started out on a trip, the moment we pulled away from the curb in front of the house, she stretched her arms wide and kicked off her shoes. Until it was her turn in the driver's seat—we switched every three or four hours. Our conversation changed, too; it became more contemplative, the two of us staring straight ahead. As I am now, with thoughts and memories tumbling unbidden, scrambling over one another to grab my attention. Inevitable, since I'm heading for the camp on the other side of the country. I look in the rear-view and swear that Basil is nodding. But he makes a smacking sound, ducks his head and settles behind me again. It's going to be a long journey back.

*

FIFTY-FIVE YEARS AGO, my first journey began. It was early 1942, and despite my young age then, I can clearly recall some events from that time. Other events have been pieced together from a jumble of images, fragments of conversations overheard, body memories, sensations. Given the intervening years, it's impossible to separate one way of remembering from another.

. My brother and sister, Henry and Kay, who have lived in Alberta for decades, know more stories from the early years, simply because they were older at the time. Truth to tell, when the three of us are together, which is not often, we rarely discuss the war years or the 21,000 people of Japanese ancestry forcibly removed from their homes on the West Coast and moved inland. A considerable feat on the part of the government and the RCMP, considering how many of us there were to round up. The numbers were greater in the U.S.—114,000 Japanese Americans having been interned at the same time. These were highly organized manoeuvres on the part of both countries, quick reactions to the Japanese attack on Pearl Harbor, December 7, 1941.

During my infrequent visits to Edmonton over the years, and while trying to pretend that we are still family, no one has ever really wanted to poke at the layers of shadow that have fallen behind us since that time. Except Lena. In the early years of our marriage, when she accompanied me to Alberta, she was forthright about aiming questions.

"They changed your names? That's an outrage! How could such a thing be allowed? What are your real names, then? Do you have two names—one English, one Japanese?"

Yes, and yes.

I remember how indignant she was on our behalf, how I'd become used to this. Henry and Kay responded politely, if not fully.

Yes, their names had once been Hiroshi and Keiko. No, they hadn't bothered to change them back. Yes, it did create confusion each time they applied for a passport. The same agencies that had taken their names away now demanded that the originals be pulled out of storage. "It's laughable," Henry told Lena, but there was an edge to his laughter. When he suddenly referred to the part of the coast from which we'd been removed as "the Jap-free zone," his outburst took all of us by surprise.

Henry and Kay did not offer information that wasn't asked for. They did not, for instance, tell Lena that my first name was changed to Benjamin by an Anglican missionary who taught some of our classes in school during the camp years—on the pretext that Japanese names were too difficult to spell and remember. *And just how difficult was the name Bin?* Or that my name was changed back to Bin when we left the camp. And changed again to Ben, by the next teacher, in the postwar school I attended. That when we moved east, I reclaimed my real name for the final time. I was the one who told Lena all of that. "Henry and Kay probably kept their English names because keeping them made their lives easier," I told her. "I never asked them why."

But perhaps I, too, am guilty of not offering information. I did not tell my brother and sister that it was Lena who requested, persisted, and finally demanded to see long-forbidden documents kept secret for more than half a century. That when the embargo on information about the internment was quietly lifted a decade ago, it was Lena who stood at the desk of the National Archives with written request in hand. As a Caucasian, she was required to present my signature as proof that she was a member of my family— hence, permitted access to the files. I had to accompany her during that first visit, but I never went back.

Locating the files wasn't easy, but Lena was not a person to give up. After weeks of following blind alleys to their frustrating ends, after tracking references and cross-references, after sitting in darkened rooms feeding slivers of microfiche into machines, after reading pages on blurry screens—whole paragraphs having been censored and blacked out—she paid for and obtained copies of everything she could turn up. When she was not permitted to see originals, she demanded copies. Of transcripts of tapes she was not permitted to view in their entirety; of auction papers concerning the fate of homes that had once belonged to my parents, grandparents, uncles, aunts, cousins. Details of fishing boats, insurance policies, beds, tables, chairs, carpets, trunks stuffed with dishes and linens, crates packed with fishing nets and tools.

Lena read excerpts to me from some of the letters, which were couched in politely firm but always condescending language, written during and immediately after the war by representatives whose job it was to explain to 21,000 people why there was nothing left.

—*It was reported that the house was ransacked. The crates you say you listed were never found at the site.*

—*The present owner of the house states that she does not recognize the Japanese interest in this property. Therefore . . .*

Yes, Lena found explanations. About the disappearance and disposal of household goods that we were forced to leave behind in our family home during the early winter months of 1942. The eventual sum, which represented total value before expenses, was assessed at $24.75. After being charged an "auctioneer's fee" of $2.48 and a "moving fee" of $3.42, our father was paid $18.85 in 1946, after the end of the war.

Eighteen dollars and eighty-five cents. A figure not easy to forget. A cheque was sent to Father, in that amount.

For an entire house. A house full of goods.

Who knows, after all this time, what really went on behind the scenes and what happened to the parts of our lives that we had to leave behind?

Strangely enough, Lena knew. Or partly knew. Lena the historian, born in December 1946, the year of the dog, one year after the end of the war, and unaware of these events until shortly before we married. She was the one who tracked my personal history.

I did not take part in the unearthing of Lena's discoveries. Having lived through the internment once, I had no desire to read through files and live through it again. Especially after hearing her rant after each day's research.

Leave the past alone, I wanted to tell her.

"How can you not want to know your own history?" she asked, genuinely perplexed. "We have a son. He'll want to read these papers someday. It's his history, too. There are relatives he hasn't met west of the Rockies, cousins he doesn't know. But most of all, the history is yours—to claim, or reclaim. Whatever!"

Did she forget that she had also told me how she'd wept over the documents while sitting at a long table inside the high-ceilinged room of the archives? A comment that made me even more determined not to know. I had no desire to weep. No desire for more anger. I had, I thought, distanced myself from the past in whatever ways I could.

Despite my determination, I admit that I listened when Lena read out details of the auction and the way the ownership of our family home on Vancouver Island was transferred to strangers who later denied that our father and Uncle Kenji had built it, board by board.

But I could not make myself open the manila folder she ultimately carried home at the completion of her single-minded search.

I could not make a move to lift it. I could not riffle the pages to see if they contained a single paragraph of meaningful information.

Lena, having finished what she set out to do, eventually stopped mentioning the folder and stowed it in my rolltop desk, where it has remained ever since. Until I crammed it into my pack this morning. Now it's in the car, travelling beside me.

Perhaps I did not want Lena's version of my history because I knew it would differ from the one I had brought to a standstill in my own memory. If I were to call it up, my version would be active. People would be on the move, changing direction, criss-crossing in my head. For decades after leaving the camps, everyone I knew was involved in the same struggle. Relocating. Trying to fit in. Moving. Moving again. Trying to find work. Dropping out of sight—sometimes for years. Maintaining an awareness of others, but silently. Sending word back, but never telling the entire truth.

Also, in my version, while some stories are unfinished, others have reached their end. Okuma-san's, for instance. His story reached its end in 1967. It was the year I left Montreal for England, on a scholarship to continue my studies in art. I was in my late twenties. I was eager; I wanted change; I wanted to learn everything I could. I wanted to stand before the great masters in the grand museums of Europe. I wanted to meet other art students. I wanted to explore the streets of London.

But first, I went to say goodbye to Okuma-san. He had retired two years earlier and was living in a small house near the river in the west end of Ottawa. I was with him the week before he died. If he knew that those days would be his last, he did not impart the fore-knowledge to me.

I hear Basil stirring, and take this to mean I should stop the car and let him out for a break, a leg stretch for both of us.

The landscape is tense and still in the frozen light. We are back-tracking into winter because the highway runs north before it angles west. Birch trees have stretched their bandaged limbs, begging for alms. When I pull over to the edge of the road and turn off the engine, Basil sends a sympathetic noise in my direction, a noise that sounds like a humpback whale, searching for a soulmate under water.

CHAPTER 5

1941–42

Although no one could have predicted exactly how or when the removal would take place, I learned later that there had been forebodings for weeks. Terrifying rumours, letters intercepted, newspapers stifled, community centres boarded up, schools closed, radios, cameras, binoculars taken away. Because we were isolated in our island community—the supply boat arrived only every ten days at the wharf near the village store—it wasn't easy to obtain information. Even so, the rumours were unstoppable. It was as if they'd been lifted by waves up and down the waters of the coast, as far north as Alaska, as far south as California and back again. There was fear of invasion by the Japanese navy or air force. There was fear that Japanese Canadian families were relaying information by secret code to the enemy. A blackout along the coast had been declared as a response to this fear and as a precaution against air raids. Every lantern, every light had to be hidden behind dark curtains in our homes after dusk.

The men of our fishing community were concerned. They gathered in small groups outside the houses and in front of the recently boarded-up canning factory. *We will be rounded up,* the rumours said. *We will be taken away.* Hadn't the men already been forced to turn in their boats under naval escort? A quick demand by authorities within days of the attack on Pearl Harbor.

Father was unhappy about the way this had been done because navy men who had no experience working the fishing boats had boarded and managed to damage many of those they'd brought in. Father was more fortunate than most. His boat, being larger, was used to tow four others, and he was permitted to remain at the helm. The boat was unharmed, but the navy men insisted that the crossing to the mainland take place at night. Both fishermen and navy men thrashed in wild wind and waves for hours in the dark, forced to approach land in the midst of terrifying swells.

After their boats were confiscated, the eight fishermen from our tiny bay were told to make their own way home from the mouth of the Fraser. They journeyed back to the west coast of Vancouver Island by ferry, by train and by mail boat. They were forced to pay their own fares. Some, more optimistic than others—Father was not one of the hopefuls—believed that their boats would be safe under naval protection.

The day the men were due home after turning in the boats, Mother watched the door for signs of Father. It was shortly before Christmas 1941. A small tree stood in a corner of our living room. Hiroshi and Keiko and I were creating decorations from paper, pipe cleaners, food colouring, and flotsam and jetsam that had washed up on our rocky beach. I could hear water lapping at the stilts beneath the floor. The tide was in. A sharp rap at the window startled us, and a man's voice shouted in to tell us that light was spilling between our curtains and could be seen from outside. Mother rushed to the window to close the curtains tightly, and she pegged them with a clothespin to keep them completely shut. Her fear was contained, but it was there and I sensed that, and I was afraid, too. At that moment, Father came in and stood at the end of the kitchen. Mother looked towards the door as if seeing him for the first time. Neither moved towards the other. Father was frowning, his face lined with fatigue.

"If you could have seen the boats at the Annieville Dyke," he said. "So many boats." He leaned against the table as if the strength had been sucked out of him, his voice a mixture of anger and disbelief. He was speaking Japanese. The two languages flip in my mind at the recollection. Until my understanding of Japanese kicks in, I always believe I've forgotten the language, though it was essentially my first—no English school having been provided in the inland camp to which we were removed, at least not at the beginning. Until the internees themselves built a school, and volunteers from the camp became our teachers.

"Ghost boats," Father continued. "The navy men didn't care if one boat rubbed another, or if windows were smashed, or if the boats bashed one another in the storm."

Of course, the boats were not returned. They were quickly auctioned off after the government allowed, in their orders, the insertion of the clause, *without the owners' consent.* A prudent look to the future, ensuring that no one would be coming back, that there would be nothing to come back to.

We also learned, some time later, that several Japanese fishermen sank their boats instead of giving them up. And Father found out about the death of one of his friends—a man whose boat had been boarded while he was on his way to New Westminster to turn it in. The man's throat had been slit and he was found on his drifting vessel, blood spattered on the floor, walls and ceiling of the cabin. He lived for a short time after being brought to hospital in Vancouver, but he wasn't able to say who had done it, who had cut the hole in his throat. He died, but the truth of his murder was never uncovered, the murderer never found.

Only weeks after the boats were turned in, we were rounded up by the RCMP. It was the year of the horse, the early winter of 1942. The mail boat, the *Princess Maquinna,* sailed into the bay to collect us. In the early morning, uniformed men made their way from house to house, banging at doors, giving warning. We were given two hours to pack. We were told to take with us only what we could carry.

And now, I have recollections of running behind Mother, my short legs tiring as I dragged and bumped a cloth bundle over uneven ground, all the while struggling to keep the pleat of her navy blue coat in my line of vision. Everyone was responsible for carrying something when we left, even the youngest. My bundle contained the heavy rice pot and *shamoji,* the wooden rice paddle, with several kitchen towels padded around both pot and lid.

My feet, arms, legs, nerves and tendons still remember the jarring and clanging of the pot, which must have separated from its lid while being dragged. How I hated that rice pot. My skin remembers the cruel curve of the lid as it clipped the side of first one leg and then the other, no matter how often I switched the bundle back and forth, no matter how I adjusted my gait or broke into a half run, always keeping the pleat of Mother's coat before me, so threatened was I by the possibility that both she and the pleat would disappear into the unforgiving mist.

No paper given up by the archives has ever documented that.

I never lost my animosity towards the rice pot, though it fed me through several more years of childhood. Later, Okuma-san had a smaller and different sort of pot, one I liked better because it evoked no memories of banging into the sides of my legs.

My ears have memory, too. They remember the harsh sound of Father's orders barked from the doorway of our house while we were packing. Father's mouth opened and closed and his shouts filled the kitchen, whereupon all other sound and movement ceased. No, not all sound, because I remember now that our neighbour Missisu—the childish word we used for Mrs., omitting her surname, which I never learned—was playing piano next door. The piece was Beethoven's Minuet in G. Notes that had been marching through the air in a deliberate and playful way began to slow, and then snagged on a distortion of mist that blurred the space between our side-by-side houses. I was well acquainted with the music, though I did not then know its name, nor did I know it was a minuet. But something happened while I was listening, something that had never happened before. I began to see milky-white colours in the air around me. A blur of waves undulated close to my body, and I was afraid I would lose my balance. I stood still while my ears listened to the notes, and in some primitive way, I understood that I was seeing sound. Sound that rippled and flowed visibly, next to my skin. And though I batted my hands in front of my face, several moments passed before the milkiness in the air went away.

Once more, I was conscious of rhythm, of music. I could also hear the emphatic tick of the grandfather clock that loomed in a dark corner of our living room. The room was shadowed by a thickness of trees on the hill that rose up behind our house and overlooked the bay, which curved in from the sea and was surrounded by mountains on three sides. The music went on, mixing and blending with the ticking of the clock. Some years later, after learning from Okuma-san what the music was called, I joined the two sounds and named it, privately, affectionately, Grandfather Minuet.

But on that particular morning, each time the kitchen door opened and shut, Missisu's notes from next door alternated between swelling in the midst of Father's shouts and then shrinking and pulling back. Notes that were loud and visible suddenly dimmed, as if their true intention was to accompany the listener to the depths of some unnamed darkness that, long ago, Beethoven had foreseen.

I had already heard the piece countless times while playing outside or while creating pictures as I sat on the boardwalk that linked the eight houses along the edge of the bay. Even then, though I hadn't yet started school, I was trying to draw, as any child does, using whatever was at hand: pencil on cardboard salvaged from the inside of cereal boxes or scraps of rough mill paper that sometimes came in on the supply boat. But never had I heard the music played the way it was that day. Missisu gave piano lessons to both Japanese and Caucasian children in our tiny fishing village, and inevitably, at some stage of learning, each student was asked to struggle through the minuet. On this memorable morning, it was Missisu herself who was playing.

But her fingers lifted off the keys before the piece was finished. That is what I remember. I was startled by the abrupt cessation of sound, and I was compelled to bring the melody to its end, silently, in my head. I was still standing in my parents' kitchen when I realized that tears were running down my cheeks, tears I did not let my brother and sister see; nor did I understand why I was weeping.

Now, in my mind's eye, I see a *tableau vivant:* Mother, Hiroshi, Keiko, frozen by Father's shouts. Mother looks up and in Father's direction. He is a full head taller than she. Two curls, one on either side of her forehead, seem to be stuck to her temples. And then—I am the onlooker inside this memory—Father, who has been coming in and out of the kitchen, turns and stomps down the outdoor steps. The dark rim of the bay is momentarily visible beyond his shoulders. Noises silenced by his anger start up again as if no interruption has taken place. Mother's slippered feet cross the room. Dishes rattle. Rice bowls, cutlery, pots, pans have been sorted on the kitchen table. What to bring? What to leave behind? The willow basket is bursting with clothes and bedding. Food for the journey is sealed in waxed paper: boiled eggs; rice balls wrapped in dark seaweed called *nori*; Mother's cucumber pickles, *tsukemono*. Along with chopsticks, *ohashi*, enough for everyone. All tucked in around the top of Mother's basket.

I hear sudden shrill voices—my brother and sister. Are they quarrelling? Is Hiroshi following Father's lead and trying to boss Keiko? Have we eaten breakfast? It is early morning, I'm certain of that. And why do I recall the stove? Bits of iron and pipe have been taken apart and are strewn around the once gleaming, now soot-covered floor. Father re-enters the kitchen, but he is no longer shouting.

"If they send us to the inland mountains," he says, addressing Mother, "we'll have to supply our own heat."

Not caring that cones of ash sift down or that there are puddles on the floor. Puddles, indoors! The unthinkable has happened. Father has been pouring buckets of water over the hot stove, and as it cools, he dismantles it piece by piece, dragging each section outside to be crated on the beach, all the while ignoring black streaks that smear one end of the kitchen to the other. No one pays attention to the heaps of mud and soot inside the house, and I begin to feel a giddy kind of danger because we have always been strictly required to remove our shoes at the outside door. The floor that Mother wipes every day with a damp mop is no longer spotless, and it becomes clear to me that what is happening at this moment in our kitchen is of greater magnitude than any stray specks of dirt we children might once have dragged in.

There is another *tableau* stamped in my memory, this from the evening before we boarded the mail boat that took us away. *Evacuation Eve*, Hiroshi came to call it. The memory is of the pyre and the dolls. Of slashes of colour emblazoned as indelibly as the bruises the lid of the rice pot formed on my fat little legs as I followed, at a run, behind my mother the next morning.

Firewood has been stacked into a neat pyramid on the rocky shore. Everyone is present, all eight families from the bay—but only Japanese. The *hakujin* families live in a separate part of the village.

It is the men who make the decision. They instruct the women to gather the dolls and bring them to the pyramid of wood on the strip of beach, which, at low tide, is awash with curiously speckled stones, tangles of seaweed, gaping oyster shells. I see now that the dolls, in some bizarre way, might be more precious than the houses we are about to leave behind. The fate of the dolls is the only fate that can be controlled in that brief and desperate time. Of course, the adults already know what the children learn only the next morning—that our homes will be looted the moment we are taken away.

Brightly coloured reds and golds, greens and silvers, jackets of silk, kimonos with permanent folds of upholstered fabric. These are the dolls that have graced the shelves of the *tokonoma*, the special corner of the living room, or that were displayed in glass cases on top of cabinets or buffets. Ceremonial dolls, dolls with real hair, black hair like Mother's, with bangs clipped evenly over the forehead. Cream-coloured faces with crescent-shaped laughing eyes and sharp, thin noses. A delicate arc of eyebrow on a face, hand-painted, as if by a calligrapher. Links to our unseen ancestors, works of art, every one—I sense and know this, even as a child. Later, I attempt to create them on paper, from memory, or I try to invent likenesses of my own.

The warrior dolls are *samurai,* with separate horse and leather armour. There are dolls for Boys' Day, Girls' Day, dolls to celebrate and honour the birth of each child. Purchased from stores in Steveston, on the mainland, or sent by great-grandparents never met. Dolls that were once lovingly packed in straw and shipped in wooden crates.

It is a symbolic fire, though the story passed down is that our parents were certain there would be no room for dolls in the bundles they would carry out of the house. It would be an outrage to think that dolls would be necessary for survival, especially during the bitter cold of that first winter in the Fraser Valley, when we ended up living in tents.

Did Mother agree with the men's decision when she carried our dolls down the steps and out to the pyre on the rocky beach? She did not. Because she defied Father and hid two of the smallest at the bottom of her willow basket. She continued to hide the dolls all the years of the war and all the years that came after, and I found out about them only after her death in 1987, less than a year before the public apology was made to us by the prime minister in the House of Commons. Mother did not live to hear those historic and crucial words. And though Lena and I were not at her funeral, when Mother's will was read, it was a surprise to everyone that the pair of dolls had been left to Lena. My sister, Kay, was instructed to send them to our home, which she did. Mother had known that it would be my wife who would unearth the family history. Even

though she had met Lena only half a dozen times—and never in
B.C.—Mother wanted our stories to be told.

On the narrow shore outside our home that evening, the dolls are
heaped onto the pyre. Each of the men carries a small vessel of *sake*,
rice wine, and sprinkles it over the pyramid of beauty, the pyramid
of art. The children are ordered not to cry, one more emotion that
must be buried, to simmer endlessly under the skin. My father, self-
appointed leader of the now boatless fishermen—wasn't he known
as "high-catcher" at sea?—strikes the first match. And everyone—
men, women, children, Mother staring straight ahead, Missisu's
eyes downcast, face expressionless—looks on in silence while cream-
coloured cheeks, elbows and fingers, upholstered pantaloons, kimonos green and gold, delicate tassels beneath dimpled bisque chins,
all, all are devoured by unstoppable, ferocious, orange licking flames.
Could I create such a scene on paper now? In my mind I see every
angle of elbow and foot, every miniature *samurai* blade.

In the morning, after we are herded onto the *Princess Maquinna*—
which brings us to Port Alberni, where a train waits to take us to
Nanaimo, on the east coast of the island, and from there to Vancouver
by ferry—we stand with our hands gripping the railings, and watch
while looters from the village move swiftly, running from house to
house as the boat tugs out of the bay. The looters cannot get inside
our houses quickly enough. They cannot wait until the boat is out
of sight.

Almost everything left behind is dragged from our home. The
grandfather clock, tables, chairs, linens, pillows, cutlery, china, sets
of dishes, photograph albums, wedding gifts and heirlooms my parents had been given at the time of their marriage. Even the toy boats
Hiroshi and Keiko and I had banged together from boards and nails,

boats to which we'd attached string, and dragged through shallow water from the safety of shore—even those are scooped up.

I retain two final images from the house of my birth. In the first, a woman's fair hair flies about her face in the wind as she exits our home triumphantly, bearing in her arms the prize of my mother's portable Singer sewing machine. The woman's eyes can barely be seen above the machine's ebony wheel. A spool of red thread is stuck to the bobbin like a traitorous flag. Another woman, older than the first, follows behind. She is carrying the curved wooden cover that slips overtop of the Singer. In their haste, they have not stopped to fit the two parts together.

In the second image, four men push and pull at an upright piano. They are trying to squeeze it through the doorway of Missisu's house, tilting it forward over the steps and onto the boardwalk. There is much shouting and shoving and swearing until, finally, they get that troublesome load down and onto a large, flat cart they have brought with them for the sole purpose of the piano's removal.

As the mail boat chugs away from the bay, the looters do not look out towards the families crowded on board. They do not even bother to glance our way.

CHAPTER 6

1997

The sensory memories, expressions fixed to the faces of my parents, a trill of notes drifting through a slammed kitchen door, a litany of conversations, that is what I have patched together. Along with random historical facts—some of which are in the manila folder, travelling on the seat beside me.

Apart from Okuma-san, Lena was the only person I ever told about the looting. How we were removed from our village. How, by nightfall of the same day, we were sleeping in cattle stalls and animal pens at Hastings Park in Vancouver. How our belongings were stolen while we watched from the mail boat as it pulled away from the wharf on the west coast of Vancouver Island.

She was silent, then angry, then silent again. "You know," she said, "it's like *Zorba*. That's what it sounds like, anyway, the ugly scene where the women run upstairs to grab the belongings of Lila Kedrova—well, Lila in the role of Madame Hortense. The looting happened after she died in her upstairs room. Everything was grabbed and fought over and torn apart while her body lay on the mattress."

I had not read the book. Nor had I seen the film, which came out in the mid-sixties, a few years before I'd met Lena in Montreal.

We watched the film with Miss Carrie, as it turned out. Lena wanted me to see it, and noticed in the newspaper that it was going to be shown on TV on a Saturday night. This was in the mid-seventies, not long after we'd moved from an apartment in Montreal to our house in Ottawa. Lena had finished her doctoral studies and had a job teaching history at the university, the reason for the move. I was trying to prepare for a solo show and was supplementing my income with freelance magazine work, doing illustrations and design. Miss Carrie had begun to stuff notes into the bottom of our mailbox at the front door; it didn't matter that our houses were twenty shuffling steps apart. She was delighted to have us as neighbours, and she liked to write notes. She did not use stamps. Stamps were for real mail—condolences sent to descendants of a shrinking group of aging friends she referred to as "the antiquarians." As she had no living relatives, Lena and I were adopted, the fact of this being undeclared. And if Miss Carrie had adopted us, we, in turn, had adopted her. The Saturday we invited her to watch the film, Lena hauled a note out of our mailbox and read aloud:

It's one of my tired days, and everything is an effort. Improved, however, over yesterday, when I had an aching back and took my own advice. I offer it to you now because someday it might be of use. Whenever possible, LIE ON THE FLOOR. Five minutes on the floor is worth a great deal. Because I am so stiffly rounded, it takes part of the five minutes to make my head lie down. But once my body accustoms itself to the position, my head lies back more easily.

P.S. The only mat I care to lie on is the small pink one.

"I'm going next door to get her," Lena said. "Even if she is having one of her tired days. She can share a pizza with us. She'll probably consider it a treat."

She found Miss Carrie in her front hall, tilted over her rickety willow walker while surveying a heap of goods in the *hellhole,* the floor space at the bottom of the curved staircase in her two-storey stone house. Because Miss Carrie had to grip the banister, hand over hand, to get down, she was not able to carry anything. So she stood on the floor above and dropped what was needed: towels for the wash, an ancient jacket shortened in the left sleeve because one arm was shrinking, a muskrat stole with hard eyes and snout that had once belonged to Mommy and was tossed below in the event that she might be invited out. Whatever was dropped landed in the hellhole with a satisfying thump. A stern portrait of Daddy in uniform looked on from the wall above the staircase; Miss Carrie had told Lena that she lowered her eyes at night when she passed it while climbing the stairs to get to the blue room, where she slept.

Lena picked up the walker with one hand and held Miss Carrie's arm with the other, supporting her until she got her up onto our veranda. Miss Carrie's bones were brittle even then. She had already suffered a broken hip and had had surgery after a fall. The items in the hellhole stayed where they were for the time being.

"I'm not giving up, I'm giving out," Miss Carrie announced as she and Lena came through our front door. "In fact, I've come to believe that my time really might be running out. A good thing, too." She lowered her chin, scrunched her forehead and peered up. "I've always thought a sudden death would make a happy corpse," she said and she laughed abruptly, a conspiratorial sort of laugh.

But that evening, she was anything but a corpse, and the three of us sat in the living room and watched *Zorba.* Lena ushered her to an armchair and propped cushions to support her hip and back. We served pizza and, later, popcorn, and Miss Carrie settled in with satisfaction.

At the end of the film, there was a long silence before our friend launched into a story of her own childhood. Perhaps she was thinking of the looting scene in the film. Her Daddy, the General, had fought in the Great War. He'd sailed to England in September 1914 along with the *Originals,* and was in theatre at the Western Front by December of the same year. He also moved his wife and daughter to the south coast of England, and there they stayed—in the tradition of camp followers—for the duration of the war. Miss Carrie had been a young schoolgirl at the time.

"We were on the coast, facing France," she said, and Lena and I settled back to listen. Of the many eras Miss Carrie had lived through, she had countless stories to tell, but never in any particular order. She criss-crossed time, described periods of innovation, buffoonery, tragedy and relief. Her stories were told with the expectation that the two of us would keep up, that we would enter the scene illuminated at the moment of its telling. We had already learned to leap from the beginning of the century and to land on our feet at its opposite end or somewhere in between, all in the same conversation.

"Daddy had to return to France that day," she continued, "because his leave was over. Mommy kept me home from school. I loved school and hated to miss a day, but I had to be present for the farewells, which were slightly formal, in the manner of the times.

"I suddenly heard the unmistakable sound of a Zeppelin immediately overhead. This was followed by a large bang. A bomb had been dropped at the end of our street, directly over the baker's house. Poof! The baker was gone! Clouds of flour rose to the sky. People raced to the scene to attempt rescue, but the baker could not be saved. Instead, they rummaged in the ruins for salvage. The rummaging continued the next day, and the day after that. The looters kept what they found."

The three of us considered. Each, perhaps, visualizing a different scene. I wondered if Lena was thinking of Madame Hortense in *Zorba*. Or if she was thinking, as I was, of my mother's sewing machine, or even of Missisu's piano, which had been hoisted with much effort on the part of the looting men.

Later, after I'd escorted Miss Carrie and her rickety walker home, Lena remarked, "Don't you sense Daddy in her house somewhere? It's as if he's still lurking. His wines are stored in the basement; his humidor adorns the walnut buffet, cigars inside. His stale tobacco is tucked into the leather pouch. And the hellhole—well, maybe that's the way she exerts defiance, now that both parents are dead. She can finally do what she wants to do. It's obvious that she managed the household after Mommy died. Probably the reason she never married—that and the fact that the young men of her generation were killed off. Has she shown you her early photos? She was petite, blonde, beautiful. There's mischief and humour in every photo. The same humour she hasn't lost, thank heavens. And—wait for this—she loves Benny Goodman! She told me that during the thirties, she danced to his band at Billy Rose's in New York. Her Benny records are stacked in a box in her basement. Along with the jazz greats. Can you believe it? Unfortunately, her record player doesn't work."

But I still hadn't caught up. I was thinking of the looting scene in the film. I was thinking of my parents, of my sister and brother. Where did the anger go? Did it find its own swallowed place to reside and brood within us, along with the shock and helplessness we felt at the time? Why weren't the parents—and the children, too—why weren't we all shouting and yelling from the railings of the *Princess Maquinna?*

We did not protest. We stood, soundless, as if we were also invisible, while the boat took us away.

I suppose it is somewhat strange that ever since that winter morning, it is the image of Missisu's piano I most easily call to mind. I have always imagined that heavy piece of furniture being pushed and pulled through time. Shoved around restlessly, continuously, within some faceless person's house. Or perhaps at a final standstill after all, collecting dust in a living room in which I will never be welcome.

CHAPTER 7

The day after we watched *Zorba* together, Miss Carrie placed a bottle of wine between our front doors. It must have taken considerable effort to transport it from her house to ours. Perhaps she let it roll around the seat of her walker. Or perhaps she shuffled to our place with the aid of her cane. A note was tied to the neck of the bottle.

There has been a rise in the price of single malt. The man who came to cut overhanging branches from the sorry old oak in my backyard frequents the liquor store and has so informed me. The wine is from Daddy's wine cellar and is meant to thank you for the film. I know it's not Scotch, which Bin prefers, but he might enjoy an ancient red. Do come and have sherry with me some evening next week, perhaps Sunday. I serve it the old way, with a fistful of croutons. I toast the croutons myself, in the oven.

A bottle of Laphroaig is with me now, so far unopened. I shove in a Beethoven tape, the Fifth Symphony, exactly right for a landscape where rock is a force, the dominant force. No escaping the fact of this since first approaching the northern part of the province. I've been travelling for hours over marsh and crag, over road blasted through solid walls of rock, in a landscape where only stunted growth survives. This is how I would depict the old, old earth in its pared-back state. Patches and furrows of salmon pink, feldspar in granite. Roots and pods, struggling to survive.

Basil raises his head at the click of the tape and Beethoven's four-note motif. What does Basil hear—apart from my thoughts? What does any dog hear? *Wah-wah-wah-wah.* He sniffs the air and settles again. I hear him gnawing at his Kong. He's content while we're moving and lets me know that he's immune to the music. Not that there's anything wrong with his hearing. At home, he hears the mail before it hits the slot and then tries to scare off the postman. Or he bounds to the kitchen from any room of the house at the sound of a yogurt top being torn off, hoping to lick its foil underside.

The music continues, three plus one, same pitch for three, the fourth pitch down a third: *Da Da Da Dum.* The theme repeats itself in insistent ways. *Fate knocking at the door.* Where did that come from? From the great man himself, who created an entire symphony around four notes. He unified themes; that was his genius. The power in the music builds and builds, never releasing the listener. Beethoven had energy and beauty inside him, and determination. Enough that he could pluck the first note from his mind and plant it to a staff, the lines of which he had drawn in one of his copious notebooks. If he'd contained the symphony unexpressed, within him, it could have destroyed him. And life wasn't easy before he wrote the Fifth. To which I could listen for days—and have. With Okuma-san when I was a boy, years after the war, when he purchased a second-hand record player. On a lumpy mattress in a long-ago student apartment on rue Bishop in Montreal. In a concert hall in Berlin. In a bedsit in London, teetering on a lopsided stool that had a splintered leg.

Beethoven once wrote to his friend Wegeler that it would be so lovely to live a thousand lives. But if given a second life, or a third, would his ears be able to hear? He was closed to the outer sound of his own music, but his inner life, his adversity, must have pushed his genius. *Listen,* Okuma-san told me. *Listen to the tapping on wood. Listen to it rhythmically. It is the music of Beethoven. His greatest works were written after he was totally deaf.*

Light is dropping from the sky. The sun has overtaken the car and I'm driving directly into afternoon glare. I've been on the road for two days and I'm still in Ontario, forced to acknowledge the immensity of one province. If I were in northern Europe, I'd have passed through half a dozen countries by late afternoon. But here I am, and I can't remember how long it's been since I've seen a motel sign. Still, the drive over the Canadian Shield is one of my favourites, and used to be one of Lena's, too. We never hurried when approaching the north shore of Lake Superior, travelling west towards the Lakehead. Lena loved hiking in the provincial parks and scrambling over bald pates of granite. To her, physical landscape was one more dimension of history. She had a deep desire to understand the makeup of the earth beneath her feet. Every time we travelled—before and after Greg was born— cobbles, pebbles, smooth stones, stones that sparkled and were studded with quartz, mica, feldspar, rattled around the floor of the car. The more sparkle, the more striations, the more pleased Lena would be.

"This is igneous," she explained to Greg when he was a tiny boy and stood beside her in his green overalls. "This is sedimentary—do you see the difference? And this one is metamorphic."

Three tiny samples in a plastic case fitted his palm perfectly. He snapped the lid shut and opened it again. *Snap. Click.*

We both enjoyed teaching Greg, and he was quick to learn. It was Lena who suggested his name the day after he was born. She was sitting on the edge of the hospital bed, her legs dangling, and she was leafing through name books while our new son hiccuped in a bassinet that had been wheeled to the room. "Vigilant," she said. "That's what Gregory means. I would like a child of ours to be vigilant."

The stones that she, and then the two of them, brought home and washed and dried and arranged on a shelf were called their *wondrous stones*. Greg moved on to volcanoes and dinosaurs before he got to whales, dolphins and other sea mammals—and remained there—but Lena continued to collect rocks and fossils, many of which are still in the spare room. Those were *her* smalls. Still undisturbed, because I've been in the room only a few times since November. It doubled as Lena's home office—and is one more area waiting to be sorted out. Maybe, maybe I'll do this when I get home.

The sun has lowered itself close to the curve of Earth, and less than an hour's light remains in the sky. I didn't hear Basil stand up behind me but a glance in the mirror shows that he's watching me, his long purple tongue hanging out.

"Okay, okay," I tell him. "I don't want to sleep in the car any more than you do."

At which he begins to turn circles in the back. A sure sign of dismay.

Last night, our first night out, we stayed in a derelict, half-empty motel that permitted dogs. I was too tired to drive any farther, and Basil slept by the door facing out, as if expecting an intruder, and then he ground his teeth for hours.

Just as I'm wondering if I should have paid more attention to the map, I see a sign at the side of the highway: OVERNIGHT CABINS. I swerve, too rapidly, and Basil lurches in the back and barks his complaint. I find myself on a lumpy gravel road and make my way up a wooded hill, following a series of dusky arrows painted on boards that have been nailed to tree trunks. A plethora of signs that makes me think of Hansel and Gretel, greedy or desperate for a place to break bread and lay their heads. Basil is making noises that I take to mean he mistrusts my judgment. From his repertoire of sounds he calls up one of his favourites, and coughs like a choking horse.

After a few minutes, the gravel narrows to become a dirt track that leads through more woods and then into a clearing at the top of the hill. I stop the car before an open space that appears to be—in this unlikely place—an old lodge, clearly on the edge of ruin. Steps of flaking concrete, a fence that leans inwards, the tips of the pointed boards teetering against a mound of dirt in the yard. At the right, a path leads to two side-by-side cabins. A rusting half-ton pickup has been abandoned beside the toppled fence. A small van is parked in front of one of the cabins.

I stop the Beethoven tape reluctantly, because it is in its third movement, which seems to be asking a series of spirited questions. Each, in turn, met with forceful response. The delicacy of the back-and-forth sequence that follows is a part I love because it moves towards strength. The theme never lets go. I have a sudden yearning for Okuma-san and wish he were beside me now to listen to this recording. If he were alive, he'd be ninety-eight years old. Older than Miss Carrie, who admits only to being born after the turn of the century, while Okuma-san was born one year before. Sometimes, I imagine the two of them meeting and I create conversations they might have had. Would Miss Carrie have made Okuma-san laugh? Sometimes, perhaps. My memory calls up his face but what I see is intensity, not laughter. Intensity and, yes, wisdom and caring.

I stretch my way out of the car and open the back for Basil, who immediately relieves himself against the fence and heads for the front steps like some hirsute cousin who is returning for a reunion after a long absence. It might be my imagination, but he looks shaggier than usual. Dirtier and smellier, too. I rap at the door, lean down and give warning: "Make an impression, will you? A good one. This is our one hope for a bed tonight."

Basil is accepted, odour and all, not only in the cabin but in the tea room, too. For that's what it is, as proclaimed by a homemade sign taped to the desk, with the inked and unexpected words: OFFICE AND TEA ROOM.

I pay cash in advance to a heavily bearded man, and an image arises: *Rip Van Winkle.* And then I think, *No, Rip wouldn't be wearing a Viyella shirt, nor would he have strands of shredded wheat lodged in his grey beard.* Strands that are so caught up, they're growing in the same direction. Not a good sign.

I utter a silent prayer that this specimen of manhood is not involved in food production. His mouth is closed, the sound of his nasal breathing like water rattling through pipes. He nods, grunts, has no words to spare, and I wonder if he's verbally challenged or if shredded wheat is lodged in his vocal cords, as well. He disappears into a back room and I go out to the car, grab a flashlight and a few things I'll need for the night, and take them to the cabin. I feed Basil a bowl of dog meal on the braided rug by the door and mix in a tin of meat to make up for the surrounds. He gobbles this in seconds, gulps half a bowl of water, lifts his hairy face and crosses the room, dripping a trail of water that I don't bother to wipe up. I pick up the book of letters I've brought to read, lock the door—which doesn't fit the jamb—and bring Basil with me to the tea room. If I leave him alone in an isolated cabin under the trees, he'll moan and bark and fling his body at the door. Or worse, tear the rug to shreds and have us evicted.

Surprisingly, we are not the only ones in the tea room. A young woman with a single golden braid down her back is chatting with another the same age, maybe early twenties. Both, I'm relieved to see, are clean. No shredded wheat in sight. They are sitting at the table nearest the entrance and nod as we come in, more to Basil than to me. The second young woman is bony and angular, with long brown hair. One of her eyes is half-closed, which gives the odd impression of imbalance. On the wall behind the cash register, a hand-printed sign has been pinned to a corkboard with an open safety pin: ANITA WILL READ YOUR TEA LEAVES.

Rapunzel and Anita, Lena would say. *Look out for the sisters Grimm. They could be in disguise.*

There are only four tables in this spacious room, which must have been a dining room in grander times. The lodge windows look down over the hill I've just driven up. There are woods on both sides of the gravel road. Woods the thickness of the ones Henry and I used to prowl with homemade bows and arrows around the camp when we were children, pretending to stalk bear and cougar. Two of the tables here offer a view of a creek below and a walking path that approaches from another angle. The creek looks wide enough to be a small river. I'll check the map later, maybe hike down in the morning and give Basil some exercise. I take a seat by the window and face the setting sun, only to be met by another unlikely sight. Two women are climbing the path. Given the shrinking light, they're in silhouette but definitely heading upwards. Basil coils himself at my feet and closes his eyes as if he wants no part of the experience. Rapunzel and her friend don't seem to be bothered by the overheated room. I sling my jacket over the back of my chair, and I'm still too warm.

The menu is handwritten and the hours of the place, which

doesn't have a name, are printed across the bottom: *Your wel-come—4 to 7 in the evening p.m.*

Rapunzel is suddenly standing beside my table, her attitude suggesting that I've interrupted her conversation. From two choices on the menu, I order a large bowl of chili and a cup of coffee. She disappears behind a painted door and I hear older female laughter in the kitchen.

Uneven light is sparkling up from the creek. I wonder about the place; it must have a history, a story, many stories. If Lena were with me, she'd amuse me by inventing her own. The women who were climbing the trail now enter the room somewhat flushed, greet me— Basil raises his head momentarily and gives a low moan—and sit at the window table in front of mine. They might be in their forties or fifties—I can't guess ages anymore, not with accuracy, though I don't know when I lost the ability. They order small bowls of chili and a large pot of tea. The tea is wanted before the meal. It's impossible not to hear every word, though they're trying to keep their voices low. It's obvious that they're staying in the other cabin for the night and were out for exercise and fresh air. The van must belong to them. From their mutterings, it sounds as if they are not pleased with the state of their cabin.

I'd like to enjoy my own silence, but it's difficult to focus on the page in front of me. Okuma-san used to talk about the more famous of Beethoven's letters that he had come across when he was a young student in Europe. Many of the letters, Okuma-san read in German; some were read in translation. When a complete set was published in English in the sixties, I ordered the set for his birthday. The three volumes came back to me after his death in 1967, along with his other sparse belongings.

But I find myself reading the same lines over and over. The letter is addressed to a child and makes a case for the true artist having no pride, only a blurry sort of awareness of how far he is from reaching his goal. I can identify with the part about the goal, but I'm unable to block out the conversation at the next table, and look up.

The women are wearing bulky cardigans, obviously knit by the same person, in tones of beige and faded cocoa. Eagles have been knitted into the design, but these once regal birds are adorned with long, limp beaks that droop like useless appendages. If I were to give the sweaters a title it would be *Eagles made impotent*. The women now shed the cardigans because of the heat of the place. The woman facing me has iron-grey hair and a too-cheery look, as if she's recently learned that every aspect of life is truly laughable. Her eyelids flutter so rapidly, I wonder if she has a neural problem. The fluttering intensifies when she speaks.

I can only guess at her companion's response to the disconcerting eye movements, because the second woman has her back to me. I look down at the page again and wonder if Beethoven was being honest when he expressed the belief that he had no pride. He did not, I know, have the love of a woman. Though he spoke hopefully and frequently of love, especially in letters he wrote during his thirties.

Basil, full-bellied Basil, stirs beneath the table when the woman facing me says to her companion, "We could have our tea leaves read. Did you see the sign at the entrance when we came in?"

"I don't think so," says the other quietly. "I don't tamper with that sort of thing."

"What do you mean—that sort of thing? What harm can be done? Come on, it might turn out to be fun."

The young woman seated with Rapunzel turns out to be Anita, the tea-leaf reader. No surprise there. She moves to the table of the two women as if tugged by a magnet, her brown hair swinging, one eye remaining half-closed, as if that is requisite for a seer. She pulls up a chair between the two.

I give up on the book of letters because a bowl the size of a mixing bowl, filled with muddy-looking chili, has been set in front of me. I feel I should have a scoop to shovel it in. I scan the bowl for remnants of shredded wheat, see none and think, *Okay, safe to eat.*

At the table ahead I hear something about a fork in the road. A decision could go either way. And I think, *Pretty easy bet, Anita.*

I look towards the creek, or river, whatever it is. In the final rays of light, last year's grasses on the cleared part of the slope have taken on a touch of gold all the way down to the water. If I could create that colour, if I could mix that colour of gold . . .

Anita's voice breaks through again. "This could go on for a long time."

"Very long?" The woman speaks with a tremor. Her head dips forward.

"It seems so," says Anita, with flat indifference.

"Maybe it means your research," says the cheery friend. "Your research never ends, and don't we both know it."

This is followed by a murmur of assent.

And then, I hear the most astonishing prediction. Anita, the fortune teller, declares in a semi-tragic voice, "Oh!" As if she has witnessed the inferno itself. She stares into the cup. "I'm sorry," she says. "Like, I have to tell you. It's as clear as can be." She pauses, for effect, no doubt. "You aren't going to live a long life."

Two small bowls of chili arrive at this moment and are set at the women's table. My body pulls up taller in my chair.

"Will she at least live happily?" This has been blurted out by the woman with the fluttering lids.

Anita shrugs—who knows?—tucks her five-dollar bill into her pocket and returns to sit with Rapunzel.

"Don't pay any attention," the woman tells her friend. "It's all nonsense, you know it is. She doesn't know what she's saying."

But the recipient of the news has stilled. She is staring out the window at what I am also seeing: the path she has just climbed; the narrow rays of disappearing light; darkness closing in; a small river that is no more than a murky blur as it curves around the base of a hill of shadows.

Should I stand up and shout? I could laugh or weep. If I start laughing, I'll have to be carried out. I spoon down half the chili, leave money on the table, grab my book and head for the door while Anita calls after me in a singsong voice, "Don't you want your fortune told? We'll bring you a cup of tea." She and Rapunzel are giggling as I push the door shut behind me.

Basil drags himself back to the cabin, reluctant to leave the warmth of the tea room. I should have intervened when I overheard the fortune. But what would I have said? And why would I interfere? Not my business.

Corpses of black bugs are squashed between tiles on the bathroom floor. I have no interest in identifying them and I don't look closely. I know that Basil will paw anything that scuttles across his path in the night. As soon as I lock the door, he plunks himself onto the circle of braided rug and glares.

There are two single beds in the room. Both mattresses are lumpy and reek of must. There is an overhead light, no lamp. Between the beds a framed, glassless print hangs at a slant: a sampan afloat on dingy water, cotton-ball clouds puffed in the sky. I have an urge to slice across its surface with a knife. Instead, I straighten the frame, if only to gain control. We are, Basil and I, in what Lena would mercilessly declare to be a fleabag. As I think this, the light flickers once and goes out. I'm standing in blackness. No light in the bathroom, no light coming in from outside. I brush my teeth in the dark, splash water on my face, stub my foot against the tin shower and crawl into the nearest bed like a lame troll.

Basil has ignored my ablutions. I snap on the flashlight and shine it in his direction.

"One night, Basil. That's all. The power outage is not my fault. We'll be out of here in the morning. Make up for lost time. And it would be nice if you'd acknowledge my conversation just once. I did not, you'll recall, abandon you at the kennel."

Basil raises his head and looks into the cone of light when he hears the word *kennel,* but he knows he's not under threat. He closes his eyes and makes it clear that I am the one, the only one, responsible for these unworthy digs.

CHAPTER 8

T here is no room to turn on this narrow mattress, so I lie on my back beneath the covers.

Why would I leave my comfortable home only to sleep in a fleabag?

Because your home is empty. Because it's bleak. Because you want to finish the last few drawings—maybe even another painting. Because you have a deadline. Because this trip might lead to anything. Because you are chasing away your ghosts. Because you are trying to open a door, any door, to some random glimmer or prospect that might be waiting to attach itself to your loneliness . . .

Loneliness.

I should bring in the Laphroaig from the car, but it's too much effort to pull on clothes and dash outside and back in again. Shredded-wheat-in-the-beard might be waiting out there with an axe.

I will myself to recall good times. Better times. At least I thought so, at the time.

In the fall of last year, just before Thanksgiving weekend, I suggested that we rent a cabin on the Gatineau River in Quebec, not far from the city, about an hour's drive. Greg had phoned to say he wouldn't be coming home. Too far for him to travel, and he'd been invited for dinner at the home of a classmate whose parents lived near campus. *A girl?* Lena and I wondered. We had always teased him about the day we'd have to find him a bride. "When you've finished school, when your student loans are paid off, then we'll start looking." *Does he have a new girl? Let's hear about her. Do we stop looking for a bride?*

Miss Carrie usually joined us for holiday dinners, but she had a house guest, the nephew of one of her antiquarian friends, a single man of fifty-eight who had arrived to visit for five days. So far—she pushed her walker to our house and related this breathlessly but with a touch of despair—so far, his entire visit had been spent sitting at Daddy's desk while reading the Bible in Greek. He'd brought the Greek Bible with him in his Gladstone bag. Miss Carrie had plans to cook a chicken for his Thanksgiving dinner. The man was humourless, she said. Hopelessly devoid. Humour could knock him over and he'd reach for his Greek Bible while lying on his back on the floor.

"I'll need to hear Benny," she said. "For survival. Will you lend me your old gramophone, Bin? Lena said it's still working. Maybe you could carry up some of my records from the basement?"

I went next door and hauled up one of the long-buried boxes—a fabulous collection, from what I could see. And helped set up the turntable Lena and I no longer used. We played mostly CDs now, except for tapes in the car. Still, we'd hung on to our LPs, as had Miss Carrie.

Lena needed no persuasion to get away for a cottage weekend. Fall term was underway and she'd been reading essays for weeks. Student appointments had begun, but she could spare three days.

She announced that she would leave all work at home. She hadn't been feeling well lately. She had a sore throat; she was tired and over-worked. "I am definitely in need of a break," she told me.

She packed lightly: jeans, running shoes, a bulky sweater, a three-inch volume of *Collected Stories* by William Trevor.

It was my job to choose the music: Beethoven for me, Goodman for Lena—nothing else would do. I took graphite pencils, paper, pen and ink. We packed the cooler with the green lid, and Lena washed a few leaves of romaine before we left. We took salmon steaks and cheese, fall tomatoes and fresh corn, a loaf of bread, a bottle of wine. Lena decided to bring the chequered oilcloth we used as a picnic-table cover, and threw it into the car at the last minute. We drove to the cabin late Saturday morning—I had found the ad in a week-end paper—and Lena, holding the directions in her lap and sitting in direct sun in the passenger seat, nodded off all the way there.

When we first sighted the cabin, we knew it was better, by far, than we could have hoped for. Basil, in the back seat, nose out the side window, released a wolf-howl he couldn't contain as I pulled up. We stepped out and looked around in wonder. A range of hills lay in soft folds beyond the far side of the river. A series of valleys was ablaze: oranges and reds, yellows and greens, one hue blending seamlessly to the next. Oaks were spaced along the water's edge, and chipmunks in the high branches chattered and tossed acorns to the ground. Squirrels darted in every direction. Brilliant clusters of red maples rose up behind the cabin. All of this, within the crisp, earthy aroma of fall. I wouldn't have been surprised to hear the blaring of trumpets.

I heard the whoop of pleasure as Lena flicked off her sandals. She rolled up her jeans and waded into the water, with Basil close behind her. He stank of river afterwards, and his legs and belly needed a rinse, but he wouldn't be held back. Nor did we try to restrain him.

Lena found a large, flat stone to stand on and rocked back and forth, barefoot in shallow water, testing for balance, surveying what she promptly named *the realm of beauty* that lay before her. Some of the rocks were slippery with moss, a vivid green that shone up through the water. But the rock Lena chose was moss-free, ancient grey and solid.

I began to unload the car and found a set of keys hanging inside the screened porch. I turned to look at Lena. Hands on hips, head tilted back, a soft curve of belly thrust forward. Her dark hair was tucked behind her ears, her skin paler than usual in the sunlight. Shadows had deepened down the lines of one shoulder. She was inhaling the scent of early afternoon, of leaves swirling down, of river itself. It was a moment of perfection in the midst of fall, one short-lived moment. I wanted to set down the cooler, the food, the chequered tablecloth. I wanted to drop everything to the grass while I drew this picture, but I didn't. I have never drawn it, though every shadow, every curve, every feeling I had in that moment is stored.

I see the picture as vertical, despite the river flowing across the bottom of the mind's frame. I see the structure of the whole. I see the shade of Lena's faded jeans; the outline of what I knew to be black bikini underwear beneath; the shape of her calves; the distortion of her ankles where they disappeared beneath the waterline; her T-shirt with horizontal stripes in cream and indigo; the way the stripes held a diagonal, rumpled pull when she stretched her arms overhead for the joy of being part of *this*. She wanted only to sink into *this,* and be thankful.

And so did I.

We had brought along a cage for Basil and padded it with a rug-end, and left it in the porch with the wire door open so that he could come and go as he pleased. He liked to sleep in the cage at night when we travelled, as long as the door was open and he knew he could get out. At home, he had a small mattress in his basket. It was only after Lena was admitted to hospital that he began to shred his bedding. But that came later.

Good things, I remind myself. *Only good things.*

The river was full and peaceful in the late glow of sun. A family arrived at the second cabin next door, a couple in their thirties with an eight-year-old daughter named Florence, who had brought along a friend, Lise. The two young girls tossed their brown hair, jumped from stone to stone in the shallow river, raced in and out of long shadows thrown by the trees. They befriended Basil and tagged after him, and collected acorns, and hooted when he held the squirrels at bay. They broke off layers of shale along the river's edge. They skipped flat stones in the water and glanced back every now and then for approval, waving to their parents and to Lena and me.

Lena settled into a canvas lawn chair, her head bowed over her book. A dragonfly dipped, rose, dipped again. With its miraculous double set of wings, it hovered above her shoulder on a current of air. Aware of me watching, she looked up, her fingers holding her place in the book.

"This man can write," she said. "Really write. Look at his face on the cover." She held out Trevor's book for inspection. "This is the way I want to look when I'm—well, whatever he was when the book was published. Sixty, maybe. I have a little over a decade to work on the lines of my face."

In the evening, our neighbours created a rock circle close to the water's edge, lit a bonfire and invited us to join them. We talked and laughed; there was nothing noisy, nothing brash. We wrapped ourselves in sweaters and listened to crickets and the murmur of flowing water.

Lena said she was tired, and we went to bed early and lay side by side in the dark, my left arm around her as always, her head against my shoulder. The curtains were closed but we could hear night sounds through the screens: far-off calls across the river; a distant, eruptive laugh; the sizzle of the fire being doused by water before our neighbours retired. There was a cassette player on the bedside table; I put in a tape and Benny's clarinet began, the volume low.

"You'd think the scale was oiled," Lena said. "The way he glides up and down it."

That was the night I told her about First Father's readings of the fates.

"What!" she said. "All these years we've been married and you've never told me any of this? I could have died and never known."

"You never asked," I said.

She couldn't stop laughing. The mattress shook, the bed shook. I smiled to myself in the dark.

"Did your father always start with Hiroshi's fate—I mean, Henry's?"

"First Father?"

"You know who I mean."

"Hiroshi was number-one son. Stronger, according to his fate. He was skilled; he was given responsibilities as a child. I was less important, being number two. Also, I was shorter, smaller, scrawnier—then."

"But more important than Keiko, Kay."

"She was a girl. That's how it was," I said.

"Thank God that's changed."

"Not entirely. Not in some families. And not only Japanese families, I might add."

"I'm a woman—must you be reminded?"

"Not at all. Never, in fact."

"Henry, born in the year of the monkey, was told that he wasn't supposed to marry a tiger—and he did?"

"He did. You know that he was divorced early in his marriage. She ate him right up."

"Oh, come on, don't blame the woman."

"I didn't take sides, I assure you. I hardly knew her."

"But you? Stubborn, yes. Protective, yes. Chasing away ghosts? I'm glad of that. But you don't weep over nonsensical things."

"How would you know? Maybe I do."

This really set her off.

"Do you lock yourself in the bathroom?" she said, between gasps. She pulled away and propped herself on an elbow. "Do you sit on the edge of the tub and weep on the other side of the bathroom door?"

"Go ahead, have your laugh."

"I am," she said.

"I see that."

"But what if the three of you slid into your fates because you knew in advance what they were supposed to be? Think of Kay, all that ambition, all the hard work. And what about the fortune? What about that? Where's my share? I'm part of your fate."

"First Father was wrong about that—the fortune part."

And this set her off even more.

She sobered then, and lay back down and said, "Maybe he was right. Maybe this is it. The fortune. What we have now."

I pulled her close.

"I mean, think of how you could use the fates," she said. "It's what everyone needs—a fate that allows us to chase away our ghosts."

And then she did one of those rapid switches in conversation, the ones for which I could never prepare.

"But it's hard to picture you weeping over nonsensical things," she said. "You've always made a supreme effort to hold everything inside. Including, I might add, any accrued anger."

"Apparently I haven't held in everything. Not if the fates are correct."

"Do you know how many times you've held my hand in public?"

"You've chronicled?" I went still, wondering. I was always uneasy when any sort of effort to probe moved in close.

"I'm trained at chronicling," she said. "It's what I do. You know that. I can give a full account. And I don't have to keep a list; it happened only once. How could I not remember? We were missing life in Montreal and had gone back for a visit. We'd been married five years. We didn't tell my family we were there, and we sneaked into the city and out again. We wanted to be tourists. It was windy, colder than we'd expected. We were walking down the hill on rue Guy, and you were about to step off the curb when you looked over and saw that I was freezing. You took off your scarf and wrapped it around my neck. Then you tucked my hand in yours and held it the rest of the way back to the hotel. It was the only time you made a public gesture of love."

"I'm subtle," I said. "Maybe you missed something. Hand-holding? How am I to know what you keep track of?"

She shifted and pressed her body into mine. I relaxed again.

"Well," she said, "there was one other occasion. This time we *were* staying with my parents; we were visiting for a weekend. We were sitting in their living room—on the couch. It was late Sunday morning and we had made love earlier, upstairs, before they'd come home from church. Bells were ringing at the end of the street. I remember melody, something carillon-like. We were downstairs in the living room when my parents came home. You lifted my hand and held it against your knee. I felt it was an emotional breakthrough.

One of the closest moments between us—because there was some-one else present. God, this is really pathetic, isn't it."

I didn't reply.

"Anyway," she said, "hand-holding in front of my parents doesn't count. We were in their house, not out in public."

Lena always got the last word; I didn't dispute it. It was the way we were together. I suppose I even relied on her for that. Benny was playing "Ballad in Blue," and I pulled her over, on top, and we made slow, careful love. And slept late the next morning, waking only when we heard Basil push at the screen door of the porch to let himself out.

Lena got up then, and pulled on her clothes and went outside, barefoot. I lay there for a few moments, thinking about the night before. Anger, public gestures of love. There was so much that was private between us. Unexpressed? In language, maybe.

I got up and went to the kitchen and made coffee and glanced outside, surprised to see a thin shroud of low fog suspended over the river. The ashes of the bonfire had been washed away in the night by a soft rain neither of us had heard.

Lena was looking down at layers of shale beneath her feet. She leaned forward, her dark hair dangling over dark water, and picked up what appeared to be a perfect stone to add to her collection of smalls. It had been washed up by the river and was lying outside the fire circle. She was so close, I could see the way the stone fitted her palm. It was round and speckled and hard, and grey lines ran through the surface like old veins. She leaned over the river again and swished the stone back and forth in the water. Patted it dry against her jeans and inspected it once more. Held it like a talisman and smoothed it against her cheek, up down, up down, an even motion.

And then, abruptly, she let go. Flung it out to the current. Gave it back to the river from which it had come. I remember thinking that she was perhaps satisfying some past—or even some future—anger of her own. Then she turned and walked up the stone path to the porch. I handed her a mug of strong, hot coffee as she came through the door. She held out her right hand, grasped the mug, and dropped it to the floor.

CHAPTER 9

1942

At the Exhibition Grounds in Vancouver, Father and the other men were separated from the women and children and taken to a different building in Hastings Park. Boys over thirteen had to join the men. Mother, Hiroshi, Keiko and I were in the larger group, and were led to the livestock building that would house us for several months. After that, trains would be taking us north and inland, far up the Fraser Valley to hastily—oh, how hastily—prepared camps. The protected zone had been declared: no person of Japanese ancestry would be permitted to live within one hundred miles of the coast. Everyone over sixteen, men and women, had been registered and fingerprinted. Each of us was identified as an enemy alien. Cars and trucks, cameras, radio transmitters, radio receivers, firearms and ammunition were confiscated.

But the Security Commission had no idea what to do with us, and there was still no carefully considered plan. They wanted us off the coast, and Pearl Harbor had given them the opportunity. They wanted the men's fishing licences, more to the point. That was the real reason. Japanese families caught too many fish and were too industrious on their farms. Get rid of the imagined fifth column, never mind that we were citizens.

All of this I came to understand much later, long after we had left the camp. And Mother told me once, but only once, how she had halted in disbelief in the doorway of the empty building at Hastings Park. It was the moment before we were led to the stables and open cattle stalls, and she had placed a hand over her mouth while being pushed from behind, certain that she would vomit from the smell. Surely a mistake had been made. Surely we were not expected to live in such a place. Not in that stench of animal urine and manure.

"Think of it," she said. "Just think of it."

I watched her private shame close over the memory.

If a mistake had been made, no one was making such an admission. Into the stalls we went, exhausted after our journey. Each of us was given bologna, a piece of bread and a drink of watered-down milk. After that, children were put to bed on straw ticks that had been laid out on bunks in the stalls. Our family was assigned two double bunks and drab army-issue blankets. There was no privacy until the women began to hang sheets as dividers between stalls.

That was the beginning wave, the wave that preceded the tide of families that followed, hundreds and thousands arriving month after month. More people than any of us had ever seen in one place. At its peak, Hastings Park was housing and feeding more than three thousand, most of us in animal stalls.

The stall we lived in reeked of horse and cow, of sheep and goat, of lime and urine and mould and dirt. Clumps of manure stuck to our feet when we walked through the building. What we saw from the doorway was a high metal gate, with barbed wire encircling the park. There was no sign of Father. The only men in sight were either

RCMP or guards stationed at the gate. Beyond the guards, I could hear streetcars rumbling by outside the park. I had never heard such a sound before, and I was fascinated by the rattle and clang of bells as sparks scattered and sizzled in the wires overhead.

In the bathroom there were ten open showers, no divisions between. A series of taps dripped above a long metal shelf and I remember a row of children's bums while we were all being washed at the same time. Hiroshi and Keiko and I stood giggling on three wobbling boards while we were soaped and rinsed, and while water ran between the boards into a drain in the floor. The toilets along one side of the room were sheet-metal troughs. There were no seats, no partitions, no privacy. Not at the beginning, not when we arrived. Only when some of the women dared to protest, only then were toilet seats brought in and flimsy partitions erected.

Our mother and all of the other mothers began to scrub. Mother's hair was damp; she was on her hands and knees and she pushed back the curls on her forehead. Day and night, water flowed past the edge of our stall through a long, connected trough that angled in and around the aisles of concrete. If someone was rinsing clothing farther up the aisle, soap bubbles floated past our stall. Whenever bubbles stuck to the cement sides of the trough, I reached over and popped them with my finger. Makeshift clotheslines were strung everywhere, and I remember running with other children under hanging clothes. We ran in and around sheets, blankets, long underwear and damp towels until our mothers came to collect us and restored order. There was little for children to do, but there was always washing going on, even in the night. Our own mother scrubbed our clothes after everyone else was in bed. When she undressed or changed, she climbed up onto her bunk behind army blankets or had Keiko hold two pieces of towel together in front of her, for privacy.

But it was the maggots that disgusted her the most. I knew they were there; I could see them swarming. And they stayed in memory because Mother talked about them for years. First, she asked for disinfectant and was given some. But even after more scrubbing, the maggots stayed on—in the pallets where we slept and in manure under the boards of the shower room. Once a week, because of damp and mould, we had to drag our straw ticks outside the building so that stuffing could be removed and new straw put in. But the maggots stayed on.

Mother wrapped us in coats to keep us warm and she draped an extra sheet to thicken the partition around our cramped living space. Other families, strangers, lived all around us. It was never quiet at night and we had to listen to the high-pitched, rhythmic sobbing of a woman whose stall was two aisles away from ours. She cried every night. And every morning she woke up with puffed and swollen eyes.

Three times a day, we were led to the poultry building, a large, high-ceilinged area filled with rows of tables made from planks placed end to end over trestles. We ate in that lime-and-poultry smell while an RCMP officer stood on top of one of the long tables and guarded us. I have always wondered who imagined that we were ripe for sabotage, a poultry room filled with women standing in line collecting bowls of food for their children. At the time, I was terrified of that long-legged, uniformed policeman high above us, a man who watched as I chewed porridge that was served in one lump in the morning, as I chewed macaroni for lunch, and chunks of tough stewing beef or fish poached in a tasteless white sauce for dinner. Everything was covered in white sauce. At night, some sort of fast-cooked rice was served, the likes of which no mother we knew had ever prepared.

Because Mother had to spend so much time standing in line to collect food for the three of us, there was often nothing left when she went back for her own meal. She wasn't the only woman who went hungry. It took numerous meetings and letters explaining conditions before the problem was resolved, and before slightly more palatable food in larger amounts was brought in.

Any news to be had was exchanged and passed on by the women in the dining room. We had not heard from Father since we'd been separated on arrival at Hastings Park, and Mother told Keiko in a flat, worried voice that he might have been taken away to a work camp. One of the rumours was that husbands, fathers, uncles and older brothers had been sent to camps as far away as Ontario and were required to wear circular targets on their backs so that they would be easy to shoot if they tried to escape. Other men were assigned to work crews and were said to be building roads near the Alberta border or in the northern part of our own province of British Columbia. And just as we thought we would never see any of the men again, Mother's younger brother, Aki, turned up.

Uncle Aki had been living and working as a fisherman on Bainbridge Island in Washington for several years. Only months before we were rounded up, he had moved to Steveston on the B.C. mainland. Now, he managed to get a message to us saying that he was close by and had been put to work as a cook in the kitchen, adjacent to the poultry building. His wife, our auntie Aya, had arrived that day, the message said, and she was in the same livestock building where we were living. Uncle Aki wanted Mother to look out for her, and Mother set out immediately, going up and down the rows of stalls to see if someone new had arrived. We did not know Auntie Aya very well because Uncle Aki had married when he was living in Washington. Whenever he had visited, he'd arrived on his fishing boat. After he'd moved to Steveston, he brought Auntie Aya to Vancouver Island to meet us, but only once. So far, they had no children.

Uncle Aki also told Mother in his message that he'd learned that Father was still in Vancouver, but was being held in a special detention centre in the city. That was why we hadn't heard from him. Every day, men were being sent away, it was true, but so far Father had not been among them. Father's brother, Uncle Kenji, had been taken to a road camp; that much had been found out. Father was doing what he could to keep our family together, and he was trying to obtain information about moving us to a self-supporting camp. To do this, he had to prove that money would be coming to him from an insurance policy and from the auctioning of his boat.

And then, one day, when rains were pounding the rooftops and while I was staring out at the barbed-wire fence, Uncle Aki came to the doorway and stuck his head inside. When he saw Mother, he called us over. He was not wearing a cook's apron and hat, but a dark suit and a long grey coat and fedora. At first, I wasn't certain who this was. He looked like an imposter who might have slipped into Uncle Aki's good clothes. But he really was our uncle. He had baked during his spare time between meals, and the guards on duty allowed him to bring a tin container filled with raisin cookies, as well as a parcel for Auntie Aya, who ran to the doorway to greet him.

Auntie Aya was shorter than Mother, and had deep-set eyes and much thinner cheeks. Auntie Aya looked more like our older sister than our aunt. Mother came to the entrance and hugged her brother, and Hiroshi and Keiko and I came running over. Uncle Aki handed us the cookies and told us we were to share with other children in nearby stalls.

For days, we talked about the taste of those cookies and how happy we had been to see our uncle's friendly face when he grinned under the shadowy brim of his hat and was recognized. Auntie Aya, however, was having a difficult time adjusting to conditions in the livestock building, and she sometimes spent hours sitting on her bunk, staring at nothing. She told Mother she couldn't sleep because of the sound of sobbing at night. It was only when a doctor was called and a baby was born in the same aisle as Auntie Aya that she roused herself and made a move to help others. The birth of the baby, a boy, had happened quickly, and the people in charge had no time to get the woman to hospital. She had two other young children and needed help. Auntie Aya was often seen after that, walking up and down the rows between stalls, the new baby bundled and held to her shoulder. She told us that she wanted a baby of her own and was getting practice. When she wasn't helping with the baby, she sometimes supervised lessons, as she had agreed to help with the loosely organized attempts to keep school-age children learning.

If Auntie Aya had at first been reluctant to get involved in other people's misfortunes, our own mother had gone into action from the beginning. There were many older women in the building, and several had become ill and needed help washing their clothes and getting to meals. I tried to stay close to Mother while she moved about, in case something unexpected might happen. Surrounded by strangers every moment, I had begun to worry about being separated from her, or from my brother and sister. I missed Father, whom none of us had seen for almost two months. Only when Mother was told that we were being sent north did we learn that he would be joining us again. But not until the day we were to board the train.

In the meantime, even more women and children had arrived at the livestock building, which meant that those of us who had been there the longest had to move on. Buses and trains were taking families away, heading to ghost towns from the former gold rush days and to camps in places named Greenwood, Kaslo, Slocan, Tashme, New Denver, Lemon Creek—as well as to work the sugar-beet fields in Alberta. Faces that had become familiar disappeared and were never seen again. And then, one morning, shortly after breakfast in the poultry building, we were told by guards that our turn had come, that Father had arranged for us to go north. Auntie Aya was to travel with us, though we did not see Uncle Aki until just before the bus arrived to take us to the train.

Everything had to be packed up quickly. Damp clothes were yanked from lines, divider sheets and blankets tugged from ropes and racks. Other families were led out of the building with us—some faces were familiar, some were not—and we were herded onto a bus and driven to a station platform, where we were to board a train. There we stood, in a huddle beside the tracks, once more clutching bundles that had been newly tied with string.

Husbands and fathers were now joining the group, and families were reunited in the confusion as everyone crowded around heaps of suitcases, baskets, hundred-pound sacks of sugar and rice, paper shopping bags, buckets and boxes, rolls of bedding coiled with rope. We were adrift in a sea of bent-over backs, a blur of shapes and colours. I moved closer to Mother, who was wearing her navy blue coat again but this time with a scarf wrapped around her head and tied under her chin. A huge black train thundered in—the Pacific Great Eastern—raising cinder dust as it puffed and wheezed to a halt in front of us. Hiroshi leapt forward, and Mother hauled him back.

"Stand still," she told him sharply. "Take your sister's hand and look after her until you are told to board the train."

I saw how tense she was when I looked up at her face.

"Hold your bundles tightly," she said, quietly now. "Don't look back. Your father will find us. Uncle Aki has seen him. He is helping the old people and he has to look after the sacks of sugar and rice. He has to be certain that the crate that holds our stove gets into the freight car at the back of the train."

Father had been brought to the station separately, but at the time we boarded, there was still no sign of him. Mother told me to lift my feet high onto the steps of the coach. A tall policeman in uniform, the ever-present RCMP, leaned forward and picked me up suddenly, as if I weighed no more than a piece of cloth fluttering through the air.

"There you are, young fellow," he said, and he set me down gently in the doorway between coaches.

I was feeling the weightlessness of the moment, the pleasurable rush of my body through air, when I heard Mother's voice below. Her refusal of help. She climbed up by herself and looked away until the policeman stepped back and offered to lift someone else.

We claimed facing double seats, Hiroshi and Keiko on one side, Mother and I on the other. I was pushing my palms across the rough bristles of upholstery, and I looked up to see a conductor and a different member of the RCMP making their way through the long aisle of the coach. One by one, the two men removed every linen square that had been buttoned to the top of the seatbacks. No dark head of Japanese hair would be touching those starched white linen squares. Again, Mother turned away until the men had passed us by.

The train began to jerk and halt, jerk and halt. Father had not found us. He had not come to the train, after all. And then, just as we were pulling away from the siding, I saw him outside, running to reach the steps at the end of the coach.

"Thank God," Mother's voice whispered above me. "Thank God we are together now."

But Father was agitated and out of breath, and he scarcely took note of the fact that he hadn't seen us for a long time. He picked me up roughly and plunked me down between Hiroshi and Keiko on the facing seat. They both squirmed and wriggled but did not dare to complain. I was trying to hear what my parents were saying, but Mother lowered her head and whispered, raising her palm in front of her lips so that she would not be heard by others crowded around us. A cold rain had begun outside and was trickling down the thickness of distorted glass in the train windows. I watched Mother as she stared over our heads while she listened to something Father was telling her. She leaned back into the seat. With no expression on her face except one of extreme fatigue, she closed her eyes.

We arrived at our destination in the evening, and pulled our bundles down from the overhead racks, only to learn that we were not allowed to get off the train. We were at a railway station beside the Fraser River, on the edge of a town we were not permitted to enter. One more rule that had to be obeyed. Father pushed our bundles back up on the racks, and snapped at us and told us to sit down again. The train backed up and stopped, dead still, on a siding away from the main tracks. Angry people from the town were parading along the length of the train, holding signs up to the windows in the fading light. They did not want us there. Not even to sleep on the train.

Wanted or not, this was where we had been sent. But no one knew what to do with us now that we had arrived. Not the protesting people from the town, not the government representatives, not the RCMP, who continued to guard the train. No one seemed capable of making a decision.

"Stay where you are," one policeman told the men. "Tell your families to be calm. Don't try to get off the train." As if we had any choice if we did get off.

It was easy to see that it was cold outside because of the way the protesters were dressed. We were told not to open the windows, but the air in the coach was worsening. It had reeked horribly throughout the journey, but now it was unbearable. Despite this, we were made to sit on the train for three more days and nights. Some children became ill and retched and cried. Odours of urine and feces and vomit mixed with the sticky-sweet smell of varnish from wood panelling inside the coach. Several of the old people had fever and diarrhea. Food was brought to the train by the RCMP, and the smell of it made the air even worse. There were spittoons outside the washrooms at the end of the coach where four or five old men stayed most of the time, bickering and talking and playing cards. It was difficult to fall asleep, even though we did our best to stretch out on seats that had been pushed back as far as they would go.

Abruptly, on the third day, we were ordered to leave the train. Once more, we gathered our bundles and left behind a place that had become familiar. A place where I had memorized every anxious face, every seat in the coach, every paint chip, every streak in the glass. Hiroshi and Keiko and I had walked up and down the aisle so that we could exercise our legs. We had fidgeted as much as our parents had allowed. Our legs were cramped, our mother's feet swollen, our father's temper barely held beneath the surface. Now we stepped down from the coach and stood in a huddle in unbearable cold, staring up at empty windows as the train pulled away and abandoned us.

I turned a full circle, feeling cinders grate under the soles of my rubber boots. Everyone was looking up because all around, in every direction, were the looming shapes of mountains. The town had sprung up in the centre of what appeared to be a four-square fold of peaks and valleys. White mountaintops glistened as if they'd been iced.

We boarded buses and were driven across the town bridge, over the swift and muddy Fraser River, arriving at a more or less flat, narrow field at the base of a mountain on the other side. Oversized tents had arrived from Vancouver on another train, and Father's name and Uncle Aki's were called out because, at their request, one large tent had been assigned to our two families.

The entire trainload of people began the business of setting up a tent village in the bitter cold of the mountains. And though we were wrapped and bundled and blanketed, I had never been as cold as I was in that place, high above a valley we had never seen, across from an angry town that did not want us on either side of the river. Mother told us to keep moving, and we clapped our hands and bent our knees and walked in circles and stomped our feet.

I could hear Father grunting, his anger visible as he pried at the boards of the crate. He had removed his jacket, his tendons taut beneath the surface of his skin. As he lifted out parts of the stove, muscles rippled up his fisherman's arms, partly hidden by the sleeves of his shirt. With a steady flow of Japanese curses and with the help of Uncle Aki and another man, he put the stove together piece by piece and levelled it on rock and damp ground in an open space not far from the tent where we would be living. Hiroshi and Keiko and I were sent to look for downed branches and dry brush on the lower slope of the mountain, at the edge of the field. While I was dragging a branch through patches of snow, I heard Hiroshi mutter, "Arse-arse-arse." Keiko began to giggle but no one else paid any attention. Hiroshi and Keiko dragged back larger pieces from blowdowns, and a fire was started in what had become, by necessity, an outdoor stove. Mother found and unpacked two pots—one being the rice pot from my bundle—and she began to melt snow so that she could boil water and prepare our meal. While we waited for the rice to cook, we leaned forward, sharing the space with Auntie Aya and some of our new neighbours. Hands and arms reached towards the burners in an attempt to capture thin waves of heat before they escaped into the mountain air.

Father put on his jacket again, and he scowled and planted his feet wide and stood behind the stove. He was taller than the other men and he wore a wool cap with earflaps, the chin strap dangling. His eyebrows scrunched as he gestured to the surrounds of ponderosa pine and Douglas fir that shadowed the slopes at his back. In places where there was no snow, the soil was a mixture of rough gravel and sand. In the woods, there was only darkness. High above, on the side of the mountain, a rockslide had left its mark, a slate-coloured vee now gathering dusk.

I shifted my weight, planted my feet in the way my father had, crossed my arms and tucked my hands into my armpits. *Arse,* I said to myself, knowing it was meant to be a bad word. *Arse-arse.*

I tried my best to remember our warm kitchen, the one we had left behind on the island so many weeks ago. I thought of Missisu's piano and I turned my head sharply as if I might be ambushed by a fog of wavy, familiar notes. I looked to Mother's face for a sign as she leaned forward to pull dishes from the willow basket.

But it was clear that Mother was not thinking about music or about our old, comfortable kitchen. I could see that she was thinking about getting food out of the pot and into the rice bowls, out of the rice bowls and into our bellies. I could see that she was thinking about warm water, which she had already begun to heat, so that she could wash the soot and train dirt off the three of us before putting us to bed on cots set up inside the heavy canvas tent.

And there we stood. Our family. The five of us captured in memory for all time, looking as if we had signed up for some bizarre adventure trek, having brought a stove with us to defeat the treachery of winter.

Uncle Aki, Auntie Aya and a few neighbours crowd into the edges of this memory. They are seeking our shared heat because no other man in camp has thought to pack a stove in a wooden crate. On the fringes of the same picture, more deadwood has been gathered. Campfires have been started all along the rows of tents. A baby wails. Food preparation has begun. The sound of high-pitched, rhythmic sobbing starts up from the far edge of the field. The same sobbing that kept us awake at Hastings Park has followed us here, to the camp. Auntie Aya shudders, and Uncle Aki puts his arm around her shoulder. Father surveys the scene and nods. Because, for the moment, our own small family is the only one that has a stove, and a poker to rattle its embers, a lifter to lift the burners and an open chimney pipe through which smoke curls up and up, into the circle of tightening darkness.

CHAPTER 10

1997

Six hundred and ninety-seven kilometres between the Soo and Thunder Bay, and I am somewhere between. I try to envisage five million square kilometres of Shield and all I can conjure is the idea of immensity. An eye looking down over lake and rock, peering into crevice to see hibernating bear, or moose knee-deep in muskeg, or wolf skulking in shadow. Water is high in ponds and craters because it has no easy place to drain. Trees lean as if a mythical wind has bent an entire forest all at the same moment and in the same direction. I feel that I'm on some vast and bumpy map, uncharted landscape from which there is no exit except the one I draw for myself. But for thousands of years, Native tribes have travelled this route. And for hundreds of years, *voyageurs, Métis,* missionaries and explorers pushed their way deep inside the continent.

I've been stopping here and there, mostly for Basil, but sometimes to do quick sketches on paper. Creeks and streams and rivers all head towards the big lake; dark waters bubble over jutting stones; circles puddle atop thin ice. And old conversations with Lena surface as I drive. A lidded eye pushes up from below, from the morass of memory that I have been holding down. I can't prevent what bursts through. I keep thinking: Lena as . . . Lena doing . . . Lena trying . . . I remember her excitement when we travelled here together. Her insistence that we stop so that she could examine the upheaval of massive slabs of rock. She wrote down the names of road signs: Widow Pond, Dead Horse Cove, Lost Boy Creek, Old Mine Road, Bear Paw Landing, Horse Thief Bay. "Every name contains its own story," she told Greg. "In the way that rivers hold stories, so do roads and pathways. Sometimes, if we dig around and listen hard, we can find out what the stories are."

She and Greg began to invent their own legends during long drives and camping trips. One day, we followed a sign for a place called Hope Lane all the way to a dead end, and Lena, peeved, declared the sign to be a malcontent's idea of perversity.

I slow to watch a fox as it crosses the road, unhurried, and disappears behind the trees. It leaves its image behind, a palette of cream-coloured fur, its winter thickness streaked with rusty red. I want to tell Lena how different the landscape is so early in the year. From the highway, it's possible to peer inside the naked forest to witness repetitive scenes of post-winter disarray. Birches have snapped and tumbled as if they've retreated in disordered haste. A month from now none of this will be visible. Deciduous trees will be in full leaf and will block the view from the road. They'll link arms with the firs and present a dense wall of forest. But for now, it's like seeing through transparent skin.

I haven't had breakfast and have to keep an eye out for town or village. Hunger is gnawing, but not enough to make me get out and dig through the cooler to see what's inside—apart from dregs of melting ice. Lake Superior is on my left—the vast Great Lake, with the United States unseen on its other side. I drove away from the cabin this morning at daybreak, and did not stop to explore the creek below. The van was gone, which meant that the two women had departed, though I didn't hear them leave. I wonder now if they left after dinner and didn't stay overnight at all. The evil fortune sticking in the craw.

A white-tailed doe, her flanks bony and thin, is feeding at the edge of the road, attracted to traces of salt left over from heavy equipment that sprayed the highway all winter. She looks up and stares as I pass. Yellow signs with images of deer captured mid-leap are posted along the road, but these gradually change to warnings of moose: NIGHT DANGER. An antlered animal is pictured: long sloping nose, left foreleg bent, shoulder to the road, challenging any driver foolish enough to be in its path while it's on the move.

The signs are a long cry from what I now begin to see in ditches to my right. Massive carcasses, evidence of collisions between moose and transport truck. The animals weigh close to a ton, and when I see the first carcass on its back, its limbs reaching upwards in rigor mortis, I don't understand what it is until I drive past another, and then another. I see four in all. Hit by trucks in the night and bounced back to the ditches to die. They are black in death, charred as if by fire. Not the majestic beasts Lena and I used to see in the forests when we were hiking, the ones that clip-clopped across the highway with their big, ungainly feet. These carcasses are sculptures gone bad, miscalculated shapes. And while I'm lamenting their calamitous deaths, I drive past a shallow gully and glance down to see a live moose looking out, a high, dark hulk almost hidden by moss and fallen trees.

When I drive past the sign for Old Woman Bay, I can't remember what it is about the place that is familiar. And then I do, and I pull over and sit there, staring straight ahead. I think of an essay I read earlier in the week and I turn the car around, drive back to the sign, leave the main road and enter a parking area where I'm at once surrounded by woods, except for a clearing before a strip of beach. The sky is big-lake sky, white and expansive, streaked with blue. Every cloud shaped with clarity. Mine is the only car in the lot, and I let Basil out the back. "It's yours, Basil," I tell him. "The entire place. Look out for small stones." But he has already taken off with a yelp, running in and around the trees, ears dragging as he follows some scent. He heads for the water, passing through beach gravel, sniffing and exploring as he slows and pads along.

I follow him down to the lake, my hiking boots sliding in and out of stone broken to millions of fragments along the edge of the bay. It was Böll's essay, Heinrich Böll, and he wrote about how one road sign, one name, could set off an outburst of memories. For me, it was this one sign that has stopped me completely: OLD WOMAN BAY.

I plunk down on a massive but smooth driftwood log. The air is cool, the sun strong. The time I cannot bypass is a summer in the seventies. The event, our first car trip, when we drove as far as Manitoba for an adventure and then aimed the car south, following the Red River for a while. We decided to go to North Dakota, then Minnesota, and we returned via a southern route home again. Southern for us, but still quite far north.

We owned a station wagon then, too. Old and clunky. We'd bought it used, at bargain price. Greg was not yet born. We travelled with a small tent in the wheel well where the spare tire was kept, along with sleeping bags and a cooler. We could be self-sufficient when we had to be. But one night we were travelling through hard rain. There was nothing around but woods and rock, and we were far from hotels and motels. We kept driving and driving until we were so fatigued it was unsafe to go on.

"We have to stop," Lena said. "It's after one in the morning. Even the windshield wipers are dragging."

"Stop where? We've been looking for hours. There's nothing to be had."

"No lodgings at the inn," she said. "But we're both falling asleep. If we continue, we're going to kill ourselves."

We saw the sign for Old Woman Bay.

I pulled into this parking lot. The same one. From the car windows we saw nothing but blackness and trees. Our headlights lit up a posted sign: NO OVERNIGHT CAMPING—STRICTLY ENFORCED.

"We'll have to spend the night in the car," I told her. "There's nobody here, so it won't matter to anyone."

The back seat was already flattened, so we climbed over and unzipped our sleeping bags. These could be used separately, as singles, or opened out flat and fitted together to make a double, which is what we did, to make a wider bed for two. We crouched low, bumping our heads against the ceiling as we zipped the outer edges and stretched out our makeshift bed. We took off our clothes and tossed them towards our feet and climbed into the padded bag, which was now spacious and warm. The car rocked every time we moved. Lena reached out a bare arm, opened a window half an inch and pushed down the locks from inside. "I don't want any bears knocking at the doors," she said.

Once inside the zipped-together bags, we lay flat on our backs and started to laugh. "Tell me a river story," Lena said. "One with a good ending, not something with cataracts and turmoil that will keep me awake."

"Let me think for a minute," I said. "Okay, here goes. A young man was once travelling through Germany, and as it happened, it was the year before he would meet the woman who would become his wife. He didn't know that then, because she was living in Montreal, still unmet, and he was in Europe, travelling alone. As a matter of fact, she was sleeping in his bed in Montreal, having rented his share of a student apartment while he was away.

"The young man was following the great rivers of Europe. He had a sketch pad in his pack, the usual supplies, and he was trying to capture something he could not quite put a name to, some understanding of the rivers he encountered. Something lost, perhaps, or something not yet found. He lingered in Bonn, Beethoven's birthplace, and visited Köln and the cathedral, and he travelled upriver to Speyer and climbed the highest hill and looked down over the ancient Rhine and watched barge traffic below. He thought he would stay overnight nearby because he also wanted to see the Neckar. He had been told that it was a beautiful river, more green than blue, with castles strung like jewels at the top of the hills. He proceeded to Heidelberg and found a hotel, and while there he bought a ticket for a boat that would take him on a new journey the next day.

"The next morning, he boarded a boat that travelled upriver through a series of narrow locks. He inhaled a breath of river air, which did not satisfy in any way because the day was uncomfortably hot. The boat had two decks, and swans paddled to the side and stretched up their long throats, demanding food, which tourists tossed down: chunks of bread, pieces of chocolate, even sausage."

"Dark chocolate? What kind of sausage?" said Lena.

"Quiet, please. People on deck were drinking beer. Small children carrying Fanta and fizzy cola ran up and down steps between decks. The boat slugged forward, but there was no breeze. And unlike the tour boat on which the young man was now captive, the passing barge traffic was remarkably swift. Colours streamed from multinational flags, towels billowed on clotheslines, bicycles leaned against shacks on broad decks. The barges sat just inches above water level, so low did their heavy loads nose through the waves.

"Across the deck from the young man was a middle-aged couple, sitting on a bench. The man was thick everywhere, squat build, large neck, rough skin. He wore short brown trousers hemmed above the knee and a pair of braces over his shirt. His wife was short, but even larger than he. Layer after layer of her body bulged from beneath a sleeveless cotton dress. She wore stockings of a bluish-white colour, as if to help remedy the swollen veins in her legs. She wiped her forehead and tried to ease herself by moving closer to her husband. At the same time, she leaned back against him. Then she slowly lifted herself sideways until she had pushed him against the inner wall of the deck. Squeezing the last bit of air from him, she turned her back, fell like a sudden blow upon him and stretched her swollen legs lengthwise along the bench.

"Jammed as he was into the corner, only bits of the man could now be seen. But he did not, as expected, push her off. Instead, he began to bounce one knee. His wife bounced and rolled with his inner tune, her eyes closed, perspiration streaming down her face. Her hand rested just below her husband's trousers, keeping time on his bare thigh. It was a moment of such intimacy that the young man, in agony, turned away. At that moment, he would have given anything to experience the kind of intimacy he was witnessing. And then he thought, *What nonsense.* But he did not forget the couple or the intimate moment between them."

"A revealing story," Lena said. "In more ways than one. A story of longing, definitely."

"But the young man was observant, you have to give him that."

"Indeed. The scene was painted quite clearly."

Observant but lonely, I was thinking, but I didn't say that aloud. The young man was always—more or less—alone.

"And this present moment," said Lena, "the one in which the young man finds himself in the midst of deep forest, is also a moment of intimacy. Too bad we don't have curtains on the car windows. What if someone drives up?"

"Don't worry," I told her. "It's so late, no one is going to drive in at this time of night. Anyway, it's pitch black and we'll be awake before dawn. How soundly do you think we'll be able to sleep like this?"

We were asleep almost before I finished the sentence.

When we woke, it was hours past dawn and sun was shining through the car windows on one side. Lena raised her head and looked out and ducked back down again.

"My God," she said. "We're surrounded. There are half a dozen cars and camper trailers. Did you hear anyone drive in? There must have been others on the highway who couldn't find a place to sleep. I didn't hear a thing all night."

But we could hear people now. The sound of many voices as families prepared breakfast at picnic tables around the edges of the parking lot. There was no way we could get dressed without being seen.

I volunteered to be the one to unzip the side of the sleeping bag, to try to gather up the clothes at our feet. I stayed low, pitched the clothes to Lena and climbed back under, and we began to dress while lying on our backs inside the sleeping bag. Not easy, I remember. And we were laughing again. The whole scene was comic because our car was parked in the middle of the lot and people were coming and going, back and forth to trailers and cars. "Who cares?" I said to Lena, through snorts of laughter. "Who bloody cares?" But every time someone walked past, we froze and pretended to be asleep.

There must have been five or six vehicles, and neither of us had heard so much as a wheel turn in the night.

When we were dressed, which took more than a few awkward manoeuvres, we looked at each other and nodded. *Ready.* We climbed out on opposite sides of the rear of the car and got back in at the front. People at the picnic tables looked over and waved. The two of us drove off.

I know the exact place we parked. Same site, same lot. I call for Basil and get him into the car, but only after offering a treat as persuasion. We are back on the highway in minutes, and I drive for more than an hour until we're at the outskirts of a small town. By the time I see a sign for a Pancake House, it's mid-morning, late, and I'm not certain I'll be served. The need for coffee is greater than the need for food, and I can probably get at least that much, so I pull in. I give Basil a drink of water and leave him in the car with the window partly down, in a parking spot that can be seen from inside the restaurant.

The place is more bar than restaurant—a sports bar or maybe a hybrid, bar and restaurant combined. There are no customers in the room. A TV on a high shelf in one corner is on but soundless. Two men are wrestling in outlandish costumes, golden cocks strutting across the screen.

A tall woman with a weary-looking face is wiping glasses and she points to a table close to where she's working. Efficiency itself, she's fast, moving from one table to another, setting places, giving surfaces a swipe of her damp cloth, creating order from salt and pepper shakers, containers of ketchup and syrup. If I were to sketch her, I'd call the drawing *Taut motion.* She wears a black pinstriped blouse and black slacks. The blouse shines like satin. Her face is thin, her long legs thin, her hip bones prominent, no extra flesh. Everything about her brings to mind the words *gaunt* and *defeated*. It's easy to see that her life, thus far, has not been easy.

But she is all kindness, as it turns out. And she gives the impression of intuiting some need, not in her but in me—a need that is blatant and personal. She brings coffee before I ask, offers the news that two moose, a cow and a calf, have been strutting through town since early morning, and that the police are in a tizzy. They've called for the local conservation officer. She hands me a menu, goes to the bar, swishes her cloth over the counter and returns to take my order. When I ask for an egg sunnyside, she says she can do egg. When I ask for toast, she can do toast. The kitchen never closes. She'll throw in back bacon as there is extra today. I can have waffles, too, if I want them. Her body leans forward and pulls back. She leaves comfort behind and disappears behind the bar and through the kitchen door. And yet, she looks so troubled herself.

When she brings my breakfast, it's a plate heaped high with food. In the centre, a double yolk in a single egg. The two yolks are unbroken, even with the cooking.

"Our lucky day, yours and mine," she says. She tilts her chin, points to the double yolk and tries to explain. "It's good luck. You know—double yolk." And then she looks at me more closely and says, "Hey, hey. It's only an egg. You okay?" She gives me a firm pat on the shoulder before she turns and goes back to cleaning up.

I stare at my plate through blurred vision and curse the fates again. And I think of Otto at the funeral, reaching over to pat at my sleeve.

CHAPTER 11

1942

There was no time to sit around and mope after our first night in the tents. Distances were marked, sticks were pounded to the earth. A month earlier, while in detention in Vancouver, Father had arranged to cash in his only insurance policy—worth one hundred and twenty-five dollars. He was also to receive, some time in the future, a small share of money from the Fishermen's Co-operative, which he had helped to set up and which had collapsed in late 1941, even though it had been incorporated only two weeks before the bombing of Pearl Harbor. Like everyone in our Fraser River camp, we would have to pay for our own internment—until the money ran out and Father found a way of earning more.

The shacks that were to become our homes were erected on a strip of land that was strewn with old sagebrush and spotted with snow, and that lay between the base of the mountain and the edge of a dirt road that led back towards the bridge—the same bridge over which we'd been driven the day before, and which we were now forbidden to cross. The strip of land was the only available space where we *could* build. Everything else was slope and mountain and cliff that hung over the Fraser River. In the other direction, the dirt road continued past us and around a curve that led to a deep canyon. If we were to travel in that direction, we were told we would face mountain ranges even higher than the ones we now stood beside. Not that we were permitted to travel; roadblocks were set up in both directions on either side of the camp and guarded by the RCMP, twenty-four hours a day.

I was shivering from cold, and looked across the wide river to the town on the opposite bank. In the daylight, I could see the railway station where our train had been idle for three nights. Smoke was rising from chimneys on the main street of a community that had heat. I saw houses spotted here and there in the hills that spread out from the town. Even in the hills, smoke was visible over the rooftops. It was clear that every bit of warmth on the planet had gathered on the other side of the river.

A meeting was organized, men and women were assembled, skills called out. There were millhands, loggers, mechanics, bookkeepers, stenographers and typists, farmers, fishermen, factory workers, restaurant workers, store clerks, cooks and accountants. When it was discovered that two men were master carpenters, it was agreed that they would supervise construction. Tools would be shared. At the beginning, someone from the Security Commission helped with the ordering of supplies. But after that, we were on our own. There was also a woodcarver among us, and he was put to work alongside the carpenters, but his main job was to help make furniture: tables, benches, shelves, stools and wooden frames for beds. Some wood had already arrived, but several more weeks passed before large quantities of rough green lumber were delivered from a mill in a nearby valley. The men in camp, along with teenage boys—Hiroshi and I were not big enough to be part of this group—sorted materials and sawed rough boards that would enable them to erect the shacks that would become our homes: three tidy rows, twenty shacks per row, each twelve feet wide, utilizing every inch of available flat space.

And shacks they were. For the most part identical. Uninsulated, with open knotholes in the wood. Each had two rooms: a main room that served as kitchen, a second room for sleeping, with a makeshift curtain dividing the two. For a very large family, a small extra bedroom was added on at the back.

But most of us were still living in tents, using kerosene lanterns to ward off the dark. The stove outside our own tent burned wood from early morning to late evening and was used not only for heat, but for boiling water and cooking food. We continued to drag dead branches and twigs and anything else that was combustible out of the woods and down the slopes. Some of the men in camp set to work cutting trees, dragging and sawing logs. Women, too, gathered wood and, during the day, stayed near open fires or inside the tents, where they bundled themselves in coats and blankets. My parents had shared the cost of a small galvanized tub with Uncle Aki and Auntie Aya, and we were able to stand or crouch in the tub and have a bath inside the tent before going to bed.

Keiko's hands became frostbitten and swollen from the cold, but there was no doctor in camp to examine her, and the puffiness lasted until summer. As for me, I was freezing all the time, both in and out of the tent. Mother gave me an extra sweater to wear, along with a strip of wool, a *haramaki*, to wrap around my torso so that my kidneys would be covered. And, finally, a long scarf to coil about my neck.

As soon as one shack was finished, a family moved in. The men from families whose shacks were complete then helped the next family to build. Each place had little more than walls, roof and a rough plank floor that snagged the soles of our feet and planted slivers under our skin. There were no doors, no inside plumbing, no electricity. Even without doors, we moved into the shacks because they offered more permanency than the tents. Four long communal outhouses were built at the back of the camp, the outhouse doorways facing the side of the hill.

After our shack was built, Father divided the bedroom by hanging a sheet. Hiroshi and Keiko and I shared the bed on the right, our parents the one on the left, a few inches separating the two. Bed frames were nailed together from raw lumber. Thin mattresses or futons were laid overtop. We had to climb into bed from the end.

Father decided that we would have two small windows at the front, the same as every other shack, but a window in the back as well, in the bedroom. He sawed and banged at the wood and made an opening in the wall, but his measurements were askew and the space for the window ended up being crooked. He made no apologies. No glass had arrived at the camp, so we had to wait. He said he would patch around the edges later. Mother hung cloths over the gaping spaces, and stuffed cracks and knotholes with strips of old newspapers that had been used to wrap the dishes we had brought with us.

At the beginning, there was no fresh water. Drinking water in covered barrels was brought in by truck from outside the camp. Like everything else, the water had to be paid for, though many people had diarrhea after drinking it. When the truck arrived, men and women brought buckets, pots, any containers they could find, and these were filled from the back of the truck. Three old people died of dysentery and typhoid within the first month of our arrival. For a while, during those early weeks, melted snow was used for cooking and drinking. When the snow on the hills disappeared, water from the muddy Fraser was dragged up the steep embankment in buckets, and strained and boiled. Water was the preoccupation of every family, and remained so during all the years we lived in the camp. Eventually, river water was pumped up from the Fraser and filtered and stored in huge wooden tanks that were levelled on boulders, but it would be a long time before the tanks were in place. Mostly, people lugged their own water and stored it in barrels that stood outside their doors. As for heat, empty oil drums were fashioned into makeshift stoves, and these were placed inside the shacks while construction continued.

The next step was to tack tarpaper to the outside of the shacks. Father dug at the winter crust of hardened earth around our new home and tried to loosen sandy dirt that could be shovelled and banked against the outer walls. He did as much as he could to prevent the winds from gusting under the shack and between cracks in the wooden floor.

In the midst of this continuous activity, Hiroshi and Keiko and I watched trucks as they drove in and out of camp. We talked about what lay beyond the mountains, and we tried to imagine the sorts of places from which the trucks had come. Hiroshi was all for talking to the drivers, asking questions, trying to help unload supplies that were too heavy for him. He managed to do some small errands, made himself useful and even earned a five-cent tip every once in a while, from one of the drivers. Sometimes, he was given a local paper by a driver, or a pack of gum. When he was given a paper, he brought it to Father, who read it by lantern light after everyone else had gone to bed.

As for Keiko, she was missing school more and more. Classes had come to a complete halt, except for the few lessons given informally while we had been at Hastings Park. Keiko also missed her friends from our old fishing village. She had made a few new friends, however, and when she wasn't required to help Mother, she could be seen with the other girls, playing school, going over old lessons they had already completed. Keiko wanted books and workbooks. She wanted a teacher. She wanted school to start up again quickly. But so far, there was no school.

In the evenings, after working on the shacks, the men met and made a plan to set aside a large field area across the dirt road, on the river side, so that by late spring the snagged tumbleweed could be burned off and communal gardens could be started, as well as an allotment strip for each family. Beyond the wide portion designated for growing vegetables, a steep cliff hung over the river below. Rules were made. Young children were not permitted past the garden plots because of the danger of falling from this great height into the river. Older children were assigned to watch over the young.

There was much discussion about how the vital garden space would be irrigated, because it had become apparent that we were stuck in a place that had arid, sandy soil. A number of experienced farmers who were interned in the camp were certain that tomatoes would grow well here. The men had been warned by the man who was leasing the land where we now lived—and who came by from time to time—that the growing season was not a long one, but the summers were extremely hot. Again, plans were made, this time to repair a damaged flume that was already on the site. Never short of ideas, the men were eventually able to divert water through a system of long wooden pipes with homemade filters. Cold, clear water rushed down from small mountain currents and from dammed streams into holding tanks and out the pipes again. This water was used for garden plots, and any extra for laundry and bathing. Every once in a while, someone hauled out a fat rainbow trout, caught in the pipes, caught between filters. A shout would be heard, and someone would pull out a trout and take it home for his dinner.

In the midst of all the planning and building, there was visiting back and forth, tent to tent, tent to shack. If the sun was strong, neighbours gathered outside. I sat on a low three-legged stool Father had nailed together, and tried to stay out of his way because he always seemed to be in a temper. Sometimes I created pictures in the dirt with a stick; sometimes I drew with a finger against my knee and traced images. All the while, I was paying attention to what people had to say because everyone had a different story to tell. The community—for that's what we were becoming—was trying to piece together details of what had happened. To ourselves and to every other person of Japanese ancestry who lived on the West Coast. A mail system was now in place. Letters addressed to the camp, already heavily censored, arrived by train in town and were driven across the bridge and dropped off in a mailbag. Camp mail was sorted on our side of the river. Letters came in from the stalls at Hastings Park in Vancouver, where friends had been left behind, from separated family members in other camps in the interior of the province, and from as far south as California. Letters also arrived from Angler, a prisoner-of-war camp in Ontario. Surprising as it seemed, and despite the number of internment camps that had sprung up in the United States and Canada, some people believed that we were in the camp under a temporary arrangement. They were certain we'd be sent back to the homes we'd been forced to leave. Others said that the worst was yet to come.

"This is the story of the two-dresser set," said Ba, and we settled around the stove to listen—as many of us as could squeeze in.

Most sat on the floor. The woodcarver whittled away at a stick of wood, and dropped the shavings into a carpenter's apron spread over his lap.

Ba and Ji were our neighbours now. They were an elderly couple whose shack had been completed before ours, just a few feet away. Elders and people with babies moved into their places first, followed by families with young children. Uncle Aki and Auntie Aya's place was also finished, and they lived directly behind us, in the second row. Auntie Aya was seldom seen outside, and Uncle Aki told us she was resting in bed because she was always tired. She was vulnerable to cold and infection, Mother said, and she did not have the energy to be outside in the mountain air for hours at a time.

Everyone was welcome in Ba and Ji's shack. Ba and Ji had owned a store in Vancouver before being detained, and they were used to having people drop by. And people wanted to hear their stories. The old couple knew more than almost everyone else about recent events in the outside world. Unlike most of us after Pearl Harbor, they had not been forced into the cattle stalls of Hastings Park. Because they were already living in the city, they had not been on the early list for removal. Not like those of us from the fishing villages along the coast. Ba and Ji were registered and fingerprinted in Vancouver and were forced to obey curfew and carry IDs, but they had been allowed to stay in their home a bit longer. Eventually, they were sent to the camp along with everyone else.

As a measure of respect, our parents told us that we must address them as Ba and Ji, even though they were not our grandparents and we were not related. They had raised a daughter, Sachi, who had married a Japanese American and was living in California. But Ba was worried. She had heard about the curfew and removal of Japanese Americans from the coast of Washington, Oregon and California. So far, Sachi had not sent any news.

Ba was the natural storyteller of the two. The skin on her face was tissue-paper thin and moved in crinkles as she talked.

"This is the story of our two-dresser set," she said again. She had told it over and over, to anyone who would listen.

"We had our store for thirty-two years." And she nodded because that was the truth. "We raised our child in the upstairs rooms and she helped out after school while she was growing up. The store paid for her education. Sachi went to university," she added, proudly. "And then, she left home and wanted to travel, so she moved to California. While she was there, she met a man who was studying engineering. They were married in Vancouver, and we were happy that our family was getting bigger. It was the way things should be. We knew when she brought Tom home to meet us that he was very smart. And because there were three sons in his family and none in ours, he took our name when he married Sachi so that our family name would be carried on. A good man," she said.

"But after Sachi had left home, we no longer needed the upstairs rooms, so we rented them to a young couple. I don't know which camp that young couple was sent to. After they moved in upstairs, Ji and I lived in two rooms at the back of the store, at ground level. Inside the store, we had a wood stove in one corner, and three benches near the stove. The old men came by in the morning to sit around and gossip with Ji. And argue," she said. "They gossiped and argued and played cards and had a lot to say about the world. They never ran out of things to say.

"And then, after Pearl Harbor"—there was a pause here—"they still came, but this time they were cautious. Some were confused. I was always listening because I was behind the counter, wiping shelves, cleaning up, serving people who came in. Who had disappeared since the day before? Was there any news? What was happening? Everyone knew that the younger men had been rounded up. Anyone between eighteen and forty-five. That's what we heard, and we became worried about the sons of our friends, all the young men we knew. Some of them were angry about the discrimination and they escaped, and police called them delinquents, and they were rounded up again and placed in custody or sent to prison camps in Ontario. We were also worried about our son-in-law in California, because everything was happening quickly and we knew that American camps were being set up.

"And then one day, we realized that the police had begun to watch our store. They treated us as if we were running a meeting place for spies. Every day, the police strolled by in pairs. They walked past the front door, pretending to be casual, and then they turned around suddenly and charged in as if they expected to uncover a secret operation. We laughed about this every time. Ji and his friends just blinked and became silent while the police snooped around. The old men got up off the benches and went back to their homes. But one by one, even the old men were taken away. And then it was Ji's turn, and the police came for him and put him in detention. I didn't see him again until it was time to board the train.

"When I was alone, I made up my mind to keep the store open. I knew people needed to buy things, even though supplies were running out on the shelves. Because there were no men left, the wives began to come to the store in the mornings. They came to exchange news and to sit and visit and sew. Sometimes, one of the women had a letter to share, and there would be news about where one of the husbands had been taken. But the police still strolled by in pairs, and they charged through the door every few days. We laughed after they left, because it was such nonsense to think that we could be accused of planning something against our country. Every time the police threw the door open and barged in, we fell silent and continued to sew. Just like the men, before they were taken away. We didn't look up until the police left the store. And then we looked at one another and we laughed. We laughed so hard, we had to hold our sides."

At this point in the story, Ba pushed her palms flat against her bulging middle to demonstrate. This was also the point at which she sat up straighter, remembering.

"I knew that we would not be able to take our belongings when it was time to leave. I could see what was happening all around. I was certain, too, that after Ji was taken we would lose the store. And when the shelves were empty, no more supplies would be delivered.

"But I did not want to give up my two-dresser set. It was polished mahogany," she said, and she paused to allow the memory of the rich, dark wood to be absorbed by the imagination of her listeners.

"Imagine. After our daughter was educated, I saved every penny to buy that set. Who ever thought that someone like me would own a two-dresser set!"

Her voice had an edge to it after this part of the story.

"Rather than have it stolen, I decided to sell, and I posted a sign in the store window. I knew that the police would be coming to take me away some morning. I knew that Ji and I would need the money. Whatever we could get.

"I was alone in the store the day the pickup truck arrived to carry it away. I was paid four dollars, the best price I could get. I stood behind the store window and watched two men load it into the back of their truck. I watched my dresser set drive away. The truck turned the corner, but for a long time after it was gone, I stood at the window and stared out. I could not make myself move."

Even though Ba had finished her story, I knew her eyes were still following the two-dresser set on the back of the pickup as it drove away from her store. She pulled herself up from her chair and went outside to stand in front of the shack. The woodcarver held up a tiny figure of a bantam rooster, head stretched and ready to fight. He placed the rooster on Ba's table, folded his apron around the shavings and carried it outside to give it a shake.

I went out and stood beside Ba. I wanted to see what she was seeing when she looked up. The mountains that had been topped with snow when we'd first arrived were now almost bare. Pine trees grew down the lower slopes in such regular patterns, they might have been planted in rows. The ground was dry, like pictures of dusky, low dunes I had once seen in a magazine that had come in on the mail boat in our fishing village. Ba looked down, and when she saw me beside her, she patted me on the head. Two puffy sacs above her cheekbones made her look as if she'd been squinting. Then she stared off into the distance, as if her eyes might be able to bore a space through the mountains so that she could see as far south as California, as far as the camp that held her daughter, who had not been heard from since the troubles began.

I went home and found a corner of cardboard, and I drew a tiny, imperfectly proportioned two-dresser set. I made one dresser high and narrow, the other broad and low. I tried to remember certain pages I had seen in an Eaton's catalogue that Mother had kept for a while in our first home, until the pages were ripped out and crumpled and twisted around kindling to start fires in the stove. From memory, I gave each dresser claw feet and drawers of different sizes. I gave the drawers an extra flourish of ornate handles, which I made up and enjoyed creating. Wishing for crayons, I shaded patches onto the sides, but this was not entirely successful. To the lower dresser,

I attached an oval mirror held in place by a thin wooden frame. The mirror tilted slightly forward in my drawing, though I had intended it to be straight.

When I was certain that everyone had left Ba's shack, I went back and slipped my drawing past the blanket that hung across the doorless entrance of Ba and Ji's home. I heard it drop lightly on a plank of the cleanly scrubbed floor. Ba must have been near the doorway, because she pulled back the blanket and bent forward to pick up the piece of cardboard. She examined it and looked at me, and then looked at it again and held it to her breast.

"You are a good boy," she said. "You are a youngest son. I have had my eye on you. You will always be a comfort to your mother."

CHAPTER 12

1997

It has taken three days to get across Ontario, but I'm headed for prairie, or almost-prairie. Somewhere outside Thunder Bay last night, Basil and I stopped at a motel where I was asked to pay an extra deposit at check-in—a damage deposit. I asked the young clerk if there was usually a rough crowd at the place but she shook her head, embarrassed by the question. I had to pay up—thirty dollars above the price of the room. And this was refunded when I checked out early this morning.

Now I wonder if the demand was made because of me, or because of Basil, who was allowed on the ground floor, end room only, but allowed nonetheless. There was even a hook for a leash attachment at the back of the motel, as well as a low wall tap, providing access to water.

The farther west I drive, the more dogs I see. I'm in big-truck country. Dogs ride shotgun or in the rear. Big trucks, big dogs. But I'll wager that few dogs are as heavy as Basil. A woman stopped to talk to him in the parking lot this morning. She leaned down as if I were not present, though I was there beside him, leash in hand. She was wearing a faded winter parka, tight jeans and high black boots that were too warm for spring weather. She made sure I was watching. She patted Basil a few times, and I was about to warn her: *If he jumps up and bounces against you, he'll bruise your thighs.* But I held my peace about her thighs. She uttered some endearments and strutted off towards her own big dog in her own big truck. Her hair swung over her face as she left. Not a word had been spoken between us. The encounter made me wonder if I've become invisible or if I've created my own impenetrable wall. Or was it an invitation and I missed the cues entirely?

By early afternoon, the clouds are thick and muted, full of moisture. Road signs have been ominous: FATIGUE KILLS, TAKE A BREAK. It's impossible to ignore the wooden crosses that mark highway deaths, most of them at curves where road has been blasted through rock. The crosses stand for speed—the kind of unimaginable speed into which some ill-fated driver accelerated before careening off on two wheels into a wall of granite. At some curves there are multiple crosses, which is even more sobering. These are adorned with painted names, red hearts, gaudy artificial flowers that have been nailed or maybe wired on. It's as if a special design exists solely for roadside shrines. On the American highways, I remember that the crosses used to be white—in contrast to the ornate creations I'm seeing on this trip.

Earlier today, after breakfast, I drove for a while and then parked the car and took Basil for a walk along the Wabigoon River. Gulls were strutting beside the riverbank, screeching after us once we'd passed. Basil wanted to give chase, but I yanked him up short on the leash. I took the leash off when we were out of town and we walked for another hour each way, invigorated by the air, the river in full spate, flowing swiftly towards its northern destination. This river's story includes mercury and poison, I told myself. And hopefully, cleanup. I had already passed the divide from the Great Lakes' drainage system to the Arctic watershed, and I wondered if the river had rid itself of mercury by spreading it north.

Basil, coiled with energy as always, raced ahead, circled back, checked to see that I was still on the path, raced ahead again. I tried to clear my mind but I kept thinking: *I have to phone Kay to let her know where I am. I have to call. She'll want an arrival date and I can't give her one, but I have to call.*

Now I'm in the car again, arguing with myself, hating the feeling of having to report. Kay knows I want to be alone but she also wants me to stop over and stay at her place when I reach Edmonton. She doesn't believe I can do this—withdraw. She's suspicious of anyone who does, because she can't, herself. Although, to give her credit, she does stay in touch. She's the one who makes the effort in the family. And she does make an effort.

I pull over and park beside a roadside restaurant. There's a phone booth inside the entrance and I drop in a few coins, thinking I'll invent the conversation after Kay picks up at her end. The coins clatter out again and there is no connection.

"Is the phone broken?" I ask the girl behind the counter.

"Nope," she says. "But most of the time it doesn't work."

Fate decrees I will not speak with Kay today, so I go back outside, where Basil is bellowing like the hound he is. Not only is he howling, but his huge paws are bouncing off the window while he lets the world know he's been abandoned. Two men are standing beside my car, trying to soothe him by talking through the crack where I left the window down.

"Your dog doesn't like to be left on his own," says one of the men, accusingly. His expression of scorn matches that of the second man, his twin, maybe. The two have matted hair, long, drooping faces, skin the colour of cold porridge.

"We don't do things like that here, Chinaman," says the other. "How long you bin over, anyway?"

There's no answer to that. I've heard it all before. To them, I could be the heathen stepping out of "Gunga Din." *This is my own, my native land,* I tell myself, and unlock the car.

I have to clear the inside windshield, it's so steamed up. Basil aims a sharp bark at the lingering twins and their self-righteous stares, and settles down again to gnaw at his Kong.

"Thanks a lot," I tell him as I start the car. "I did leave your window down, you know. You have air, you have food, you have water, you have my company twenty-four hours a day. And if you behave like this again, I'll marry you off to Kay's little scrapper, Diva. Would you like that? Would you? They marry frogs in Bangladesh to stave off drought. Don't think I can't arrange your marriage to Diva to stave off petulance."

He raises his head, pulls another sound from his repertoire and yips like a fox. He stares at me with innocence and continues to chew.

As I drive, I'm seeing the faces of indignation left behind. I don't care to think about what the two men were trying to protect. They probably don't know themselves. Is it about being better? Is it about owning the right to belong?

I can't pretend I haven't wondered about Greg since he left home. The unposed questions about belonging. It was Lena, not I, who marched right into his classroom when he was in grade four and had been called *slant eyes* by a boy at his school. Maybe the protest did some good, maybe not. An assembly was held the next day by the teacher, no mention of the name-calling, no finger-pointing. Instead, a discussion on uniqueness and celebrating differences, which Greg told us about when he came home. Who knows if the discussion changed anyone's behaviour?

That was when Greg was a child. And what about now? If he has learned anything from my behaviour, he has learned to keep the insults buried. Maybe I've let him down in that department, but there aren't any rules.

I see a gas station and restaurant ahead and decide to try phoning Kay again. If I get through to her, she'll know enough not to press. But she'll be wondering about my whereabouts. She and Hugh will be having conversations, trying to figure out exactly where I am. They'll have a map laid out on the dining-room table; they'll be making guesses. They'll be discussing Lena, too. And First Father. I don't even want to imagine what they're saying. I don't want their concern or their pity. *Go and see him,* Kay will say. *Why won't you ever forgive? He has to see you. How much time can he have left? He's eighty-four. It's easy to find the place. It's on the way into Kamloops, on the outskirts of the city. A small house on a dusty road off the main highway. Mother always took good care of it. He used his redress money for the down payment after the Apology. It's a shame Mother didn't live to own the house she'd rented for years, but they never had the money. Of course, when he made the move to purchase, we helped him out.*

Of course.

I don't want their interference. Not that they're interfering right now. How much more alone could I be than in a car travelling a straight line across the country? If there's something to work out, it's called grief. It's close and it's sorrowful and it's something I haven't put a name to. Anger, maybe. At everything. At Lena. She shouldn't have died of a stroke. She had warnings and didn't pay attention. She didn't tell anyone. She didn't tell me and she didn't tell Greg. And now we've both lost her. Was she frightened? Did she have a foreboding? Did she not understand the danger, or did she understand it all too well?

The worst part to think about is that if she *had* paid more attention—or if I had—she'd be with me now. There was medication in her purse, untaken. I didn't know she'd seen the doctor, didn't know she'd been advised to control her blood pressure. I didn't know her blood pressure was high enough to need controlling. Everything was kept private. When her hand let go of the coffee mug at the cabin door in October, I thought it was because the mug was slippery. We swept up the glass and mopped the coffee and I filled another mug.

Lena was about to celebrate her fiftieth birthday. Child bride, she used to call herself, jokingly, being in her twenties when we married—while I was in my thirties.

Three and a half weeks after the scalding coffee splashed at her feet, three and a half weeks after Thanksgiving weekend, she had the final stroke that killed her. A cerebral vascular accident, the doctor called it. CVA. That happened in hospital, after I called the ambulance, after her speech began to slur and both of us stopped believing that this was about overwork and fatigue.

So here I am. One more person in my life has disappeared. And I'm heading back to family, first family, and at their bidding.

But not quite yet.

The terrain is changing. Big open spaces have begun. Basil, behind me, is making horse sounds again and I can tell that he's enjoying this outlet for his energy. I stop the car and let him out at the side of the road. I keep him on a leash because there's a bit of traffic—

not much—and I look around while I receive the generosity of sky from every direction. While I'm pulled over, a freight train moves along the bottom edge of sky into my line of vision, far off, south of the highway. Prairie train, long trail of flatcar, boxcar, train that seems not to move but *must* be moving out there, along that never-ending space.

Basil does his business beside the road and leaps into the car again. Once he's settled, I decide to keep on, get through Winnipeg and out the other side, branch north a bit, aim for Saskatoon and then north and west again. I want to drive and drive. I want to pass ranch and wheat farm and watery slough. I want to be numbed by the early flatness of prairie before I reach rolling hills. I'll stop when I have to, when I can no longer go on, when I feel myself falling into the dark.

When Lena and Greg used to tell stories in the car, sometimes they started with a chant:

In a dark dark wood, there was a dark dark house
And in the dark dark house, there was a dark dark room
And in the dark dark room, there was a dark dark space
And in the dark dark space, there was . . .

They took turns filling the dark space. I didn't need to. I had enough dark spaces of my own to fill. Or so Lena reminded me, when I disappeared into gloom.

"Where do you learn these things?" I said to Lena.

"Childhood. I make up the endings. We both do, don't we, Greg?"

Stare stare like a bear
Wearing Grampa's underwear

Greg was giggling in the back seat.

"What about your childhood?" Lena said. "Tell us the stories you learned."

"Not *Goldilocks*. Not *Hansel and Gretel*. More like *The Spider Weaver* and *Kachi-Kachi Yama*."

"Tell us," they both said at once. "Tell us! Please!"

The train is still there, to the south, and gives the impression of being miles long, travelling a path parallel to mine and at the same pace. It's a cardboard silhouette, pushed by some force that comprehends enormity, patience, space. At one point, the distance between road and track narrows and I can make out the image of a moon on the side of each boxcar, each moon missing a chunk, as if it's been bitten out. And then, as my car surges ahead, I hear a long, slow whistle from the train. A greeting in this limitless land. *I am here and you are here and I salute you.*

Beyond the western edge of Winnipeg, it begins to snow. A quick, harsh blizzard that takes me by surprise. I drive through it and half an hour later I'm under afternoon sun, wondering if the storm happened at all. But here's the proof: horizontal chunks of snow, trapped and unmelted at the base of the windshield. The air as cool and fresh as it was in Ontario, but the landscape so vastly different.

Weather can be visualized in all directions here. Sun ahead, cloud behind, blue above. There it is, the primary colour between green and indigo, background for migrating geese to stroke a wide-stretched vee across an otherwise unbroken sky. One puffball cloud appears to have been catapulted from an earthbound slingshot. The scene keeps changing. A visible rope of rain stretches taut in the northeast, tethering cloud to earth. Spindly baby calves huddle close to their mothers in a muddy field close to the road.

I switch on the radio and listen to an American talk show from across the border for a while. The topic is aging and how old people are treated in today's world. "If I'm in the way, put me on a piece of ice and push me out to sea," says one old man who phones in. "There isn't any sea around here," says the host. "Then take me out to the back forty and shoot me," says the man.

I switch to CBC and hear the tail end of an interview with a British mystery writer who talks as if she has a rag in her mouth. Finally, I turn the radio off. And think of Greg, young; I can't remember exactly how old. Maybe eight, nine. He had heard the word *cremation* somewhere and brought it to me, asking for explanation. I did my best, tried to describe without alarming him. He took in the information, gave a little chuckle and said, in a deep, low voice and with immense bravado, "Well, they can just lay me down on a sailing ship and set fire to the sails and let me drift out over the ocean." And then he laughed as if this was the funniest image he'd ever conjured. In fact, the two of us roared with laughter, tears running down our cheeks.

Since Lena died, I've sometimes found myself praying when I think of Greg. "Please, God, let him be safe. Let him grow and thrive and have a life. Let him be happy. Please." Praying when I've never prayed before. Praying that things will be all right for my son.

I look to the sky ahead and suddenly wish for a canvas. A flexible surface, responsive to the pressures of the brush. It's been weeks, months since I've painted. I have only paper with me now. Still, the urge is there, or was, fleetingly. A good sign. Hopeful.

I fumble with tapes and push in Symphony No. 3, *Eroica,* and still my thoughts as the music begins. The first movement does that to me: it says, *Listen.* It's the second movement that makes me believe Beethoven heard many voices crying in his head. Well, it's the funeral march, after all. But the entire symphony keeps breaking expectations. There is a grandness to its fragmentation, its emphasis, its yearning. As I turn up the volume and settle back to listen, the one long curve in the road—the only curve on this part of the prairie—makes me understand that I am on the extreme edge of a rim of orb called Earth.

THE FATHERS

Water spilt from a tray never returns to the tray.

CHAPTER 13

1942–43

The sixty shacks were completed during our first summer in the camp. In ours, the opening Father had made for the window in the bedroom wall was now covered by a blanket that Mother had nailed to the frame. The blanket helped to keep out the cold air at night, but Hiroshi and Keiko and I still sought one another's warmth, our legs and feet intertwined in sleep beneath the blankets that were heaped on our bed. Doors and panes of glass were taking a long time to arrive in the camp, and complaints to the Citizens' Committee had not yielded results.

The Citizens' Committee, comprising a dozen interned residents, was the main committee in camp, and its representatives did their best to solve problems and complaints that arose in the community. An RCMP office was across the river, and the Mounties in this office acted as a liaison between our camp and the town. Although we were supposed to be self-sufficient, we were all registered with the Mounties, and we had to rely on the town for supplies. It would be a couple of years before we would be permitted to cross the bridge and enter the place ourselves, so families had to shop by catalogue or by mail. For groceries, lists were made and sent over to the grocers in town every two weeks. Most of the time, people made do with what they had at hand.

Despite the hardships, much had been accomplished. The field that had held nothing but sagebrush when we'd first arrived now contained the lives and the comings and goings of more than two hundred people. With daylight hours being longer, the air was warmer, especially in the middle of the day, and more and more people were seen outside. The fire in our stove was allowed to go out after breakfast. Keiko and I were sent out to pick dandelions, and Mother prepared these with sugar, sesame seeds and *shoyu,* the soy sauce we had brought with us. But the supply of *shoyu* was running low and had to be watered down until more could be ordered.

Once the shacks were finished, a meeting was held to finalize plans for the schoolhouse, which would be located at one end of the field. It was to have a long, divided room for classes, as well as a community room. Every family in camp pledged to contribute to the building in some way, because everyone wanted the children's education to start again. The school year had not resumed after being interrupted the past winter, after our removal from the coast. For now, older girls in the camp who had recently completed high school and any young women who had studied at university were approached by a school committee to see if they would be interested in being teachers. Information about correspondence courses began to arrive from the Department of Education in Victoria, and some training was promised for would-be teachers the following summer, in New Denver. The carpenters had begun to make desks and benches for the school, and so far, the supplies consisted of a blackboard, a few pieces of chalk, scribblers with multiplication tables on the back and pencils without erasers.

Keiko longed to be back in the classroom again. She played school, and she acted at being "teacher" when she had any time left over from helping Mother or after doing her share of weeding in the garden plot. She hauled me in as her "pupil," and it became her mission to teach me to read and do elementary math. She also encouraged my drawings. Sometimes we made puppets and miniature puppet theatres together. For materials, we used whatever we could find in the woods and any remnants of cloth or paper or cardboard that had been discarded around camp. For glue we used grains of cooked rice, moistened with water, and we pressed these flat with our thumbs. Other children joined in, but Hiroshi refused to participate in Keiko's classes, held in the shade of softly scented pines up the slope behind the camp. There was a plateau there, partway up the mountain, a flat area that everyone had begun to refer to as the Bench. From that height, we could look directly down on the entrances to the outdoor toilets below, and watch people go in and out. It was said that ghosts hung around the wooded area behind the outhouses, and a girl in her teens who joined us one day told us she'd seen the ghost of one of the old people who had died of dysentery when we'd first arrived, a woman in her seventies. The ghost of the woman had no feet but it had been prowling in and around the trees, even with no feet.

"Bin can chase away ghosts," Keiko told the others. "It's part of his fate. Father said."

Sometimes I was persuaded by the older children to run down the hill, arms outstretched. They all laughed as I ran, but I did not laugh. I had not seen any ghosts. Still, I ran down the hill, shouting at the top of my lungs, pretending to chase the ghosts away.

The main problem in the camp was always the supply of clean water. Several of the men chipped in together, and after obtaining permission from the RCMP office across the river, they purchased an old truck. The mechanics in the camp kept the truck running, and it was used for everything from early cartage of water barrels to much later delivery of tomatoes that would eventually become the main source of income for the camp. Special permission was needed before leaving the camp area, but there was no place to go. Our movements were restricted, and the road blocks were still in place. We weren't allowed in the town. We could walk along the road to the end of the bridge on our side of the river, but we were not allowed to cross it. That was as far as we could go. There was nothing but canyon and river and mountain everywhere else.

The heat of summer, as we had been warned, was as extreme as the cold had been during the winter months. Some people were having difficulty moving about because the temperature soared higher than 110 degrees Fahrenheit. Despite this, no one could stay inside for long because of the work that had to be done in the gardens. Seeds and budding plants had to be watered in the dry, sandy soil. Most families had a long stick or broom handle with an empty can attached at one end, for the purpose of watering. Until a workable irrigation system was set up, full buckets of water had to be carried to the garden area. The stick-and-can device was dipped into the bucket and used to water the plants, one at a time, row by row. All the while, men and women, girls and boys could be seen climbing the hill from the river below, carrying full pails of water suspended from yokes they wore across their shoulders. Some families devised their own filtration systems, using layers of sand and homemade charcoal above their water barrels. In our home, we were still boiling water for drinking, and we collected rainwater at every opportunity.

One morning, the long-awaited shipment of doors and windows arrived by truck. The men in camp stopped work on the gardens and the schoolhouse, and immediately began to work on the shacks again. Within a short time, every shack had a door with a latch and real hinges, and windowpanes in the two front windows.

But Father had wanted the extra window for our home, and he had made the crooked opening in the bedroom wall at the back. Now he had to cut an extra pane of glass. He went outside to try to fit the glass to the frame, and lost his temper when the frame splintered and a thick chunk of wood fell to the ground. He let go of the glass and it, too, dropped and shattered.

I was outside, at the corner of the shack, sitting on the low stool I had dragged out from the kitchen. I had a piece of cardboard on my lap and I was drawing a picture with the stub end of a pencil. I was trying to draw a horse, but I was having difficulty. I had a picture of a horse on the ground in front of me, torn from an old calendar that Keiko had found. When the window glass hit the ground, I looked up and blinked.

"What are you staring at?" Father shouted. "Why are you sitting there making foolish pictures when you should be helping?"

I looked down unhappily at my picture, which did not in any way resemble the calendar horse. Especially the distorted hind end.

"Arse!" I shouted. And then, out of nowhere, came "Arsehole!"

Father picked up the chunk of wood that had splintered from the frame and threw it in my direction, hitting me squarely on the forehead, directly over my nose and between my eyes. I heard my own cry and became aware of something gushing down my face. I reeled back and put my hand to my forehead. I saw a red splash on the sandy ground and another against the tarpaper on the outer wall. Mother came running outside, and a sudden, abrupt shout hung in the air between my parents. I was helped into the house, and after that I remembered nothing except waking in my bed after dark.

It was Keiko, later in the evening and under the blankets, who whispered and told me what had happened next. Both she and Hiroshi were astonished that I had sworn at our father. I did not mention my bad drawing of the horse. Of course, the story grew and grew and we went over its details many times after that, but always out of earshot of our parents. What happened after I was laid on the bed became Keiko's story because she had been there when the pane of glass had fallen.

Father went to get another pane of glass from the camp supplies, and returned to the back window to try again. Mother was in the bedroom, looking after my wound. Keiko was sent to get clean water from the barrel outside the door. Hiroshi had missed the whole event because he was working in the garden, watering plants.

Ji, who had heard the commotion, came over from next door to help repair the broken frame and fit the glass. Through the hole in the wall, the two men could see directly into the bedroom while I was being cared for. Father was scowling while they moulded and packed putty in and around every crack, until the glass was finally fitted. Still, it was awkwardly set because of the way the opening had been made in the first place, and nothing was going to change that. But Father didn't care, and Ji did not comment on the crookedness. Nonetheless, Ji stood back and smiled at the patchwork and the finished product. He liked perfection. He'd had carpentry experience in his youth, and long ago, he had built shelves and a deep counter in the general store he and Ba had owned in Vancouver. He pulled out a rag, which most of the time hung from his back pocket, and he wiped remnants of linseed oil from his fingers. His tough old hands were creased with rivulets of cracked skin. He patted Father's shoulder as if Father needed encouragement. And then he soundly told him off because of the cruelty he had shown his younger son.

When Ji went back to his own shack, he sent Ba over to look at my injury. The bleeding had stopped, but she examined the wound, went home again and returned, carrying a small bowl of egg white, runny and raw. This was applied to the split in my forehead while I lay in bed, and then she covered the wound with a strip of clean cloth.

When Ba was finished, she patted the pocket of her dress and pulled out a letter and showed it to Mother and Keiko. It was from an internment camp in California. The name of the place sounded peculiar and magical on her tongue: *Manzanar, Manzanar*. Ba's daughter, Sachi, and her husband, Tom, had been moved to this camp, which Sachi wrote about. She said it was a large and lonely place, with barbed wire around the edges and guards with guns in towers to keep watch over the inmates inside. Thousands of Japanese Americans had been taken there from the coastal regions, and thousands more were to come. Sachi and Tom were sharing a small apartment in a barracks building with another young couple. The two couples were not entitled to more space because, as yet, they had no children. They ate their meals in a mess hall. The camp was surrounded by desert, and there were mountains in the distance.

Mother and Ba sat together in our kitchen and drank green tea and went over and over the letter, discussing every detail of the place that Sachi described as Manzanar. There were a few censored lines in the letter, but Ba now had an address to write to, and she was going to answer the letter this very day.

Ba returned to our place every day for a week to apply egg white to my forehead and to change my dressing. Each time she came, she made sure Father was there so that she could give him a tongue-lashing because he had injured his child. Father did not argue with an elder; he looked away and waited for her to finish. The rest of us had never heard Father spoken to in such a way, and

I was secretly glad to hear Ba scold him. I was happy to have the attention of Mother and Ba while they patted the dressing to my wound. But what I remembered most from that time was Father being punished for his bad temper.

For a week of sunny days, I sat outside on my stool with my head tipped back, egg white running down my forehead. In time, the wound healed and everyone, including me, continued to believe the story that I had called my father an arsehole. The scar, of course, remained.

Two weeks before the new school opened for classes, a Chinese grocer drove his truck across the bridge from town and arrived, unannounced, on our side of the river. The slanted boards on the side of the truck shook and rattled as he turned off the dirt road and entered the lumpy, muddy grounds. Because it had been raining early in the day, he had thrown a canvas overtop of the boards to make a temporary roof to keep his supplies dry. People came out of their shacks and crowded around. The man told us his name was Ying. That was his last name, but everyone called him Ying, he said. He lowered the back of his pickup and showed what he had for sale. He told us he had a new store at the end of town near the bridge, and he promised to drive to the camp every Monday so that people could put in their orders. On Wednesdays, he would return with the deliveries.

In the back of the truck and on display were ginger root and Chinese cabbage, yeast and green tea. He even had *shoyu*, our kind of soy sauce, along with rice and flour, sugar, buckets of lard, oatmeal, baking powder, sesame seeds, crackers and eggs. He had a few oranges, and he had nails, cast-iron skillets, brooms, pails and chicken wire. People began to buy, and the items in his truck were soon gone. When Ying drove away, the noise left behind sounded as if the muffler on his truck had fallen apart.

The following Monday, he returned, as promised. The women came outside and placed their orders. Ying put on small, round glasses and recorded every order in his notebook. There was an air of gaiety about the occasion.

"One pound *chimpo* sausage," a woman piped up from the crowd around the truck. "Don't forget to add *chimpo* sausage to my order when you come back. A big one, too."

The other women began to laugh.

"*Chimpo* sausage, Ying," they called out. "*Chimpo* sausage! Don't forget!"

Ying laughed, too, and Hiroshi and I looked at each other and grinned. We could tell from Ying's expression that he didn't know *chimpo* was a slang word for *penis*. I smiled to myself and backed away. After Ying left, Hiroshi said, "*Chimpo*. He doesn't even know what it means."

Every Monday, when Ying drove his truck to collect the orders, the women continued to make a joke of *chimpo* sausage. When Ying found out what it meant, he carried on with the joke. I guess he was enjoying it, too.

One afternoon, Ji came to our shack and began to build a wooden sink for our kitchen. He also built a shelf beside it to hold the small bucket of water that we kept just inside the door. Mother often helped Ba and Ji. She sent baked treats to their place; she helped Ba to hang her wash outside; sometimes she helped them in their garden plot. She knew that Ji was trying to help her in some way, too. He built the sink from cedar and made it with smooth and beautiful joints. Mother rubbed her hands over the surface and bowed slightly to Ji to thank him. She couldn't wait to try out the sink, and they each poured a glass of water through the drain, but not before setting a pail underneath to catch the same water again. They laughed as if they had shared a great joke, and then poured the captured water back into the bucket.

After the sink was in place, Ji became more ambitious, and suggested that he and Father build a bathhouse to be shared by our two families. The bathhouse, raised in an enclosed wooden shelter, became a separate structure between Ji's shack and ours, with short paths leading to it from both homes. The wood that lined the bath was as smooth and beautiful as the wood in the sink. The bath had a galvanized metal floor and a wooden platform across the bottom to keep us from being burned. Ji had designed it so that a wood fire could be kept going in a chamber beneath the tub.

Now that we had our own private bathhouse, we were able to have a real bath every night, an improvement over standing or sitting scrunched up in the galvanized tub. After Hiroshi and Keiko and I scrubbed with soap and rinsed and climbed in for a hot soak, it was our parents' turn. Even during the winter months, we soaked every night in our newly built tub.

Uncle Aki and Auntie Aya wanted a bathhouse, too, and Ji showed Uncle Aki how to build one. There were many such projects going on in the camp, along with logging and chopping and sawing wood for the coming winter. Like hauling water, wood gathering was a never-ending job, because no one could survive winter without a large supply.

But we had survived so far. We would never have running water; we would never have electricity or refrigeration. But produce from our garden fed us, and Mother pickled and preserved beans and cucumbers and tomatoes for the cold months. Our root cellar, dug out of the earth, was stuffed with carrots and cabbage and squash. Many families had begun to raise chickens, and the men caught fish in the Fraser and shared it out. Every two days, Mother and Keiko and Auntie Aya made bread together. Auntie Aya, who had stayed inside so much when we'd first arrived in the camp, was expecting a baby the following summer. Uncle Aki ordered wool from the Eaton's catalogue, and Auntie Aya began to knit and sew. She wanted a baby boy. She wanted their first child to be a son.

All the while, Father was reading about the war whenever he managed to get a newspaper in his hands. He was never in a good mood after reading about bombings and invasions and the sinking of ships. The more he read, the more he scowled and said that we would be in the camp for a long time. At the dinner table, he railed on about the war and snapped at us if we weren't paying attention. Mother did not comment. She did not argue with Father; nor did she stick up for us when he was in a bad mood.

Father and the other men talked when they were outside, and passed on news that came to camp. Everyone was interested in knowing what Japan was doing in the war, because whatever Japan was doing could also affect us; it was as if we were somehow to blame.

After another cold winter in the camp, everyone was anxious to have warm weather again, especially Hiroshi, who had one of the biggest jobs of all—carrying water up the hill. The large communal tanks were in place and that made the job a little easier, but the tanks were across the road and partway down the hill, towards the river. Every family needed its water barrels replenished daily, for household use. In our family, from the beginning, that had been Hiroshi's job.

The worst time for carrying water was during the winter, because the path down the side of the hill was slick with ice. Father had made attachments from rope to provide traction for Hiroshi's gumboots, and those fit at grip sites around his ankles and beneath the soles of his boots. Every day, he had to slip and slide down the hill and back up again. When the school year was in progress, he lugged water before and after classes. Father made him fetch water for Ba and Ji, too, because they were too old to do so themselves, especially during winter on the icy path. But when Father was out of earshot, Hiroshi swore. He swore with words I had never heard before. Nor did I know where he had learned them. All winter, he called the path to the water tanks "that goddamned icicle hill."

I knew I would be taking over the chore of the goddamned icicle hill when I was older, and I did not look forward to that day. Father kept telling me I had to work at strengthening my arms and back, and this worried me. I did not give much thought to the job Hiroshi would move on to when it would be my turn to take over icicle hill. Whatever the job would be, I knew Hiroshi would complain and swear even more.

When Father was not around, when I was alone or with my brother, I went to the lean-to where the wood was stored and practised placing the Jack-pine pole across my shoulders to test the amount of weight I could bear. There was a nail at each end of the pole and I tried to balance a bucket on each side, the way Hiroshi did.

"You can't do it!" he shouted at me. "You're too scrawny. Anyway, why bother trying? You have to grow bigger before you can do what I do."

I did not say what I thought. That he sounded full of anger, just like our father.

One morning in spring, I got up at the earliest light, while the camp was still quiet. I slipped out of bed and dressed and began to walk up the sloped path behind the shacks. Hiroshi and I sometimes came up here together, and sat on tree stumps and played *Rock-Paper-Scissors— Jan-Ken-Po*. Because I was alone now, I skirted the trees behind the outhouse buildings, where the ghosts gathered. A few people were outside their shacks, and some men were already up and working in the garden across the road. I continued up towards the Bench, and heard a sudden noise above me. Before I could react, I was startled by horses that burst past me at a gallop. I jumped to one side of the path and watched in excitement as the wild animals raced to the camp below. Maybe I had disturbed them; I didn't know. They galloped in and around the shacks, circled back, raced through again and disappeared up a trail that curved around the mountain at the far end of camp. There were shouts as people ran outside to watch. I counted the horses as they raced by. One, two, three . . . eleven in all, tangled manes flying.

I had not tried to draw a horse since the year before, when Father had thrown the chunk of wood at my forehead, but I decided I would try again, this time using a real horse as my model. Hiroshi and I began to stay outside as much as possible so we could keep a lookout for the horses, each of us for a different reason. Our vigilance was rewarded when the horses came back several days later, again without warning. I counted eleven, and this time they arrived in the early evening, nervous and alert. They slowed and pawed at the earth and snorted and nickered and began to graze on green shoots that were coming up along the edge of camp. When they had eaten enough, or for some other reason we could not discern from our safe distance, they took off abruptly and all together, and galloped away.

Hiroshi began to boast. He had seen several Native children around, higher up in the hills, and one of the older Native boys had been riding bareback on a wild horse, using only a homemade bit and reins made from rope. If someone else could do this, so could he, Hiroshi said. He wasn't certain how the boy had tamed the horse. Nor was he certain that he would be able to ride without a saddle, but he was going to give it a try.

I, too, wanted to ride, maybe one of the smaller horses—a colt, perhaps—but most of all I wanted to draw one of these beautiful animals. I had a pencil with an eraser, and I tried many times to capture the likeness, always starting with a suggestion of mane and the long, sloping lines of the neck and head. Every time I tried, I ended up erasing more lines than those that remained, and my drawing became a mass of smudges. I wanted to create an animal mid-gallop, nostrils flared, head stretched forward, eyes looking directly out of the picture—the way the horses sometimes looked at me as their bodies hurtled past.

I tried to draw on cardboard, and I drew on small fragments and chips from the ends of lumber that were strewn around the edges of the camp. Sometimes, I drew with a stick, scratching lines in the dirt. When I did have a piece of paper, it was usually brown and bloodstained, old wrappings that had come from Ying's store with coiled-up *chimpo* sausage inside. I was careful not to press too firmly, in case I had to erase and start over again. I tried not to make holes in the paper. I drew over the top of old newsprint that had been used for packing, and I filled the narrow borders of catalogue pages. I edged closer to the horses and composed a foreleg bent and off the ground, almost meeting mid-air with the hind leg when the horse was running. I tried to draw a horse that was at a standstill, peering around its long, flat forehead to look sideways at me with a large dark eye. I drew a horse straight on, with its front legs looking like knobbly stilts. I drew a mane that parted over the ears and swung over the highest part of the horse's face, above its eyes. I tried to capture the dip in the horse's back and its scraggly tail. I drew legs that were half dark and half white.

I spent much of the spring and summer trying to draw those wild horses. And I found that I had to study the animals again and again to observe the angle of their legs and if they moved in the same way all together, or if the front joints were different from those at the back when the horses were in motion.

Hiroshi had found a long, rusted railway spike in the dirt on the garden side of the road, and he scrounged for a length of old rope and then tied the rope to one end of the spike. He told me that if he could figure out how to get the rope attached to the other end, the sharp end, and if he could make the two stay together without the rope slipping off, he would get his homemade bit into a horse's mouth. He kept an extra length of rope handy for a rein. He had already chosen the animal he wanted to ride: the tallest, one that had a reddish coat and mane. He did not want Father to know about this, so he hid the spike and rope under his pillow and slept on top of them every night. Sometimes he forgot them in our bed in the morning, so I brought them outside and told him I would tuck them behind the woodpile. When the horses came, Hiroshi ran to the woodpile to get the spike and rope. But when he tried to edge close to the herd, the horses skittered off, left and right. Eventually, after several weeks, he grew tired of this and gave up. But I did not stop trying to draw them.

One night, I was awakened by a noise that sounded like an explosion, a huge snorting sound. It was a warm night, and because of the heat, Mother had left the door open with only a thin blanket hanging from the frame, hoping that a bit of breeze would come in around the edges. I was lying on the mattress beside my brother and sister, and I heard the snorting sound again, but I could not understand why the others weren't awake. How could they sleep through such noise? Because I was at the edge, I slid silently out the end of the bed and went to the kitchen. There, in the open doorway, was a horse's head, a huge dark head tangled in the blanket, tossing back and forth. The front of the horse's body was almost inside our kitchen. I stood where I was, unable to move.

In an instant, Mother was beside me, pulling me out of the way. She crossed the narrow kitchen and waved her arms, and this startled the horse so that it backed out of the doorway and galloped off, its hooves slamming the earth as it ran.

I knew, even in the dark, that Mother was shaking. She did not light the lantern. She composed herself, and rearranged the blanket in place over the doorway while the others, even Father, slept on.

"Shhh!" she said. "We won't wake anyone. Go back to bed now and don't make a noise." But before I returned to the bedroom, she pulled me close to her and held me tightly, as if she might lose me if she let go.

In the morning, I wondered if I had dreamed the horse in the doorway. But I saw from Mother's face that what had happened in the night was not a dream. The horse was real, its sudden, frightening presence a secret between us.

CHAPTER 14

1997

I reduce speed as I enter a small Saskatchewan village, more of a crossroads than a village, really. A few buildings, including a squared brick tower with four walls bulging, as if the tower has been fattened up from inside. And then, as the speed limit changes again, a church with a signboard displaying a message in large white letters against a black background: WE'VE BEEN IN THE FOR-GIVENESS BUSINESS FOR ALMOST 2000 YEARS.

I drive past a farm where two mares stand behind a fence, one with head drooped at a telltale slant, a rich, dark mane sliding forward. It has been a long time since I thought of the wild horses in the camp; a long time since I've drawn them. They were so much a part of life there. In the background, circling, galloping through camp, all that energy and beauty. A long time, too, since I thought of my father chucking a piece of wood at me. Instinctively, I raise my hand to my forehead and feel the indent. There isn't much to see, but I can still detect a slight depression.

In the seventies, in the early years of our marriage, Lena ran her index finger lightly down my forehead, tracing the scar. "How did you manage that?" she said. "I've asked before, and you've never really explained. It's so vertical. The perfect scar. Vestigial. Like a genetic marking."

"I was learning the rudiments of hand-eye coordination," I said. "Trying to draw the back end of a horse. It's a long story. Somehow connected to a place called Manzanar."

We were side by side, sinking into the middle of a couch that had a deep sag. Closer than we would have been had we chosen the hard chairs that Lena was now eyeing, and that had been taken by others. It was an uncomfortable position, but I liked our bodies touching through our clothes: side, arms, thighs. It was our private circle of closeness, the one that was comforting and familiar. It was a warm fall night and we were in the basement of a house belonging to a couple we did not know well, but who lived at the end of the street. We had accepted the invitation to a barbecue because we were trying to be neighbourly. Lena and I were still new to the city, having spent the first five years of our marriage in Montreal. Lena was beginning to meet her colleagues at work, and I was alone in my studio much of the time, painting. Except for exchanging quick greetings with some of the neighbours, we had so far met only Miss Carrie on our street. And now we were at a barbecue, and the party had been rained on, a sudden storm.

Our hosts, Pete and his wife, Petra, ushered everyone inside and down the chewed-up basement steps to the rec room below. Pete stayed outside on the patio and dragged the barbecue under an overhang so that he could tend the charcoal. He was turning kebabs on long metal skewers, and every five minutes or so he appeared at the top of the basement stairs and shouted words of encouragement to the rest of us.

The other men in the room were big and heavy-set. A room of giants, taller than I. Six two and more, to my five nine. I'd have looked undernourished in a lineup beside them. Pete was an accountant; the other three men worked for him, in the same small company. They all bantered back and forth as if they knew one another well, as did their wives.

Despite the familiarity among them, Petra seemed unsure of how to keep the conversation going. The place smelled like basement, damp and mildewed; there was no pretending. There was a bar across one end of the room and a pea-green shag rug on top of the cement floor. We were all hungry and the men were showing signs of being tired of waiting for their food. Pete was taking a long time to cook the beef over charcoal.

One of the men, Ron, stood up across the room and came over and squeezed himself down into the edge of the couch next to Lena, which meant that our positions were suddenly altered. I was now higher than the other two, and it was Ron's arm and thigh that were pressed into Lena's—on her other side.

"I came over to talk to you," Ron said, ignoring me, "since we're neighbours now, more or less. I work at the sweatshop with those characters." He gestured to the other men. He wore dark-rimmed glasses, and the lenses were so flecked with white specks or with food crumbs, I couldn't understand how he could see. *He probably can't,* I thought, unkindly. *He probably uses his filthy glasses as an excuse to make blundering moves on other men's wives.* I disliked him instantly.

No one seemed to know how to talk to me; they behaved as if I were an exotic whom they couldn't be expected to understand. It seemed a surprise to them that I spoke English. They were careful and polite, and spoke loudly when they addressed me, as if I were partially deaf. And then, a series of strange confessions began. Ron's wife offered up the information that her mother used to eat Chinese food once in a while. She ordered it from a takeout, she said. I took this to be some sort of nod in my direction and did not dare to look sideways at Lena.

One of the other wives, after a pause, said that she liked fortune cookies the best. As no one else had any further Oriental offerings, she added that she ate three rosehips every day before breakfast, rain or shine. While thunder crashed and boomed overhead, Petra gave up the information that she was a Roman Catholic, and that during her childhood, her mother had kept inkwells filled with water blessed by their local priest. This holy water was sprayed around the house during electrical storms to prevent lightning strikes and fire. Between storms, Petra's mother sent her back to church with the inkwells so they could be replenished and blessed again. There had been a "coloured" family in the congregation, she added, and they were very nice people.

At this point, a thin yellow dog appeared, and yipped down the steps. Petra, talking rapidly and with a nervous laugh, told us the dog had taken to chewing the basement stairs, and had already chewed part of the first and second steps. Lena and I exchanged looks without being caught. Petra went up to the kitchen and came back down with a small, clear bowl of salted pretzels. She passed the bowl around and the other men dug deep. The pretzels were gone in an instant, and Petra set the empty bowl on the bar without offering to fill it again. Everyone in the room was sipping at a half glass of wine. Ron pulled his weight up off the couch and clomped up the stairs and returned with a bottle of Scotch. I had noticed the bottle earlier, in a kitchen cabinet behind glass doors, when I'd first come in. Ron poured a stiff drink for himself and offered it around. Petra looked positively frightened by this raiding of the house liquor supply, and then relieved when she heard a shout from Pete, above, saying that he was ready, that she should bring on the plates.

She went upstairs and Lena followed, offering to help, and five minutes later the two women reappeared, carrying dinner.

Pete, the other three men and I had been apportioned three cubes of beef, one medium potato and four green beans. On the women's plates were two cubes of beef, half a potato and three beans. I tried to imagine the conversation between Pete and Petra while they were doing the calculations, but I couldn't come up with the words. Ron barrelled down the steps with a new bottle of wine and served it out among the men.

We all bent over our laps, and the plates were emptied in moments. Except for Pete, the other men stood in unison and began a silent, undeclared hunt for food. I followed. Up and down the steps, into the kitchen and back again. The word *hunger* was not mentioned. Nor were the words *second helpings*. Ron went over to the bar, licked his index finger and wiped it across the bottom of the empty pretzel bowl, gathering the last grains of salt. Another man and I went outside to the patio to tackle scrapings on the barbecue rack. No one had thought to ration or hide the remaining liquor, and all of us, finding no more food, settled down to drink. There was still wine—each couple had arrived with a bottle—and an almost full bottle of Scotch.

And then, as if on cue, a chain of events familiar to everyone but Lena and me began to unfold.

Petra announced, "Button-button time," and the men tromped up the stairs and called out to me to join them while the women chose a hiding place for a large black button. The only rule, according to Petra, was that the button must stay in the basement.

Back we came. I looked at Lena, who was still on the sagging couch, and I reached down and squeezed her hand. If the game was meant to be fun, no one was laughing. The men were milling about, searching for the button. Ron was on hands and knees, his thick palm groping beneath an armchair. I stood like a statue. Others were crawling across the floor while Petra and another woman called out, "Warm! No. Cold. You're freezing. Ice!" And then, in sing-song voices, "Someone in the room is boiling. You're hot!"

Lena, expecting equal humiliation for the women's round, sat stiffly while giant men peered into shadows like caged animals trying to escape. Fingers grazed upper ledges and shelves. Lena and I both understood that this was a continuation of the search for food. We watched helplessly.

And then, I decided to rescue us. I announced that we had to check in on Miss Carrie before it was too late in the evening. She had asked us to drop by, and we'd promised to do so on our way home.

"Miss Carrie," Petra murmured. "We never see anything of her. She's the old woman who lives at the opposite end of the street, isn't she? A bit dotty, I think."

Lena and I turned away, not daring to speak. The yellow dog yipped as we blew our goodbyes back to Petra and Pete, who saw us off at the side door. Lena tucked her arm in mine until we reached Miss Carrie's house. The lights were off. Miss Carrie had not, of course, asked us to check on her at all.

"I feel like waking her up and telling her about the party," Lena said. I could tell that she was upset. "Is that why we love her—because she doesn't judge us?"

"She's been around for a long time, since the beginning of the century," I said. "She was born shortly after Queen Victoria died. She's wiser than most people; she measures things differently."

We continued on, to our own front door. The storm was over. Lena tilted her head back and took in a long, slow breath of damp air. "Curtains of blue, curtains of black," she said. "Just look up there."

I followed her gaze upwards. No stars were visible, but there was an eerie beauty to the chill and the darkness.

"It's too much," she said. "How long will it take before people will be used to having someone different in their midst? And *how* different? The same under the skin."

"I'm used to it," I said. But we knew that already.

"Ottawa is a small city," Lena pronounced. "A *white* city, mostly."

That was true, too. But we'd also seen graffiti scribbled across a subway wall during a recent visit to Toronto, which was *not* an entirely white city. DEATH TO MIXED RACES we read as our subway car rolled past. Random hate, it seemed, could be anywhere.

And in Montreal, hadn't we kept our own marriage ceremony small, only five people present? The two of us, the minister, and Lena's sister and husband as witnesses. Our world wasn't ready for mixed marriages, but that hadn't stopped us. And Lena had been protecting wounds of her own. Her sister, whom she loved, had drawn her aside just before the ceremony. "What about children?" her sister asked. "Have you given enough thought to that?"

As if any future child born to us would belong to a stigmatized breed. The question, Lena told me later, had come from love and she understood that, but the underlying message had been: *You still have the chance to change your mind.* Lena had fought her sister off on her own terms.

We walked around to the back entrance of the house so that we could prolong our time in the night air. We unlocked the door, headed for the kitchen, opened the fridge door and closed it again. We were past hunger, wobbly from drink. Lena began to laugh as we climbed the stairs. Once started, she couldn't stop.

"You looked like hunters and gatherers on the prowl," she said. "If you could have seen yourselves. All the big men trying to fill their bellies. And button-button was the last straw." She was doubled over now, and I joined in. "The poor yellow dog," she said. "No wonder it's eating the basement steps. It's starving."

We went to bed and turned out the lights. Once more, Lena ran her finger over the scar on my forehead. And then, so lightly I scarcely knew her hand was there, she traced every feature of my face, ending with my lips.

"You're going to have to tell me how the scar got there," she said, through a yawn. "I need to know." And she fell asleep.

I was thinking about Ron squeezing himself onto the couch next to her, and I reclaimed her now and pulled her towards me. She was still asleep, but she turned to her side and slid her thigh over mine. And then she woke again.

The next day, Miss Carrie announced that she had decided to fly to Winnipeg to visit her antiquarian friend Lill, who was recovering from surgery. A few days later, Lena and I drove her to the airport, helped with the tan-coloured leather luggage that had belonged to her Mommy in another century, and promised to pick her up on her return. She intended to stay four weeks, because she wanted to be useful. Letters began to arrive soon after her departure, and we were entertained with a letter a week, for the next month.

Thank you for seeing me off, even though I had to travel without the items that refused to turn up, including extra spectacles and favourite garters. Lill has recovered from her operation, but yesterday she tripped and twisted her foot. She sprained her ankle and must walk with a stick. She insists on bending forward to pick up the many things she drops, even with her foot newly swollen.

An old aunt, age one hundred and two, lives in a room beyond the dining room, where I am not to go. An attendant comes and goes, unseen, through a side door. The aunt eats behind a heavy curtain; perhaps she splashes or has spills. Lill and I sit at an extended dining table, which I crawled under and latched from beneath because of its precarious state of balance. Lill pretends that every part of this is normal. The aunt belongs to the family of Lill's late husband, Beau. I'm told she has thin hair, wears a "piece"—not her own. Since my arrival, she has been grinding her teeth behind the curtain. Lill says Beau's side of the family all had good teeth in their day. I deduce that the strain of my visit is the cause of the grinding.

The second letter arrived soon afterwards:

The Reverend from Lill's church announced that he was coming to visit, and I pondered what to wear. Fortunate that I climbed to Mommy's cedar closet in the attic before departure and dropped a 1936 dress into the hellhole, where my open luggage awaited. It's a good dress, hand-sewn, turquoise and gloriously fashionable again, with large sleeves. I wore it with great success. The Reverend made it clear that he'd be staying awhile, so Lill brought out her game of Scrabble. I had never played, though the game has been around for years. The three of us sat at a small table in the living room. Lill can't see enough to play well but I did not bring this to her attention. The Reverend spelled O-V-A-R-Y. I could scarcely believe my eyes. Nothing was said. Lill peered at the tiles but did not seem to notice ovary. We carried on.

After the Reverend left, we talked about friends who have died during the past year. Then we talked about a talent party I once hosted when we were young. Everyone who attended was required to perform. A trifle party, too, in the same year. I chose a handsome young man to serve the wine. He arranged green and red cherries across the trifle, moments before it was served. The world was young and gay then. Now Lill and I are the only two left. The handsome young man disappeared into the next war. Most of the other young men we knew died in the first.

At night I lie in bed in the guest room with my eyes wide and think of the people I've known, dead and alive. My head fills with ghosts. The furnace clicks on and off as if it were January. I can feel gusts of air in the room around me. Lill keeps the house far too warm. Occasionally, the old aunt snorts, down below.

And the third:

The church we attended—Anglican—was hung in scarlet, for St. Simon and St. Jude. I took Lill's arm to prevent her from falling up the steps. The Reverend recited the longest prayer he could concoct and Lill nodded off. She said she enjoyed the outing nonetheless.

On Mondays, Thursdays and Saturdays, a young maid arrives to clean and prepare dinner. When she is not here, we fend for ourselves. I sew and read the newspapers aloud to Lill. At the moment, I am relining a nice old dressing gown she found in a back closet—1920s or earlier.

Every morning I prepare breakfast, my chore and my pleasure. Lill manages tea. I made cookies one day when the coast was clear. And ironed scarves. I am Busy, capital B. Blind and partially blind people require attention, though Lill will not admit to either condition. Who are we if we aren't here to help one another in life? And, I suppose, in death.

Weather is holding and I am due to depart in ten days. I shall be flattened by the time I am home and will not be lunatic enough to travel again. One trip every quarter century is enough.

Lill has employed a boy to cut the grass for the last time before winter. I see him from the window, making careful rows. The aunt grinds on behind the curtain. When we enter the dining room, Lill calls out, throwing words ahead of her so as not to startle.

Now I stop. Said grass cutter will mail this as he departs.

P.S. There is art on the walls here. Good art that Bin would want to see.

The final letter of the trip arrived the same day Miss Carrie returned home. We met her at the airport.

Lill invited a friend to tea, a retired officer of some regiment or other, old and ill and sorry for himself. I had already met him, when he was a dozen years younger. He was better company then as retired officer than he is now in the role of dying man. He was once attractive and interesting; now he is bent on dying.

Fortunately, Lill's young niece had also been invited, and this provided diversion for everyone. She brought her young man, to whom she is engaged. He was on display, but he was awkward and has not yet learned to be charming. He has a mother, like everyone else, but has not been instructed. He wore a three-piece suit, has a beard—urban, not prospector. He did not look like a provider. SHE carried the tray into the dining room, but he plunked down on the first chair he could see. The dying officer looked on, amused at last. I wrote a note to the niece this morning: "A young man is at a definite disadvantage if he is seated when a lady enters a room for her tea." I sent it off by the afternoon post.

"This is how I want to get old," said Lena. "With spirit like Miss Carrie's. Connected. Engaged. With people of every age. Even the ones who are dead."

We loved receiving Miss Carrie's letters, and she had more stories to tell on her return.

And Lena and I had something of our own to tell: Lena was pregnant, due the following summer, 1976. Our first and only child, conceived the night of the barbecue. Our beautiful son, our beloved little worrier, Greg. Born old, in a daze of humidity and heat.

CHAPTER 15

1944

Auntie Aya's baby was born in the early summer. It was a boy, and she and Uncle Aki named him Taro. He was delivered a few weeks before his due date, and he had black hair, a squarish sort of birthmark on his neck and dark eyes like Auntie Aya's, eyes that stared up into mine when I went over to meet him. He was small, and his toes and fingertips were cold and dusky blue, but Uncle Aki held him up proudly in the doorway so he could be seen by callers who stood outside to congratulate the parents.

Ba was the one who assisted with deliveries because, for many years, she had helped the midwife in the Vancouver area where she'd lived during the time she and Ji had owned their store. She was the only one in camp with that kind of experience, and as there was no doctor among us, she was kept busy the three and a half years she was in that place. She called for my mother to help with Auntie Aya's delivery, and when Mother came home that night we heard her whispering to Father, behind the dividing sheet in the bedroom. Ba was worried, Mother said, when the afterbirth came, because she knew there would be difficulty ahead.

The birth was cause for celebration because Taro was a first son. Our father opened the small red book and read aloud the fate of a baby born in the year of the monkey. After I saw Taro, I drew a picture of a horse as a gift, and Uncle Aki tacked the picture to the wall in their bedroom and told me he would give it to the baby when he grew older. It was somewhat of a stick figure, but I was pleased with the drawing nonetheless, because the slope of the neck was better than my earlier attempts.

But Ba's prediction bore out, and Auntie Aya began to bleed heavily within twenty-four hours of the delivery. She had to stay in her bed and did not seem to be getting better. Some said it was because of the extreme cold she had endured during the early months of the past winter. Others said she had breathed the terrible choking fumes from lime that had been dumped into the holes of the outhouses during the first hot spell. That was the problem, they said. It was not a good thing for a woman expecting a child to breathe such fumes. All of this we children overheard, even though the conversations were whispered.

Auntie Aya became more and more ill. The bleeding turned to haemorrhage. Mother came home one afternoon after helping Ba, and she sat on a chair and looked at the floor and we could see that she was crying. She told us that our aunt was weak and had lost a lot of blood. She had been lying on her back in bed and had told Uncle Aki that she was slipping away; she could feel herself leaving.

Uncle Aki began to run frantically from shack to shack, but everyone knew that there was nothing more to be done. Father decided to send one of the teachers with a message across the bridge, to let the doctor in town know that a woman on the east side of the river was dying. After many hours, someone drove up in a small, dusty truck that had a running board. The driver was not the local doctor but a veterinarian. He went into Auntie Aya's home and spoke with her and gave her an injection, and that gradually stopped the bleeding. She was weak for a long time because she had lost so much blood, but eventually she recovered.

Little Taro, however, was not so fortunate. He died not long after Auntie Aya's bleeding stopped. He had looked so perfect when he was born, but because of the condition of the afterbirth, he did not have a chance. That is what Ba told everyone. All those months he had survived inside Auntie Aya's womb, but when he was born he lived only seven days.

When Baby Taro died, he was dressed and wrapped in a blanket and carried to the cremation site that had been established in a small clearing surrounded by woods on the side of the mountain. The sun was sparkling; the trees around the edges of the clearing were dappled with light. I looked up and saw the wild horses grazing on the plateau above us. Auntie Aya was too weak to stand, and a chair was brought for her so that she could sit during the service. Uncle Aki stood behind her, and they wept openly.

After the cremation, after the smouldering ashes had cooled somewhat, after the mourners had returned to their shacks, Hiroshi and Keiko and I were taken back to the site by Father and Uncle Aki. Each of us was given a pair of special chopsticks, and we were told that we had to sift through the ashes to pick up any tiny bones that remained. We had to be especially vigilant for a fragment that might resemble a teardrop shape. As cousins of Baby Taro, that was our duty. Keiko was handed an empty baking powder tin, and with the chopsticks, we were to drop the pieces of bone into the tin.

I was worried that my chopsticks would slip and I would get into trouble, but Father and Uncle Aki crouched down and said that this was important and we must not let a single piece of bone fall back to earth. For our baby cousin's journey, we must not.

Although I was very much afraid, I helped Hiroshi and Keiko pick out every tiny fragment we could find in the cooling ashes. Father and Uncle Aki stood by to ensure that nothing was dropped. The fragments in the baking powder tin were carried by Uncle Aki back to his home, where Auntie Aya awaited.

Auntie Aya was to keep the fragments of Taro's bones for many years, until long after the war was over and there could be a proper grave in a real cemetery. But more and more, Auntie Aya was seen sitting outside on a low stool in front of her shack, even in the fall, when the days became cold and we were in school. She spoke less as people came by to see her. Uncle Aki often came to our place to visit, and I overheard him tell my parents how worried he was. At night, when my parents were in bed and thought I was sleeping, I heard Mother say that Ba had told Auntie Aya she must never become pregnant again. She was not strong enough to carry another baby inside her. Father did not comment; I never heard a reply from him when Mother was telling him what went on in Uncle Aki and Auntie Aya's house. He listened in silence and he did not say what he was feeling.

Some days, Auntie Aya got up off her stool and stood in her doorway and called out to anyone who would listen. She called out that she could hear Baby Taro's bones knocking against the inside of the baking powder tin. The bones were knocking against the sides, she said, because they wanted to be free.

Shortly after Baby Taro died, an old man came to live in our camp. Not old like Ba and Ji, but older than our parents. He had been hiding in Vancouver and caring for his sick wife ever since December 1941, when Pearl Harbor was bombed. After his wife died, the man wandered out onto the street and was picked up by police. No one knew how he had escaped detection for so long. The adults said that he must never have gone outside, that he must not have left the rooms he was renting in Japtown. They said he must have had help from Caucasians, his *hakujin* friends, to get food and supplies. They said that after his wife died, he didn't care anymore about being seen. He went outside and was immediately detained and then sent to our camp above the Fraser. Ba and Ji told Mother and Father that he was known to the Vancouver community, and that he was an educated man who had once played the piano and knew a great deal about music. Everyone had assumed that he had been sent to a road camp somewhere in northern British Columbia and had been put to work building roads.

The old man's shack, at the end of our row, was built with the help of Father and some of the other men. They worked quickly because they had to return to work in the gardens. The communal gardens had become large and productive, and everyone helped so that money would keep coming in from the sale of tomatoes, which were shipped to Vancouver by train.

The old man's home was slightly smaller than everyone else's because most of the ready building materials had already been used. With his arrival, the camp now had sixty-one shacks and a population of two hundred and seven.

Every day and evening, Hiroshi and Keiko and I saw the man outside his shack, chopping wood for kindling. When he was not chopping wood, he was tending a garden plot that he had started late. In the evenings, he went for long walks alone up to the Bench and around the hills behind the camp. Sometimes I saw Father speaking to him at the end of our row, and they had long conversations.

It was rumoured that of the many boxes that had accompanied the man when he arrived, several held books. These were unpacked and lined up on rough shelves in his shack. Some of the books contained pages of musical notes. Why, the neighbours wondered aloud, would anyone use an allotment of space for books? He could have brought bedding, or tools, or an extra bag of rice.

The old man's name was Okuma-san, and not long after he arrived, he killed a bear. No one knew how he had done this, because no man in camp was allowed to have a gun. Father told us that Okuma-san's name meant Great Bear, and that it was fitting he had killed such an animal.

Hiroshi and Keiko and I spoke about this among ourselves.

"He probably set a snare," Hiroshi said, insisting that the old man must have read about snares in one of his books.

We all wondered if this was so, and if it was possible to learn how to catch a bear by reading a book. When Hiroshi asked Father about this, he said, "It is surprising, it is true, but Okuma-san is a wise person and he must have studied the habits of the bear. He knows that bear follows the same trails, over and over. He knows what bear likes to eat and where he takes his rest."

The bear was hung with a rope around its neck in a rough and open woodshed that Okuma-san had erected behind his shack. Everyone came to see, knowing that after the carcass had hung for a few days, the meat would be shared out among the neighbours. With high summer temperatures and no refrigeration, fresh meat had to be eaten quickly before it decayed.

The day after the news of the bear went through the camp, I walked by myself to the end of the row and stared up into the cavity of the bear. Its belly was slit all the way to its groin, its organs removed, and I could see the thick lining of beige and milky-coloured fat that showed how the animal had begun to prepare for its long winter sleep. The bear's eyes were open and its pink tongue lolled out the side of its jaw. The old man came out of his shack and asked my name, and I replied, giving my last name first. "Oda," I said. "My first name is Bin. It's short for Binosuke."

Okuma-san nodded and repeated my name, and I was surprised to hear the softness in his voice. He told me that he had met my father, and that they'd had long talks. That was all he said, that and my name, and then the two of us stood in silence before the open woodshed, and despite the foul odour coming from the bear, we admired its beauty. I wanted to look through the window of Okuma-san's shack so I could see the books that were rumoured to have pages of notes, but I was shy and I turned and went home without asking.

The next day, before nightfall, I returned to look at the bear. This time, I hid in shadow of the trees so I wouldn't be seen. To my surprise, the bear's hide had been removed and its body flipped end to end. Now it was hanging by its hind legs, which had a stick between them to keep them apart. In the dim light and from where I stood, the carcass had taken the shape of a human without a head. Only a bit of fur remained around its paws. I was so shocked by the sight, I couldn't keep myself from shouting out. I stumbled and fell in the dirt, and picked myself up and raced for home.

For the rest of the summer, I dreamed of the headless bear that had once ambled alive and free over the Bench up on the side of the mountain. The dark mountain that cast its shadow, and that stretched up and up above the camp and the turbulent river.

CHAPTER 16

1997

"Does the river have voices, Dad?"

Greg.

A fisherman in hip waders was standing in the middle of the river, casting for trout. The kind of sports fishing First Father had never done—probably never had a chance to do. I watched as the flyline snapped forward, back, forward, back again, curving in on itself and out again, lighting, finally, on the surface of a small dark pool downstream. Amazing grace. Motion efficient, appearing effortless. Line at a standstill mid-air, yet moving again, again. Grace. Amazing.

"Voices?"

"You know. Like it might be trying to tell you something."

I was trying to still the motion, the snaking of the tip through space, and yet create the illusion that the line, the movement, was about to thrust itself off the edge of the paper into—what? Imagination? Extension of imagined space?

It was the early eighties, I recall, and we were in Prince Edward Island beside the Dunk, a river so narrow we could toss a stone from

one bank to the other. There was a muffled dampness to the surrounds, the result of strong rains the night before. Branches along
the banks drooped over one another like crossed swords. We had
walked the trail for a mile or so, no problem for seven-year-old Greg,
who loved being outside in his rubber boots, loved to examine life
along the trail—underbrush, wildflowers, plants and weeds. He was
listening, that day, to the river.

"I do hear the river," I said. "I listen because it has a story to tell.
Sometimes many stories. What does it tell you?"

"Well," he said, seriously, "I hear it say my name when it's rushing by. It sounds like *gregogregogrego.*" He looked down sheepishly,
then smiled, more to himself than to me. "I can hear the sea, too. I
sure heard it in that big storm last night." He added this bravely, and
raised his chin to look up so he could check my reaction.

The storm last night. It was the end of August and we'd rented a
cottage—our first family visit to that province. But something about
the sea and the excitement of being there stayed with Greg from that
time and never left. No surprise that he's a science student now, and
that his graduate work will be in marine studies.

The cottage we'd rented on the north shore of the island was
actually a mobile home—a large trailer, though we called it a cottage. It was about thirty feet back from the edge of a cliff, set at the
bottom of a long, narrow field owned by a bachelor farmer named
Albert. We were in the wide part of the Gulf of St. Lawrence, the
part that is expansive and so almost sea, it *is* sea. The storm the night
before had been fierce, and we had been witness to the gathering
of forces the entire day. Breezes changed to winds, winds to almost
gale, low-lapping waves to fierce whitecaps rolling over the surface
of the water. I ran outside to the car to get a map, and the car door
snapped back against my legs after I'd pushed it open. The sea was

flowing rapidly into dips between dunes below the cliff, as if there were empty vessels to fill all along the beach. By nightfall, the trailer was shaking so badly I wondered if we were experiencing the tail end of a hurricane that had swept up the Atlantic coast from Florida and Georgia and the Carolinas, and was now blowing out to sea. There was no radio in the place, no phone, no warning system. We were a mile from Albert's farmhouse and the nearest human.

While being tucked in at bedtime, Greg looked up, white-faced but with small, perfectly round patches of red on his cheeks, the tell-tale sign of excitement—and worry.

"Are mobile homes stable enough to withstand hurricanes?" he asked. His voice was thin and earnest, but trusting, always trusting.

Lena and I came out of his room together. She whispered, "He *will* think up every adverse condition. He has no idea he's unearthing my deepest fears. This damned wind sounds as if it will lift us right off the cliff and into the waves. I don't like it one bit."

Greg called us back to his room. "I don't like the way the cottage shakes when you both walk down the hall at the same time," he said. "It frightens me."

We bundled him up and brought him out to sit with us in the narrow living room, and looked outside—though all we could see was blackness—and told stories while the arms of the wind battered at the long sides of the trailer, which felt so fragile from within, the place might as well have been made of tin. Lena brought out a lamp from our bedroom and tried to find a place to plug it in, but the power went out and we had to light candles. We told stories about bravado and trickery and good humour. By the time the worst part of the storm had passed, Greg was asleep. Shadows flickered behind me as I carried him down the hall to his room and tucked him in for the second time. And heaped blankets overtop so he wouldn't be cold in the night.

In the morning, we woke to a strong breeze, this time from the northwest. Puffs of clouds, plump and grey, hung from a line above the horizon. A far-off haze made the sky look as if a triangular chunk had been removed. The rain stopped, and from the window, we could see surf crashing in sideways. Humps of sand-covered seaweed shaped the outline of the beach for miles. I suggested that we give the sea a chance to calm down, that we drive inland, away from the wind and in shelter of the woods, a trail walk along the river. Lena said she would stay at the cottage because she wanted to read for a while. Later, she would prepare a picnic supper to take to the beach in the evening, if the wind had died down by then. Easy foods that we could carry over the dunes. Island corn, sandwiches, marshmallows to roast. We made a plan to collect driftwood high up on the sand later in the afternoon so that we could make a night bonfire at the base of the cliffs. If the wood was too wet, we'd use the supply of dry wood that Albert had left under a shelter. The weather turned quickly on the island, and we hoped for a calm sea by nightfall.

I had been working with watercolours, trying something new, wanting to capture sea, sky, shore; tough marram grasses that bound the sand; the shadow of a hawk that hunted in the afternoons along the edge of the field; a mix of quick and dramatic changes. The light around me altered every time I looked up. I had already begun to move away from my early work, and now every stroke I made was stretching towards some new form. Here, it was stretching against the threatening bulge of dark sea. "Sombre," Lena said when she came up behind me one morning. "Moody, moody." I wondered what she saw, but I didn't ask. She was right, though. A sombre tone was creeping in from underneath. The only other comment she made was after we had returned home. "There's been a change," she said. "Almost as if the sea left its mark on you. The shapes seem to disappear into the painting itself, and yet some part of them is still there—if you know what I mean."

I did. I understood what she was telling me, and it *was* because of the sea.

Greg and I returned to the cottage that day, after our inland river walk, and we stood on the cliff looking out over a long stretch of surf that was now somewhat diminished because the winds had lowered. The waves were still white-tipped but safe for leaping, and exciting for a small boy. There were four people in the water below, two of them children. We watched as they waited for the exact moment a wave peaked to dive headfirst into the foam. From where we stood, we could hear their voices drifting up as if from an old recording, bumpy and muffled, only the odd-pitched cry getting through.

Greg raced to get his bathing suit, and we changed and hurried down to the beach and into the cold water. Tiny smooth stones were being tossed pell-mell at the edge of shore. We swam, and jumped waves to get ourselves out deeper, and rode larger waves back to shore, and fought against them to wade out, and rode them in again. I couldn't keep from laughing aloud while Greg shrieked his delight. When I finally persuaded him to come in, his slim body was hard and blue with cold. I rolled a big towel around him and sat him down so that I could massage his legs.

That evening after our picnic supper, we sat below the dunes around the fire and we were rewarded with a moving-picture show of the aurora borealis against a dark wall of sky: vivid, miraculous, an infinity away. Great vertical sheets of light. The breeze had dropped completely; the sea was calm, its bulge ominous as ever. Foam slid in over sand that had been pounded flat. The red blink-blink of a buoy flashed and bobbed far out. We listened to the slow wash of waves and watched in awe as the sky's colours rushed past on their way to somewhere else. Shades of deep green to lighter shades and back again swept over the huge stage of the night. There were greens I have never seen before and have never seen since.

Greg told Lena, "All that moving colour in the sky makes me feel like shouting, Mom. It makes me feel like running underneath." And then he shrank into himself. "It makes me feel like a tiny speck." He started to drop off to sleep and, barefoot, I carried him over hard-packed sand and up steps that had been dug out of the dunes but managed to change shape in every weather. I tried to be careful of my footing, but it wasn't a smooth climb and Greg woke before I could brush the sand off his legs and feet and get him into bed.

"You know, Dad, when I grow up," he said, looking straight up at me, "I'm going to be all Japanese like you, instead of just half." He snuggled deep into the covers, and then he added, "This has been the happiest day of my life." In an instant, he was asleep.

When I told Lena, she said, "It's because you went in with him. You could be bothered. You went into the sea, which he loves, and you jumped those fabulous white waves alongside him, and he'll never forget."

But I was thinking of the mirror, of the reflection that had stared back at me, the one I could not escape as a child or a young man. The hope that by the time I grew up, somehow, in some miraculous way, the mirror would turn me into someone else.

CHAPTER 17

1944

"Follow," said Father.

It was mid-morning when we left the shack for our end-of-summer picnic, our big outing before school started up again in the fall. We walked single file, Hiroshi behind Father, then Keiko, then me. Mother was last in line, keeping an eye on us from behind. We waved, called out to Ba and Ji, and fell silent after we crossed the dirt road. We walked past the communal tomato gardens, past rows and rows of eggplant and radish, carrot and cucumber, melon and squash. We skirted the edge of the cliff and made our way through foliage and undergrowth, and found the zigzagged trail that descended the embankment. Down and down we went, always in shadow of the mountain, the sounds of our progress echoing back as we stumbled over gravel and root. The day's heat pressed against the earth; the air was still. Sun poked through slits in the treetops and planted blotchy patterns of shadow and light over the trail. The lower parts of the path were hot and dry and sandy, and shifted each time a foot touched down. At the bottom, there was river, only river. That, and a small island in the midst of rushing water.

The moment we reached the chosen spot, Mother began to clear a space for our picnic. Father set down the bundles he had carried and he stood, hands on hips. We fell silent while he examined the river with a fisherman's eyes.

"I thought the banks would be more exposed," he said. "This water is dangerous and high. Higher than it should be so late in summer."

He looked out again and I had a moment's worry that he might lead us back up the trail without the picnic happening at all. But he did not look tense or angry, and it was clear that he, too, enjoyed being here, close to the great river.

"My arms are aching badly, really badly," Hiroshi complained, filling the silence. He knew the complaint would get him nowhere, but he made it anyway. He had carried the gallon water jug all the way from the shack. Father glanced over at Hiroshi, but he did not reprimand. Carrying water was Hiroshi's job, whether he wanted it or not.

Keiko's job in this season was to help Mother with the canning and preserving, but she also worked in the gardens, picking tomatoes. There were no more classes held by Keiko on the slope above camp, but she continued to find and share materials for drawing and copying, and she helped me with reading and printing lessons. She and her friends had also persuaded an eighty-four-year-old woman in camp to teach Japanese dancing. At night, when the chores were done, the girls went to the community room to learn from the woman, who had once been a dancing teacher in Vancouver.

My own chores were not difficult these days. I, too, picked tomatoes. I also carried armloads of wood into the shack for the stove, and

I stacked wood outside after Father had finished chopping. Most of the time, Father was after me to stop daydreaming. Sometimes he rapped my head with his knuckles because I wasn't paying attention. "When you aren't so scrawny, when you grow taller and bigger, you won't be spending hours over your scribblings," he said. "You'll be taking your share of family responsibility, like everyone else."

But he kept me busy, all the same. There were summer days when I worked for hours stacking wood into tidy rows behind our shack. If even one log or piece of kindling stuck out crookedly, he came out and knocked the woodpile apart and made me start over again.

Despite Father, I did find time to draw. Mother helped by putting away bits of cardboard for me, and these were hidden under the edge of the mattress. Sometimes, during the summer months, I was able to get away from the whole family and climb the trail to the Bench. I sat up there by myself on a tree stump on the side of the mountain, and I looked down over sagebrush and rolling tumbleweed, the outhouses, the rows of shacks, the gardens on the far side of the dirt road, the water tanks with wooden bungs in the sides and the river in the deepest part of the ravine.

From high up, it was easy to tell which shack belonged to my family because of the neatness of the woodpile and because of the crooked window at the back. Sometimes I would see Hiroshi come around the side of the house with our bows and arrows, and he would look in all directions, searching for me. If I didn't feel like playing in the woods, I ducked back into the shadows before he had a chance to look up. And there were others to watch, too. Our community was in perpetual motion: people walking or standing in different attitudes and postures; sixty-one shacks to observe and draw, some with oddly proportioned additions—lean-tos, wooden bathhouses, overhangs to keep woodpiles dry, pits dug for earth cellars, tiny rooms or shelves added to the side or back of a shack when there was extra space and spare lumber. There were many chicken coops now, too, including ours. Chicken manure was never wasted, and was used as fertilizer on the gardens. Because of the smell, the coops were kept at a slight distance from our homes.

I watched children my own age and younger playing on pathways and in the open space beside the schoolhouse. I once saw Hiroshi rolling a large stone down the hill below me, then hiding when it crashed into the roof of one of the outhouses. I saw Auntie Aya sitting dully on the low stool beside her door, her head tilted back as if to trap the sun on her face, her bright, lacquered combs shining as her head moved forward and back. There were days when she banged the back of her skull rhythmically against the tarpaper of the outer wall. I watched Uncle Aki come outside and soothe her, or sit beside her for a few moments and take her hand. I watched him climb a homemade ladder and replace boards on the side of his bathhouse, all the while keeping an eye on Auntie Aya, never letting her out of his sight. When he was working in the garden, he brought her to stay with Mother, who helped her with meals and with the preserving of vegetables for winter.

People greeted one another in the camp and I observed how slowly their bodies moved in the oppressive summer heat. I watched the way they crossed the road, and I watched the angle of their backs as they bent over plants in the garden plots. Voices could be heard in the mountain air: some in laughter, some in argument or irritation. Always, there was a murmur of rising sound.

When I returned home with pictures on cardboard or wood or bark—rarely on paper—Father reminded me again: "Drawing will not put rice in the pot. Drawing will not buy food from the back of

Ying's truck. Everyone in the family must contribute. Everyone must work, no matter how young."

In fact, earlier on our picnic morning, before breakfast, I had painstakingly drawn two wild horses on a piece of boxboard, but my drawing was yanked from my hand. It disappeared and was probably tossed into the stove. I was sorry Father had taken it away from me, because I'd wanted to make it better. I had drawn the eye of the larger horse to make it look alert and ready to bolt if startled. The head of the smaller horse was tucked under the neck of the larger, but the nose of the small horse had turned out looking like the fat, long beak of a giant goose. I knew everyone would laugh at a horse that looked like a goose; I knew my drawing was a complete failure.

But on this once-a-year day, I was not going to worry about a picture that had been yanked out of my hand. Everyone in the family, including Father, was taking a holiday, and our day at the river was meant to be enjoyed.

Father completed his careful study of water conditions and now pointed downriver to fallen rocks that jutted out near the base of the cliff. These, he said, would provide shelter from the current. He led the three of us away from Mother and showed us a gravel bar where we were permitted to play in the shallows. He chose this place not only for safety; a bit farther along, he planned to throw out a line for sturgeon.

We followed again, and watched in silence while he selected a branch from the bushes and sank it into the sand. He tied a length of fishing line around the tip so it would twitch up and down if a fish was hooked, and then he anchored the line to the trunk of a cotton-wood tree. Two feet from the end, he attached bait to a large hook, and then weighted the line with an oblong-shaped rock. He lobbed it out in a high arc, and the rock sank down into the deepest part of the river.

"Now," he said, and he was even smiling, "we will attract a big fish. Agreed?"

Hiroshi and Keiko and I nodded agreement, and then we went back to the gravel bar to play while he returned to the picnic site along the bank.

When it was time to cross to the island, Father stood and called out to us. Because I was youngest, I was left behind in care of Mother on the main shore while Father swam breaststroke alongside Hiroshi, eldest and tallest, and helped him across. Mother put her hands on my shoulders from behind, and we watched while Father returned for Keiko and swam with her to the island, where she stood beside Hiroshi. Finally, he came back for me. Because I was small and he was big, he hoisted me onto his back and began to swim through the dark current, out and out to the island and the swiftest part of the river.

But I was already slippery from playing in the shallow water, and because my arms did not reach all the way around to his chest, I was terrified that my fingers would let go. If I put pressure on his neck, he would be sure to make an angry noise. So I hung on and hung on, certain that I could do nothing to save myself if I slipped off. I knew that Father was strong, and I willed the muscles of his arms to push the swirls of treacherous water behind us. At the same time, I knew that I would never forget this moment, and my exhilaration became tangled up with the fear of sliding off my father's back.

While one part of me believed that the journey to the island would never end, another part of me was watching the colours of the river. Ever since that day, I have been able to describe them as if I were once again in its middle. First, there was a surprising change from muddy brown to marble green. Then from marble green to sparkling turquoise. We neared a second gravel bar and I was relieved to see the river bottom, clear and close. Before I had time to be thankful, I was lifted in one strong movement and set on my feet in shallow water. For a few seconds I stood, lightheaded, and then I realized that while I had been worrying about slipping off Father's back, I had forgotten to think about Mother.

I turned to look, and I was surprised to see that the dark channel of rough water had so easily divided our family into two parts.

"Mother!" I called out. "Swim across. I'll wait for you."

But she only smiled and waved, and stayed where she was.

The midday light had made its way down to the clearing, and when I scrunched my eyelids almost shut, golden needles of sun glinted against the blackness of Mother's hair. Her hair was long but she had bangs and, always, the two curls, one on either side of her forehead. She seemed to be thinking about something when I called out, but she shielded her eyes with one hand and motioned to me with the other. Her fingers flicked forward to tell me to follow Father, who was striding off, leaving me behind. Hiroshi and Keiko were already out of sight; I could hear them talking and laughing as they explored. I turned again to glance over my shoulder, but Mother was small now, far away. She had leaned forward, perhaps to unwrap one of the food parcels she'd carried down the embankment, perhaps to stare at the ground or to look at a rock or an insect that had caught her attention. I knew I had to join the others, and I reluctantly followed their voices and rounded the curve of the island. Sharp rocks jabbed the soles of my feet, and I tried not to yelp as I ran to catch up. I pushed the image of Mother away. Just because I was the youngest didn't mean I was a baby. Nothing could make me look back again.

When I caught up to Hiroshi and Keiko, they were splashing about in the water on the far side of the island, turning over clams and pebbles to search for treasure, specks of fool's gold they hoped to scoop up and carry home. I lagged behind and then waded the few feet back to shore. I reached up to a low tree and snapped a branch that felt exactly right to my palm. I returned to the water and poked the end of the branch under a flat rock, flipping it over so that I could see the array of living creatures attached to its underside. The rock, I told myself, had extended an invitation, had offered protection, a shadowy place to hide. And some of the river's smallest creatures had accepted the invitation and decided to stay.

The summer before, during our annual end-of-summer picnic and while we were still on the main shore, Father had explained to me that a flat rock in the river was always a guarantee of something beneath: tiny minnows with large heads and protruding bead eyes, minnows that darted towards my toes and could take me by surprise; cased larvae bonded with grains of sand and bits of pebble and stick; raised black dots that might be some sort of egg.

What sort of egg? I had asked at the time.

But Father didn't know.

I wanted an answer. A year later, I still wanted an answer. Thinking back, I kicked at loose gravel and watched my feet disappear as the bottom turned to murk and cloud. I inhaled the smell of river deep into my lungs.

"*Are! Are!* Come see! Come see!"

My concentration was broken by the shouts of my brother and sister, and by the terse voice of our father. I was curious to know what they had discovered, but I stayed where I was because I had found treasure of my own: a resting caddis fly, its wings folded in the shape of a peaked tent, the tiniest tent imaginable. I squatted to stare, and I marvelled.

When at last it was time to leave the island, Father called me to his side. I might have been last over, but because I was the youngest, I would be first to go back. I thought of Mother again, and looked anxiously across the channel, relieved to see her sitting on a rock shelf, her legs stretched out. So seldom did I see her outside, sitting idly like this, I wondered for a moment if the person on the far bank was the same one who stayed inside most of the time, cooking, baking, sewing, knitting, washing and mending clothes, sweeping, keeping our place clean. Indeed, it *was* Mother, and she was staring downriver as if her eyes were following the current as it swept along on its journey to the coast.

Father hoisted me up with a single hand, as if to remind me that I weighed no more than a dried and brittle clam. Back we went, over turquoise and marble green and muddy water, until I was handed into the outstretched arms of my mother. She wrapped a towel tightly around me and began to rub at my heels because she knew, without being told, that my feet were stinging with pain from playing in the cold river. Father returned to the island and swam alongside Keiko, and then he went back for Hiroshi. Finally, we were all safely returned to the main shore.

Mother had set out picnic food, knowing how hungry we would be, and she lifted a square of damp cotton to reveal thinly sliced strips of omelette. Earlier in the morning, Keiko had helped to make *nigiri sushi*—balls of rice pressed to diamond shapes, with black sesame and dried seaweed sprinkled overtop. There were homemade pickles, *tsukemono;* thick radishes from the garden; and for dessert, a large hot cross bun for each of us, decorated with thin lines of white icing. Hiroshi was sent to fetch the jug that had been set in scooped-out gravel at the outlet of a cold spring that fed into the river. I watched as Mother added sugar to the water and then poured in the contents of a corked vial, which she shook end to end, dispersing a thick and oily lemon extract. She tilted the jug until the yellow colour had spread throughout the liquid, and then she held it to the sun. Satisfied, she poured the lemonade into our waiting cups.

Father kept urging us to eat, to finish every bite of the food we had carried down the embankment. With his chopsticks, he passed me an extra helping of *sushi,* and then he offered me half of his hot cross bun. He had never done this before, and I glanced up at Mother to see if I should accept. She nodded yes, and looked towards the river while I ate my own and then half of my father's dessert. Hiroshi and Keiko looked on in envy.

As soon as we finished eating, Father told Keiko to stay with Mother to help clean up. Hiroshi and I were to follow him along the bank while he checked his fishing line. As we approached the cottonwood tree, we could see that the line he had attached to the branch was badly shredded.

Father nodded darkly and said, "Only a great fish would break such a line."

Hiroshi nodded, assuming the same expression.

I looked up at Father and saw a quick flash of anger, but I saw something else, too. Respect for the great fish. The summer before, I had watched him and several other fishermen haul in a large sturgeon, longer than my own body. I had shrunk back, out of the way, awed by its gaping gills and slow-moving tail, by the ridge on its back, by its mottled, purplish-pink skin. I had seen respect then, too, on the faces of men who were no longer permitted to fish in coastal waters. They fished below camp in the mighty Fraser and with makeshift equipment—their own having been stolen or auctioned off. But this was not the ocean.

In the late afternoon, our picnic came to an end for another year. Fatigued, sated with food and sun and fresh air, we began the slow, steep climb up the sand-and-gravel trail towards our shack. My head was filled with images of rock and canyon and river below, though the picnic site could not be seen once we had crossed the garden plots and the dirt road.

Mother seemed preoccupied when we were home again, but she warmed some green tea and gave us a snack and, just before sunset, sent us up the trail to the Bench so that we could pick berries before bedtime.

I knew exactly where to find raspberries and currants on the plateau, and I scrambled up behind my brother and sister, knowing that other children would be there, too. We spread out, intent on filling our buckets, and I wandered away by myself until I came to a thick clump of raspberry canes. The silence of the mountain settled around me, though I was aware of occasional spurts of laughter and a low murmur of voices drifting in and out of the evening air.

I tried to remember all that had happened since early morning: the excitement of waking on picnic day; the walk down the steep trail; the wriggling, darting creatures of the Fraser; the changing colours of the big river; the scent beneath the cottonwoods; the feel of the branch in my palm when I poked and prodded under rocks. I thought of Mother's arms reaching for me when I was first to return across the channel on Father's back. I thought of the way she had rubbed at my heels to warm my feet. I thought of the perfect yellow lemonade and the sticky-sweet taste of hot cross buns and the extra portion I had been given by my father. I looked down over the fast river, which could be seen from the height of the Bench, and I told myself that this had been the happiest day of my life.

But my cocoon was broken harshly by a shrill voice shouting, "Bear! Bear!" and every one of us on the Bench, every child, including me, raced down the slope. By the time we reached bottom, laughing and calling out, no one knew if a bear had actually been seen or if fresh droppings had been sighted, but the cry of "Bear! Bear!" had scattered us and sent us running down the hill to our beds.

When we returned to our shack, we saw that we had a visitor. Our parents were standing side by side in the kitchen, the room bloated with silence. Father was rigidly tall and looked uncomfortable, as if something had gone wrong. I had never seen an expression on his face like the one I was seeing now. Mother's face appeared to be crumpled and small. Her eyes were red and I could not think what could possibly be wrong at the end of our day of days, our picnic of picnics. I handed the bucket of raspberries to Mother, who did not seem to notice that it was only half full. She placed the bucket on the shelf beside the smoothly jointed sink that Ji had built for her.

The third person in the room was standing across from our parents. A bundle of clothes was on a chair, along with blankets and a small pillow. I recognized a sleeve from my knitted sweater sticking out of the bundle. I looked to Hiroshi and Keiko but they did not know what was happening any more than I did. Hiroshi sat down on the bench against the wall and waited. Keiko looked from Mother to Father and was about to speak. But before she could get a word out, we were told why the adults had been waiting silently for us to come down the hill.

My father, who had two sons, had made the decision to give me away. I was to be given to Okuma-san, the man from the end of the row, who lived alone and had never been fortunate enough to have a son of his own to carry on his family name. He had come to collect me, and it was then that I was told that my surname would no longer be Oda, and that I would be taking the Okuma name as my own.

Keiko burst into tears and was crying loudly. Hiroshi banged his bucket to the table, spilling the raspberries he'd picked, over its surface. I stared at the berries because they were rolling in slow motion to the edge of the table and dropping to the floor, one by one. Hiroshi, after this outburst, opened his mouth but seemed at a loss, because no words came out. He slammed the door and disappeared outside.

As for me, I knew now why I had been given the extra dessert. My parents had known the entire day what was going to happen. And no matter how much I wept, no matter how much my mother and Keiko wept, I was sent out of the house of my family and moved to the home of my second father. The man I thought to be old, the man who owned an entire shelf of books that had pages of notes, and who was quietly known to everyone as Great Bear.

TOMORROW'S WIND

Have a walking stick ready before a fall.

CHAPTER 18

1944

Okuma-san did not raise his voice, nor did he threaten. He spoke softly, with an evenness of tone I was not accustomed to. He told me that I would be able to play with my brother and sister as before, and they could visit me whenever they wished. We would all be back in school when classes resumed the following week, and we would see one another every day.

I knew that Hiroshi and Keiko would be at school, but they would be with the older students in grades five to eight, on the other side of the divided classroom. I was in grade two, on the side of the room that held grades one to four. I would see my brother and sister only at recess and lunchtime. After school, they would be doing their chores—water-carrying for Hiroshi, while Keiko had to set the table and help with the cooking. We would all have homework; I would be doing mine at Okuma-san's. I still did not know what was expected of me there.

There were fifty-two children in our school now, and three teachers. One of the teachers, who had a university degree, volunteered to work with the boys and girls of high school age. The students who would be graduating at the end of the school year were going to be permitted, for the first time, to write their final exams at the town high school across the river. Until now, they'd had to write exams by correspondence.

I liked my own teacher, Miss Mori. She had taught me the previous year, as well, and she knew that Keiko had helped me learn to read and print before I'd started school. Miss Mori sometimes asked me to draw pictures on the blackboard, and she let me use some of her precious supply of chalk. I wondered if Miss Mori would say something about my name changing from Oda to Okuma on the attendance sheet. I hoped that one of my fathers had let her know before classes were to begin.

I knew that Mother was spending time at Uncle Aki's house in the afternoons because Auntie Aya was not able to look after the work by herself. Sometimes, she stayed in bed all day. On good days, she sat outside the doorway. Some days, she tried to cook; other days, she did not. She liked the catalogues that arrived in the mail, both Eaton's and Simpson's, and she kept them by her side and read them as if they were storybooks. She lingered over the pages that had pictures of babies and baby furniture and clothing, and there was always a sadness about her.

The first day I spent at Okuma-san's, he prepared our meals and set two places. He asked me to sit opposite him at the table, on a bench that had been hammered together from pieces of pine. I sat, but I had no appetite. I ate no breakfast or lunch, nor did I want food ever again. He did not seem surprised.

In the evening, when it was time for our supper, he said, "Perhaps tomorrow your appetite will come back. Would you like to look at a book while I am having my meal? There is a book on the chair for you, over there. You might not have seen this one before. I know you have learned to read, and I can help you if there are big words that are difficult."

I shook my head and did not look towards the book or the chair. I had seen few books since we'd arrived at the camp, except for the ones lined up on a shelf at the back of our classroom. I did not feel like looking at a book now. I wanted only to return home. I missed the cooking smells in my real home, and I missed the calming presence of Mother and the way she silently looked out for me. I wondered what my own father was doing at that moment.

"Some other evening, then," said Okuma-san, still speaking softly. "There are many more books." He gestured towards the shelves. "They will be waiting for you."

I did not look at the place he was gesturing, but this did not seem to bother him either.

"I am going outside for a walk," he said. "I will leave a snack on the table in case you become hungry later."

When he had finished eating, he went outside, and I watched as he crossed the dirt road and began to walk slowly up and down the rows between garden plots. While he was gone, and with an eye to the door, I lifted the cover from a plate he had left on the table. It held a small trout, a slice of tomato and some cabbage. Beside it was a bowl of rice. I ate quickly and finished before he came back.

He looked at the bones on my plate.

"*Neko shirazu,*" he said. "What about the part the cat can't find? The cat is unaware of the fat morsels in the cheeks. He walks away from the bones of the fish but he leaves the best part behind."

I picked up my chopsticks and poked at the bones and found little pads of trout in the cheeks, like miniature hidden scallops.

The next morning, I ran to my own house and stood in the doorway. I knew that First Father would be out in the gardens with the other men, harvesting and packing, preparing tomatoes for pickup by trucks that would come from across the river to take the flats back over the bridge—some to the town cannery and some to the railway station, where they would be loaded onto a train. The communal gardens in our camp had become known in only two years, and there was a steady market for our produce. The people of Vancouver wanted good tomatoes that grew fat and red and abundantly.

Everyone in camp who was able to work had to put in extra hours during harvest time, picking tomatoes and filling the big red pails. I could read the print on the sides: BURNS' SHAMROCK PURE LARD. After each pail was filled, it was carried to the end of a row and the tomatoes were dumped gingerly into the flats. Tomatoes had become the main source of income in our camp, and everyone had to take care that the ones that did not go to the cannery were not bruised during packing. At this time of year, people were extra busy because individual family plots had to be tended as well.

Mother was standing by the stove when I opened the door. She was wearing a loose summer dress patterned with overlapping ovals of a soft grey colour, and a red apron overtop. On her feet were open-heeled slippers that First Father had woven from straw. He had made a pair for each of us the first winter so we wouldn't get slivers in our feet from the plank floor.

I could smell *shoyu*, the familiar aroma of soy sauce. Mother had been adding drops to something she was stirring in a large pot. The two curls on her forehead looked as if they'd been lacquered, because steam was rising straight up out of the pot. I knew she had heard me enter.

"Bin." She said my name carefully. "Father said you were to stay with your new father." I could see that she was forcing herself to speak these words.

She did not move from the stove, but I saw her glance quickly out the window in the direction of the tomato fields.

She came to me in the doorway then, and put her arms around my shoulders and my back. She pulled me close, and when I looked up, I saw that she was crying without noise. She pushed me away gently and said, "Go now. Don't get into trouble. We will see each other every day. Go and find Hiroshi and Keiko. They are picking tomatoes, but they are probably watching for you. They are still your brother and sister, don't ever forget. And I am still your mother, though we will no longer live in the same house."

I edged back slowly, casting a glance around the room at all that was familiar: the homemade table and bench, the few chairs, the low three-legged stool, the curtain in the doorway that led to the bedroom, the beautiful smooth sink and shelf that Ji had made for Mother, a hastily constructed cupboard that held our blue-and-white rice bowls and plates and chopsticks and kitchen utensils.

"Hurry!" Mother said. "Go and look for the others. And be sure to show your new father respect. He is an educated man. A good man. I am certain of it."

She returned to the stove and stood without moving. She did not look in my direction. I had no choice but to let myself out the door.

As I walked away from my mother's house, Ba called to me from her doorway.

"I've been watching for you," she said. "I thought you would come back this morning. Try not to be sad. This is the way things happen sometimes, when one family has no sons and another has more than one."

But I could see that she looked sad herself.

"Sit at the table," she said. And she set out a green bowl and cut an orange into slices for me. "Ji is in the garden," she added, when she saw me looking around for him. "He will be glad you were here to have a visit with me." She sprinkled some raspberries around the orange slices in the bowl. "Finish them all," she said, "and I will read my letter from Manzanar while you are eating."

She patted the deep pocket of her dress, where she carried every letter that had arrived from her daughter, Sachi, in California. The letters were creased and flattened and had been read many times. When a new one arrived, she always took it over to read it aloud to Mother and to anyone else who was there. I had not heard the latest one, which had arrived the previous day. It had been written in the early summer, and had taken months to come from Manzanar because it had to go to the censor's office before arriving at our camp. Ba sat on the chair across from me at the table.

"This letter slipped past the censor," she said. "It must have been put in the wrong pile. There isn't a single mark on it." She laughed, and then she began to read.

Dear Mother and Father

> *Tom and I are okay. There are so many people around us every day, it is like living in a city, even though our "city" is surrounded by guard towers and barbed wire and it happens to be in the desert and there are men with machine guns in the towers.*

> *Although some people are beginning to leave now, there have been as many as 10,000 here at one time. Much bigger than the camp you write about in your letters. Also, we have electricity here, and running water, and I am sorry that you do not. That must be a great hardship after living in Vancouver so many years.*

Tom is still teaching apprentices about electricity and plumbing, but he volunteered his extra time to work on the new park I wrote about before. It's in the middle of the main camp, inside the first round of barbed wire. The park has ball diamonds and even an outdoor stage. The schools here are huge—kindergartens, a high school, elementary schools—and we have a hospital now, with an operating room.

My own job at the co-op keeps me busy. I've been working there for a year, and it's grown so much! What started out as a mail-order business has become much more, including a department store, where I'm to be found most days. My experience at our old Vancouver store while I was growing up has really helped. I still miss the store, don't you? All the gossip that was exchanged over the counter, the stove people gathered around, I miss it all.

The farm outside our main camp, still inside barbed wire—don't for a minute think anyone is free to walk out the gates—is so productive that we are able to ship a surplus of food to other prison camps. How about that for self-sufficiency? We grow every vegetable you can think of, and we raise cattle, pigs and poultry, too. Well, I don't, but the farm workers do.

The churches and YMCA are still up and running, even though the rumour is that they will close as more and more inmates depart. What we'll get, on departure, is $20 each and train fare to our destination. Great pat on the back! But most people have no place to go. The best way to get out of here is to have a job waiting in some state that wants us. Tom and I do not want to pick sugar beets. That's one job that's being advertised in our Manzanar newspaper. We'll be staying a bit longer, until we know what we're facing on the outside. I'll let you know as soon as we decide.

Love to you both, and please stay healthy,
Sachi

Ba was lost in thought over Sachi, and I waited until she folded the letter along all of its creases, and replaced it in her pocket alongside the other letters. I thanked her for the orange and the berries and went across the road to the garden.

Hiroshi and Keiko were waiting.

"What's he like?" Keiko said. "To live with."

When I didn't answer, Hiroshi said, "Your new father." And then he blurted out, "Is he kind?"

"Yes," I said in a soft, low voice, not unlike Okuma-san's. "He is kind."

I was aware of people in the rows around me, staring. Everyone seemed to know.

Keiko reached into her pocket and pulled out two Ritz crackers she had brought from home. She pushed them into my pocket and said, "For later. If you want a snack."

I picked up an empty lard pail and began to drop the ripe tomatoes on top of one another, not caring if they became squashed or bruised.

CHAPTER 19

In the evenings, Okuma-san read books by the light of a kerosene lamp. Sometimes, he lit candles. Every evening, he left the same book for me on the chair after the supper meal was finished. Sometimes I stole a glance at the book, but it wasn't until several weeks after school began that I opened the cover.

Okuma-san pretended not to notice.

There was a strange picture at the beginning of the book. A baby boy with a pleased expression on his face was inside a round fruit that looked like a peach. He was stepping out of its centre, where the pit should be, and the peach had split open. The boy held his fat little arms above his head as he strode out of the peach. He looked ready for adventure, and I began to wonder what the story was about.

Okuma-san peered over my shoulder and said, "Ah, yes. This is a story I was told when I was a boy about the same age you are now. It begins with an old man and his wife who are lonely because they have no children."

I did not want that kind of story.

I ignored Okuma-san and turned the page. I saw a river. It was curving its way out of hills that had been drawn to look far away on the page. There were wavy lines on the surface of the river, and a large peach floating on its current. An old woman kneeled at the edge of the river. Beside her was a washtub filled with clothes. I turned the page to see that the peach had drifted to shore and was lodged next to the washtub. The old woman and her husband were smiling as they looked down at a baby curled up inside the peach, which had split open. I could see that pictures were helping to tell the story, but I did not know what the story was.

I looked at every page. A monkey and a dog were dressed up as humans and fighting with swords; a boat was sailing on a sea and heading for an island. I decided to read the story by myself. But there were a few big words I did not know.

When Okuma-san went outside for his evening walk through the gardens, I examined the pictures in the book again. Two were in colour. Others were shaded in black and white, as if they had been drawn with a pencil, or maybe with pen and ink. Okuma-san had three pencils in his shack, and these were kept sharpened in a small jam jar on the shelf. He had ink and a long pen with a nib that he sometimes dipped into a small bottle. The ink was dark, almost black. He had told me the name of the colour—indigo. In winter, the ink in our school froze on the coldest days. The teachers lined up the stubby bottles on a small table close to the stove, but it took hours for the ink to thaw. On those days, we wore our winter jackets all day, at our desks.

After Okuma-san returned from his walk, he said, "Would you like me to read the story to you?"

I nodded, though I was careful not to let him think I wanted to live with him, just because he owned a book that had pictures of a monkey and a dog dressed as humans.

We sat at the table and I learned, for the first time, the adventures of Momotaro, the boy who floated down the river inside a giant peach and washed ashore, only to be discovered by an old man and an old woman. I especially liked the part about the treasure Momotaro won. This included a hat and coat that made him invisible and a hammer that could turn objects to gold by striking them. If I had such objects, I thought, I would arrange my life so that things would turn out differently. I would start by wearing the hat and coat to make myself invisible. I would slip into the home of my real family and I would stay there. I would remain invisible so that everyone would think I had disappeared and would feel badly. Especially First Father, who had given me away.

That night, when I lay in my bed—a narrow cot that Okuma-san had built across the room from his own—I pulled the covers up around my ears and thought about my first family. I missed them all but I didn't know if they missed me. Then I thought about the story of the river, which was also the story of the old man and the old woman who found the boy inside the peach. That boy was happy to be found. I wondered what the other stories in the book were about and tried to remember the details of the pictures. I decided that I would draw a story of my own. The next day would be a Saturday, and I made up my mind to ask Okuma-san for permission to hold the long pen with the fitted nib, and to dip the nib into the squat round bottle of indigo ink. I would look for a bit of cardboard or a piece of board as soon as breakfast was over. I was going to draw the great river below the camp. I was going to draw the island in its middle, the one I had been taken to on First Father's back. But I would change the story. I was going to give it an ending of my own choosing.

In the morning, before I had a chance to ask about pen and ink, Okuma-san went to the corner of the small room that was both kitchen and living space, and lifted a plank that had been propped at a slant against the wall. I'd noticed this when I had first arrived in his house, but had not asked what it was. Okuma-san was not a big man like First Father, and his shoulders were slightly stooped. When he lifted the plank I could see that it was almost as long as he was tall.

"An old tree has given up this gift for me while I must live in this place," said Okuma-san, as he turned the wood so the flat side faced up. "This is my keyboard and it is made of ponderosa pine, a tree that can live to an old age, four or even five hundred years. Imagine what the earth was like when the tree that gave this wood was no bigger than a tiny seedling. It is the kind of tree that likes to stand tall, and sends out a long, long root."

He gestured in invitation, and I reached out to feel the wood and rubbed my fingers across the surface. The keyboard had been smoothed and sanded, right to its edges.

"At first, the wood was sticky, maybe more so than Douglas fir, but when I saw it, I understood how it would show its beauty. It was dry when I chose it. That helped. That and the sanding. I began to work on it soon after I arrived here."

The clear and even grains of the plank, face up, were visible even through the black-and-white keys that had been painted on its surface. On the underside, bits of bark were still attached, as if to remind that this had once been a tree. The bark was as it had grown in the forest, grooved in thick, hard plates. The underside, in its natural state, was as beautiful as the sanded surface.

"Do you see where I have drawn the keys?" he said. "I have made this my instrument. When I lived in Vancouver, I had a piano that was beautiful in both appearance and sound. I played it every day until it had to be sold. But here, if I want to play and have no piano, I must practise some other way. I can do this, as long as the music is inside my head and my heart. Do you see the keys?"

I nodded, but I had never heard anyone say they had music inside their heart.

"There are fifty-two white and thirty-six black keys along the length of the pine. That adds up to eighty-eight—a full keyboard. Have you ever heard anyone play the piano?"

"Missisu," I said. "I listened from our step. Sometimes I looked at the piano in her house."

When I saw the question on Okuma-san's face, I explained. "Missisu lived beside us in our fishing village. That was before the Mounties told us we had to leave. *Hakujin* men who lived in the village took her piano away on a cart with wheels when we were on the mail boat. Missisu was sent to a different camp before our family left Hastings Park."

Okuma-san nodded. "I see. And what was it that Missisu played on her piano before it was taken away on the cart?"

"I don't know the names of anything. She taught other children and I listened from the step. Sometimes I could hear her from inside our kitchen."

"I, too, taught children at one time," he said. "Grown-ups, too. But there were no students after Pearl Harbor was bombed."

I did not tell Okuma-san about the morning we left our home by the sea, when the whiteness of sound from the piano drifted in front of my face and had to be batted away. I did not tell him about the tears that had rolled down my cheeks while I'd listened to Missisu play. I did not tell him about the hated rice pot banging into my legs while I followed Mother's navy blue coat, or about the fates that First Father had read aloud so many times. He did not have to know everything.

Okuma-san sat on a rough kitchen chair and placed his home-made keyboard in front of him across two small trestles he had fashioned from tree stumps. The trestles were solid, and narrow enough to stow beside the plank when it was propped in the corner. He inched the keyboard back and forth until it balanced to his satisfaction. Then he adjusted his position, tucking his knees beneath the wood, raising and lowering his heels, planting his feet several inches apart. When both feet were firmly on the floor, he shrugged his shoulders exaggeratedly, closed his lips and nodded. His arms hung at his sides in relaxed fashion. Then both hands came up over the centre of the board, acting as if they were not truly connected to his arms.

"Watch closely," he said. "Watch my hands. Maybe your neighbour Missisu played this."

He looked towards the pine plank, then tilted his head back and closed his eyes. He had been sitting straight in his chair but his upper body dipped forward suddenly, as if he were entering a place that could not be seen. His fingers began to move against the wood and seemed to be following a familiar path. What I heard was rhythmic and insistent, a rapping against pine. Although both hands were in motion, the fingers of the right were moving more quickly. Okuma-san's left hand paused briefly and then struck the plank emphatically several times. I strained to hear any sort of melody, but there was nothing to discern, apart from fingers rapping on wood. The sound filled the room of the shack.

Both hands came down at the same time and stopped abruptly. He rubbed at his left hand and shut his eyes. I wondered if he was in pain, but then he spoke again.

"It is a minuet. Minuet in G. Not a long piece, but a good one for piano students to practise once they have already begun to study."

Okuma-san's hands were once more suspended an inch or two above the plank, his fingers relaxed and extended. At any moment, they might drop back to the painted keys and begin their race up and down again.

"The man who gave this minuet to the world was called Beethoven. Can you say that?"

"Bait-o-ven," I ventured.

"Good. He created this minuet 150 years ago. He was a great artist but he did not have an easy life. There were many problems that had to be faced. But he did not give up just because he had problems. He continued to create so others would always be able to listen to his music, even though he could not hear it himself. Because, you see, he was deaf from the time he was a very young man. The deafness made his life sad and empty sometimes, and he felt cut off from the people around him."

I tried to imagine this, but it was difficult to picture a man called Bait-o-ven making music he could not hear. I wondered if Okuma-san was mistaken, or if this was another made-up story like the one about the boy inside the peach.

Okuma-san's hands dropped to the keyboard and he began to play again. This time, however, he hummed in accompaniment to his own finger-tapping. To my astonishment, I recognized the melody that he was humming. I knew the entire piece in my head. It was the same one Missisu had played the morning we had been taken away on the mail boat. Having recognized the melody, I also remembered the noise of the grandfather clock and the way it had ticked emphatically in the background, merging with the drifting notes.

"Grandfather Minuet," I said softly, more to myself than to Okuma-san. I was able to follow now, tap by tap, as his fingers moved against the wood.

"I see that you do know this one," said Okuma-san. "Then I guessed correctly."

He lifted the plank so he could get his knees out from under it, set it on the trestles again and walked over to the bookshelf. He chose a large, thin book that had a faded brown cover and loose pages, and he opened it carefully on the tabletop. He turned each page with two hands so that the paper, which was fragile and thin, would not tear. He pointed to a page that held row after row of markings and notes.

"This is what the minuet looks like on paper," he said. "The one I have just played. I have owned this for a long time. But it is only a small part of the creations that came from the heart of the great man."

He placed the sheet music back on the shelf. He sat me down at the end of the table and brought down the pen and the nib, the squat bottle of indigo ink and a small square of blotter. I did not have to ask him for any of these. He set his three sharpened pencils beside me, along with an eraser.

"You are very good at drawing. I have learned this about you. I have heard it from many people in the camp, and from your teacher, too. Perhaps it is something you can do while I am practising at my keyboard."

I looked around for something to draw on.

"Ah," he said, "I have forgotten the most important thing." He reached up to the shelf and opened a different book. Four sheets of paper had been inserted inside the back cover. He put one of these in front of me. The paper was thick and cream-coloured.

"Take your time," he said. "And I will take mine. You may draw what you wish."

He went back to the shelf and chose another book of sheet music. He opened this and propped it against a wooden support he had nailed together to hold the pages upright. The support rested on a low cupboard. There was a small wind-up alarm clock on the cupboard. It was white and had a nickel finish and an oversized bell on top. Beside the clock was a photo of a woman in a small frame. She was wearing a traditional kimono, and she was smiling. This was Okuma-san's wife, who had died; he had already told me that. She had been a singer and she had loved music, and sometimes he had played the piano for her when she had performed.

Okuma-san sat between the trestles now, and faced the propped-up pages. He adjusted the plank all over again until he was happy with its position. He raised and lowered his shoulders, shrugging a few times, preparing. He settled back and began to move his hands and fingers rapidly up and down the painted keys. I did not know what he was playing.

I looked at the blank paper on the table, the first I had ever been given only for the purpose of drawing. The paper was beautiful—too beautiful to use all at once in a single drawing. I folded it, and folded it again. I slid the blotter nervously towards the ink bottle, dipped the nib and tapped it against the rim as I had seen Miss Mori do in the classroom. I crouched over the paper. In the lower right-hand corner, I began to make small dots and lines that I hoped would resemble the river. My drawing might be part of a story; it might not. I only had a feeling that I wanted to put on the paper. If the feeling turned into a story, I did not know what the ending was going to be.

CHAPTER 20

No longer did I hide my drawings under a corner of the mattress. No longer did I receive knuckle raps to my head because I was a daydreamer. Even so, when I drew, I crooked my elbow, ready to cover the page with my arm in case anyone came to the shack and tried to see.

The paper I was given was sometimes a blank page that Okuma-san removed from the back of one of his books. He used the thin, sharp blade of a knife and did this painstakingly, so as not to further damage the book. If there was a blank page at the front, he removed that as well, to provide me with extra paper. Sometimes he folded the paper and, with the same knife, slit it in two. There were days when I returned home from school in the afternoon to find a new sheet of paper lying on top of my bedcovers. On one rare occasion, Okuma-san procured a long strip of paper from Ying's truck. On the Monday, he had passed Ying a coin folded inside a strip of cloth and quietly asked him to bring what he could. On delivery day, Wednesday, the long rolled sheet was passed to Okuma-san after the women had finished gathering around the truck, after they had paid for and collected sugar and flour and thread, after they had laughed about extra-long *chimpo* sausage. When I held the oversized sheet of paper, I folded and refolded and divided it so that I could do many small drawings instead of one large one.

Sometimes, on a Saturday or Sunday, Okuma-san took me for a long walk up the side of the mountain or down the trail to the river. He pointed out plants and bushes and birds along the way. If neither of us knew the name of a species, we brought a leaf or a twig back with us to the shack, and tried to identify it from books, later.

Now that the harvest was over, money was distributed from the proceeds of the sale of produce, especially tomatoes. Families were ordering winter clothing from catalogues, which were passed around and shared. Okuma-san traced an outline of my foot on a piece of cardboard, and we had a long and serious discussion about ordering new shoes from Eaton's and how many sizes larger than my foot the shoes should be. We decided on a pair a full size longer, but of a type that would lace past my ankles, so they wouldn't fall off my feet. He also ordered a pair of thick socks for me, and he laughed about not being able to knit. I knew that Mother would knit socks for me; she always did, just before the snow came.

She and the other women in camp were busy now, pickling, preserving, knitting socks and mittens and scarves, lining winter clothes, everything done by hand. The men were making improvements to the root cellars near the shacks, and they dug more cellars out of the side of the hill and reinforced those with planks. Everyone, in some way or other, was occupied with finding wood, chopping wood, clearing deadwood, stacking wet wood, storing dry wood. Huge logs were dragged from the surrounding forest and sawed with a crosscut saw. Having enough wood for winter was important to every family, and the woodpiles grew higher and higher.

I helped to keep Okuma-san's woodbox filled to the top, day and night. Unlike the real stove First Father had crated and brought with us on the train the winter we arrived, Okuma-san's stove was like the others in camp, a converted oil drum that rested horizontally on low cradle legs made from iron. A large kettle was filled to the top so that warm water was always available.

Every day, when I came in from school, a snack was waiting for me on the table: crackers, sometimes a bowl of canned peaches. Fish was salted and dried, sometimes canned. We ate it with rice and with vegetables from the garden. On rare days, a special treat from Mother was waiting on the kitchen table: *sushi,* or part of a cake she'd baked earlier in the day and delivered while I was at school. There was always enough for both me and Okuma-san. If First Father knew about this, no one said. I did not see First Father often. When I did, it seemed to me that he turned away, as if he didn't want to speak to me. He did speak, sometimes, if I happened to be with Hiroshi or Keiko, outside.

"Are you behaving well?" he said to me one day. "Are you learning new things?"

I nodded. By now, I knew what was expected of me at Okuma-san's. What was expected was that I would learn. Learning, reading, drawing and music were honoured in his home. I had a sudden urge to blurt out the name *Bait-o-ven* to First Father, but he had moved on.

In the late fall, our first camp wedding took place. Miss Mori, my teacher of the past two years, married a man whom everyone knew as Tak. Tak was in his twenties, and had been living with his parents in our camp for the past six months. He had been sent to a work camp in 1942, to build roads near the Alberta border, but after a year he was permitted to join his parents because his father had become ill. Few young single men were ever allowed to remain in the inland camps; they were either sent to Ontario prisoner-of-war camps, to work camps to build roads under supervision, or—if they could find jobs—they were permitted to move east to work. Even the young male teachers in the other internment camps in the interior were eventually sent east, after being told by the Security Commission that they could no longer keep their teaching jobs.

Tak remained in our camp until his father was well again, and by then, he and Miss Mori had decided to marry. They planned to move to Ontario after their wedding. They had been promised work in Hamilton, and had received permission to travel by train across the country. Tak's parents would leave with them, and that would mean the first empty shack in our community.

I was sorry to lose Miss Mori partway through the school year. She had always given me extra challenges. It wasn't difficult for me to learn work from the third grade because I could hear the lessons around me from the next row of desks. I was doing both grade two and grade three work at the same time. Miss Mori also taught songs to the four grades on our side of the room. There was no instrument to accompany our voices, but that didn't stop her from teaching us to sing. There was one special song we planned to sing at her wedding, but that was to be a surprise.

Miss Mori was replaced by Mr. Blackwell, a Caucasian missionary from the Anglican Church, a man who had once taught English and Bible studies. He was living in Vancouver when Miss Mori announced her departure. When the school committee found out about him from church contacts, he was invited to teach at our camp. He agreed to take over grades one to four for the rest of the year, and he found a room in a boarding house across the river. He had an old black car. Every day, he drove it across the bridge, right up to the school door.

Everyone stopped work for the wedding, which took place outside on a sunny fall Saturday afternoon. A canopy had been created and decorated, and Miss Mori and Tak stood under it and were married by a minister from across the river. The minister left immediately after the ceremony. With the temperature cooling down, we all moved inside the schoolhouse to celebrate in the community room. Many of the women had baked, and Mother had made a special cake in the oven of her stove. Other families had donated butter and sugar to help with the cake.

At a signal from one of the older girls, Miss Mori's pupils, including me, gathered quickly in one corner of the room. We stood, tall and proud, and sang to the new couple "Don't Fence Me In," a song Miss Mori had taught us the year before. Miss Mori wiped at tears while we sang, but at the end of the song, she joined everyone in the room as they clapped and cheered.

I had made a special card for my departing teacher, using a precious sheet of thick paper from one of Okuma-san's books. I folded it across the middle and drew a mountain and a schoolhouse. I tried to make these look like our mountain and our schoolhouse. Across the bottom, in indigo ink, I drew the river. I wanted Miss Mori to remember me and I wanted her to know that I was going to miss her. Okuma-san stayed at my side much of the afternoon, and he presented the new couple with a book of Japanese legends from the two of us.

School carried on, and as always, we started the morning by reciting the Lord's Prayer and singing "God Save the King." Mr. Blackwell had brought a large rolled map with him from Vancouver, and this was hung on the dividing wall between classrooms. He used a pointer, and pointed to all of the pink areas and said, "This is the Empire, and we are proud to belong to it." There was a round globe on a stand on the other side of the classroom, and Keiko sometimes pointed out the names of countries as we spun the globe during our breaks for lunch or recess.

Mr. Blackwell was a kind teacher but he insisted that we work hard. He also decided, that year, to give us new names. He told us it was difficult for "white" people to pronounce Japanese names, so he gave us English names. I was called Benjamin Okuma the rest of the time I was at that school. Sometimes, he called me Ben. The following year, Mr. Blackwell stayed on and taught the upper grades. That is when he changed Hiroshi and Keiko's names to Henry and Kay. Okuma-san and the other children continued to call me Bin. I did not like being called Benjamin at school, and sometimes I forgot to look up when Mr. Blackwell called out the English name he had given me.

All our lessons were in English now, even though Miss Mori had sometimes spoken the Japanese language when she was teaching. Mr. Blackwell, however, insisted: English in the classroom and English in the schoolyard. Some children did not speak Japanese at all; others began to learn English only when they first started school.

There were evening classes now, too—these provided extra help for high school students—as well as community classes for adults. Classes were offered in drama, dance, sewing, carpentry, singing and calligraphy. Uncle Aki had persuaded Auntie Aya to take one of the classes, and she said she would try calligraphy. She had done this before, when she'd lived in Washington, and she would try again. But only if Uncle Aki accompanied her to the classes.

At Okuma-san's, once my homework was done in the evenings, I was permitted to do as I wished until bedtime. There were books on his shelves, perhaps even more books than there were in my classroom. The textbooks and readers at school had to be shared because there weren't enough to go around. These were the same texts that every other child in British Columbia was using, and they had been ordered through the Security Commission's purchasing office. But in Okuma-san's shack, the books were different in every way.

I began to take them down, one at a time, to examine them closely. There was one about animals I especially liked, and Okuma-san read the accompanying stories to me. When I was alone, I turned the pages slowly and made up my own stories to go with the pictures. These were not animals such as the ones that lived in the woods and mountains around the camp. These were not wild horses that galloped between the rows of shacks on spring and summer mornings, or chipmunks that darted among tree trunks, or black bears that ambled up on the Bench. These were not loping coyotes silhouetted on the ridges of surrounding hills. This book was populated by monkeys and badgers and hares and crabs and foxes, and sparrows that danced on their tails and held fans tucked to their wings. Some animals wore kimono-like robes and *geta*, wooden clogs, on their feet, and some were full of mischief. They especially liked to trick one another.

Okuma-san told me what he knew about these creatures. He also told stories that were not in his books, but that he had heard as a boy. Sometimes he talked about people he had met long ago while travelling in the big world I had never seen. When he spoke about his travels, I pictured the spinning globe in the schoolhouse and imagined Okuma-san in a small boat, paddling over its round surface, crossing seas with ease, pulling up on the shore of one foreign land after another.

★

OKUMA-SAN HAD BEEN an only child, born in Victoria just before the turn of the century. His parents were importers of silk and tea, and they had owned a store that did very good business. The school he attended in Victoria had divided classrooms: Japanese and Chinese children on one side, Caucasian children—*hakujin*—on the other. The same divisions existed in the play area outside. A fence split the schoolyard down the middle: Japanese and Chinese children at one end, *hakujin* children at the other. That was the way things were then, Okuma-san explained. He had always hoped that the *hakujin* children would accept him as he grew older, but Japanese children played together and *hakujin* children did the same.

After supper, in the evenings, Okuma-san's father liked to sit on a chair by the front door outside the small bungalow where they lived in Victoria, smoking a cigarette and watching the goings-on of the street. The cigarettes he smoked were hand-rolled and inserted into the end of a yellow-stained ivory holder. The father smoked one cigarette per night, always after supper. He puffed slowly and did not allow anyone to disturb him while he smoked. If it was raining, he stood in the doorway to stay dry.

When Okuma-san was nine years old, his father decided to travel to Japan to visit the companies he dealt with in his business, and he took Okuma-san along to learn something about the country of his ancestors. They sailed on a freighter, and Okuma-san described that stormy voyage with huge waves crashing over the ship's bow. He was told to stay below in his bunk, and was not permitted to climb the steps to the outer deck because the wind was so strong he might be lifted off his feet and blown over the side. When he became seasick, one of the crew members gave his father a chunk of ginger root and told him to have Okuma-san drink warm tea made from the grated root. After he drank this, the seasickness went away.

When he and his father arrived in Japan after the difficult journey, they visited the village where his late grandparents had been born. He was told stories of his grandfather, who had gone out in a boat every day to catch fish. The grandfather had been a fisherman all his life, but he couldn't bear to touch the scales and skin of the fish he caught. He could not bear even the smell of the fish.

Here, I interrupted. I knew about fishermen and how they came in and out of the bay in the fishing village where I had been born. I knew about the stink of fish on First Father's clothes when he used to return to our house after fishing up and down the coast for weeks.

"Well, then, if he couldn't touch the fish, how did your grandfather get them off his boat?" I asked. "He would have to sell them, wouldn't he?" I had never heard of such a fisherman.

"I was told that he wore special gloves made from rubber when he handled the fish," Okuma-san replied. "And when he became ill from the stench, he leaned over the side of his boat and emptied his stomach. But he remained a fisherman because it brought him a good living."

It wasn't the sea that claimed the lives of Okuma-san's grandparents. They had died of a contagious disease, the name of which he did not know. He thought it might have been cholera. They had died within days of each other.

During that trip to Japan, Okuma-san was taken to Osaka by his father, who made the decision to leave him there so that he could attend school for a year. Okuma-san boarded with an older British missionary couple. Okuma-san's father wanted him to learn about Japan in school, but he also wanted him to continue to speak English.

His father said he would be back in one year to bring him home. He promised that Okuma-san's mother would accompany him when he returned the following year.

Okuma-san was amazed to live in a place where everyone was Japanese, and he enjoyed walking through the streets without being noticed. It was the first time he had not been surrounded by Caucasian faces, even though he was living with a *hakujin* couple.

But at the Japanese school he attended, things did not turn out quite so well. His teacher, his *Sensei,* was ill-mannered and short-tempered. He had dark eyebrows like bushes grown thick to keep outsiders from peering in to see the world of his thoughts. Okuma-san did not like the teacher or the school. He was taunted by other Japanese boys because he was different, and because he had come from a land across the ocean where none of the other boys had been. The Japanese he spoke was unlike that of the others, and this, too, gave him trouble. He had a hard time making friends. The man and woman with whom he boarded, a childless couple by the name of Dowson, were kind to him and treated him like a son. Still, he looked forward to the day his parents would return so that he could leave the school he disliked so much. His father and mother sent him two letters during the year: the first told him how much he was missed; the second gave their approximate arrival date and the name of the freighter on which they would be sailing. His father was going to meet with new business partners, because he had decided to import Japanese dishes, as well as silk and tea.

But the freighter never arrived in Japan. It went down in a storm in the Pacific, and Okuma-san became an orphan before his tenth birthday. The missionaries, Mr. and Mrs. Dowson, tried to get information, and when it was finally confirmed that his parents were dead, they decided to adopt him. It was not difficult to obtain permission, because they were British and he was Canadian, and because he had been born in the Empire. They taught him about England and travelled with him to that country in the same year. After that, his education took place in the great capital of London.

I interrupted again. "I know where London is," I said. "King George lives there. Keiko showed me on the map at school. We have a picture of the King and Queen on the wall in our class and we sing 'God Save the King' every morning."

"Well, London is the place I lived," said Okuma-san. "And I sang the same anthem when I was a boy, and I walked past Buckingham Palace, where the King and Queen live, many times. When I was young, two other kings lived there: King Edward and a different King George."

But life had turned out differently for Okuma-san, because in London, he was still an outsider. He did not look like anyone in the streets or at school. He learned to be quiet and to stay out of trouble. Whenever he could, he stayed indoors and read books in the library so the boys would not taunt him in the schoolyard.

I had never been to such a place, and Okuma-san told me about the library at his London school and the public library not far from the house where he had lived with the Dowsons. He had walked through rooms lined with shelves from ceiling to floor, every shelf stacked with books. More books than he had ever seen.

From the time Okuma-san was first adopted in Japan, and later, after moving to England, Mrs. Dowson recognized his love of music and taught him to play piano in her home. When he was in his early teens, he was sent to an advanced teacher. After the end of the Great War, his adoptive father died. Mrs. Dowson was left with little income, but she sold her house and moved the two of them to a smaller place. Knowing it was Okuma-san's dream to continue to play piano, she provided him with enough money to travel to Vienna, where he spent the next three years studying music. He took extra classes in the German language at night. When his money ran out, he wrote to Mrs. Dowson to tell her he would have to come back to England. But the letter was returned to him by Mrs. Dowson's brother, who told him she had recently died. That was when Okuma-san decided to return to North America. Now that he was a young man, he wanted to see if he could make a life for himself in the country of his birth.

I listened to these stories because I had never considered the fact that Okuma-san had once been a boy. Now I was forced to learn that he had lost not one set of parents but two. I did not like the way parents kept dying in his stories, nor did I like to think of him as an orphan, which was what I considered myself—even though my first family lived just along the row of shacks, a short walk from our doorstep. But one thing was different. When Okuma-san was adopted, he had been allowed to keep his Okuma surname, whereas I had not been allowed to keep the surname Oda. Nor did I want to, not anymore. If First Father did not want me, I reasoned, then I did not want his name.

Although I listened carefully to the things that had happened to Okuma-san, I was also waiting to hear a different kind of story. I thought about how he had arrived late at the camp, almost two years after everyone else. I did not ask about his wife, the singer, because he seldom talked about her. I had heard Mother say that the lines in his face were there because of grief over his wife's death. But too many people died in his stories, and I did not want to hear more about death.

Then I thought of something else.

"Tell me about the bear," I said suddenly. "How did you catch the bear when you first moved here to the camp?" This had been on my mind for some time, but I had never asked. I wanted to go to school and tell Hiroshi and Keiko that I had finally found out.

"Ah," said Okuma-san. "It was fortunate for me that the bear cooperated."

But that was all he would say.

Two wooden blocks clapped together. The clean knock of sound arrested all other noise in the room. An unseen hand wound the camp gramophone and set the music spinning. Unrecognized fathers took their places on the raised wooden platform, and I knew that First Father was among them. At school, Hiroshi had told me that Mother had been sewing a costume during the past several weeks, helping to prepare for the *shibai*, the winter play.

The storyteller stepped forward slowly, an air of magnificence about him. He made us wait, taking time to settle himself on a stool at the edge of the lantern-lit stage. A black curtain slid away from a painted backdrop and fell into darkness. No longer did I see a rough platform on wooden props. No longer did I see fisherman, farmer, mill hand, carpenter, cannery worker, storekeeper, factory hand. Instead, I saw imposing figures, the whirl of dark robes, makeup and mask, watercolours, banners of calligraphy fluttering before my eyes.

The story unfolded; a brand-new script had been created. All the roles, including women's, were acted by the men. They had been practising for weeks, ever since the end of harvest. In the school-house, after hours, props had been constructed and painted, and these had been pushed against the walls of the community room and covered over so we could not see what was on the backdrops before it was time for the performance. Even Okuma-san had put on his heavy coat and disappeared on weekends, working in secret alongside other men who were painting and nailing boards and planning the entertainment for this December night.

How we laughed, how we laughed, how our hands flew to our mouths. Between scenes, while backdrops were being changed, two men came out and sat at the front of the stage. Each man wore baggy trousers, *hakama,* and *tabi,* split-toe socks. They faced each other and held a running conversation and told jokes that made us laugh some more. One man held out a ripe banana, began to peel it slowly and carefully, and then tapped the side of his hand. A neat slice fell off. He tapped his hand again and another slice fell, the same size as the first. Everyone in the audience was roaring with laughter, but while I was laughing, tears rolled down my cheeks. The second man began to catch the slices, until finally, the banana skin was empty. How could this happen? I wiped my eyes. I couldn't understand. It was only when I was older that I was shown the trick of piercing the skin of an unpeeled banana in layers, beforehand, with a long needle, making a steady stitch all the way around—an invisible stitch that would not be seen by the audience.

Auntie Aya and Uncle Aki were seated in the row in front of me, and Auntie Aya was wearing a new navy dress with a sparkly belt that Mother had made for her from material Uncle Aki had ordered from Eaton's. It was the first time I had seen my aunt all dressed up. In the winter months there was no place to go anyway, except to visit from one shack to another. Apart from her calligraphy classes, she rarely left her shack. When she did go out, Uncle Aki was right beside her, hovering near, as always.

When the second act of the play was over, everyone clapped and clapped and protested and called for more, but the curtain was pulled and closed. The actors had run out of script. The jokes had been spent. The evening had come to an end.

When we'd entered the crowded community room at the beginning of the evening, Okuma-san had ensured that I would be seated next to Mother and my brother and sister. Ba and Ji were farther along in the same row. Ba had patted her thick pocket, where the end of a new envelope could be seen sticking out—another letter from the place called Manzanar. She was extra happy this night, because Sachi and Tom had written that they were expecting their first baby in April. This would be the first grandchild for Ba and Ji.

While we were all enjoying the entertainment, I had not once thought about missing my family. In fact, in the crowd of people and without thinking, I had inched my chair closer to Mother, as if I were part of my first family again.

Everyone was in high spirits at the end of the play, putting on coats and mittens and scarves, waving and calling out farewells, heading for the door. First Father remained behind in the community room because he had been one of the actors. As we were leaving, he was sprawled on the platform stage with the other players, half in and half out of costume. They had already begun to celebrate, some of them having stored homemade potato *sake* for this special night. For weeks, it had been brewing and fermenting with lemons and sugar, hidden away in heavy crocks in earth cellars dug into the side of the hill.

When we were outside in the cold again, I automatically followed Mother and Hiroshi and Keiko. They were ahead, halfway down the row, before they heard the crunch of footsteps on the snow behind them. They stopped, and Mother half-turned. When she saw me still making my way towards her, she shook her head, almost imperceptibly. When I caught up, she put her hands on my shoulders and turned me to face the direction from which we'd come. I looked back towards Okuma-san's shack, which we had passed at the end of the row. My second father was standing by his door, staring at us, looking as if he had lost his way. His head was wrapped in a scarf, his face expressionless. I felt a small push between my shoulders and heard Mother's voice say softly, "You are sure to sleep well tonight, Bin. It has been such a happy night for all of us."

She continued on her way and I was left, caught between the two shacks.

I stood without moving. The mountains leaned in on all sides. The other families had quickly disappeared inside their homes, and I was alone on the path. I had to force myself to drag my feet towards Okuma-san. The excitement that had pulled me along behind my first family now deserted me, and I was stranded like an island in the midst of cross-currents that overlapped in the same stream.

The wind was blowing hard as Okuma-san and I stomped the snow from our boots and went inside. I began to prepare for bed, and climbed under the covers without saying good night. I was feeling badly, but I didn't know what to say. As I lay there, I could hear the rattling of loose boards up and down the rows of shacks. The wind always howled more at night, and Okuma-san once suggested that I listen to it as a kind of music. Wind music that played against the roof, the tarpaper, the ill-fitting floorboards with frost on the nailheads, the doors, even the trees. For him, he said, the wind swayed and rocked the trees as if they were outdoor instruments being finely tuned.

From behind the curtain that divided bedroom from kitchen, I heard his footsteps, followed by a dragging sound and a creak, which I knew to mean that he had lowered himself to his chair and was balancing the keyboard. As if I were beside him, I could see in my mind how he would be relaxing his shoulders, adjusting his knees, wiggling his feet and planting them flat to the floor. His upper body would dip forward, the way it always did when he began.

If he was about to play what he said was called the Hammer-klavier, I knew his head would be bowed. I tensed then and waited for the sound of his hands to come down hard against the plank. The fierceness of the beginning always startled me, no matter how prepared I tried to be. Then I heard his hands moving in a different way as they made a hollow tapping up and down the length of the silent keyboard. Not silent, because playing against wood was far from silent, even from where I lay in my bed. Okuma-san's fingers were entering what I had come to think of as a frenzied race towards a place so far away it could not be reached, not even by him. This rapid movement of fingers and hands went on for some time and then there was a pause, and after that his hands slowed and paused and slowed again.

I was becoming sleepy, and the sound of the wind began to blend with the insistent rapping of fingers. I thought of Hiroshi and Keiko getting ready for bed in their shack farther along the row. I imagined them wearing the same kind of pyjamas I had on—the ones Mother had made for the three of us from flannel sheets. I knew that Keiko had her own bed now, because she had told me so at school.

"My cot is at the end of the kitchen," she had said. And then she'd laughed and added, "At night, I'm the warmest one in the family because I sleep closest to the stove. Hiroshi still sleeps in the bedroom. Where we all used to sleep before . . ."

She'd stopped abruptly, as if she had blurted out too much.

I pictured all of this while I was buried under the blankets I had pulled up over my ears. I pictured First Father getting home after the celebration, maybe staggering a little as he checked the stove, his last ritual before sleep. I knew that he, like Okuma-san, would have to get up in the night to add more wood.

Not so easy to conjure at this moment was Mother, who had turned me away, even though I had pushed my chair close to hers during the play. I knew that she was still my mother, and that there was no mother in the house of my second father. I listened to the wind both inside and out while I was thinking of her. And as I was dropping off to sleep, I wondered if, at exactly the same moment, she was also thinking of me.

CHAPTER 21

1997

Sweeping along Saskatchewan prairie, I am surrounded by the sounds of the *Missa Solemnis,* the great and glorious Mass. *From the heart! May it go to the heart.* Beethoven's message, written in his own hand above the Kyrie. As I do every time I listen, I wait for the burst of passion that marks its beginnings.

In the camp, Okuma-san said, "When we are out of this place"—he had been trying to tell me about the Mass—"you and I might someday hear this wonderful music together. When you are older, we might even be fortunate enough to attend a live performance. The beginning of the *Missa Solemnis* has a way of entering the spirit all at once and then holding it captive until the last note."

It would not be until the late fifties that I would hear a Toscanini record of the Mass, when Okuma-san and I listened to what seemed to be sounds funnelled from many places into one place, the choir swelling into the room where we sat. And now it's as if I am compelled to hear this, and every one of Beethoven's works, through Okuma-san's ears and in the context of his stories. *It is a big work,*

222

Beethoven wrote. Simply that. Nothing about the nearly four years of its creation, the dedication, the countless delays. By the time it was finished, Beethoven was in his fifties. I've sometimes wondered what he felt at its completion. Numbed, perhaps. When I listen, I think of how he had to witness its performance in Vienna. He was unable to hear a note of it. Three years later, in 1827, just when the music was finally being published, he was dead.

As the *Missa Solemnis* soars inside the car, I open a back window slightly and let the music escape outside. I had been thinking of a drawing Greg worked on one Sunday morning when he was a child. Lena and I were still in bed and he was patiently waiting for his breakfast. He drew a man lying on the ground, an ambulance door open beside him. A light on top of the ambulance, with rays to denote flashing, had been filled in with red crayon. The caption read: IT IS BEST TO KEEP A PRSON WARM WEN HE HAS A HART ATTAK.

I listen again and look out at the prairie landscape. I have driven north as far as I want to go on this cool and sunny day. I stop the car, turn, and begin to travel south and west again, mainly west, where I'll rejoin the main highway that leads to Alberta. For some time now, I have been passed by snow geese that are holding up the limitless sky, line after wavering line, as they migrate north. Now there are more and more, and they begin to land in farmers' fields on both sides of the highway, the vees overlapping until they've become an assemblage of sinuous shapes.

While this is going on around me, Basil begins to pace. He starts dashing from one side of the car to the other, sniffing the air repeatedly. He keeps trying to force his nose into the gap where I've lowered the back window. If I stop again, there's no telling what he will do. Run to the fields, ears flapping, bellowing for sure. I'd never get him back.

A new sound begins to break the silence of earth and sky. It is a chattering of thousands that can be heard from more than a mile away. The earth where the geese land becomes a moving mass of white. Then an entire field seems to rise suddenly into the air. The geese have been startled, perhaps by a fox. And though many separate flocks are on the ground, they surge upwards as if they are one, and swerve in a wide U-turn to regroup. It's as if a lasso has rounded them up in the sky. There is a jostling of position while they assume the same direction, and then they land again. Their continuous noisy chatter can be heard inside the car, even over the Gloria of the Mass.

I wish Greg, with his love of the natural world, were able to witness this astonishing sight. But he is on the East Coast, witnessing his own astonishments. And here, above Basil and me, the migration goes on all day, thousands upon thousands of white geese, black wingtips flashing.

I slow, take my time and listen to the sustaining power of the final movement—described as the prayer for inner and outer peace.

*

DURING THE LAST EVENING of that first trip we made to Prince Edward Island in the early eighties, the three of us took a walk along the beach for a mile or so. "To say goodbye to the sea," Greg told Lena as we stepped out of the mobile home and made our way over dunes and down the side of the cliff. "But only for now. Because I'm going to remember this place, and hold it inside of me until we come back next year. We *are* coming back, aren't we?"

To which Lena replied, "I see it all now—and for the rest of time. I'm living with a man who is obsessed with rivers, a boy who loves the sea. We'll be planning every holiday from now on around rivers. Or oceans. Or rivers that empty into oceans."

The sky was dull when we set out, the vaguest of suns showing itself in a haze at the approach of sunset. Strips of horizontal cloud were stretched across the western sky like iron bars. The bottom half of the sun disappeared all at once, leaving the upper half stranded in an inverted silly smile. It was the only notable shape in that vast grey space. Cormorants flew low over the waves, their migration having begun. Greg was thrilled that he had recently learned to identify them. While tagging after Albert on the farm, he'd been taught to differentiate between cormorants and geese.

"They both fly in vee formations," Albert had told him, pointing out past the shore. "From here, they look pretty much the same size, do you see? But the wild geese never coast. Their wings never stop flapping. A cormorant will pause now and then, and coast. That's how you tell them apart."

There was still a bit of light during our walk, and Lena said she was turning back because she wanted to start in on the packing. The sky was changing again, and clouds had begun to spin out from the setting sun. Greg and I continued for a while, sandpipers scurrying ahead comically, miniature busybodies with white rings around their necks. We were intent on reaching a promontory where the red cliffs jutted sharply into the sea. Mostly, we were silent, listening to the ebbing waves and paying attention to what had washed up on the sand since our last walk. Just before we reached the point, we came across a tidal pool that was shrinking rapidly but, at the same time, creating numerous shallow puddles some twenty or thirty feet back from shore. In the puddles, hundreds upon hundreds of small herring were trapped. The tide was going out quickly. The once wide rivulet through which the herring had swum in from the sea had left its outlines, but it was now clogged with sand and the exit was blocked. It was obvious that the herring were doomed, because the pools that contained them were too far back from shore. There was no hope of reopening the rivulet; it had closed long before we'd arrived. And now that the water was being absorbed, hundreds, maybe thousands, of small fish were abandoned on the surface of the sand.

Greg began to scoop them up, his bare hands turning to liquid silver as he ran to the edge of the sea to dump them in. Back and forth he raced, saving as many as his small hands could hold. When he saw how little progress he was making, he tried to scoop the flopping bodies into his sunhat, running to the sea and returning to the shrinking puddles. I helped him for a while, sickened by the hopelessness of the drama we'd become a part of. We could not keep up. There were too many tiny fish. Too big a school, too many stranded.

In exhaustion, and finally acknowledging what I already knew, Greg plunked himself down on the sand. His knees were bent up, his head down. His skin was almost nut brown from the sun and he looked like a sea creature himself.

I heard a curse. "Goddamn," he said. That tiny, lean boy. He was struck down in defeat. It was a defeat for me, too, because I could not see any way to help him. He'd have been insulted if I had said, "It's an accident of nature and we have stumbled upon it and we are witness to it and there is nothing more we can do."

I thought of Okuma-san, who had always been there in the background when I was a young boy. Somewhere near. Instructing, caring. Hovering, the way Uncle Aki hovered over Auntie Aya. What would Okuma-san have done in this situation? He would have allowed Greg the dignity of silence.

It was dark when we turned and made our way back, the living-room light in the trailer acting as a beacon on the cliff to guide us forward. Greg's narrow heels dug into hard, damp sand, leaving a trail of dogged footprints.

At bedtime, my son, who had been born old, looked up from his pillow and said, "I'm not so sure I want to live in an unjust world."

To which I had no reply.

The death of the herring did not deter Greg. His love affair with the sea having begun, he became all the more determined to learn about the creatures that live within. Lena and I supplied books and recordings. He began to take tapes to school, sharing songs of the humpback whales. At home he sat in the reading chair, wearing oversized earphones while leafing through his new books and singing heartily along with the whales. In an exercise book he brought home from school, he printed: *I have a reckrd with sownds of a humpback whale. I'm going to be a marine bologist. I love sea mammals. They are frendly that's why.*

When the teacher asked the class to make two lists, one of things they could do and one of things they couldn't, Greg printed in his book:

THINGS I CAN DO: think, sing, giggle, subtract, swim, love the sea

THINGS I CAN'T DO: fly, juggle, drive, hate the sea

At dinner one evening, he crossed his hands over his chest and declared that in place of his heart were whales and dolphins. That was where he was holding his love.

CHAPTER 22

1945

By the beginning of 1945, the windows at Okuma-san's had frosted over and we would not see through them again until spring. Thick needles of frost had built up inside the walls; Okuma-san held a chair and steadied it while I stood on the seat and broke off the larger brittle needles near the ceiling. Like every other tarpaper shack in camp, ours was not airtight, though Okuma-san had done what he could to seal the cracks. At night, the boards snapped and groaned and the place breathed with a hoary rasp. I'd become used to the winter noises here, in the way I had been familiar with distinctive sounds in my earlier homes: the tide seeping up under the house of my birth on Vancouver Island; the winds gusting through the boards and knotholes in the home of my first family.

There had been recent changes in our camp. Four families had packed up their meagre belongings and departed the first week of December. They left their homemade furniture behind and travelled together, all of them heading for Ontario. Their shacks were now being used for storage of wood and for food that could be kept frozen.

The United Church had helped these families to find work—two of the older girls would be domestics; their parents were to be caretakers and short-order cooks. One man was to have a job working for a laundry, another for an optical company.

Ba and Ji had received a new letter from California. Sachi wrote that half the population, almost five thousand prisoners, had now left Manzanar. Unlike Canada, the United States had decided to permit Japanese Americans to return to the West Coast. Despite this, many were moving east because their homes in the coastal regions were no longer available to them, and their jobs were gone. Sachi's husband, Tom, had applied for a job in Nebraska, using his engineering background, and that was where they were heading. Although Sachi was expecting the baby in April, she was going to try to get temporary work as a steno, to help with the income after they settled.

Since Christmas, two babies had been born in our camp. Ba had helped with the deliveries, and both babies were girls. The parents had to keep the wood in the oil-drum stoves piled high and burning constantly to make certain that the new babies would be warm enough.

Also, a man had died of pneumonia—one of the elders. I hated to use the outdoor toilets at any time, but when someone died I became worried about the footless ghosts that were said to gather in the woods behind the building, even though I still hadn't seen one.

As for the war, it wasn't any easier than before to get news about what was happening either in Europe or in the Pacific. There was still no radio in camp. We did learn, from letters, that many Japanese Canadian men had been recruited to work with the British and Australian armies. And that the Canadian army needed men to teach the Japanese language to soldiers who would be working in Pacific operations.

For a few days, our worries were set aside because New Year's Day was the biggest celebration of all. It was the custom for families to visit back and forth for two or three days over this period. On New Year's Eve, I ran back to the house of my first family because I was allowed to bathe in the bathhouse with Hiroshi and Keiko on this special night. We scrubbed extra hard, remembering the warning of the adults: anyone who forgot to bathe before midnight would turn into an owl.

Everyone in camp, including Okuma-san, had been making special foods and there was a festive air, despite the bitter cold. Mother came to visit, and helped with *sushi* making. Okuma-san put a chicken in the pot—our contribution to the larger celebration that would take place in the community room of the schoolhouse, where lanterns were hung from the ceiling and long tables and benches set out for the feast on New Year's Day.

My gift from Mother was a shirt, one of Hiroshi's that had been cut down and resewn. She also gave me a new pair of thick knitted socks and a navy blue bow tie. If the tie had been cut down from one that had belonged to First Father, I was never to know.

Okuma-san had something for me when I woke on the first day of 1945. It was a surprise, hidden on a shelf behind his books, and I wondered how I had not known it was there waiting for me. After I dressed on this special day, and put on my bow tie, and wet my hair and parted it with a comb, Okuma-san presented me with a small brown box, about four inches long and two inches high. He took it down from the shelf and held it out in both palms. He placed it in front of me, on the table.

"Lift the cover," he said. He was smiling.

A half-moon indent on either side of the box permitted me to lift the lid with one hand while holding the bottom section in the other. Tucked inside was cream-coloured paper, tightly rolled and shaped like a cylinder. So neatly did this roll fit the space, the box had to be turned upside down to free it. A thin black ribbon attached to the outer edge had been wrapped around the roll several times to keep it from unravelling.

"This is a scroll, a scroll painting," said Okuma-san, not without pleasure. He helped me unfurl the crisp, curled paper, and showed me how to use my right hand as an anchor. With my left, I rolled the scroll down the length of the table.

"I think you will want to see what this artist drew a long time ago. Eight hundred years ago. Can you imagine so much time going by? It is a famous piece of art in Japan. And here we are, sitting at a table in this camp in British Columbia, looking at the work."

I said to myself, "Eight hundred years." But so much time was a vagueness that was not easily pictured.

Okuma-san went on. "The artist was probably a priest. He might have lived in a monastery. This is not the original, but a copy. I treasure it because it was a gift from my father when he first took me with him to Japan when I was a boy. It was given to me before he boarded the ship to return to Canada. As I have told you, my parents were lost at sea during their voyage back to get me the following year." He added this so softly, I wondered what else he was remembering from that time. But he continued.

"The artist drew the scroll with brush and ink. What we have here is the colour of charcoal. The paper is darker than it was at one time, because I opened it so many times when I was a child."

I was anxious to keep unfurling. My right hand was secure as an anchor, but as the scroll opened, it became longer than my left arm could reach. I saw, too, that at the centre, a wooden dowel was attached to the inner edge. The wood for the dowel, said Okuma-san, had come from a cherry tree. He helped me to steady the unravelling scroll so it would not spring closed suddenly or fall to the floor. Once it was open all the way, he held the dowel and rewound the scroll so that we could start at the beginning again. This time, I scrolled left, slowly, by myself, and paid more attention to what the artist had drawn and to what the story was about. The opening images were of grasses and shadowy lines suggestive of hills and tree trunks. Animals were playing in water, perhaps a lake. The water then narrowed and might even have been a rolling river that flowed in the background.

The animals that splashed and played were rabbits and monkeys and frogs. Two monkeys were scratching each other's back. The rabbits—hares, Okuma-san called them—were diving and swimming around the edges of the scroll. There were hills on either side of the wavy lines that depicted the river. The hills were drawn in simple strokes, soft and grey.

I stared. How was it possible to show a tree blowing in the wind this way, with only a few dark lines and a bit of shading? I watched the animals frolic down the length of the table while Okuma-san helped reroll the parts I had already seen. In this way, the two of us controlled the speed at which the pictures were displayed and, at the same time, kept the scroll from slipping off the edge of the table. A monkey raced in and out of the scene, among the frogs and hares, holding a switch in his hand while he ran. The river faded; a road began. A fox at the edge stood like a human and held his full, bushy tail between his legs. A large frog was shouting at the fox, and another hare suddenly appeared. I continued to unfurl, and saw a large lily pad tied to a frame made from branches. The lily pad was being used as a target for bow-and-arrow practice. Hares and frogs were in separate groups, aiming their arrows and testing their bows as if for a competition.

Leafless trees showed the passage of time and distance; these were deliberately spaced and rugged and blowing helter-skelter. After that, the hares began to dominate the activity. There were long-whiskered hares with short-tufted tails; hares with fans, or with cages they carried suspended from long poles; hares with fishing rods made from branches; hares talking, laughing, running, leading a deer with a long rein, inspecting a tied and captured boar. Badgers and monkeys squatted comically, wearing loose robes. A dead frog was sprawled on its back. There was a chase, a dance, tiny mice peering around the edges of the scene. I felt that I could make up my own story. I could create many stories from the pictures. Trees and shrubs began to leaf and flower as the scroll went on, but a single line of hill was always constant in the background. And then, all the animals in the foreground began to roll on the ground with laughter. Or so it seemed. A sober monkey sat smoking; a frog in the lotus position sat on a tabletop. An owl perched on the branch of a gnarled tree; a series of dots and marks showed the owl's feathers. An outdoor feast was set up to the left of the tree. Picnic foods were spread out on a table and the spread continued along the ground.

I loved the simple lines of the scroll, the frenzy of activity, animals posing as humans, reading, smoking, eating, singing. The last of the figures, a solemn and important-looking frog, was carrying a rolled scroll that looked very much like my own.

Okuma-san was pleased that I liked my gift, I could tell. And I had something for him. Something I had drawn in secret at school and hidden in my desk. It was my own childish picture of the bear. Not the dead, upside-down hanging bear, the one that sometimes opened its jaws and gnawed its way into my nightmares, but a living bear. One that had raised its large head only a moment before to sniff out some danger that could not be seen with its small, dark eyes.

After the holiday, when school started again, rumour, confusion and fear were once more being stirred up. The war would soon be over. Japan was going to be defeated. The camps would close. The camps would not close. We would be allowed to return to our homes. We would not be allowed to return. Other people, *hakujin* people, lived in our houses now. Fishermen's lives had changed forever. Japanese Canadian fishermen no longer had licences to fish. No one had boats; no one owned a car. If we did move, where would the men find work? Where would we move anyway, if the war did end?

And then, not many weeks later, something that was not a rumour had to be talked about. RCMP officers arrived from the town and asked to meet with the heads of families. Word was quickly sent around from shack to shack, and the men gathered in the community room. They were told that every family would have to sign a paper offering two choices: the first was "repatriation," which meant authorized expulsion and exile to Japan, a country only a handful of people in the camp had ever seen; the alternative was to agree to "relocate" east of the Rocky Mountains.

Of course, everyone was upset by this turn of events. Four men who lived in the camp came to our shack after the meeting, because they wanted to talk things over with Okuma-san. I opened the door for them and they sat around our table. One of the men looked over at me, but Okuma-san said, "My son knows what is going on. He may hear whatever we have to say. Our decisions will affect him, too."

What were the men to do? They were angry. No one understood this new demand. It was clear that we weren't wanted in the province, but why would anyone be sent to Japan? That was not our country. We were citizens here. We had agreed to move into the camps and get off the coast because we were given no choice after Pearl Harbor. What more was wanted of us?

Okuma-san listened quietly as the men said what they were thinking.

"We have to have more information," he said. "I will do what I can to find out more from the RCMP, the next time they come to the camp."

After the men left, Okuma-san took out his own worries on the keyboard plank. Every evening now, after our supper meal, we went through the ritual of clearing the table and washing the rice pot and storing the dishes. Okuma-san placed paper and pencils—sometimes pen, nib and ink—before me at one end of the table. When my homework was done, I could draw or read until bedtime. I was expected to say if I needed help with homework. Otherwise, he pulled out the keyboard, settled it on the trestles and once again began to practise the piece he returned to most often, the Hammer-klavier, the one with which he was never satisfied. This was a "sonata," he had told me.

What the sonata meant to me was the rapping of fingers for an extraordinarily long time. When it was in progress, Okuma-san was in a dream state and I was kept far outside of this. I knew he was unaware of me watching. At times, a look of melancholy—perhaps even pain—came over his face, and at first I was worried. But then his face would be calm again, as if he could hear, at that moment, what no one else could. I was always glad that we had eaten before he began, even though I stayed at the kitchen table, not daring to speak during the better part of an hour. I looked at the clock, and the hands were not moving. I fidgeted a little in my chair, but it was clear to me that even this distraction was not acceptable. If I were to ask a question, it would not be answered. Okuma-san was not present, not really. So I drew, or watched, while his fingers raced up and down the ponderosa pine. If a book had been placed on the table, I pulled it towards me and turned the pages as silently as I could.

There was a pause, another pause, and then a gentle flowing movement over the painted keyboard. This movement, the one that made his hands almost float, sometimes made me think of the great river below the camp. At other times, one of his hands seemed to reply to the other. For a while, his fingers trilled against the plank so rapidly I could not keep track of any particular rhythm. At other times, the sense of peace was so overwhelming, it filled the room.

The left hand rumbled up the keyboard from the lower end. Okuma-san's foot made an involuntary forward movement. His hands came to rest. There was stillness.

Again, he was not satisfied.

"I hear the music," he said softly. "But my hands do not move the way they should. That means I do not perform the way I want to. It is my left hand that gives me trouble, a foolish fall many years ago. It happened suddenly, but a bone fractured and then rehealed. It meant that I would never again play the way I had played before the fall. But even before that, the piece was always difficult to play."

He went on. "Think of the many times you have tried to draw wild horses, or even the big river. It is like that with music, too. If you draw the river, you want to transfer what you know you have inside yourself to a single sheet of paper. You want to work with the white space of the page; you want to create light and flow, mist and current. You especially want to capture spirit. But as you have already learned, these things are difficult, which does not mean that you stop trying. There is good reason to try again, to move forward, to make the attempt to accomplish what you have not been able to do before. There is always good reason to keep trying."

I did not know what to say. I thought of the river and my feeble attempts to draw it. I thought of the island, where I had been taken on First Father's back. That time was far away. The picnic with my previous family was part of a world I had dreamed. Like our fishing village on the coast. That, too, belonged in a world entirely different from the one in which I woke up in a freezing shack every morning.

Okuma-san turned back to the keyboard. Most of the time when he tried to play this sonata, he looked at notes on the pages of sheet music. Sometimes, he tried to play parts from memory. He told me that even though the sonata was called the Hammerklavier, that was not what Beethoven had intended. The great composer, he said, had wanted the German word *Hammerklavier* to be used for his piano sonatas, instead of the Italian *pianoforte*. But the word became attached to this particular sonata, No. 29, and it was thereafter referred to as the Hammerklavier.

"One hundred and six," he said. "That is the opus number. Do you know what *opus* means?"

I shook my head, knowing the answer was coming.

"Numbers are assigned to the works of a composer," said Okuma-san. "This sonata was given the opus number of 106. Beethoven wrote it during a period of poor health. He was in so much pain all the time, a substance made of tree bark was put on his arms. But then he couldn't move his arms. Herbs were put on his belly. He took cold baths. There was humming and buzzing in his ears. And he had little money to support himself. Of course," he added, "by then, he was deaf and he had become reclusive, but his genius could not be held back."

Okuma-san's left hand occasionally became swollen because of connecting with wood that had no give to it, on painted keys that did not depress in response to the pressure of his fingers. At those times, he asked me to soak a towel in a basin of warm water and to bring it to him, especially after the Hammerklavier. Sometimes I watched the clock. And when I recognized the rhythmic raps on the keyboard and knew the ending was near, I poured water and brought the towel before I was asked. I watched while Okuma-san wrapped it around his hand to let the moisture soothe his skin and help the swelling go down. Streaks of red appeared along the length of both thumbs and on the inside of his wrists. His palms, which became mottled, remained like that for hours, but he did not seem to notice.

Throughout the long winter, the stove was lit all the time and the air inside the shack was dry. So dry, the edge of one of Okuma-san's thumbs split open. He went to a shelf and took down a tin can with a lid. Inside was his sewing kit: a thimble, a package of needles and two spools of thread—one black, one white. He sat on a chair by the table, and with coarse black thread and a needle, he sewed his own thumb, forcing the needle through his toughened skin. Once the needle had punctured the edge of the open wound, and before he could bring himself to push it through the opposing edge, his partly sewn hand pulsed in the air, palm up. A low moan, "Uh uh uh," came from his lips and I scrunched my eyes, believing, sometimes, that I was feeling the needle, too. He closed his eyes and pushed the needle through again, repeating the process until enough stitches crisscrossed the wound and closed it.

All of this became an ordinary part of my life during the winter

months: to sit and draw; to read or dream while listening to the rapping of music that my second father heard inside his head, and that
came out on the smoothed plank of pine through his moving fingers
and his swollen, stitched hands.

CHAPTER 23

1945–46

The weather was warmer, the season changing. With the approach of spring, there was much to talk about. The paper every family had to sign had become real and threatening. The paper represented what was known as the "dispersal policy." All conversations, no matter what else was being discussed, ended with talk about the demands made and how to act in response.

Okuma-san asked if I wanted to go to the river one Sunday, and the two of us set out after lunch. On our way past the communal gardens, we greeted several men who were burning heaps of tumbleweed that had blown in and around the rows during the winter months. Flames leapt high as they crackled, and there was a sweet scent around us while the brittle weed scattered sparks into the air.

We hiked down the steep trail, with Okuma-san in the lead. He had placed a special order for me with Ying several weeks before, and Ying, in turn, had sent to Vancouver for a thin sketch pad of real art paper and a small box that held four sticks of charcoal. The entire pad was to be used for no other purpose than drawing, and it was the first sketch pad I had ever owned.

When we reached the bottom of the trail, I saw Okuma-san look intently towards the place where a small boy had drowned three weeks earlier. This was near the spot where First Father had once fished for sturgeon. The boy had fallen in and was swept away, his body never found. There had been a service in the community room of the school, and everyone in camp attended, crowding the room, the hall, the doorway, even the outside steps. I tried not to imagine the boy thrashing in panic in the water, but I could not keep the image from my mind. As if we were having a conversation of thoughts, Okuma-san now said, "Rivers sustain and nourish, yes, but they can also take life away." I did not reply. I did not know what *sustain* meant but I knew what it meant to say that a river could take someone's life. I had seen death in the camp: my baby cousin, Taro; several old people who had been cremated; and even the dead bear that had hung upside down behind Okuma-san's shack. Now there was another death: the boy who had fallen into the river and would never be returning to his parents' shack. This was one more ghost to worry about, a child ghost, footless, joining the others.

I settled myself on a flat rock and smelled the air around me and thought about this same rock shelf where Mother had sat and stretched her legs in the sun. I opened my new drawing pad to the first page and began to shade until lines resembling a riverbank appeared on the paper. Okuma-san stayed close by, reading a book while I drew. I tried first of all with a thick pencil and then I added charcoal, rubbing it sideways across the paper. I was thinking of the scroll I'd been given at the new year, and about the river that ran through it from end to end. Even though the river could not always be seen in the scroll, there was somehow a suggestion that it was there. Sure enough, a bump or a wavy line would reappear as the scroll was unrolled, and there it was again.

I was also thinking of Okuma-san telling me once that there were many different ways to draw. That it was all right to change the shapes I made on the page, that it was all right to alter them from what they started out to be. What I drew did not have to be the object that happened to be in front of me. It did not have to have the same edges or shape. I could look at the object as a starting point and use my imagination in any way I wished.

It was peaceful in that place, even with the roar of river beside us. And just as I was attempting to create an outline of the island, I heard footsteps crunching on the grit of the pathway that descended the embankment. At once, I recognized the father of the boy who had drowned. He stood near us and stared out over the river, which, when I looked, now appeared sullen and dark. He and Okuma-san quietly exchanged a few words and I heard them discussing the paper that everyone had to sign, choosing one path or another into the future. There was to be a meeting later that afternoon, in the community room in the schoolhouse. "Alone or together, we are helpless," the man said. "There is no place we are wanted."

"But it is pointless to allow the rage," Okuma-san said. "If we allow the rage, it will consume us."

The man shrugged and then turned to me and asked if he could see what I was drawing.

His request took me by surprise, and gave my drawing a sudden importance I did not want it to have. I was aware of his sadness, which could be seen on his face, but I became unsatisfied with what I was doing and did not want to show the page in my sketch pad to him or to anyone else. I closed the pad and turned it face down on the rock, and even put my hands over it, fearing that he would pick it up, or that he would take it away from me and examine the drawing.

Of course, he did no such thing. He smiled sadly and stood on shore for a few more minutes, looking out over the water. Then he turned and made his way back up the path.

After he left, I asked Okuma-san which family I was to be a part of when the important paper was signed.

"You are my family now," said Okuma-san. "You and I will remain in Canada. This is our country, and we will not be forced to leave."

I was glad to hear this, but I wondered about my first family. I did not want them to be on the other side of the wide blue stretch I had seen on the globe at school when I'd spun it around and stopped it abruptly, my finger landing on the Pacific Ocean. I did not want them to be so far away that I would never see them again.

Later that afternoon, after Okuma-san and I climbed the embankment and returned to the shack, I ripped out the page I had worked on by the river and crumpled it in my hand. I threw the drawing into the fire and burned it, right after Okuma-san left for the meeting. The men were to have one last discussion about the dispersal policy and the paper that had to be signed.

The next day, Hiroshi and Keiko came to me at school, and I learned that First Father had decided to take his chances and had signed the paper, agreeing to be sent to Japan, over which bombing raids were now in progress. He was going to take Mother and Keiko and Hiroshi with him. He had been planning this for some time, Keiko told me, because she had begged to have a haircut that was more stylish, with shorter hair. First Father refused to allow this because he said she would have to have long hair when they went to Japan so that she would fit in with girls her age and not look like a foreigner. She recounted all of this in the schoolyard, and then she told me what had happened next.

Mother, in a surprising and unexpected burst of defiance, declared that she was not going to leave. What would she do in a foreign place, even if it was the country of the ancestors? Hadn't she been born in Vancouver? Hadn't she attended school in that city as a child? Wasn't she entitled to raise the children in their own country?

The final comment had come from next door. Ba and Ji heard the argument and came in to take Mother's side. Because they were elders, they had no worries about interfering. Ji declared that any child sent to Japan after the end of the war would be in danger of dying of illness or starvation.

Mother, given support from the elders, would not change her mind. "Whether we are wanted here or not," she said, "we should stay. If we move, we won't see Bin again. Okuma-san will never agree to go to Japan. He has already said."

Keiko's eyes were puffy from crying, her cheekbones flushed. She said she'd been frightened when Mother's voice was raised in argument against First Father. Hiroshi, too, was unhappy about what was going on around him. But Father had signed the paper, and now the paper had to be unsigned.

Mother, with Ba and Ji's help, won the argument. A new paper was signed and my first family was not among those escorted to the coast to board a ship that sailed to Japan after the end of the war. But as Okuma-san later explained, the politicians were successful in ridding the country of thousands of Japanese Canadians. In the spring of 1946, the first shipload of exiles, immunized and with papers signed, sailed away from the West Coast and headed for Japan. In all, some four thousand people left Canada. Some were from our camp. One man told everyone he was glad to leave after being interned for years. He hoped for a life better than the one he'd been living since the bombing of Pearl Harbor. Other families were caught up in the atmosphere of chaos and had signed the paper out of fear.

First Father now became undecided about what to do next, and I often saw him outside, pacing around, engaged in bitter arguments and rantings with the men who remained. He was not the only one who had lost everything he had ever worked for. His boat and licence, his business, the house he had built in our fishing village, his honour and now, perhaps, his country. He had received a letter from his brother, our uncle Kenji, who had been sent to a road camp just after we'd been removed from the coast in early 1942. Uncle Kenji had spent eighteen months separated from his family, who were living in an internment camp in New Denver. He was with them now because he had finally been permitted to join them the previous year.

Uncle Kenji wanted to return to fishing, but that was impossible. Like the rest of us, he wasn't allowed back on the coast. In the letter he wrote to First Father, he said that he'd heard about work being available farther south, maybe at a sawmill not far from where we were now. He did not want to leave British Columbia, which had always been his home. None of us had seen Uncle Kenji since we'd been taken from our homes in 1942.

I worried about all of this. For a second time, we had to move out of our homes. One family after another began to depart. Some arranged to meet relatives who had been detained in other locations. Some left on the running boards of trucks that were filled to capacity with people on the move. Most were leaving the province and heading east, disappearing to different parts of the country—everywhere but to the West Coast. None of us was allowed back there—not yet. That would not happen for another four years. When Japanese

Canadians were finally allowed to vote in 1949, that was when we were allowed to return to the coast. But by then, of course, most had been dispersed elsewhere.

For now, the places people moved to were mainly chosen by chance. Someone had heard that a job might be found. Two rooms were offered in a city in Manitoba or Ontario. A housekeeper was wanted here or there. A minister from a church arranged for several families to move and found work for them on Ontario farms. A mushroom factory was hiring and said it would take internees from the camps. The sugar-beet fields in Alberta needed more workers. Some older Japanese children were being accepted into regular high schools. University students were in classes in the East. A Japanese doctor had been asked to work in a rural area that had no hospital or physician.

In the camp, in the middle of August 1945, this is how we learned more about hate, and about victory over Japan and about what would become known as VJ Day.

On a hot day, cars from across the river were heard approaching the camp. Most of the adults, including Okuma-san, were working in the communal gardens on the other side of the road. Some of the men were down at the river, fishing. Hiroshi was up on the Bench, picking currants. Keiko was with me because she had come to borrow a book from Okuma-san's shelf and had stayed on to read and keep me company. Keiko had short hair now, and shiny black bangs like Mother's, but without the curls on her forehead. She was laughing out loud while she was reading a story in the book.

There was suddenly so much noise from the road, we went to the doorway to see what was happening. Some of the mothers were running towards the shacks and bringing their children inside. We became frightened because many cars driven by men from the town had begun to circle through camp. Keiko and I banged the door shut and pushed the table against it and pulled the curtains tight so it would be dark inside the room. The two of us kneeled on a bench by the window and watched through a tiny crack. Our whole camp, within minutes, appeared to be deserted, but we were all there, hiding inside.

The men in the cars drove round and round, back and forth on the road and up and down the rows between shacks, blasting their horns and shouting through the car windows they had rolled down. "Have you heard the news? We dropped the big bomb and we won the war against you goddamned Japs!" This went on for about fifteen minutes until, finally, the drivers and shouters seemed to tire of roaring through a silent camp. The cars turned and went honking back to the bridge and towards town.

We knew then that Japan had surrendered, and we were glad, too. A few weeks later, during the first week of September, we heard about the formal ceremonies and final surrender of the Japanese military aboard the American battleship USS *Missouri*. But on that hot August day, when the news first came to the camp, we had been forced to hide behind the walls of our shacks because Canada, our country, was no longer at war.

Newspapers were brought from across the river. News of the terrible bombs that had been dropped on Hiroshima and Nagasaki had greatly disturbed everyone, and no one knew the extent of the destruction. People were being more cautious about their decisions now. Okuma-san decided that he and I would stay on until the end of the next school year, even though we were now free to move east. He was watching and waiting to see what would happen next. He sent letters to Vancouver friends he'd had before the war, knowing that he would not be able to teach or even travel back to the West Coast. He hoped that someone might be able to help him find work in some interior location of the province, even though we were being pressured to move east of the Rockies.

Hiroshi and Keiko and I met frequently up on the slope behind the camp and talked and played *Jan-Ken-Po,* and told one another of any changes or plans that had been overheard within the two families. But nothing changed for a while. Until Ba and Ji left.

Ba and Ji had been like family to all of us, but we had to make the best of their departure. They cried when it was time to leave, but they laughed, too, because they hoped to be reunited soon with their daughter's family. Sachi and Tom were now living in Nebraska, where they'd moved from Manzanar, and their baby had been born, a son named after Ji. The baby had Ji's first and last names, since Tom had taken Sachi's surname when they'd married in Vancouver before our expulsion from the coast.

Ba and Ji planned to travel across the country as far as Winnipeg. They would stay there with a family friend until Sachi could arrange for them to join her. Ba wore a grey dress and black gloves and a black hat with a short veil over her forehead for the train journey. The letters from Manzanar she had once stored in her pocket had been replaced by a photograph of the new grandson. She kept the photo of the baby in an envelope and pulled it out of the pocket of her dress to show everyone one more time before she left.

The numbers in camp were steadily shrinking, but First Father carried on with the gardening, as did Okuma-san. The sale of tomatoes was still bringing in enough money to support us. The school stayed open for another year, with one Japanese teacher and seventeen students. The Caucasian teacher, Mr. Blackwell, had gone back to Vancouver at the end of the war. And then, finally, in 1946, it was decided that the school would have to be closed at the end of the term. There would be only a few families remaining in the fall, not enough to keep the building open any longer.

Okuma-san and I remained in our shack until the end of the summer of 1946, after most of the tomatoes had been harvested and sold. Ying had been bringing newspapers from across the river all the while, and Okuma-san read these and told me that we must be patient because it looked as if some of us would be able to remain in the province after all. A few Caucasians had begun to stick up for us and there had been public objections to politicians who were trying to force us to relocate. Employers had come forward to say that they needed help on farms and in their orchards and sawmills and canning factories. They needed to keep up with demand and production, and there was a shortage of workers.

People from the town across the river began to come over to our camp, offering a few dollars to take the deserted shacks apart so they could salvage the lumber. It was around this time that my first family announced that they would be leaving. Uncle Aki and Auntie Aya would leave with them. Auntie Aya did not want to be far from Mother, who had helped her so much throughout the years in the camp.

The evening before they left, Mother came to our shack and knocked on the door. She brought with her an armful of clothing that Hiroshi had outgrown. She also brought a basket of food that could not be taken the next day. After Okuma-san and I had put these things away, she asked me to come for a walk.

My mother and I crossed the dirt road and went past the gardens, all the way to the far edge of the cliff that looked down over the great river. There was a narrow path along the edge, and we walked back and forth on this path. She took my hand in hers and I remembered, afterwards, how warm and small her own hand had been. We stopped several times to look at the wildflowers, and when we came close to the gardens again, she exclaimed over the huge size of the pale green cabbages still left in the rows.

It was a warm evening, and Mother had on a yellow cotton dress with a raised pattern around its bottom edge that reminded me of delicate rows of puffed corn. She wore a pair of sandals that First Father had made for her from leather, and as we walked, she stopped every few minutes and held my shoulder for balance while she shook out the sandy grit that was trapped under her toes.

"Bin," she said. "You know that you will always be my son. Okuma-san has adopted you because your first father thought it was best. But I will always love you and we will see each other again."

"When?" I asked. "When will we see each other?" I knew that there was little money, and that people like us did not go travelling.

"When we can," she said, and she looked down over the river as if it were far away and not flowing swiftly below us, at the bottom of the cliff. "We will see each other when we can."

In the morning, Mother, First Father, Keiko, Hiroshi, Uncle Aki and Auntie Aya were picked up by Ying in his truck. Keiko was trying not to cry, but tears rolled down her cheeks. She looked so much older now, with her short haircut. Hiroshi and I said goodbye, and he threw out a hand in *Jan-Ken-Po* and I did the same, and we both did *Scissors* so neither of us won. Hiroshi looked away, towards the town on the other side of the river. First Father put a hand on my shoulder and a low sound came from his throat that sounded like "Huuuh."

The goodbyes were not prolonged. I watched them push their bundles up into the back of Ying's truck and I watched as they climbed up beside them. First Father thumped the cab to let Ying know he could pull away. Okuma-san stood beside me. Mother had her navy blue coat over her arm, the same coat she had worn when we'd arrived almost five years earlier.

First Father did not look back. I saw him only in profile as he departed. He looked resolute and unrelenting about this decision and any he would make in the future. The last image I held of the others was of them looking back at me as if they were trying to fix me in memory. Their faces became smaller and smaller and finally disappeared as Ying's truck bounced and rattled along the dirt road. Ying drove them to the bus station across the bridge, and they were gone.

Two weeks later, we received a letter from Mother telling us they had found a place to live in a valley about forty miles south of the camp. First Father and Uncle Aki were working in a sawmill and they would stay there until they were able to save enough money to move again. Uncle Kenji and his family had arrived there, too. There was a school a mile down the road, she wrote, and Hiroshi and Keiko—now called Henry and Kay—would be attending with our cousins, in the fall. That was all she said, apart from giving an address care of the local post office.

This postwar move undertaken by my first family was the beginning of many. Uncle Aki and Auntie Aya stayed in the mill town until 1950. They waited a year after they were allowed to vote in federal elections—which also meant that they were free to go to the coast—and then moved to Vancouver. It had become clear that Auntie Aya needed help from the kind of doctors that were available in a large city.

First Father and his brother, Uncle Kenji, both accomplished fishermen, drifted for years in the interior of the province, from village to town, from town to village, always far from the coast, seeking work in mills and orchards, staying overnight in flea-infested bunk-houses, trying to find places to live, making repeated and thwarted attempts to search for what would never be recovered. My first family moved so many times, I had to check the envelopes that arrived from Mother and Keiko to learn their latest location. It was only after Hiroshi and Keiko and our cousins had grown up and left home that First Father and Mother moved one last time, even farther inland, to the outskirts of Kamloops, near the North and South Thompson Rivers, where the two of them remained. Uncle Kenji followed right behind them, and had a house nearby.

CHAPTER 24

1946

Summer was almost over when Okuma-san made plans for the two of us to travel to a town in southern British Columbia. We were among the last few families to leave the camp. A friend he had in Vancouver, a Caucasian, had written to say that he had heard from a cousin, a Mr. Boyd, who lived south of the Okanagan Valley and needed someone to do odd jobs related to his business. He was willing to hire Okuma-san. The job had nothing to do with music, but it might be a way of biding time until more freedom of movement was allowed and until communities were more welcoming.

The cousin, as it turned out, owned a market garden that had grown too large for him to handle. His property was located on ten acres at the edge of a small town and there was a building where we could live on the property itself. Okuma-san was warned that the building would need some attention. In the letter, his friend also said that a school would be within walking distance for the child.

We travelled by bus, which really meant three buses, as we had to change twice along the way. Because there was a two-hour wait between the first and second buses, we sat on a bench outside a garage in the first town and kept to ourselves. At the entrance to the town we had both seen the sign welcoming visitors, posted by the roadside. Directly below the welcome sign, a second sign had been nailed to the post: JAPS NOT WELCOME. I had no difficulty reading this and did so, silently, to myself.

Okuma-san bought two more tickets when it was time to change buses again. There was another wait and again we stayed outside, sitting on a low wall at the back of the station parking lot. Okuma-san dipped into the food basket he'd packed for our journey, and gave me a rice ball that had almost dried out, some strips of omelette and an apple. He had made lemonade before we left the camp and we drank from a jar with a tight-fitting lid.

It quickly became clear that people did not like the look of us sitting there. Okuma-san spoke to me in a low voice. "Look straight ahead," he said. "People are sometimes afraid. Maybe of themselves, maybe because the war ended only a year ago and they want to blame someone who is nearby. Don't be ashamed. We have done nothing wrong and we still have a long way to go."

No one spoke to us, and eventually, the final bus arrived. After we boarded and took our seats near the back, I closed my eyes and wished for nothing but sleep.

*

I HAD NEVER BEEN to a *hakujin* school with all Caucasian children. It was early September and Okuma-san and I had been trying to fix up an old chicken coop on the property owned by Mr. and Mrs. Boyd, Okuma-san's new employers. The Boyd house was at the front of the property and the gardens lay beyond—acre after acre of rich, dark soil where vegetables, tomatoes and strawberries were grown. At the far end, there were more than a dozen apple trees. Off in the distance I could see a range of dry, golden hills.

Although the Boyds had not raised chickens for half a dozen years, they had never torn down the chicken coop on the property, and this was now put to use to house us. It had been swept out and modified before we arrived. A door had been put in, and the wire fencing surrounding the chicken run had been ripped out. The rest was up to us.

This required days of scrubbing, getting rid of feathers and dust and insects. Okuma-san painted the inside with white paint. Two metal cots were provided. The rest, Okuma-san bought secondhand when Mr. Boyd drove him to a junk store on a back street of the town. We had a kitchen table and bookshelves made from apple boxes and a counter that contained a dry sink and a low cupboard. A room at the back of the chicken coop was the bedroom. Okuma-san bought a small table so that I would have a place to do my homework, and this was put along the wall in the main room, which served as kitchen and living area. The place was smaller than the shack we had just left, and not as clean. There was a pump in the backyard, and the pump handle croaked up cold, clear water for drinking. Water for bathing was heated on a wood stove. The toilet was an outhouse near the fenced edge of the property. It had not been used for years, because the Boyds now had indoor plumbing in their own home. Mr. Boyd had hooked up a power line to the chicken coop, and this meant that for the first time since 1942, we had electricity. Okuma-san walked back to the junk shop and purchased a brass desk lamp and set this on my homework table, which wobbled unevenly and had to be levelled from below with a thin wedge of wood.

At the beginning, Okuma-san worked both outside and in. Not only did he help with gardening, but he was also asked to keep track of invoices that were impaled on a sharp spike on a desk in the enclosed back porch of the main house. Mrs. Boyd had been looking after this task until we arrived, entering the figures in a black ledger. She showed Okuma-san what was expected, and he spent long hours over the invoices every week. Old furniture had been stacked up and pushed together at one end of the porch so there would be room at the other end for the office desk and the shelf above it.

Two local men worked in the gardens, and these men lived within walking distance in the town. Their jobs were to weed and harvest and look after the sprinkling system during the evening hours. One man was responsible for pruning the apple trees. He showed me how he had made inroad paths that allowed for both harvesting the apples and the reach of the sun. He showed me, too, the place where asparagus plants pushed up next to the trees, and he told me that in the spring, he tended them and kept them healthy. At night when I went to bed, there were new sounds and I could hear the rhythmic swish-tick of irrigating, the hum of water as it paused in the air before it fell to the parched rows all around.

Okuma-san pitched in outside wherever help was needed, and I helped, as well. All of this meant that there was little time for any other activity. The plank keyboard had followed us by bus to the Boyds' address, and had arrived at our chicken coop one hot, dry afternoon. So far, it had not been touched. Nor had I opened the sketch pad that was tucked into the shallow drawer of my homework table.

Okuma-san did take an hour off work, however, to accompany me to school on my first day. We walked from the Boyd place at our end of the town, crossed a short field to reach Main Street and continued to the other end, where the school was located. It was a large two-storey building and contained classrooms for primary, middle and high school combined. High school students used the upper floor, all other grades the lower. I was to be in grade four.

Several laughing, playing children were standing around the entrance for the younger grades on that first day. Some of the smallest students were accompanied by their mothers, but most children were on their own. They were talking excitedly in raised voices, darting in and out of small groups and calling to one another. As we approached, everyone became silent and the crowd stood back to let us through. Most of the mothers looked at the ground when we passed, but the children stared at me and I had an uneasy feeling at the pit of my belly. I wondered if I might be getting sick. If so, that would mean I wouldn't have to attend school after all.

Okuma-san ignored the stares and the averted eyes and walked into the building as if he knew exactly what to do and where to go. He led me down a long hall and around a corner to a second, shorter hall. He stopped outside a classroom that had a brass number four nailed above its doorway. The door was open, and I followed him into the room. We had not spoken since entering the school, and this made me uneasy because I wondered if he had been guessing the location of my classroom.

A young woman was standing behind the teacher's desk and she looked at us and said her name was Miss Paxton. She seemed to be expecting us, and this surprised me. Her cheeks flushed as Okuma-san bowed slightly and presented her with an envelope that contained my report cards from the camp. The contents were supposed to be proof that I belonged in her class, though from the look on her face, I thought she was on the verge of denying this.

"This is my son, Bin," said Okuma-san. "He has completed grade three, but he has also done much of the grade four work because he was in a mixed class last year."

Miss Paxton looked at the envelope that had been deposited in her hand, but she did not open it. Instead, she pointed to a row of desks and told me to take a seat at the back. The other desks were spoken for, she assured Okuma-san, though he had not commented on this. He bowed his head slightly as he departed, and when he reached the doorway, he half-turned in my direction and nodded, making certain that I looked him in the eye before he left.

There was no time to think about my abandonment in this large, strange place because a bell rang out loudly and the building expanded like a bellows in response to the sudden noise. Children came from every direction, through the doorway and into the class-room, but they slowed when they saw Miss Paxton. They became completely silent when they saw that I was already in my seat at the back of the room. After one quick glance around, I knew that there was no one like me in the class—no other child with a Japa-nese face.

Every child seemed to know exactly where to sit. Perhaps some order had existed before school began. All I knew was that within seconds, every desk was filled. Order prevailed until a girl in my row held up a note and said she had to be near the blackboard because she couldn't see properly. Miss Paxton nodded while she read the note, and had the girl exchange seats with a boy in the front row.

Miss Paxton then called for complete silence. We stood, sang "God Save the King" and recited the Lord's Prayer, and the school year began.

To start off the day, Miss Paxton said, "Let's take turns, class. As you all know, on the first day of school, we stand beside our desks, one at a time, and say our names out loud. Both names," she reminded. "Last and first. I'll begin. My name is Miss Paxton." She said this as if Miss was her first name, and then she printed MISS PAXTON on the board.

As I was in the last seat of the farthest row, my turn came after everyone else had finished. I stood, pressed a hand to the back of my desk and said, "Okuma, Binosuke," putting my last name first, because I was not certain what I should do. I sat down quickly.

The children laughed so loudly, I became confused and wondered if, instead, I should have given the surname of my first, and not my second, father. I stood again and the room went silent. I blurted out, "Oda, Binosuke," and my cheeks felt as if they had been slapped.

"Did you just say two different names?" said Miss Paxton. She looked down at her attendance sheet and then back to me.

I nodded and sat in my seat.

"And how do you come to have two sets of names?" she said.

I told her I had two because I had once lived in the family of my first father.

"Stand up again," she said. "How many fathers have you had?"

"Two," I said, and quickly sat down again. All of this sitting and standing made the class laugh even harder.

"What kind of names are those, anyway?" Miss Paxton said. "What kind of names, class? Shall we hear them again? Stand up and tell us, so that we can understand."

"My name is Bin," I said, thinking that if I gave only my shortest name, no one would laugh.

"Bin," said Miss Paxton. She printed *B-I-N* on the board in giant letters with white chalk, and she drew an even bigger *X* through my name.

"Bin is not a name we use for children in this country," she said.

"We say bin for dustbin or garbage bin, but it is not a name we give a child. We'll assign a name that we can remember, an English name. We will call you Ben. Can you remember that?"

"Yes," I said. And I wanted to leave this room and never come back, even knowing that Okuma-san would not let me stay home from school.

Miss Paxton printed *B-E-N* on the board and erased my crossed-out Japanese name.

When the day was finished, I walked out the school door alone. Behind me, I heard a boy's voice mutter: "So long, rice paddy. Don't bother coming back."

Okuma-san was waiting for me at the end of Main Street as he had promised. When he asked how the day had gone, I said, "Fine." I told him nothing about Miss Paxton, nor did I tell him that my name had been changed back to an English name again.

But that was only the beginning. On my second morning, Miss Paxton said, "Stand up, Ben. Stand beside your desk and tell the class your mother's name."

I had only one mother, but I wasn't certain if Miss Paxton was laying a trap. I did not want the class to know anything more about my family, so I stood and spoke quickly. "My mother's name is Oda, Reiko."

And the entire class, as well as Miss Paxton, laughed as if they would never stop.

Every morning, for the rest of the week, Miss Paxton made me stand and say the name of my mother aloud so that the class could start off the day with a good laugh.

Miss Paxton was my *Sensei*, my teacher, and I knew that I had to show respect and do what she told me to do.

No one else in the class was asked to stand and say the name of a parent.

Miss Paxton was not able to make me cry.

That was my first week in my new school.

CHAPTER 25

1950–51

I had never had a school art lesson until the year I was in grade eight. It was 1950, and an announcement was made at the beginning of the year that art classes were to start on Friday afternoons in late November. When I heard this, I felt an excitement that was physical, an excitement I had not known before.

On that first Friday morning, my heart beat faster. I raced through morning lessons. The clock slowed, intentionally. No one in our class knew who would be giving the lessons, but it was rumoured to be one or the other of two veterans, each of whom had fought overseas during the war and had returned to take up teaching again.

I had already had an encounter with one of the veterans, Mr. Abbott, and I was hoping he would not be the one to teach art. His regular class was geography, and he was also responsible for physical education. After gym class one day the previous June, a boy complained that his wallet had been stolen from a bench in the locker room on the main floor. I was accused of the theft. Mr. Abbott believed the boy and, despite my protests, took me to the principal's office, where both he and the principal tried to force me to admit my guilt. But I would not; I was innocent. My pockets were turned inside out and my desk was searched, but the wallet was not found. "I've dealt with these Japs before," Mr. Abbott told the principal. "I'll get it out of him yet."

While I was being threatened that a letter would be sent home to my father and that I would be expelled, an older boy came running into the office and said the wallet had been found in another boy's locker. Mr. Abbott turned and left the office. No apology was made. The principal sent me back to my classroom. I never learned if the real thief was punished. I do know that for several days, in the schoolyard outside, the boys chanted, "Stealer! He's a stealer!" when I came near.

I recounted none of these events to Okuma-san. Nor did I tell him that the covers of war comics occasionally turned up in my desk drawer in the classroom. There was always a Japanese soldier depicted on these covers. A soldier with an ugly yellow face, large buck teeth, eyes squinting behind thick glasses. I ripped up the covers and learned not to react. If someone started a fight outside, I did not run away. I did have a few friends, boys my age, and though they did not join the taunting, they did not come to my defence. It was too risky for them.

Occasionally, letters arrived from Mother. Keiko wrote, as well. She and Hiroshi were both in high school and doing well. Our camp school had not let us down. I had kept up my own marks, and was at the top of my class every year. When Mother wrote and asked about my grades, I reported back. But whenever a letter came from her, I fell into a dark mood and brooded for days. Our old lives were far away. I had not seen my first family since 1946. No one had the money to travel.

Okuma-san was saving money to move us to Ontario the following year and had been promised work in Ottawa as a music teacher.
Letters had been coming and going. The job was at a small college,
teaching music to students of high school age. He would be giving
both group and individual lessons. One of his conditions was that I
would be able take my high school studies at the same college. Of
course, a piano would be available to him. Okuma-san had always
kept up his practice on the plank keyboard, which had a permanent
place against one wall of our chicken coop. After years of listening to
Beethoven rapped out on ponderosa pine, I could tell almost as soon
as he began which piece he was playing.

One day in the early fall, when I came home from school scuffed
from fighting, I walked into the chicken coop and saw a small refrigerator tucked in behind the door and plugged in overhead. Okuma-
san had purchased it secondhand. Mr. Boyd had picked it up in his
truck and had helped to carry it in and set it up.

We had nothing to keep cold in the refrigerator that afternoon,
except for one egg. We set the egg on a shelf by itself and laughed
as if it were the funniest thing we'd ever seen. The refrigerator rattled and buzzed every time we opened the door. Okuma-san said he
would buy cold food the next day, milk and butter and meat. He did
not comment on my appearance, though it was obvious that I'd been
in a fight. The two of us kept opening the door to look at the egg.
During the night, I was wakened by the rattle and I heard Okuma-
san in the kitchen, opening the fridge door again. I pictured the lone
egg in that cool and empty space.

Another afternoon, Okuma-san had a secondhand turntable to
show me when I came in from school. He had bought it that day,
along with a great find, a record of Beethoven's Emperor Concerto
that someone no longer wanted, though it was almost new. Okuma-

san prepared our supper and I set the table, and the two of us sat in silence while the music surrounded us. Okuma-san could not keep his fingers still. Every inch of space in the room was filled with glorious and noble sounds. Hands and fingers played real keys. The second movement was so beautiful it seemed to float into the walls of the chicken coop. When it was over, we listened again as if for the first time. Had we been seated in one of the grand concert halls of Europe, we could not have enjoyed it more.

That evening, Okuma-san told me about the *Heiligenstadt Testament,* which Beethoven wrote when he was thirty-one years old. He had addressed it to his brothers, one of them by name, but it was never sent and was discovered among his papers after his death.

"It is a sad document," said Okuma-san. "Very sad. Because in it, Beethoven finally accepted his permanent infirmity, his deafness. Imagine, at thirty-one and with the kind of genius that was inside him. Who knows how he was able to triumph over those devastating conditions? Maybe his deep love of life and his love of God allowed him to continue."

The kitchen was almost dark by then, and I went to bed feeling that the music was still inside me. I did not want the feeling to escape.

On the Friday that art classes began, I had begun to worry about the possibility that Mr. Abbott, the gym instructor, would walk into our classroom and announce that he was the teacher. I knew he could make my life as difficult and as complicated as he wished it to be. It was a relief to me when the other veteran—there wasn't a student in the school who did not know which two teachers had fought in the war—Mr. Owen, walked through the doorway and announced, "Today we will begin the study of art."

Mr. Owen had fought in the Battle of Hong Kong and had been

wounded. A bullet had gone through his cheek. There was a large scar on the left side of his face. His left eye was lower than the right, as if it had been mangled in the process of being wounded. He had been taken prisoner in Hong Kong by Japanese soldiers and was sent to Japan to work in a factory. Everyone knew how weak and sick he had been at the end of the war, when he'd finally returned home.

Our first class was a drawing class, and that was fine with me. Mr. Owen wanted us to draw either a horse or a dog. He handed out art paper and then he began to draw on the board with chalk, demonstrating a model of ovals and circles that could be created into a horse's head and belly and back. The outer lines could be erased after a likeness had been found.

The demonstration of the dog began with two ovals and a circle. The circle was positioned behind the oval and transformed into a long, floppy ear on each side of the head. Another oval was positioned on its side and became the dog's seated body. Legs and tail were added at the end.

I drew the horse, but did not need circles and ovals to help me. From memory, I drew one of the wild horses from the camp.

Mr. Owen walked up and down the rows of desks, looking over our shoulders. He was impressed with what I had done.

"It's good, Ben. It's really very good. You didn't need any of my teaching aids to get started. And as you already know, there are many ways to draw a picture."

He asked me to stay after class that day.

"Ben," he said, "have you ever looked at real paintings in a gallery? Would you like to borrow some of my art books? I have quite a library at home. It's important, when you are an artist, to look at the work of others and to know what has been done before."

I agreed, cautiously. I was not accustomed to excessive kindness from teachers. But a friendship between us began that day.

Mr. Owen helped me to pay more attention to the natural world. He encouraged this so as to provide me with grounding. To start with basics but to be aware of every aspect of my own creations. "Look at what is around and between the objects you draw," he told me. And I did. I began to focus on the spaces between, the angles and shadows, the fragmentation of light. I even began to wonder if I could draw these on their own: the shapes and groups of shapes above and between and below—instead of the objects themselves.

It was almost a decade later when I experimented in earnest this way, divorcing myself, freeing myself from being bound to actual objects, appreciating abstract shapes, real and imagined, and the ways they could exist for their own sake.

Along with Okuma-san, Mr. Owen helped me at the beginning of this journey. He challenged me to believe that every new drawing and painting deserved the excitement I gave to it as I searched for new forms that might bring it to life. Even when I was in grade eight, this was deemed to be important.

Some days, during those Friday afternoon classes, my classmates would ask Mr. Owen to tell us about the war. One time, he spoke about being a prisoner in Japan.

"I was weak," he said, "and I had lost a great deal of weight. More than fifty pounds. My clothes were ragged; I had no shoes; there was little food to be shared. One of my jobs was to take deliveries from the factory in which I worked to a second factory, more than a mile away. I was given a heavy knapsack that was filled with metal parts, and told where to deliver it. I did not have to have a guard because there was no place for me to escape. If I had tried to hide, some of my comrades would have been killed in my place. In my weakened condition, barefoot, it was a long walk for me at the time. I had to pass through a remote village on the way. The village was poor and it was obvious that the people who lived there were barely scraping by.

"One afternoon, while I was walking past a small house, I became dizzy from hunger and from the heat, and I had to sit down at the edge of the road. An elderly couple came outside and offered water. Then they went back inside and came out with a small scoop of cooked rice. They helped me to stand, and I was able to continue. The scoop of rice and the water kept me going."

Mr. Owen stared out the classroom window for a long time before he continued, but none of us spoke or tried to interrupt.

"I can never adequately explain to you what that meant to me," he said. "Apart from the obvious fact that I stayed alive one more day.

"The old couple looked out for me after that, and helped me whenever they saw me on the road between factories, carrying the heavy knapsack. When they had extra food, they shared it. Sometimes it was nothing more than a fish head pulled from a watery stew. Sometimes it was a rice ball. They were probably putting their own lives in danger by giving me food, and I have always felt badly that I had nothing to give in return.

"When the war ended, before I left, I sat on the floor of my bunkhouse and made a drawing of the two of them, the man and his wife. I took it to them and said goodbye. I was able to leave them a ration kit, given to me by American soldiers. Many of my comrades had died from starvation and abuse in the prison factory. But I am alive today and standing in this classroom because one elderly Japanese couple who had almost nothing themselves were humane enough to help me."

It is possible that after Mr. Owen told his story, I found myself in fewer fights at school. Certainly, my classmates and I remembered the story, because we talked about it several times, among ourselves.

I did borrow art books from Mr. Owen that year. Week after week, month after month, until I had gone through most of his library. One of his books was about Japanese woodblock prints, and some of the representations within reminded me of the scroll I had been given by Okuma-san. I took the book home to the chicken coop and showed it to Okuma-san, and we delighted in turning the pages, examining the uniqueness of the art. I was especially captivated by the way water had been drawn. Some waves looked like hard chunks of river. Others showed as soft ripples or shadows. I began to understand that there could be a soft or hard look to water, that there could be many ways of depicting rivers, that this was a matter of technique and of choice.

Mr. Owen also introduced the use of watercolours to our class, but I found this to be a difficult medium. We had many discussions—just the two of us—about the artists I had read about in his books. He gave me hope that some day I might be fortunate enough to stand before some of the great paintings I had seen on the pages, and witness them for myself.

At the end of the year, on the report card that would be presented to the college I was moving to in Ontario, the one where Okuma-san and I would once again restart our lives, I was given an A plus for my work in Mr. Owen's class.

The two of us talked after our last class, Mr. Owen and I, and he told me, "Ben, there will be a great deal of pressure put upon you to be ordinary, to follow the norm, never to raise your head. Because of this, your art will become the most private part of you. The secret possession that you will guard the most."

Okuma-san and I left the plank keyboard behind in the chicken coop, and Mr. Boyd drove us to the train station. Before we departed, I walked to Mr. Owen's house and presented him with a watercolour I had painted. It had been a struggle, but I had done my best and I had created my own representation of the golden hills that edged the town. The golden hills and the sun-hazed sky that fell upon them. I signed the painting *Bin Okuma*, using my real name. It was the first time I had ever signed anything I had drawn or painted. Never again did I use any other name except my own, after that day.

CHAPTER 26

1997

I haven't been successful in reaching Kay by phone, but I leave a message on her answering machine and tell her I'll phone from the next stop. Basil and I are in Alberta now, just beyond the border, sitting in the sun at a picnic table that's next to a gas station and truck stop. Basil has been well fed but he's eyeing my hamburger, watching me chew as if he's about to expire from starvation. We're both happy to be out of the car, enjoying the spring air. It's warm enough to be outside here, as long as I keep my jacket on.

A family, parents and two children, a girl and a boy, come out with hamburgers and fries, and join us at the picnic table. The boy, maybe twelve or thirteen, reaches for Basil, runs his fingers through his coat, and Basil responds with his groaning, contented noise, mouth open. When the boy lifts his hand, Basil nudges him for more, and then gives himself a good shake.

"His hair is pretty matted," I tell the boy. "We've been on the road for over a week and he needs a good bath."

The boy tells me they have a dog at home, a Dalmatian named Putty. Basil is on his best behaviour with this family. The boy tells me he's going to study to be a veterinarian after he finishes high school. His mom and dad are ranchers, and his younger sister rides. She has her own horse and that's what interests her. She gives me a shy grin and looks down, and she, too, gives Basil a few pats. The boy is so comfortable and easy around his parents, and around Basil and me, he reminds me of Greg not so many years ago.

When we're back in the car again, I think of Greg the year he finished middle school. That would have been 1989, and Miss Carrie had invited us for dinner—a family night I had not forgotten.

★

HE IS A GOOD CITIZEN, Greg's homeroom teacher wrote in a note home, the day final reports were given out. *What a pleasure to have him in my class.*

"I've heard of parents writing teachers to thank them, but not teachers writing parents," Lena said. "Do you realize that's the second teacher who has written to us with the same message, both using the word *citizen?*"

I'd noticed, yes. And Greg was listening, smiling to himself.

"What was it like at your schools, Bin, when you were a child?" Miss Carrie asked. "After the war, I mean."

Three faces looked at me, waiting for an answer. But I rarely talked about my schools.

"I learned to use my fists," I said. That was all. But my mood had changed and I had altered the mood at the table as I'd tipped into darkness. Too late to catch myself. Lena watched as I shut down.

"Pass your plate," said Miss Carrie, promptly changing the sub-ject. "We're having plain stew. No luxuries, I'm afraid, even though it's a celebration: Greg finishing middle school with straight A's; the butcher donating bones for the stew; you returning home after being out and around the Empire."

At the word *Empire,* Lena rolled her eyes and laughed out loud. We were seated at the long walnut table in Miss Carrie's dining room. Despite her claims about no luxuries, there were ample chunks of beef in the serving dish, along with the donated bones. The stew, one of her specialties, was thick with dumplings on top, and potatoes, onions, carrots and tomatoes under the steaming surface.

I had recently returned from a trip to both Malta and Gibral-tar. I was still earning part of my income from magazine and book illustrations—especially from two loyal editors. They knew I would travel, and they sent work my way or sent me away to the work. My paintings had been selling, and I was buoyed by that. But I was looking forward to a time when I would not have to rely on outside work at all. I was obsessed with supporting the family—Lena told me often enough—even though we both had earnings. I was also trying not to repeat myself on canvas, feeling frustrated just as I was trying to move in a new direction. I had had two exhibitions of my own, both held at Nathan's gallery. I had participated in many group shows, but other responsibilities had a way of moving in on my time. I had a show coming up and Nathan had great hopes for it, as did I—although, as always, I had doubts. There were always doubts.

After dessert, we moved to the living room and Miss Carrie brought out an unopened bottle of Daddy's decades-old brandy. For Greg, she had made fruit punch. There was an upright piano along one side of the room, but the cover had always been pulled over the keys. This night, the cover was rolled back and the ivory keys exposed. Miss Carrie saw me looking that way and remarked that the piano had been purchased before she was born. She had taken lessons as a child, but the piano had been placed in storage when Daddy marched off to the Great War and she and Mommy followed as far as England.

"We rented this house for the duration of the war while we were away," she said, "but the piano was never the same after coming out of a damp warehouse. We kept it, nonetheless, and I'm glad I still have it. I suppose I'll sell it someday, when I can no longer pay my taxes. I wish I had learned to play properly when I was a child. But I was more interested in what was happening around me than in practising scales. The teacher Mommy sent me to before the war provided lessons in her living room, and for years I was compelled to go to her house every Thursday after school. Heavy maroon drapes were pulled across the double windows right next to her piano, and not a speck of natural light was permitted in the room. There was a musty odour, too, disagreeable and depressing. I felt that the drapes had sealed in the century before mine, and now I can't help but associate piano lessons with that jowl-cheeked woman and the smothering odours of cheek powder every time she squeezed onto the bench beside me in that airless room. Still, our own piano was played after the war. This old house hosted many parties, and there was always someone who knew how to play. We even hosted the famous war ace, Billy Bishop, one evening. He was staying at the Château Laurier, and Daddy bumped into him there and invited him. A dashing officer. His uniform is in the War Museum here but whoever arranged the display did not do justice to the great pilot." She looked back to the piano. "Bishop stood in that very corner during a singsong at one of Mommy's parties."

"I took piano lessons for a while," Lena said, and Miss Carrie and Greg and I looked at her in surprise. Lena shook her head. "Oh, not that many years. I insisted on playing everything by ear, and that did not please my teacher. I studied as far as grade eight in my conservatory exams, so I have the piece of paper. I played to amuse myself, mostly. I miss it, I suppose. But I haven't given piano playing much thought, because I'm so busy teaching all the time. And we have so much recorded music to keep us company at home."

After we returned home, Greg went straight to bed—*Did Miss Carrie really know Billy Bishop?* he asked. *Didn't he fight the Red Baron?* And we assured him, *Oh, yes, if Miss Carrie says so, it's true.* Lena and I were preparing for bed, undressing, talking about the evening.

"Every emotion you've ever learned," she said, as we got into bed, "has been turned inside. Locked in. But it will come out, even the anger. It has to. How can it not?"

I knew she was talking about the reference to my fists over dinner. But I was past anger—I thought. And the old anger I had carried around for so many years had not been about school. Not really. It had been about—and I had to face it—it had been about everything. Removal, exile, dispersal, being on the outside. Being given away— now *there* was a reason to be angry. Perhaps none of those things had been dealt with. Not in the way Lena meant. And what would be the point, anyway?

"You've told me some things that happened in your past," Lena said. "And I know I haven't heard them all. You have a right to be angry. The anger is part of your story." As far as she was concerned, everything that happened to a person was added on to the cumulative story.

She continued. "All of those things that happened, they've also made you different from everyone else. They've made you the fine artist you are. But there are times when your dark side hangs over you like a mantle, a heavy cloth. We hardly ever talk about this, but there have been days when I've wanted to yank off that mantle, drag it away and shout, 'Move over! We all have pasts, we all have backgrounds!' Sometimes, when I'm trying to understand all of this, I get angry myself," she said. "So figure that out."

Silence.

But she wasn't going to stop there. "If the moods always trace back to your first father," she said, "remember that you've also had choice. Two role models. One who seethed with anger—with good reason. Another who had the same reasons to be angry but managed to create peace around himself and everyone else. Maybe, just maybe, you ended up being a better father yourself because you were able to choose. You are a father, a good one."

To love a child. Yes. I understood what it was to love a child.

But to give one away?

Having two fathers had always created a complex double measure. And if all I had to do to be a father myself was to love Greg, then I had been doing that. But my intent was also to keep our family of three, now four—three plus Miss Carrie—safe and close, and I did worry about that. I knew there was no reason to worry, but I did. I was always trying to protect everyone. It was part of the fates. There could be sudden losses—every Japanese Canadian knew that.

And then there was Lena's family, unlike mine in every way. Her family had come from one place, Montreal or close by. Too close, she sometimes complained, only a two-hour drive away. Whereas my family was scattered forever: uncles, aunts, cousins, brother, sister, nieces, nephews, anywhere and everywhere in the country, unseen and no longer really known. Except through Kay. She was the one who had the information; she was the one who tried to round everyone up, if only in her head. She was the one who informed me that Uncle Kenji's son, a cousin younger than I, had finally moved back to

Vancouver Island's west coast and now fished for a living. That Uncle Kenji, who still lived near First Father in Kamloops, drove to the coast every spring—a full day's journey by truck—to visit his family and to go out on the boat with his son.

Auntie Aya now lived in a long-term residence for psychiatric patients in Vancouver, and Mother's brother, our Uncle Aki, lived in an apartment nearby so that he could visit her every day. Sometimes, she came out on a pass for two or three weeks, but she always had to go back to receive the care she needed. I wondered if, for Auntie Aya, Baby Taro's bones had ever fallen silent, or if they still rattled in the baking powder tin. There had been something fragile about Auntie Aya from the beginning, but after Baby Taro's death, whatever broke inside her was never put right again.

My brother, Henry, had moved from job to job for many years until the mid-eighties, when he'd found something he was good at. He bought a small truck stop, expanded the diner and turned it into an excellent business. He couldn't wait to retire and had told me over the phone that he'd earned his retirement. I wasn't sure how he would spend his extra time. Travelling a bit, perhaps. Or driving back and forth between Alberta and B.C. Most of my relatives kept their heads down, stayed below the radar, as far as I could figure. Whole lives spent with their heads down.

As for Mother, we'd had visits with her at Kay's home several times, because Kay had arranged for her to be there whenever we'd visited Edmonton. But now, Mother was gone. I did not attend her funeral. Kay sent the ritual photo, Japanese funereal style, of family members standing around Mother's coffin. First Father, taller than the others, stared grimly into the camera eye. I couldn't bear to look at that photo. It disappeared, and is probably mixed in with other family photos and papers.

But even though I had seen Mother from time to time, for me she had always remained as she was during the last evening we spent in the camp in 1946. The image I carried around had scarcely altered with time, both before and after Mother's death. It was always Mother with black hair and bangs, a curl on each side of her forehead, wearing her yellow cotton dress and taking me by the hand to walk back and forth on the path at the edge of the cliff that looked down over the Fraser River. I could still call up the sensation of her hand pressing down on my shoulder when we paused so that she could shake out the grit from her homemade sandals.

The truth was, I had never really said goodbye, not even when we were all still living in the camp. She was the one I had missed the most, ever since the day of the picnic, when I was given away. The memories of her were the ones buried deepest, but that had happened while she was alive, not after her death, when I was an adult. I had hunkered down, buried the connection—perhaps to protect it—and I rarely brought it to the surface.

But I had done what artists do. I had painted. There was one canvas I had never put in a show or offered for sale. I used acrylics and mixed my own colours to create deep indigos and browns. It was an abstract that contained a heaviness of feeling but with a single fine edge running along one side, an edge of the palest yellow. And a mass of white that took up a third of the canvas, and that I could hardly define. Lena loved the painting when she saw it, but I did not tell her how it had come about. I could scarcely articulate the genesis to myself.

And First Father, well, apart from the photograph that Kay sent after Mother's funeral, I had not actually seen him since the day in 1946 when he left in the back of Ying's truck. Lena and Greg had never met him and I did not consider him to be Greg's grandfather. He was never at Kay's in Alberta because he refused to leave British Columbia, the province that had once tried so hard to remove him. Perhaps he still held the suspicion that if he were to leave, even this long after the war, he would not be allowed back in. As for me, I was the only one in the family who had not re-entered B.C.

Maybe First Father was the most stable one of us all. He was the one who had staked out his territory. But the years went on and distances stretched farther and farther. After the Redress Agreement was signed in the fall of 1988, after the public apology was made by the prime minister, First Father received his cheque, as we all did. Mine was banked and invested for Greg's education. First Father's payment, Kay had let us know, was put towards buying the bungalow he and Mother had rented for years, on the outskirts of Kamloops. But Mother was no longer alive to enjoy the fact of ownership. Nor did she live long enough to hear the Apology.

I had been going over all of these things in my mind and had turned away from Lena after our conversation about moods. I was lying on my side with my back to her. I knew she was not asleep; I could tell by her breathing. But I had nothing to offer.

"Listen to me," she said into the dark, and she brought me back. "You and I started a new chapter. Our own chapter. One that has nothing to do with war. A chapter that began with love and opened enough space to let in hope."

I turned to face her. "You know I haven't forgotten those years, Lena. But I don't waste time feeling sorry for myself."

"I know you don't," she said. "But there *are* those moments that rear up every once in a while."

I did not say what I was thinking: that *those* moments were about the threat of chaos, the threat of loss.

"Everything happened a long time ago," I told her. "I know I'm blessed to have what I have now, to have the family we have. I'm blessed to be able to practise my art. And tell me, what was that about you playing piano—when we were at Miss Carrie's tonight? You've never said a word about that before. What about the silence around that?"

"You're just trying diversionary tactics," she said. "As usual. Anyway, it wasn't really a silence. There wasn't anything to say. Piano was something I studied as a child, that's all. How could that measure up to your stories of Okuma-san and the keyboard of ponderosa pine?"

"Well, I never learned to play," I said. "In fact, for me, Beethoven was first learned in silence. Not exactly silence. Silence shaped by rhythm. Hands, fingers, tapping, rapping. Long before I knew what the actual music sounded like. Except for Minuet in G. Grandfather Minuet."

I had already told Lena about the music from Missisu's piano entering our kitchen the morning we were uprooted from the coast.

"Would you be able to identify music if I tapped it out?"

"Maybe. As long as it's Beethoven. Who knows?"

"Turn on your side again," she said. "There. I don't know every note, but I can do part of this by ear. It will be awkward, but stretch your imagination. Don't move, now."

I waited. Tried to push the memories away.

Fingertips on my naked back. A moment of stillness while she thought, and then rapid pulsing, very rapid. And steady, from the left. Movement, sudden and light, from the right. Both hands, even and quick. More rapid movement, melody on the right, quickly up and down the scale, a pause, steady pulsing again.

She stopped.

"Again," I said, and she repeated the pattern in exactly the same way.

"Waldstein Sonata," I said. "No. 21, first movement. The entire sonata lasts close to twenty-five minutes."

"Incredible. I can hardly believe it."

The camp, the shack, the cold. Sitting at the table with a piece of cream-coloured paper in front of me, paper that had been slit from one of Okuma-san's best books. Indigo ink, a fine nib, a corner of blotter. The clock on the cupboard. His head nodding forward just before his hands came crashing down on ponderosa pine. The mottling of the skin afterwards. The dryness. The splitting of his thumb and the way he sewed it back together with black thread. Me, with my eyes scrunched, looking, but trying, at the same time, not to see.

"Okay, here's another. From the beginning."

One chord on bare skin. Both hands. One-two-three-four, one-two-three-four, one-two-three-four . . .

I knew it at once, but she continued.

"Piano Concerto No. 4, first movement," I said. Hearing every note in my mind, as she was.

"A symphony, then."

"Maybe I can guess which one before you start."

"Do you realize that we could go on the road?" Lena said. "Side-show—I could be your manager. We could make our fortune this way. I could quit teaching."

"Play."

"Light touch, playful, steady beat, non-stop, bit of melody, steady, steady, rock-rock, rock-rock, tah-tah, tah-tah, tah-tah."

"Easy. Maelzel had invented the metronome and I think Beethoven was having a bit of fun. Symphony No. 8, second movement. Tah-tah, tah-tah. He fought with Maelzel, one of the feuds that lasted. Maelzel, the inventor, even made several mechanical hearing aids, but Beethoven said they didn't work. Any collaboration between the two was not a happy event. Beethoven considered the man ill-bred, someone who was trying to infringe on his rights."

"How do you know all this?"

"Okuma-san. The stories he told. All those nights in the chicken coop after we left the camp. He bought an old turntable our last year in British Columbia. And records, one at a time, as he could afford them—usually secondhand. All the while, he was salting money away so that we could move east, where he could teach and send me to art school. It was one of those nights in the chicken coop when I heard a recording of Beethoven for the first time. The light was fading around us. I felt the music enter my soul, I swear. We listened under that low ceiling, in a building that should have been condemned . . ."

"Please don't talk about the chicken coop," Lena said. "I can't bear it, not tonight. Here. I'm going to play the last one. Ready? This will be difficult. Focus. Identify."

Her hands, resting on my skin, all fingertips. Slowly, slowly, floating, one side to the other. Pressure, even pressure on my back. Pause. Into the skin, all fingers again, forward and back. Pause. So many pauses. My body reaching to meet the silhouette of melody, the music shaped by rhythm. And then, the fingers of her right hand, only the right, slowly picked out, slowly. Disjointed taps. What? What? I feel as if she's swaying now. And I.

The rage, Okuma-san said. *We cannot allow the rage. If we allow it, it will also consume.*

As it consumed First Father. As it broke Auntie Aya after the burning of Baby Taro. As it left its marks, forever, on me.

"You have to concentrate," she said. "I'll start again, from the beginning."

Slow floating fingers across my skin, the pauses.

The beauty of the music in my head. The powerful surge of realization. The unmatchable creation that would always be there for every race, for every generation, for all time.

"Adagio. Second movement. Emperor," I said, so softly I didn't know if she had heard. It had been the first Beethoven recording I had ever listened to.

I turned to face her again. We fell asleep, clinging to each other. The music was in my body. I was clinging to life itself.

REQUIEM

Life's wayfarers drink from one and the same stream.

CHAPTER 27

1997

Y ou're driving straight through?"

"That'll work out best, I think."

Kay has picked up the phone as if she had her hand out, waiting for it to ring. She's not happy about this new plan of mine. I don't tell her I'm already on the other side of Edmonton.

"I'll be stopping at your place on the way back," I tell her.

"Hugh went out to get extra groceries," she says, as if this will change my mind. "And I told Henry I'd call him when I knew which day you were arriving. He's planning to join us for dinner. I'm making *teriyaki* chicken. Henry has a serious friend, I don't know if he told you. I haven't met her yet. Someone he met after he sold his restaurant. Or maybe he met her while he still owned it. Anyway, they were friends before. She's Japanese. He's on the pension now, you know. The first of the three of us. Next year, it will be my turn. Aren't you glad you're the baby of the family?" She laughs. "Henry has taken up weightlifting, too," she adds. "At his age."

"Impressive," I say. "But look, I'm sorry for the delay. All it means is that I'll be arriving four or five days later, something like that."

"I had no idea how far you'd be driving each day. I didn't even know if you had my work number. Though the academic year is winding down and I'm not at the office so much. You could get one of those cell phones," she says drily. "Then we could get in touch with you when we need to."

It's always about need with Kay. Her needs, Hugh's needs, my needs. And of course, First Father's.

"What is it that you're looking for?" she says, changing tactics. "Searching, searching, you travel around the world, but for what? You don't light long enough to find whatever it is."

Ah, I wasn't expecting this. But that's her job. Identify the problem.

"Your room is ready. And what about Basil? I thought you wanted to drop him off with us while you went on to the camp."

I look through the wall of the phone booth and see Basil watching for my next move. Big, sloppy, happy Basil. He's drooling against the car window as I speak. And he does love the company of other dogs, even Diva; he's more sociable than I am and can fit into any existing hierarchy. Though a few years ago, when he was younger and we were visiting Kay, Diva, after two days, had had her fill of the interloper. She dragged Basil's bed out to the yard and dumped it on the grass.

The real truth is, I'm not ready to face sister, brother-in-law, brother or his new friend. My own silence has been exactly right throughout this trip, and I need to protect it a bit longer. Well, there it is, what I need.

"What about Kamloops?" she says suddenly. "You have to pass through there to get to the camp, or very close by. I've already warned

Father that you'll be driving to B.C. after you leave Edmonton. He'll be sitting in his chair, staring at the door as always, but this time he thinks it's you who will be walking in."

A man who won't leave the province. Another who won't enter. Until now. I imagine a painting, panels, a diptych maybe, some sort of split canvas. If I were in it, I'd paint myself out.

"I don't know why you did that, Kay. I haven't decided about that." A long sigh.

"You never knew," she says. "Well, how could you? No one ever told you. After we left the camp, while we were on the move from one town to the next, some nights after Henry and I were in bed, Father mourned because he had given you away. It was terrible. He keened, a high-pitched wail. My God, it was terrible."

Did I hear correctly? Did she say keened? First Father, keening.

"There was no keeping him quiet," she said. "It was disturbing to all of us, but to Mother especially. Her grief was quiet and contained. But just as terrible all the same. There were other people around, too. In the mill towns. Other Japanese families, just a few. We lived in such close quarters; everyone knew everyone else's business. No one was happy about the noise."

"What are you trying to tell me, Kay?"

"How do you think Henry and I felt? You were his favourite. You always were. He had hopes for you. The biggest hopes. He loved you so much. Can't you see that? He always loved you best." She sounds like a child as it spills out of her. "Why do you think he gave you to Okuma-san? My God, Bin, figure it out. You're not a stupid man. He wanted more for you. What he couldn't give. A future. Any future at all. But he missed you. He even said, several times, that he was going to go after you and bring you back. Long after you and Okuma-san left British Columbia."

I swallow hard at this. I'm the target of the ambush: words coming at me from all sides.

"But he didn't come after me, did he. If he'd wanted me, he wouldn't have given me away in the first place. Anyway, by then he'd have lost face—if he'd tried to take me back. Okuma-san *did* legally adopt me, you know. He *was* my father."

I haven't intended anger, but there it is.

"I know all that," she says sadly, and I suddenly understand that what she's telling me is probably true. Every bit of it.

Why didn't he let Mother visit me when I was a child? I don't ask. Okuma-san and I were living far away from them, in the south of the province. Even before we moved to Ontario, there wouldn't have been enough money. A trip would have been unthinkable.

All the emotions withheld. First Father, having made his decision, would have had to banish any thought of changing his mind and trying to get me back.

All the feelings concealed.

All the stories never told. Fifty-one years of stories. Fifty-one years since Ying's truck drove my first family across the bridge and dropped them at the bus station on the other side of the river. I have no idea, I realize, how they lived their lives. I know only how Okuma-san and I lived ours. I received Mother's letters, and Kay's, but did the letters reveal anything? They never wrote about the details: how much my sister and brother had grown in a year; if they had to wear tight shoes; what they endured at their schools; if their hand-me-downs were ridiculed; if Henry was often in fights, as I was; if they had enough to eat; if they ever knelt inside a church to pray. Did they have trouble finding their first jobs? How did Kay get herself to university? She must have worked so hard. And what was Mother's life like during those years, before Kay and Henry left home? Hard-working, of course. I found out later that she had worked as a domestic in the home of one of the mill owners. Trying to contribute earnings to feed and dress her children. But no one was in a position to give Mother what she did not have. A different kind of life. A family undivided.

"Look," I tell Kay, "I'll go. I'll visit him. I'll drive right up to his goddamned doorstep. Give me the directions."

"You don't have to swear," she says. And there's a sudden softness to her voice that makes me remember her as she once was, up on the slope behind the camp, trying to teach me to read, helping me to collect pine cones to decorate, admonishing when she heard anyone say a swear word, urging me to run down the hill to chase away the ghosts—something I've never quite managed to do.

But you can, Lena's voice says, suddenly, in my head. It's as if she's beside me again. *Put the fates to use. Chase away your ghosts. This is your chance.*

I wonder for a moment if Kay is crying.

"I'm sorry," I tell her. "I didn't mean to swear. It's just that I hadn't made up my own mind about seeing First Father—not yet. Give me the directions."

I take them down and write them on the back of Otto's new business card, which I've pulled from my wallet while standing in the phone booth. I flip the card over and see an engraved chrysanthemum in one corner, symbol of the Imperial family. Otto's publishing address and phone number are prominent. With Japanese characters I don't know how to read down one side. A prelude to his retreat with the Buddhists in Japan. And now, directions to First Father's house on the back.

I continue west through miles of rolling hills. I had phoned Greg immediately after talking to Kay.

"I might be able to get back to Ottawa for my twenty-first birthday in the summer," he told me. "Unless you can make it to Cape Cod. If you can swing it, it might be easier that way. Everything will depend on the dates around my program. And there's someone I want you to meet—you and Miss Carrie, too. Her name is Caitlin; she'll be at Woods Hole with me. We managed to be accepted into the same program. I've been seeing her for a while now. She's in two of my classes here," he said. "She's great, she's just great. You're going to like her, Dad. And she doesn't like to be called Kate. Full name only."

I felt his happiness. I felt happiness for my son. And Lena's voice prods me again.

Greg will be fine. And you won't have to look for a bride. He'll do it on his own, when he's ready. All in good time.

I keep on until suddenly, starkly, I have a thrilling view of what appear to be walls of black slate. Pushed up by the earth's internal forces. Dark silhouettes on my left, snow peaks on my right. A bit farther, and I see that some of the mountains are heavily treed. When I'm close to Jasper, several plump bighorn sheep bound past the car as if in welcome.

Something is settling into place. Neatly, the way Greg's case of rock samples used to go *snap, click* in his palm. A familiarity roused from deep sleep as I drive farther into the mountains. As real and subtle and deep-down present, as if I had never left.

Uncle Kenji, I now recall, helped to build this road I'm on, the one that eventually became the corridor, the Yellowhead Highway. Uncle Kenji's first camp was a road camp.

I drive and drive. Basil, content to look up from time to time, sniffs the air, looks out at shapes that block the sky, settles back.

"This is what it comes to, Basil," I tell him. "I haul out a map of this outrageously vast country and get into my car and pack my friend the dog, and carve a route from east to west, and come upon an amazement of eruptions that have been thrust up out of our recent geologic past. And we drive through them as if there's nothing that cannot be accomplished, as if there's no mountain that cannot be moved."

I hear a snuffle from the back. Look around again. I am in British Columbia and the sky has not fallen; the mountains have not crumbled. This is the province of my birth; the province of the birth of my parents, all three.

After a day's drive, when I drop south, I realize that anything could be waiting on the other side. Mule deer, for a start. I see them standing under shelter of the trees. Yellow wildflowers, brash and sturdy, everywhere I look as I descend into Kamloops, my ears popping, out of the higher hills and into the lower hills. This dry and sunny climate. Sunny, well into the evening hours. The wide valley looking as if the mountains on all sides slid back voluntarily and allowed the North and South Thompson rivers to meet.

I pull over to a roadside restaurant, feed Basil at the edge of the parking lot and go inside to find food for myself. I order a steak, mashed potatoes, a cheese salad. But when the food is brought to my table I see that it was a mistake to stop here. The steak is too bloody; the mashed potatoes are instant; the cheese salad has no cheese. I question the waitress and she tells me the cook ran out of cheese.

I know when to give up. I order a coffee and pull out the road map, pull out Otto's business card, match Kay's directions on the back of the card to the map and see that I'm not far from First Father's house. Probably not more than five or ten minutes away.

The car is steamed up from Basil's barking, and I wipe a rag down the windows. I start the engine and brace myself. The road is dusty once I leave the highway, but hard-packed and wide enough for two cars. There aren't many houses, and they're small; they look as if they've been gathering dust for a long time. I pull over to check directions again, see the mailbox painted black, a low-slanting roof, outside shutters closed over south-facing windows. Exactly as Kay described. There's a good-sized garden at the side, which she did not mention.

The house is smaller than I imagined. Can't be more than four rooms at most. But no truck in sight. And then I remember Henry telling me that First Father and Uncle Kenji purchased a truck together years ago and share the use of it. They get their groceries together, their supplies, whatever they need, whatever they drink—I have no idea. The truck must be at Uncle Kenji's.

I go to the door and face an uneasy silence. I trip over the step, worn smooth and sliverless. He'd have heard me drive in—or maybe not; he might not hear well. *He's eighty-four,* Kay reminded me on the phone. *He'll be in his chair, facing the door. The door is never locked. The way he sits, he looks as if he never gets up, though he must, to cook and eat and sleep.*

I rap at the door and there's no response. I push it open and step inside. There's the mat, set out to receive shoes that will never touch the surface of the inside floors. It all comes back, like a sudden gust of winter. And a heap of shoes farther inside, but not all belonging to one person, surely. When I look more closely I see that they are slippers. Some meant for visitors. Slip out of one pair and into another.

No lights on. I flick a wall switch and a spartan kitchen jumps to life. Rice pot on the counter, an electric rice pot, its cord haphazardly wound. A blue-and-white rice bowl I recognize, chopsticks beside it on a bamboo pad. A bottle of *shoyu* on a shelf. A bad print of Mount Fuji on the wall.

Mother's willow basket is on the floor, in a corner by a chair. The same basket that was stuffed with as much she could carry the morning we boarded the *Princess Maquinna,* the mail boat that took us away from the coast. The same willow basket that hid the one pair of dolls that escaped the burning pyre. Now it is filled with papers and magazines. There's no other reminder of Mother, that I can see. And there's First Father's chair, with cushioned seat and wooden arms. The place smells like childhood, and part of me is reeling.

"Hello," I call out. "Hello. It's Bin."

No response.

I push open the bedroom door. This room is as spartan as the kitchen. A double bed, roughly made. Dresser, closet, bedside table with a book on top, a badly frayed palm-sized book with a red cover.

He never discussed his own fate, I now realize. That wasn't part of the ritual.

I go out to the car and bring in my bag. I leave the shoulder pack in the car. The manila folder is still in there, but I haven't looked at it since I left home. It's almost dark now. The mountains have stretched into their heights to shut out the light; I'd forgotten how quickly it happens. I'll stay overnight, sleep on the couch—if he has one. I peer into the living room and see that there's a pullout against the wall, with several blankets folded on top. Probably where Kay and Hugh sleep when they visit. A second chair faces a TV. There's a small bathroom, off to the side. First Father must be at Uncle Kenji's. Maybe he's having his supper there.

Basil takes up position beside an unlit wood stove in the living room. A wood stove means a woodpile, somewhere. It must be outside the back door. And the night chill has begun to drift in.

I return to the kitchen and see the note on the table. I don't know how I could have missed it the first time through. A message, hastily scrawled, written in ballpoint.

BIN

> *Kay phoned to say you might be coming here, but your uncle Kenji came to pick me up. He finally persuaded me to go to the coast with him. Vancouver, and then the ferry over to the island. Your cousin will take us out on his boat a few days. Might be my last chance to try out my fisherman's legs again. Our old house on the coast was torn down, they told me. It gave more than a few men a hard time when they tried to knock it apart. I built it to last. On our way back, Kenji and I will look for you.*

The note is unsigned, and there's no date. So matter-of-fact I want to tear it to shreds. But I don't. I fold it over and over, stare at it in my palm.

> I bring in the Laphroaig. And the piece of mat that Basil sleeps on.
> I pour a bowl of water and watch Basil drink like a camel.
> I pour myself a two-finger Scotch. Make that three.
> I slump into a chair.
> What did I think I was expecting?

I'm in the living room, drinking my third Scotch, thinking of the lousy meal I was served at the restaurant. And then I think of the Japanese food Kay used to prepare whenever Lena and Greg and I visited. Everything tasted a bit fishier, a bit saltier than the food we ate at home. Kay's food tasted like childhood and looked like childhood. Even the stacks of prawns with their heads and beady eyes, though we never had prawns in the camp. And *sushi*, so many kinds, and green tea—homegrown—and *tsukemono*, the thin but crunchy pickles Mother and Kay used to prepare together. The smell of brine, *shoyu*, cucumber, some sort of mash made of rice bran, stone weights pressing it all down. There's no aroma like it. Which sets me to wondering if the large crock that once stored them has been stowed somewhere in this Kamloops house. There might be a basement.

I find a door off the kitchen and steps going down. Small house, small basement. The ceiling is low. But there's a workshop down here, and a workbench with a vise at one end, a chunk of wood clamped in its jaws. Tools are laid out neatly, the way I lay out my own brushes. A tall homemade stool has been pushed close to the bench.

Above the bench, at eye level, something hangs on the wall. Something vaguely, faintly recognizable. A piece of cardboard, box-board, a faded pencil drawing nailed to the wall, the nail hammered through its top edge to hold it in place.

Two horses, or attempts at horses, one large, one small, the head of the smaller horse tucked under the neck of the larger. An alert eye, an animal ready to bolt. The head and nose of the smaller horse resemble the beak of a grotesque giant goose. A child's drawing.

Yanked from my hand.

Disappeared, the day I was given away.

Kept more than fifty years.

I don't bother to open the pullout. I lie on it in the living room and pile on the blankets. Basil, the hound who knows the scent of grief when it's all around him, drags his mat over and settles at the end of the couch. I reach out a hand and rub the coarse coat of his back, the soft and silky part of his ears. The warmth of him. The life of him. He groans, and rolls over heavily, an animal who no longer wants the burden of memory.

CHAPTER 28

1996

Lena woke and saw me standing beside her, looking down. She was lying on her back on the floor, on a small pink mat laid on top of our own carpet. Miss Carrie had seen her drive in, rolled up the mat and wheeled it over on her walker, insisting that Lena borrow it; it was her remedy for almost every ailment. A pillow supported Lena's neck; a thin blanket was pulled up to her chin.

"You're home," she said. "Come and tell me about the fates. I was thinking about them. I want to hear them again."

"I thought you were at the university all day."

"No classes Friday afternoons, remember? I had a bit of a headache, a bit of dizziness, and decided to come home early. I'm glad it's the end of the week. Who invented the week, anyway? Why does time have to be divided into days, weeks, months, the school year? Anyway, I'm home. And this mat is so comfortable, I don't ever want to get up."

It was November and I'd been to the National Gallery, and had stopped to see Nathan on the way back. *Figure out a title*, he said. *If we're planning to do a show, you have to come up with a title.*

There was a book on the floor beside Lena. On top, a large book-mark with a message—BAN LAND MINES: NO PRODUCTION, NO EXPORT, NO USE, NO STOCKPILES. One of Lena's causes. She was frequently recruited by others at the university who looked to her for support.

"Tell me about the fates," she said again.

She looked tired, despite having had a nap. Tired, unfocused, something else I couldn't put a name to.

I sat down on the carpet beside her.

"First Father," I began, "took the red book down from the shelf. He read back to front, top to bottom. He always started with Hiroshi . . ."

"Hir-o-shi," she said, interrupting. She slowed the syllables and stared at the ceiling, as if seeking approval for her pronunciation. Then she added, "Henry."

"Because he was number-one son."

"Skip to your fate," she said. "Never mind the others. Yours is the one that makes me laugh."

I leaned back against the chesterfield and thought, *Laugh? When did laughter ever exist?*

"First Father said, 'Bin, you are youngest, number-two son, born in the year of the tiger. A tiger may be stubborn, but can chase away ghosts and protect.'"

"Tell me the end part," she said, knowing already.

"'But because your time of birth was at the cusp of the year of the rabbit . . .'"

"You are destined to be melancholy, and you will weep over non-sensical things." She recited the rest, smiling. I ventured a hand over the familiar bones of her wrist and felt the pulse of my wife. It was rapid, too rapid, as if she'd been running in her sleep.

"Who were you *not* supposed to marry?" she said.

"First Father didn't tell me that part. He probably didn't think my marriage fate would be important."

"But it is important. You chose me. Tiger chose dog."

"Other way around. Dog chose tiger."

"Is that the way it happened? Are you sure?"

"I'm sure," I said. And wondered who had chosen whom. At the time it hadn't seemed like choice. More like inevitability. It had seemed right. Was right. A good match. She was smiling again. I looked past her and through the living-room window. A child of the sky had taken a thick marker and looped a line of gloom around the base of each cloud.

"Do you remember," she said, switching topics, "when we drove to the cabin on the Gatineau River? An hour's drive from here." She spoke as if it had been years ago instead of only a few weeks. "We took the cooler with us—the one with the green lid. I packed the oilcloth with the red-and-white squares, hoping there'd be a picnic table at the place."

I continued where she left off.

"Another couple arrived, and stayed at the only other cabin. They were accompanied by two young girls: their daughter, Florence, and her friend Lise. There was a softness to the distant hills on the other side of the river. That was the view we saw from shore. The visual suggestion was one of a series of far-off valleys, each folded to the next, the muted wrappings of red and gold."

"Say that again, will you?"

"Which part?"

"The visual suggestion. I want to hear you say it."

A moment preserved.

We were both silent, and then she said, "That was the night you told me about the fates."

"I remember how you laughed."

"I'd never heard any of that before. You'd been holding on to secrets. What else haven't you told me?"

"If I'd known the fates would amuse you so much, I'd have told you earlier."

"I'm glad nobody ever tried to predict my fate," she said. "I'd have been menaced. I *am* menaced. My head feels as if there are lines criss-crossing inside my skull. Slicing up my brain. Sorry," she said. "Sorry for that unnecessary dark moment."

Basil chose this moment to do a circuit through the room, dragging his mattress in his teeth. The past few days, he'd begun to lift the mattress out of his basket and drag it around, ensuring that he'd be seen.

Lena called him over for a pat.

"Come here, you outrage," she said, and he dropped the mattress in the doorway between living and dining rooms. He took up position beside her. She tried to reach for him, but her arm wouldn't move.

"What's wrong, Lena? Have you seen the doctor?" Something inside me had gone still.

"I called," she said. "I have an appointment first thing Monday, before classes."

But the words came out slurred, and she closed her eyes and I saw what was happening, and I ran to the phone.

Emergency response was fast. Miss Carrie stood at the top of her veranda step when she saw the flashing lights, but I had no chance to speak to her. Other neighbours had come outside and were standing on the sidewalk as Lena was carried out of the house on a stretcher.

I was told which hospital she was being taken to, and followed in my car. My heart was racing; my throat was dry. I hadn't stopped to phone Greg, or leave him a message. Everything that was happening—Lena's faltering attempts to speak, Basil's frantic barking, the solemn faces of neighbours as I pulled away from the house, the streets through which I drove, which suddenly seemed hostile and unfamiliar—everything was telescoped, as if each part of the emergency had conspired to occupy less space and less time than real space and real time. The ambulance left me far behind and Lena was already in Emergency by the time I parked my car and ran to the entrance.

It took me a few minutes to find her, to find out which curtain she was behind, and another few minutes before I was permitted behind the curtain with her. The doctors on duty were blunt. From the Emergency Room, I phoned Greg and told him to come home at once.

A bleak smile from her hospital bed. A grim one from me, in response. Bleak information delivered and received. She moved her left hand, gestured towards her body beneath the covers. There was an IV hooked up to her arm.

"Look at me. I'm pulled down in a heap. Like one of your fractured and broken smalls."

But I wasn't protecting her now. I hadn't kept her safe.

She had difficulty speaking. "I have so much to give up," she said. Tears running now, unchecked. "You and Greg."

"He's on his way," I said. "He's coming. He'll be here tomorrow."

"He'll carry on doing what he's already begun," she said. "He loves his life."

I leaned my forehead into the sheets, felt the ridge at the edge of the mattress. Closed my eyes. I wanted to banish the encompassing gloom.

"Don't give up hope, Lena. Please don't," I said.

I felt her drifting.

She brought herself back. But her look was so distant, any bit of hope I'd had now drained away.

Her condition changed quickly. There was no time to think of what more to say or not say. *A word once uttered is beyond the reach of four galloping horses,* Okuma-san had always told me. But I had no words to utter that could save her.

In the morning, I went home to feed Basil, to change clothes, to speak with Miss Carrie and to pick up Greg at the airport. Lena was now in Intensive Care. Miss Carrie immediately took a taxi to the hospital and said she would stay on the unit until Greg and I arrived. At home, Basil had taken up position at the top of the stairs, his head over the top step. He was keeping watch over the front door below, and he was upset. He hadn't kept his pack together. His disintegrating pack. I knew how that felt.

While I was collecting the few items I needed to take back to the hospital, Basil began to drag his mattress again. It seemed that no matter which direction I looked, he was crossing a room or passing through a doorway, the mattress in his teeth.

Before I left for the airport, I sat on the edge of the bed for a moment and looked at a framed photo of Lena on the dresser. I stared, but what I was seeing was fragmentation. Because of the lighting at the time the photo had been taken, only half of her face was visible, the left. It was obvious that she was ready to explode in laughter. How could I tell, from her left eye, from the shadow of her lip, from the vertical line of her nose to her darkened chin?

I could. I just could. I removed the photo from the frame and stored it. The Lena I had left at the hospital had no laughter, no smile. And I wanted her refocused; I wanted to make her whole.

When Greg and I returned from hospital that night, after Lena had become unconscious and had not reawakened, after she had died of a massive stroke, we saw the lights on at Miss Carrie's and we went there first, to tell her. The three of us stood inside Miss Carrie's front entrance, next to the hellhole, and held one another, and wept for what we could scarcely believe, wept for what each of us had so suddenly lost.

Greg and I let ourselves into our own home. When we turned on the lights, we saw that Basil had methodically ripped every bit of his mattress to shreds. Pieces of white wadding were scattered in every room over the entire main floor.

CHAPTER 29

1997

K *eep river as your focus,* Lena always told me.

And there it is. The deep canyon, the great Fraser River on my left, teeming with its own life, cutting its way through mountain, rock, soil, eroding as it flows.

I've decided to take a long route from Kamloops, and I approach from the south. The highway has been narrow and winding, hugging the side of the mountain for miles. Warnings of rock slides have been posted along the way, and I grip the wheel and glance up, wondering if I'd be able to shoot ahead, even if I had warning. It's easy to imagine tons of loose boulders up there, hanging by threads.

I have been listening to what Okuma-san described as the last masterpiece written by Beethoven, the last string quartet, op. 135, the one Beethoven finished the year before he died. I chose its fourth movement to be performed at Okuma-san's funeral, and now, it is perfect for this day, the notes floating to the highest peaks. I left this valley fifty-one years ago on a bus with Okuma-san, and now, I listen to the music he loved. There is a delicacy to this quartet, a reminder of contrasts, of opposites, the more so while I'm surrounded by the majesty of the mountains. Everything comes together. Perhaps everything Beethoven knew. Maybe he had some grand vision of humanity. *Muss es sein?* he asked. Must it be? And he answered his own question. *Es muss sein*. It must be.

*

IN THE LATE SUMMER of 1967, I was about to move to London, England, on a scholarship. I had finished a degree in fine arts several years earlier and had been living in a small apartment in downtown Montreal. I was painting, and sharing the apartment with an artist named Peter. We had become friends, and we both had part-time jobs. I worked at an antiquarian bookstore west of Atwater during the day, and attended classes at the Museum of Fine Arts in the evenings. Peter worked for a private gallery on Sherbrooke Street and attended the same classes. Each of us had submitted a painting to the jury for the museum's spring exhibition, and we were ecstatic to learn that our work had been selected. It was the final exhibition of that type, and it was my first painting to be accepted for a large exhibit. It was also the year of Expo 67, when the world came to Montreal. Every chance I had, I took the Metro to the Expo site and visited the gallery, the outdoor works by Giacometti and Henry Moore, the photography exhibit, the many splendid pavilions. Everything seemed possible that year.

In August, I travelled by train to Ottawa to spend a week with Okuma-san before departing for London. He had made a life for himself in Ottawa. It was a quiet place, and it suited him. Although he had retired from teaching two years earlier, he had remained active in the music world. He had bought a piano and he played for himself, but not publicly. The pain in his left hand had worsened over the years and he suffered from arthritis. But he listened to music constantly and he had become known as a Beethoven expert. He gave talks and lectures and wrote program notes and published a number of important papers. I had met most of his friends. They attended concerts together and performed, and some were members of the church Okuma-san attended in the west end of the city.

He had also accomplished what he had set out to do: he had ensured that I completed my formal education; he had sent me to university; he had helped me to begin the exhilarating study of art. He had provided me with a home, and he had supported me in every way.

The week I spent with Okuma-san was the last week of his life, though I did not know this at the time. He had a friend, Mari, and the three of us ate most of our meals together. Mari was a widow, and she and Okuma-san spent much of their time in each other's company. During that week, he and I walked the pathways along the Ottawa River, talking, discussing music and art. He was curious to hear about my latest enthusiasms. He also wanted me to visit Paris, Florence, Berlin, Vienna, Rome, Amsterdam, the great cities of Europe. He spoke about the birthplace of Beethoven in Bonn, the life mask, the ear trumpets, the grandfather clock, the four-stringed piano, all of which I would later see for myself. I had saved as much money as I could towards travel expenses, and Peter had found a McGill student named Lena to take over my room in Montreal during the year I would be away. I did not meet Lena before I left the country, but Peter told me she was a history major, a Montrealer who wanted to move out of her parents' home so that she would be closer to the campus.

Two days after I said goodbye to Okuma-san in Ottawa, I was in Montreal, packing my belongings in a trunk that was to be left behind with Peter. The phone rang and it was Mari. Okuma-san had died suddenly, from a heart attack. I was on a train, returning to Ottawa, within hours of the call.

At the funeral, I sat beside Mari, who had arranged for the musicians—all friends of Okuma-san—to play the last movement of the String Quartet in F major. It was performed expertly, the grace and power of Beethoven flowing into every sorrowful space inside the church. From the oak pew, I thought about the grace and power that had also been Okuma-san's. He had met adversity with stoicism and with hope. He had set the example of never giving in to anger, even though he knew I had anger of my own inside me. He had provided strength in my background, and I had relied upon him for stability, for support and for love.

As I sat there, I could not help but think of the shack in the camp, with its brittle needles of frost inside the ceiling and walls, the worn plank keyboard of ponderosa pine, the bruised hands, the attempts at the sonata, the cream-coloured paper he had slit from his best books so that I would be able to draw, the lone egg in the refrigerator, the first time I heard a recording of the Emperor Concerto and how we listened to it twice in the same evening in the fading light of the chicken coop. I wondered, too, if the plank keyboard even existed. We had left it in the chicken coop the day we departed British Columbia, and it might be there still. I doubted that any other tenant lived in that place after we left in 1951.

I thought of all the parts of our lives that Okuma-san and I had shared as father and son, for twenty-one years. And I was grateful.

Muss es sein? Es muss sein.

After the funeral, Mari gave me an envelope that had been found with Okuma-san's papers and his will. Whatever he owned had been left to me. I opened the envelope later, when I was alone, after the mourners had departed, after the *sushi* and sandwiches had been served, after I had returned to the house in the early evening. *My Dear Son,* I read,

> *I have been troubled by a heart ailment for some time, and there is nothing more to do that has not already been done.*
>
> *I am ready, but you have your entire life before you. You will be a fine artist, I am sure of this. Remember, always, that I have been grateful to have you as my honorary and beloved son.*

The music has ended; the road widens. I am able to loosen my grip on the steering wheel as the car descends into the valley. I park at the side of what, surprisingly, is now a paved road. Why should this come as a surprise? It's been more than half a century since I lived here.

Basil clambers out and we stand together and face the camp. Or what would have been the camp. But could sixty-one shacks have fit into this narrow space? I walk forward into the field where the huge tents were set up the fourth day after our arrival by train. At first, this is confusing, and I wonder if I can be in the right place.

Any structure we left behind has been razed to the ground. The field is run through with weeds and shrubs grown wild. There are bushes with red berries I don't remember, and sagebrush and tumbleweed at the edges of the field. The slopes hold only a thin layer of trees. The ground is lumpy, but when I look more closely I see outlines of scooped-out places, now covered with tufted grass. And there's the town, on the other side of the river. This has to be the camp. But the winds of fifty years have swept through and it has become a barren place.

I stand still and try to gather memory. Recognition comes slowly. My eyes follow contours and outlines on the surface of the field. I open a mental map and unfold it, square by careful square.

This is it, I tell myself, and I pace forward. I'm at the edge of a rounded hollow filled with clumps of earth, and I see a couple of pieces of old tin. I look to the left. A plank led to the bathhouse here. Ba and Ji's shack there. Uncle Aki and Auntie Aya's behind. At the foot of the hill, the site where the outhouses used to be. Outhouses with their snow chinks in winter, and always cold as fear. The trees have been cut down in the place where the ghosts were said to gather. There isn't so much as a board anywhere, but I can trace the community; it's all here.

And now that my eyes have adjusted, I see tarpaper fragments, a shallow indent hardly more than six feet square. I pick up a stick that fits to my palm, and use it to dig. And suddenly I'm unearthing a half century's drifting silt. The end of the stick hits something that clinks, and I keep digging. Pieces of china now, and some heavier Japanese porcelain. A blue-and-white rice bowl that matches the one I saw in First Father's kitchen last night. This one is whole except for a large triangular chip missing from the rim. Miraculously, I find the chip as well, and I stow both pieces to take back with me.

Bin, protector of fractured and broken goods.

This is the place. The buried place. With no trace of path worn smooth between three rows of shacks; no trace of bathhouse, outhouse, schoolhouse. No trace of Jack-pine pole, of water tank, of woodshed where a headless bear once hung upside down. No sign that a community endured, that Auntie Aya gave birth, that Baby Taro died and we searched the ashes for his teardrop shape. No sign of the funeral pyre, or of graves in the woods. No sign that elders died, that children played and shouted, that Ba waited for letters from Manzanar, or that Ying drove his truck to camp every week and laughing women gave orders for *chimpo* sausage. No sign that Mother wept, that First Father raged, that Hiroshi and Keiko and I and all of the others, young and old, had to set aside our dreams and our hopes.

I look up now, to the flat Bench where we picked berries on summer evenings. The camp was hemmed tightly between road and Bench here, the mountain rising up behind. But I'm astonished to see, beyond that, a second mountain behind the first. Another mountain was there all this time and I didn't know, because I was too small to see. All those years and the mountain behind the mountain could not be seen.

I tug my shoulder pack from the car, lock the door, cross the road and search for the trail that leads to the river below. Basil, sometimes in front, sometimes behind, has no difficulty following the steep path. He is remarkably stable with his low centre of gravity and his large feet and claws.

There is the gravel bar. There are the jagged rocks, the muddy green water. I don't need to look, not really. The river, the mind's companion—fast and hard and unrelenting—is where it has always been.

There is no mist hovering, no rope of cloud stretched along its length. The small island, in the middle of the channel, has eroded along the edge but otherwise is much the same. I sit on the flat rock on the riverbank and open my pack. I should have brought Lena here a long time ago. I should have shared this place with her. I'll bring Greg. We'll manage a trip before long. And when he's with me, we'll keep going, all the way to the Pacific, to the coastal village on Vancouver Island where I was born, even though the house is gone. Or maybe we'll start at the sea and work our way back. For now, this has to be enough.

From my pack, I pull out the manila folder that has Lena's signature written across the cover. I begin to leaf through papers, copies of documents she was never able to persuade me to read. The ones from the archives. The ones with whole paragraphs censored and blacked out.

But Lena has highlighted lines of her own in faded blue, and these I *can* read.

—The file reveals that no crosscut saw was inventoried.

—The file reveals that no sewing machine was located.

—The file reveals no mention of a grandfather clock.

—When the area was visited by officials sent to appraise the property, no property could be identified at the location described.

—As you did not reply to our letter, it was understood that you agreed to the $8 value of the skiff, which was sold.

—The fishing vessel previously owned by you was sold through the Japanese Fishing Vessels Disposal Committee, the vessel having been requisitioned by Naval Service.

—Supervision costs of $41.50 have been charged to you. An additional $68.90 has also been withheld to cover possible repairs, and has been deducted from the sale price.

And the ultimate, repetitive replies to persistent requests after the war, also highlighted by Lena: *The items found on the property were declared to be of no value.*

I cram the papers back into the folder. Basil is joyously splashing, running from water to riverbank, from riverbank to water. I step down to the edge and raise my arms and I hear Lena's voice.

You're drowning your history, Bin. Think about it. This is your own history.

And I reply, "But maybe this is the way I can, finally, for all time, get rid of the ghosts."

I pause for a moment, and then I let the folder fly. Papers scatter on the waves and bob and swirl as they rush downriver. The same direction as the body of the small boy who drowned and disappeared during the last year of the war.

Back up the bank now, I sprawl out on the rock shelf where Mother once sat in the sun. I take out the wooden box given to me by my own beloved son. I take out a charcoal pencil and the pad that has the thickest paper and I begin to draw. It is like naming, I think. And Lena's voice says, *Yes, but which name? You, for instance, have had so many.*

I look around at the mountains and at the turbulent river rushing past on its long journey to the coast. I inhale the air, cool and clear. I think of the people I love and have loved, living and dead, and I think of the camp that once existed here but is nothing but shadows now, and I decide: REQUIEM. That will be the name of my exhibition. I'll phone Nathan and Otto later this afternoon, and I'll let them know so that they can get things moving at their end.

I focus on my drawing now. And listen to the soft, scratchy, satisfying sound of charcoal against paper. I look up, and then down again. This is what I have always known. This is what river is.

There is a familiar sound behind me, the crunch of footsteps on the trail. At first, I don't look back, and then, as the noise becomes louder, I stand and face the path. Basil, alert, is at my side. First Father is wearing old fishing clothes and rubber boots; Uncle Kenji, his brother, is right behind him. They lumber down the path like two bears who have had no guidance in subtlety. Uncle Kenji's face is unreadable. First Father speaks my name.

"Bin," he says, and he moves towards me.

Do I take a step back? First Father's voice an echo, a warp through time.

"We're staying across the river," he says. "We're on our way home, and there's only one hotel in town. Keiko called to say you might be here today or tomorrow, so we drove this far and watched for a car at the camp. We booked a room at the hotel for you, just one night. We'll leave for Kamloops in the morning. Is that your hound?"

His hand grips my shoulder. I feel the warmth of his fingers pressing down.

"We caught fish," says Uncle Kenji, determined to fill the spaces. "We were out on the boat. At sea again. You'll have to come with us next time. And bring your boy. We haven't met your boy."

First Father is still a large man. Stooped, but not frail. Never frail. He doesn't bother to wipe the tears that are streaming down his face.

I move towards him. Both of his arms pulling me in. A son, after all. Again. A father, a son.

ACKNOWLEDGEMENTS

On the subject of the expulsion and internment of approximately 21,000 Japanese Canadians and 114,000 Japanese Americans (total numbers on the West Coast at the time of the bombing of Pearl Harbor, December 1941, being approximately 22,000 and 120,000, respectively), I would like to acknowledge some books in particular, though my entire library on this subject contributed to background knowledge. *Justice In Our Time* by Roy Miki and Cassandra Kobayashi; *Democracy Betrayed* by the National Association of Japanese Canadians; *The Politics of Racism* by Ann Gomer Sunahara; *Nikkei Legacy: The Story of Japanese Canadians from Settlement to Today* by Toyo Takata; the very moving *Teaching in Canadian Exile* by Frank Moritsugu and The Ghost Town Teachers Historical Society; *Manzanar* by John Armor and Peter Wright, photographs by Ansel Adams and commentary by John Hersey; *Spirit of the Nikkei Fleet: BC's Japanese Canadian Fishermen* by Masako Fukawa, Stanley Fukawa and the Nikkei Fishermen's History Book Committee; *Japanese Proverbs* by Otoo Huzii, Board of Tourist

Industry 1940, Japanese Government Railways; *Sleeping Tigers,* a National Film Board of Canada documentary; various issues of *Nikkei Voice.* I thank members of the second and third generations, Nisei and Sansei—including family members—who agreed to be interviewed and told their stories to help me understand the impact of the experiences endured between 1941 and 1950. I'm especially grateful to my late mother-in-law, Sumako (Oye) Itani, who, in interview, many years ago, unflinchingly recounted her experiences as a young woman uprooted from her home on Canada's West Coast.

I acknowledge *The Fraser* by Bruce Hutchison; *The Letters of Beethoven,* 3 vols., collected, edited and translated by Emily Anderson; Heinrich Böll's essay "The Place Was Incidental" in *Missing Persons and Other Essays.*

I appreciate the love, support and expertise of my husband, Ted, and my children. For answering my many questions about music, thanks to my son, Russell Satoshi Itani. To my daughter, Sam Itani, thanks for constantly checking in and for responding to my queries about the natural world. Also, for advice, love and support sent my way, I thank composer Yehudi Wyner, and conductor Susan Davenny Wyner, both in Massachusetts; composer Gabriela Ortiz in Mexico City; pianist Emily Upham in New York. Many thanks to the Civitella Ranieri Foundation in New York, which generously provided me with a fellowship and residency at an Italian castle in Umbria: a wonderful retreat where I had the support of director and staff, and the company of fine artists in residence at the time. My gratitude and special thanks go to stroke expert Dr. Antoine Hakim, to artist Bobbie Oliver and to actor Eve Crawford. To artist Norman Takeuchi, I so appreciate our many discussions and the visits to your studio. I thank legal expert, Ilario Maiolo, who helped me to understand the laws of the period and what constitutes a Crime Against Humanity. Also, special thanks to: Craig Smith; Aileen Bramhall Itani; Joel Oliver; Judy Oliver; Orm and Barb Mitchell; Paul Kariya; Terry Gronbeck-Jones; my former professor Gordon Hirabayashi; Caroline Page and the original "Basil." A few incidents in *Requiem* first saw the light of day in an earlier story called "Flashcards." Resemblance to any person living or dead, or to any names found within, is entirely coincidental; this is a work of fiction. If there are errors in background or historical information, I take full responsibility.

Finally, with great affection, I acknowledge my agent, Jackie Kaiser, and my editor and publisher at HarperCollins, Phyllis Bruce. I know it's there, always, during these long journeys: your unwavering support. I thank you both.

A NOTE ON THE TYPE

This book is set in Dante, the first versions of which were the product of a collaboration between Giovanni Mardersteig, a printer, book and typeface designer, and Charles Malin, one of the great punchcutters of the twentieth century.

Mardersteig drew on his experience of using Monotype Bembo and Centaur to design a new book face with an italic that worked harmoniously with the roman. Years of collaboration with Malin had taught him the nuances of letter construction, and the two worked closely to develop a design that was easy to read. Special care was taken in the design of the serifs and top curves of the lowercase to create a subtle horizontal stress, which helps the eye move smoothly across the page.

In 1955, after six years of work, the fonts were used to publish Boccaccio's *Trattatello in laude di Dante*. The design took its name from this project.

A GROVE PRESS READING GROUP GUIDE
BY BARBARA PUTNAM

Requiem

Frances Itani

ABOUT THIS GUIDE

We hope that these discussion questions will enhance your
reading group's exploration of Francis Itani's *Requiem*.
They are meant to stimulate discussion, offer new viewpoints
and enrich your enjoyment of the book.

More reading group guides and additional information,
including summaries, author tours and author sites
for other fine Grove titles may be found on our
Web site, www.groveatlantic.com.

QUESTIONS FOR DISCUSSION

1. On Vancouver Island, Father and Uncle Kenji have shored up their fisherman's house with skill, foresight, and giant stilts. It is proof against the tides, "but all the while, hidden undercurrents had been making their own incursions with the tides, in and around and under the house" what are these insidious incursions (p. 3)? How much warning does the family have of impending doom?

2. Kay asks Bin, "What is it that you're looking for? . . . Searching, searching, you travel around the world, but for what? You don't light long enough to find whatever it is" (p. 288). And asking himself why he set out on a long, often uncomfortable trek, Bin answers himself: "Because you are chasing away your ghosts. Because you are trying to open a door, any door, to some random glimmer or prospect that might be waiting to attach itself to your loneliness" (p. 71). What is Bin hoping to find—or to give—on his grand westward journey? Heart's ease, from his loss of Lena? Clarity about his exhibition? Rivers, yes, within the abstracts, but he needs an organizing principle, a title. What else has propelled the trip?

3. Bin, packing for the journey to British Columbia, is aware he needs to get serious, to face up. "But facing up also means admitting the dark places that are only too ready to seep from the shadows" (p. 13). Shadows, ghosts, anger—what are the demons for Bin? "Anger is not so easy to disguise to the self" (p. 13). Is it surprising that with his innate (and learned) Japanese reticence that he keeps anger repressed?

4. What is it to be Japanese? About the looting in their wake leaving the island, Bin recalls, "We did not protest. We stood, soundless, as if we were also invisible, while the boat took us away" (p. 58). Later, years later, Bin reflects, "Most of my relatives kept their heads down, stayed below the radar, as far as I could figure. Whole lives spent with their heads down" (p. 277). What does the reader learn about the culture and behavior of the Japanese from the story?

5. "I think of the years I looked into the mirror, never liking the person I saw, wishing to be anything—anyone—but." (p. 19). How have the borders of identity shifted and blurred in the postwar years? Otto and Miki? Bin and Lena? How is identity a double-edged sword in the novel?

6. Does Okuma-San further Bin's Japanese identity? How does he do this at the same time he is making Bin into a citizen of the world? How does Okuma-San teach Bin to respect himself despite attacks from the outside? How is Bin's art finally allowed to flourish? What other teachers make a difference in the boy's growth?

7. With no regard for their Canadian citizenship, the Japanese are systematically dehumanized. How do the authorities achieve the stripping down of dignity? In Vancouver? (Can one help thinking of Jews in Europe?) In the camp? "Like everyone in our Fraser River camp, we would have to pay for our own internment" (p. 105). What are the conditions in the shacks they build for themselves? What is their source of information for five years? Wartime mail?

8. Years later, at a neighborhood party in Ottawa, Bin meets a more civilized (or sivilized, as Huck would say) form of estrangement. "No one seemed to know how to talk to me; they behaved as if I were an exotic whom they couldn't be

expected to understand. It seemed a surprise to them that I spoke English. They were careful and polite, and spoke loudly when they addressed me, as if I were partially deaf" (p. 149). Have you seen this kind of distancing for other marginalized people who may seem "exotic"? In another instance, a parking-lot encounter with two men who call him "Chinaman," Bin tries to figure out the animosity. "Is it about being bitter? Is it about owning the right to belong?" (p. 121). Are these usually elements of bullying?

9. "During my infrequent visits to Edmonton over the years, and while trying to pretend that we are still family, no one has ever really wanted to poke at the layers of shadow that have fallen between us since that time. Except Lena" (p. 36). How does Lena the historian prod Bin to search for his roots, for documentation about the internment? How successful is she? Were you surprised the embargo on internment information was not lifted for a half century? Do you think the locked files represented ongoing prejudice? Guilt of a government?

10. In his somewhat quixotic quest, how is Bin dependent on the realist Basil as his Sancho Panza? What is Basil's last commentary on his loss of Lena?

11. Which is more arduous for Bin, the camp or his new school afterward with all the hakujin (Caucasians)? What are his other trials in the years after the war?

12. After the years of deprivation in the camp, what are some of the new glories for Okuma-San and Bin?

13. How has Beethoven been a lifeline for Okuma-San on several levels? How does the music bring him and Bin closer? Before they even have the used record player to enjoy together, think of Okuma-San's playing the ponderosa pine plank keyboard,

with only the rhythm of Beethoven's "Minuet in G" or the Hammerklavier sonata to be heard. (In later years, how does Lena physically evoke these pieces for Bin?)

14. Do you see Okuma-San's keeping up his piano technique as a symbol of the courage and grace of Japanese people in their internment? Describe their superhuman efforts to provide food and shelter in these years. Dutiful Japanese children also did their share—think of Hiroshi in his Sisyphus role of hauling water up icy hills for his family and the grandparent figures next door.

15. After Lena's death, Bin turns to Beethoven for solace. In the *Leonore Overture III*, "Joy rising from an underground spring . . . Always the flute, beckoning and bringing a glimmer of light . . . that would be Lena, all of those things. I am the receding part" (p. 28-29). At one point, when Bin is facing his anger ("removal, exile, dispersal, being on the outside. Being given away"), Lena intervenes. "'Listen to me,' she said into the dark, and she brought me back. 'You and I started a new chapter. Our own chapter. One that has nothing to do with war. A chapter that began with love and opened enough space to let in hope'" (p. 279). Talk about what Lena has brought in the past and continues to bring to Bin in memory.

16. The respect of Japanese for their elders (alive as well as dead) is legendary. How is that theme recurrent in *Requiem*? Do older people in the book earn that veneration? First Father? Okuma-San? Miss Carrie? The eighty-four-year old who teaches traditional Japanese dance in the camp?

17. The mystery of Bin's last name and the term First Father is held in abeyance for over half the novel. Does that narrative device work to further the story? Was your curiosity assuaged by the revelation on page 183?

18. Water: how has it been central to Bin from the beginning of his life? Lena notes, "You always bring me to water. . . . No matter what you invite me to do or where we do it, we end up walking trails beside a river. Or crossing a bridge and staring down at one" (p. 29).

19. Bin speaks of things falling into place with a click. How does his riverside epiphany of "Requiem" link his life events with a similar click?

20. In lieu of a musical requiem, Bin offers his exhibition. What does he wish to lay to rest? What losses, angers, ghosts? What remembered joys?

21. "I look around at the mountains and at the turbulent river rushing past on its long journey to the coast. I inhale the air, cool and clear. I think of the people I love and have loved, living and dead, and I think of the camp that once existed here but is nothing but shadows now, and I decide: REQUIEM. That will be the name of my exhibition" (p. 313). And then, as if Bin has finally unlocked a door, what is the ultimate revelation?

SUGGESTIONS FOR FURTHER READING:

Obasan by Joy Kogawa; *A Child in Prison Camp* by Shizuye Takashima; *Snow Falling on Cedars* by David Guterson; *Years of Sorrow, Years of Shame* by Barry Broadfoot; *Manzanar* by John Armor and Peter Wright; *The Jade Peony* by Wayson Choy; *The Ghost Brush* by Katherine Govier; *Guernica* by Dave Boling; *Deafening* and *Remembering the Bones* by Frances Itani